# CHERRY HILL

A JONATHAN CROWLEY NOVEL

JAMES A. MOORE

ISBN 978-1-63789-286-2
Macabre Ink is an imprint of Crossroad Press Publishing

For information address Crossroad Press at 141 Brayden Dr., Hertford, NC 27944
www.crossroadpress.com



First Crossroad Press Edition - 2025

# Prologue: 1971

Gary Harper barely even noticed when the man stumbled into view, staggering at the edge of the road not a hundred yards from the squad car. It was the motion of the stranger's uneven gait that caught his eye. The object of his attention was easily into his sixties, with lean features partially hidden by a new growth of salt-and-pepper facial hair and a buzz cut of the same colors growing on the top of his head.

He looked drunk, but it was hard to say for sure. All he knew for certain was that the man had probably had better days. He wore a pinstriped button-up shirt that had become a mess of wrinkles, with a few small tears along the sleeves. Ken was sitting next to Gary in the cruiser and had been messily chowing down on a sandwich from over at Carlino's Diner. He stopped chewing and stared through the windshield.

"You seeing what I'm seeing?" Ken asked through the pastrami still trapped in his mouth.

Gary nodded and turned on the flashers. He might have been willing to let the man go about his business, but the lack of pants or shoes made him change his mind. The only thing stopping the man from being fully indecent was the length of the dress shirt. It fell below his middle thigh. The poor, old bastard was obviously a few bricks short of a full load. He looked again and shook his head at the synthetic gleam that ran across the man's left leg below the knee. He'd heard of artificial limbs, of course, but never actually seen one. The strange gait was caused by the stranger having to throw his fake leg forward and settle on it just the right way in order to avoid falling on his face.

The old man walked with his head down and muttered to himself; he was too far away for Gary to hear the words. If he even noticed the police car with the flashing lights, he managed to hide the fact.

Gary shook his head and got out of the squad car. He didn't want to deal with a half-naked man while eating his lunch, but there wasn't much choice in the matter, not in the long run.

The man stumbled and fell, catching himself on the palms of his hands. He got back up even as Gary started in his direction and kept going, not even noticing the blood running across the palms of his hands.

"Mister? You all right?" He felt stupid asking when it was so obvious that the old man was not, in fact, anywhere near all right, but he asked anyway. He heard Ken climbing out of the Crown Victoria and felt a little better for it. Not that he was scared of an old man; he just didn't want to be the only one dealing with restraining the guy.

The man kept walking, and Gary hesitated. He had a chance to look at the crazy nudist's face and was taken aback by the fury he saw in the geezer's expression. Still, he was damned if he'd let an old man intimidate him. Gary squared his shoulders and moved a little faster, ready to haul the man in for public nudity and any other charges he felt necessary.

He put his hand on the man's shoulder. "Mister, I don't know what's wrong or where you think you're going, but you have to come with me."

For the first time the stranger looked at him and his already feral face grew wilder, more enraged as he shrugged Gary's hand away.

"Don't touch me." The words were hissed.

Gary froze for a second, taken aback by the pure viciousness of the man's demeanor.

Ken wasn't as slow to respond. He sank his fingers into the old man's shoulder, the same spot that Gary had gripped a moment before, and opened his mouth to issue a sterner warning.

He never got the chance. The bony elbow that slammed into his mouth and busted both of his lips wide open stopped him from talking. Ken staggered backward, both of his hands covering his bloodied mouth, and cursed through the red spittle.

"I said don't touch me, you shithead." There was nothing frail or deranged in the tone of voice, merely angry.

Gary drew his nightstick and decided it was time to end this mess before it could get worse. The old man was still looking at Ken, eyeing him warily, and standing with his arms at his sides and his legs—real and false alike—slightly bent.

Gary swung the club in a hard arc toward the back of the lunatic's head and let out a small squeak when the old bastard moved fast and blocked the blow, his aging forearms slamming into Gary's wrists and knocking his aim off.

Before he could do more than let out a protest, the old man was on him, striking him in the temple with the edge of his hand and knocking his vision into a star field. Surprisingly strong fingers wrenched the nightstick from his hand and tossed it aside.

"You get away from me, boy, before I have to get nasty." The old man was staring at him now, and Gary made sure not to let his eyes show any sign that Ken was getting ready to tackle the geezer.

The half-naked man shook his head and, without bothering to look back, did a spinning kick that was nearly flawless. The only problem was that he'd apparently forgotten he had a fake left leg, and that was the one he tried to balance on. The look on his face was comically surprised as his foot slid out from under him and dropped him on his side across the cracked pavement. His heel almost connected with Ken's jaw, but as the old saying goes, almost only counts in horseshoes.

The old man started to get up, and Ken drew back his own leg and kicked him in his stomach, lifting him off the ground. Ken wasn't one to accept being manhandled.

The mad stripper grunted and coughed as he rolled over. Ken moved closer, maybe just a little too confident that the fight had been knocked out of the man on the ground. With unexpected speed and strength, the man bucked his body back a bit and put all of his weight on his bloodied palms. Then he arced his body up and off the pavement and brought his right foot around in a vicious kick that connected with Ken's jaw. Even from a few feet away, Gary heard the bones in his partner's face break. Ken hit the ground like a dropped side of beef and stayed down.

"Sonuvabitch!" Gary took three steps back and drew his .38. Old man or not, he wasn't about to take any more chances with the sort of opponent that could drop his partner in a fight. Ken was one of the biggest men on the force, and he had spent several years when he was a wee bit younger as an amateur boxer.

The old man managed to land on his good leg and roll into a standing position. His eyes bored into Gary's and he smiled what had to be the most savage smile the police officer had ever seen. "Told you not to touch me. That went for your partner, too. Now, why don't you head on your way and we can both forget this whole, messy business before I have to get nasty with you."

Gary looked from the man to his revolver and shook his head. "You're kidding, right? Put your damn hands on the top of your head."

"Not happening, Junior. I have things to take care of." That smile stayed firmly in place, and the eyes looking at him kept boring inside Gary's head like they were trying to see if there was a brain hidden somewhere deep in there.

"It wasn't a request. You just took down a cop. You're not going anywhere."

"Guess again, sunshine."

"You make one move, old man, and I'll take you down."

The old man took one step forward and raised his hands above his head, hooking his fingers into wiggling claws. "BOO!"

Gary flinched. Unfortunately for both of them, the finger squeezing the trigger of his revolver flinched too.

The bullet pounded into the man's stomach and blew out through his back, sending him staggering back with a shocked look on his face.

"Oh fuck oh fuck oh fuck oh fuck!" Gary moved forward, all caution set aside, and dropped down next to the half-gutted man. His hand jumped up to his radio and he called in for two ambulances after making clear that there was an officer down.

The old man's skin had gone an unhealthy shade of gray and he was wheezing, his lips moving softly.

Gary leaned in closer to hear whatever it was the man might say.

The man's teeth were bared in an expression of raw pain as he leaned up just a bit to be heard well. "You moron," he hissed with hatred straining his words. "You could have at least gone for the heart."

That was the last thing he said before the ambulance arrived.

# Chapter One

The Cherry Hill Sanitarium was not, on the best of days, a cheerful facility. Established in 1843, the place had seen more than its fair share of tragedies in the one hundred and twenty-seven years it had been functional. What had started as a nice, exclusive facility where the wealthy could hide away their less savory family members had degraded over the years to become a privately owned asylum for the criminally insane.

The building was situated five miles from the closest township, on land that had been selected long ago for its inhospitable nature. Despite a small oasis of solid ground, the entire place was surrounded by swampland and littered here and there with the occasional pit of quicksand. There was no one who wanted the land, and that had been true even back when the original facility had been founded.

There were reasons for that, as we'll examine when the time is right. For now, it's enough to know that the structures built on the land were not happy places. How could they be? The very nature of the Cherry Hill Sanitarium leant to unhappiness. The minds they worked to treat were not merely injured, but usually shattered somewhere along the way. The asylum did not merely hold the delusional and the depressed, but the criminally insane. No inmate who came into the facility was there for anything less than extreme acts of violence against another human being. There might have been a few exceptions, true, but due process in a court of law said otherwise.

The campus was shaped like a wagon wheel, with a central hub and seven spokes running outward toward the actual rim of the wheel, said rim made of fortified stonewalls and barbed wire in this case. The exterior of the buildings was a façade of brickwork that lay hidden behind thick runners of vine, the better to hide the bars in the windows on the lower levels. The vines, while decorative enough, were kept trimmed down to avoid any possible use as a natural hand or foothold should anyone get through the two-inch-thick bars and wire reinforced glass of the actual windows. No chances were taken when it came to escape.

The interior of the wings was concrete and cinderblocks, painted an institutional shade of green that allegedly helped soothe the patients locked inside. Most of the people locked inside the building would have pointed out that the color was obnoxious, but no one would have listened to them in any case.

The central hub of the facility was slightly better, being the original building and a holdover from less industrial times. Though the rest of the compound was built with an eye toward security, the oblong central structure had been designed to be aesthetically pleasing. Large, spacious rooms held the visiting stations and the main offices for the doctors and nurses assigned to treating the wretches who came to dwell within the asylum.

In the largest of the offices, Doctor Roger Finney kept his desk, his files, and his world. At fifty-two years of age, he was considered one of the leading experts on criminal psychosis and was still thought of as something of a maverick when it came to treatments. If it was new and improved, he was one of the first to give it a go, and had, on a few occasions, come up with new methods of gaining insight into his patients' minds.

None of which mattered the least bit to him. The good doctor was, to be kind, obsessed with his work. To remind himself of this simple fact—as if he needed any reminding—he kept one of his favorite sayings posted on the wall, just below his calendar of M.C. Escher pictures. The saying was one of his own comments from his doctoral thesis: "The human mind is an oubliette, carefully hidden away within a labyrinth. There is no easy way to explore it or to discover its many hidden depths." His reason for having the saying on his wall had less to do with arrogance—though he could be very cocky when it suited him—and far more to do with reminding himself to be patient.

He always wanted results faster than was humanly possible. It was a weakness that he acknowledged and did his best to work around.

At the moment he was looking at one of the doctors under him, Phillip Harrington, who was not working out as well as Finney had hoped he would. Harrington was dressed in a gray suit with a crisp, white shirt and a red tie. He was doing his best to look in control of his own destiny, but he was failing. Maybe it was the sweat gleaming on the growing bald spot where his hair had receded, or the way he kept nervously chewing at his mustache. Despite his best efforts, he looked wretched. So far they'd sat in absolute silence for almost ten minutes, while Finney composed himself and Harrington did his best not to fidget too much.

That made Finney very happy, though he did his best not to show it.

"So…" Harrington spoke softly, almost as if he were afraid of being heard.

"Phil, I've been looking over your list of patients. I have to say, I'm not sure about a few of the decisions you made." He gestured to the stack of files on his desk and frowned. "I think we need to talk about your methods."

"I don't understand what you mean." His voice was calm, but the look in his eyes gave away that the man was nervous. "I've been following accepted protocol from day one."

"No, you've been going through the motions, Phil. I haven't seen a single case where you did more than you absolutely had to for any of your patients." He paused to let his words sink in, knowing full well that his comments were falling on deaf ears. "I've seen little more than doses of Thorazine for any of the people under your care, and that worries me."

Harrington stared at him blankly, but it was a ruse to buy time. Finney was a near master at reading human expression and he knew Phil well enough to understand when the man was trying to work out a proper answer in his head.

The phone rang on his desk and both men jumped a little. Roger grabbed it up before it could ring a second time. "This is Finney."

"Doctor Finney? This is Bob Wilkes." He nodded his head and held up one hand for Phil to wait a moment.

"Hello, Bob. What can I do for you?" He already knew the answer, of course. Wilkes was the head of security at the asylum and that meant he took care of seeing to every new arrival. The first order that Roger had put in place when he took over the asylum was that every person who came into the institute was to be met by him as soon as they were signed for.

"Well sir, the new patient arrived just now and you said you wanted to see him."

He said his thanks and then turned back to Harrington. "Let's finish this a little later, Phil, okay?"

The man looked at him and nodded. Roger pushed away from his desk and moved past the other doctor, barely even acknowledging him any longer.

The well-polished linoleum floors almost blurred as he walked. Roger did not believe in walking slowly to his destinations. Travel time reduced his ability to be properly effective. He moved down toward the receiving area and to the single room he kept there for the purpose of interviewing all new patients.

The interview process was important to keeping his hospital running smoothly. He had to assess each person for himself if he was going to understand who was best qualified to handle the new patients. Besides, his methods make it easier to keep up with the frequent reports he demanded of his staff.

The room where he met the newcomers was Spartan, having only two chairs and a small table. The chairs were bolted down and so was the table. The closest thing to a decoration was the metal ring that was also bolted into the concrete, a small concession to the need for security. Once a new patient was brought in, the cuffs they were wearing were chained to the bolt to stop them from getting overly enthusiastic. The first time he'd actually interviewed a new patient the man had tried to attack him. Even with chains in place, he'd managed to kick Roger in the face. Twelve stitches had taught him that the people he treated were in a maximum-security asylum for a reason.

He did not believe in letting the guards overhear the sessions between doctors and patients. Some of the topics discussed were exactly the sort of things that could cause the average person to want the patients lynched. So despite his desire to make the new arrivals as comfortable as possible, he still used the anchor and the chains for his own protection. A man had to know his limits.

The new patient was already in the room when he got there. The guards were positioned outside of the door and nodded to him as he approached. "How's our new client, gentlemen?"

"He's a quiet one, Doc." Bob Wilkes was a man of few words, another thing that Roger liked about him. The man was slim and in shape, an ex-military policeman who had earned Roger's trust and respect.

"Well, let's see if I can get him chatty enough to tell me his name, shall we?"

Wilkes opened the door and Roger walked in, taking his seat across from the stranger.

He was older than Roger expected, with short gray hair and a lean, hard form. His face was long and his nose was slightly hawkish. Roger had trouble reading his eyes, mostly because the man was staring hard at the floor.

"Well, welcome to Cherry Hill." He smiled politely.

The man nodded his head, but otherwise made no gesture.

"Can you tell me your name?" No response.

"Can you tell me what you did to get yourself sent to my facility?"

The man chuckled softly. "Yeah. I got bitchy with a few police officers."

Roger let himself smile at that one. A "few police officers" in this case meant a total of seven: two when he was initially arrested and several more when they took the man out of the hospital. Naturally he'd read over the case files and then studied the court transcripts. John Doe was very obviously not sane. He was here for the same reason that most of the people were here, because no one knew what to do with him. During his time in an actual holding cell, he'd broken several other prisoners' limbs and in one case, broken a man's back. The problem was, despite his actions, he showed little sign of being a dangerous person unless he was put into a confrontational situation. Apparently the man whose spine he'd ruined had been attempting to rape him at the time. Most of the others had started with small attempts to establish a pecking order and ended with near riots by the time it was all over.

Too violent to actually keep with the general populace, too crazy to be left to his own devices, and too unpredictable to leave in a regular prison, he'd been deemed criminally insane and sent to Roger.

"I'd really prefer to have your name, sir. I can call you John Doe if that's your preference, but honestly, what harm is there in letting me know who you are?"

Once again, the man's only response was silence.

"Why did you attack the police officers?"

"Because I told them not to touch me and they didn't listen."

"That hardly seems an appropriate response to an officer of the law, surely you realize that."

The man looked at him for the first time, and despite all of his training, Roger flinched when he looked into the new patient's eyes. They were nothing spectacular, plain and brown and unremarkable, but the intensity of the gaze was surprising, even for a man who was used to looking into the eyes of madmen.

"Let's give you your revelation for the day, shall we, Doctor? A little something to make you feel like you've done your job and made progress in the examination of your newest patient." Roger stared hard, taken aback not only by the fury in John Doe's expression, but also by the cultured, educated phrasing. "I was minding my own business and trying to sort out the things that have gone badly in my life just of late. I was bothering no one and simply wanted the same courtesy, because, I have to tell you, my life has gone to shit in the last few months. I was having one of the worst days of my very long life, Doctor, and because they were bored, a few officers of the law decided to get fussy about me not being properly dressed. All I can say to that is I found the clothing that I could. There wasn't much left after the plane crash, you understand."

The man stopped for a moment, his face perfectly calm except for the rage that seethed from his eyes. "I didn't want help, and I didn't want trouble. So when I told them not to touch me and they did anyway, I lost my temper. Oh, and those fine, upstanding officers of the law? They were using nightsticks. I was using my hands and my one good foot." His hands reached down and tapped his left leg, which gave off a clearly artificial sound, even over the rattle of his chains.

"I was defending myself. Was I maybe a little rude? Oh, yes. But I was still only defending myself."

Roger leaned over onto the small table and placed his elbows on the edge as he focused on the man. "One of them shot you in the stomach, didn't he? Why was that?"

"I said 'boo' to him and he panicked."

"That was all?"

"Well, I'd just knocked his partner down and he was a rookie."

"What plane crash, John? I'm not aware of any plane crashes."

The man shrugged "Small commercial jet. Went down a day or two before the incident with the cops. I was one of the passengers."

"I don't recall any notes on that."

John Doe grinned for just a second, a wolfish expression that changed the shape of his face. "I haven't seen any of the notes, Doctor. So I wouldn't know what you've heard."

"I think I would have remembered hearing anything about a plane crash."

"It might not have come up."

"Do you remember the flight number of the plane?"

"Not the vaguest clue."

Roger nodded and jotted himself a few notes. That was the sort of thing that could be researched, and that could, maybe, tell him who was on the plane that crashed, if there had actually been a plane. He was dealing with an unknown, after all.

"Are you sure you won't tell me your name?"

"Doctor, what makes you think I even know my name?"

Roger had to think about that one for a while, so he ended their session. Afterward, in his office again, he looked over his notes and decided that he'd keep close tabs on John Doe. He wasn't sure that he wanted to take the case for himself, but he would definitely keep watch.

A smile played at his lips when he made his final decision. Harrington would have the case. He needed something out of the ordinary to shake him up. John Doe might just be exactly what Phil needed. Roger had a strong feeling that Doe would not be as easily handled as some cases.

---

The guards handled their new charge with a modicum of respect, but mostly because he was old. He shuffled on as best he could and said nothing to anyone.

He didn't want to be here, but then who would? The place was about as comfortable and homey as a prison. Each of the doors they passed as they entered the North Wing was made of heavy-grade steel and had a number stenciled above it. His new home for the foreseeable future bore the number 29 and had a small window with wire mesh at the right height for sneaking peeks at him as discretely as anyone wanted to. A simple handle with a deadbolt lock and a three-inch-thick steel bar to slide across the door should he suddenly decide to go traipsing through the hallways in the middle of the night. Closer to the bottom was an access port for sliding his meals in.

The interior was just as lovely, with a thin mattress and a pillow, as well as his very own toilet, also made of steel. Aside from that, there was nothing, not even a desk.

He knew why, of course. He was considered a dangerous man. Those days were over. He would accept his time at the asylum and call it a blessing. This would be a nice enough place to die.

One of the guards walked into the room with him and had him sit on the mattress. Once he was down, the man unlocked the cuffs on his wrists and ankles and stepped back to the door.

"Listen up, sport. If you're smart and don't do anything to make waves, this isn't the worst place to be." Oh yes, this was the welcome speech. He managed to suppress a smile. "Don't try to attack anyone and we'll all get along fine. We'll be coming once a day to get you a shower and a shave, and if your doctor says it's all right, you'll be allowed outside for a bit. Other than that, this is your new home. Make the best of it."

He liked the guard. The man was direct and honest and didn't feel the need to beat his chest to show everyone who was boss. They'd probably get along just fine.

A few moments later, the door was closed and locked and John Doe leaned back on the cot and settled in for rest.

The screams from one of the other inmates lulled him to sleep.

---

The air in the room smelled bad, but that was to be expected. On the lowest level of the asylum was the wing where the least functional patients were kept, and the man sitting in the small room qualified as barely smarter than a carrot these days.

After more violent episodes than anyone else in the history of Cherry Hill, Dr. Phillip Harrington decided that Alex Granger was too dangerous to himself and to others to be left merely drugged out of his mind. Electroshock therapy had failed to make him more agreeable and so had locking him in an isolation chamber. Thorazine and every other anti-psychotic they used seemed to keep him calm for about ten minutes before he went into another hyperactive assault mode.

After the third time Granger escaped from a straitjacket, the most extreme measures had to be taken. He was lobotomized. A small, sharp implement was used to frappe his frontal lobes in an effort to make him calm down. By God, that had the desired effect.

These days Granger stared at the walls and rocked back and forth when he was feeling frisky. Most of the time he simply stared and drooled.

Alexander Anthony Granger was nineteen when he was delivered to Cherry Hill. He was arrested after a long string of murders led figuratively and literally to his front door. Police in Philadelphia had spent months seeking any sort of evidence in connection to a cannibal killer who apparently hunted and then mutilated the bodies of his victims.

Alex was found coming home with a head gripped in his hand, held by the long hair of the teenager he'd decapitated. Michelle Ellis was the last person he killed, but a quick look inside the basement of the home he shared with his grandmother made clear that she was not the first. He'd kept their heads, leaving their bodies to rot wherever they dropped.

Granger didn't resist when the police took him in and he didn't have much to say when he was questioned and later taken to trial. He was another case where the only real way to handle the situation was to have him locked away where he could harm neither himself nor others.

That hadn't worked so well and the end result was the lump of flesh now sitting on the mattress in his room, stewing in his own wastes.

The interns and nurses came around and cleaned him every day, changing the plastic sheets on his mattress and helping keep him as tidy as they could. He ate the pureed foods they gave him and behaved better now than he ever had before the operation.

Whenever anyone looked in on him, he was as quiet as a mouse and as docile as a newborn babe.

Granger fell back on his cot and his body twitched a few times, his eyes rolling back into his head as his muscles danced to their own tunes. To date no one had ever seen one of his seizures, or felt the sudden chill that came into the room, or heard the whispers that surrounded him when they happened.

No one saw the smile that twisted those bland features into something frighteningly like the expression Granger wore before the lobotomy. And the instruments that could have recorded his massive surge in brain activity hadn't even been invented yet.

The doctors would have been amazed to see what was growing in place of his frontal lobes. They would have made him famous with their careful studies and the copious notes they would have taken.

But Granger was a model patient these days. He never made a sound and he never caused trouble.

Maybe if he had, they would have known what was coming and been able to prevent it.

Or maybe they would have just died violent deaths, instead.

Some things are more careful about hiding.

What was growing inside of Alex Granger was newly formed and young, but more cautious than Alex Granger had ever been.

# Chapter Two

The leakage started slowly. It almost always came as a trickle first, and by the time he knew about it, whatever had caused the problem was ready to break the pipes into shreds. Currently, there was a pool of water soaking his knees as a reminder of that sad fact.

Billy Hague always hated that part of his job. He stared at the toilet in cell number 31 and scowled. "You just know that sombitch did something to it on purpose. Every damn time I come to his cell, I find the worst things stuck in this here bowl."

Wilkes chuckled and nodded his head. "Know why he does it, Billy?"

Hague pulled his plunger from its spot on his cart and looked back at the security guard. "Why don't you enlighten me while I find out what he used this time?"

"Because there's only two places we're gonna take him in this sort of situation. Either he gets to go to the park or he gets to sit for an extra hour in the cafeteria."

The custodian nodded his head. "Which one is he doing today?"

"He's in the park." The park was what everyone in the place called the patch of grass, benches and two stunted trees where the inmates could go for a spell.

"Well, I guess I can't begrudge him that one. Got to beat staring at the same four walls." He attacked the clogged toilet bowl with the plunger, doing his best to force the water down hard enough to dispel the clog. It was a stubborn lump of whatever, and after a few tries he gave up and reached for the coiled steel snake designed for just such an emergency.

"That's why we let him get away with it, the poor old bastard." The man in question was a flabby, pasty slob who had tried to prove his love for a woman by killing her entire family. Aside from that one miscalculation, he'd never hurt a single person. Understandably, the woman whose family he'd set ablaze didn't seem to find the gesture overly romantic. Hague couldn't remember the man's name, but he'd long ago started calling him "Cupid," because of the literally thousands of love letters he'd written over the years.

No one seemed to have the heart to tell him his paramour had died ten years earlier. Hague wasn't about to be the one to spill the beans. He could have changed his mind when a wave of water splashed his legs and soaked him a little more than he already was.

"Christ on a bike!" He pushed and prodded the blockage, but couldn't get it to move.

"Giving you a little trouble there, Billy?"

Hague shot him a withering look. "Yeah, you could say that." It was time to go for the big guns, and he didn't hesitate. He grabbed a different, more elaborate contraption that he'd picked up from a friend who was a plumber a few years earlier. The rooter was half an inch thick and ended in a set of pinchers that could clamp down and pull back out of the toilet damned near anything that was put in. If this didn't work, he'd be forced to actually remove the toilet bowl, and that wasn't an idea he liked very much. Cupid was rapidly getting on his nerves, love letters be damned.

Wilkes gave out a low whistle of appreciation. "Guess he got a little serious this time around."

"He gets any more serious, I'm gonna shove this thing up his ass and pull his liver out." The device slid in and Hague worked it until he found the blockage. Once he was sure he had the thing in place well enough, he used the grip on the far end and clamped down on the obstruction. It was tough, whatever it was. He could feel the obstruction giving a little, but not as much as he would have liked. Whatever the hell the man had shoved into the toilet wasn't ready to move without a serious fight.

Hague pulled hard and felt the stuff move toward him, the snake sliding forward by an inch before it stopped. Wilkes shook his head and moved closer. "You need some help?"

"I won't complain. You need to stop giving that sonovawhore things to write with."

"Oh, quit being such a wimp and move over." Hague slid a little to the side and the guard braced one foot against the commode as he grabbed the snake. The two of them counted to three and put their backs into it. Whatever was in there slid forward again, giving a little, but not enough to pull it loose.

"Damn." Wilkes shook his head. "Why isn't the pipe just busting?"

"For all I know it is."

"That's not funny, Billy."

"You hear me laughing? No, I didn't think you did."

"One more try?" Wilkes looked dubious, but Billy wasn't about to turn down the help. Again they counted to three and gave it the old college try, this time with more success. With both of them straining and holding the snake tightly, the blockage suddenly slid forward, spiking more water from the toilet bowl on the floor. Billy cursed as his already soaked pants got wetter, but at least they'd managed to snag the blockage.

It came out of the toilet in a rush, and the stench made both men gag. Hague coughed and looked away for a moment, but Wilkes looked at the lump and then backed away quickly. "What in the name of God?"

The clamps at the end of the snake held their prize for both men to see: a dark gray, putrid lump of meat, raw and rotting. Hague saw three fingers in the tangle of decay and dropped the snake right then and there. A wedding ring glistened on one of the digits.

"There ain't no way I'm seeing that."

"Back away from it, Billy." Wilkes put a hand on his shoulder and urged him to move. "It's time to call in the cops."

Hague broke policy and reached for his smokes, lighting up as he sat at the far end of the room and stared at the remains of a human hand. Wilkes joined him a few minutes later, both of them forced to wait for the police to show and start asking questions.

They were both still there several hours later, after the police removed the toilet bowl and began extracting the mangled human body that was blocking the pipes. Despite their best efforts, the only way to remove the mortal remains was to take it out in bits and pieces.

Billy Hague turned in his notice just after the question-and-answer part of his day was finished. He wasn't a superstitious man, but he couldn't bring himself to work at a place where anyone or anything could manage to cram a grown man into a four-inch-wide pipe.

---

Phil Harrington sat in the room provided for dealing with his patients and stared at the man on the couch. He had no reason at all to be scared about the meeting; the man was once again in cuffs that were anchored to the floor, but he was scared anyway.

Something about the man was just creepy as all hell and he knew in his heart that as much as he was assessing his new patient, the man was taking his measure.

"So, John, why don't you tell me about yourself?"

"I'm really amazingly boring. Mostly I sit in my cell and stare at the wall. There aren't even any interesting water stains to look at."

"Would you like some paper and a few markers?"

"I don't draw much. Mostly I whittle." The man looked his way and winked. "I'm guessing there isn't much chance of getting some wood and a good whittling knife."

Harrington chuckled, feeling a little more at ease. "No, that's not really likely to happen for a while, but I could get you a few bars of soap and couple of plastic knives. You'll have to work with them carefully, they break easily, but I could arrange that."

"Do that, and we'll be friends for life."

He made a quick note on the legal pad he had across his leg. "Consider it done. Now, in return, tell me about yourself."

"What do you want to know?"

"Everything. Are you married, what do you do for a living, do you have kids, how did you lose your leg."

"I was married. Now I'm a widower. I had three children. They're all dead. For a while I was a professor of theological studies with a side of parapsychology, but it got boring. I lost my leg in Korea, where I made the mistake of stepping on a mine."

He looked at the man in absolute silence. That was the most John Doe had spoken to him. "How did your wife die?"

The man sat up straighter and looked him in the eye. "I really don't want to discuss that."

"John, how can we work on making you better if you aren't willing to share the information that we need in order to find out the problems?"

John Doe smiled at him and leaned forward, placing his elbows on his knees, like he was just going to have a nice, casual conversation. The smile was the sort that said he could easily take a bite out of Phil's face, as if he were a ripe, tasty apple. "We're going to get this out of the way. I'm going to tell you this once, Dr. Harrington, and then we'll move on to other things, am I making myself clear?"

"By all means, John." He prepared to take all the notes he needed and looked at his patient.

"My wife is dead. My children are dead. They lived happily and I was happy with them. But I made a mistake and that mistake came back to haunt me." Harrington opened his mouth to speak and his patient held up a hand to stop him. "Let me finish and then you can ask me five questions. I suppose you can ask more than that, but I will only answer five."

Harrington nodded.

"Now, I did some very dangerous work a while back and I quit that work. I gave up that life when I decided to get married and settle down. Someone I thought had been removed from the picture came back into my life and murdered my wife and my children. When that was done, that special someone tried to kill me. I'm tougher than I look."

"I'm sorry for your loss, John. When did all of this happen?"

"A few months ago."

"Right before you were incarcerated?"

"That's right. I was still trying to work it all out in my head when I had my unfortunate run-in with the police."

"What happened to the person who killed your family?"

"I think I killed him."

"How did that make you feel?"

"The murders? Like my life was over, which it is. Killing him?" He shrugged. "Like there was still a possibility for joy in my life."

"Were you wanted by the police for killing him?"

"No one ever found the body. Believe me, no one will ever find the body."

"Do you believe in God, John?"

"Sorry, Doc. That was five questions. You're all out of answers."

They sat in silence for the rest of their appointment.

---

He sat in his cell and stared at the wall, infuriated by the audacity of Harrington. It didn't matter that the man was supposed to ask him questions. It didn't matter that he knew the head doctor was only trying to help. He didn't want to talk about his past. His past was best left behind.

He couldn't escape from the things that had happened, but he could fake it if he tried hard enough. Every time he closed his eyes he saw the remains of his family scattered across the inside of his house, ripped into bloody pieces and strewn about as if they were mere trash for the garbage heap.

"Stop thinking about it," he warned himself. "If you think about it, it's real."

When he closed his eyes he could hear their voices, see their faces and almost feel them.

But that was impossible after what had been done.

John Doe closed his eyes and settled back on his mattress. Three doors down the hallway, the man he'd already come to think of as "The Screamer" was wailing out agonized cries and begging somebody to leave him alone.

Even at full volume he was less of a distraction than he would have been in the outside world.

Doe looked at the pills they'd given him to swallow earlier, the ones he'd fake swallowed after his evening meal. He knew what they were, that they were designed not to cure a psychosis but to dope him to the point where he couldn't be violent on a bet.

He didn't believe in anesthetizing his mind. It was the one asset he still had that could be useful in his life. Still, it was his mind that was haunting him, making his existence more miserable than he wanted to be.

The Screamer stopped wailing and settled down into a much softer crying jag, his sobs echoing down the hall in waves of desperation.

Something dark and menacing slipped through the wall in John Doe's room and looked at him for several seconds, taking his measure. It was not natural, he knew that immediately.

Doe sat up and stared at the thing and it in turn stared back, surprised that he could see it.

The thing took one step closer and thought about reaching for him; a spectral hand moved away from the pool of darkness that made up its body and stretched in his direction.

"Now then, do you_*really*_want to do that?" he spoke softly, but knew it heard him.

The thing flinched just a bit and then slid out of his room, fading through the wall as if it were nothing but a thin mist.

John took the pills to the toilet and flushed them, watching as they were caught in the currents and finally knocked down into the sewer pipes.

"No pills for you, old fellow. Not yet anyway."

He settled in for the night, lulled by the sounds of the Screamer crying.

---

The Cherry Hill Mental Health Institute rested as well, the doctors reduced to only two for emergencies and the patients fed their nightly doses of medication.

The lights that normally burned throughout the day were still lit, but they flickered at one-third the brilliance, leaving just enough illumination to let the guards walk their beats and ensure that no one being held in the place got stupid.

Ernst Holbrook was the night watchman on the North Wing. He seldom had any troubles, aside from people like Lawrence Poole screaming away half the night. Even Poole was being quiet for a change.

Just after midnight he made his usual rounds, starting at the top of the fourth floor and working his way down level by level, he looked into each of the rooms and made sure no one was misbehaving.

On the third floor he pulled out his cell keys and held them tightly in his fist to ensure no one would hear them jingling. The third floor was the women's ward, where most of the cells were empty. There were only seven patients in all of the rooms, and few people would have willingly called any of them human if they knew the truth about what they had done. Sandra Dennings had stabbed her husband of seven years over fifty times, claiming that he beat her and made her do bad things. He couldn't defend himself, being dead and all, so the choices were to let her go or lock her away. Somebody decided she needed a mental overhaul and now she was a guest on his ward. She'd been a looker in her time, but that was all in the past. Before they upped her drugs the last time around, she'd taken to ramming her face into the wall. She'd shattered her chin, her left cheek and four teeth before they restrained her. What was left of her face had taken on all different contours when she was done healing.

Eloise Fischer was only three cells down from Sandra of the mashed face. Ellie had taken a can of gasoline and set her house on fire. She was still inside when it happened. She didn't try to move or struggle until the firefighters came to her rescue. She fought the firemen for every inch of burning space they dragged her from. They got to her, but not until she'd suffered third-degree burns over half of her body. It was touch and go as to whether or not she'd live for a while, but they saved her. Well, her body at any rate. Her mind was as gone as gone could be, and no one had managed to make her talk since her arrival.

They found the bodies of over four hundred cats inside her house. As he understood it, some of them had been dead for years.

Leslie Anne Hampton was in the cell at the end of the wing. He still didn't know why she was in the place, only that she was. Leslie Anne was thin and pretty in a mousy sort of way. Best of all, she went out like a light when she was given her meds.

He opened her cell and checked on her, locking the door for the safety of everyone concerned. She was alive, but deeply unconscious. Ernst took advantage of the situation and had his way with her. She didn't complain. She never did.

When he was finished and had cleaned her up properly, he left her cell and moved on down toward the second floor. The stairwell was better lit than the corridors and he started down them with a spring in his step.

For a moment, just as he was setting his foot on the landing where the stairs turned back on themselves, his skin pulled tight and the hairs on his neck rose in a wave of gooseflesh.

Ernst looked all around, half certain that he'd heard or seen something, but not sure exactly what it was. He listened carefully and scanned everywhere, fully expecting to find a patient walking the stairs and trying to hide.

There was nothing to see and nothing to hear, so Ernst moved along, rubbing his hands over his arms and suffering from the distinct feeling that someone was watching him.

Something was, of course, doing just that. It watched him when he took advantage of Leslie Anne Hampton and it watched him as he checked all of the cells on the second floor of the North Wing.

It watched, and decided it did not like what it saw.

But now was not the time. Soon, it promised itself, but not just yet. Maybe tomorrow night.

When it was properly hungry again.

# Chapter Three

Roger Finney answered the questions to the best of his ability, and even though he had done nothing wrong, the police detective intimidated the hell out of him. Detective Branaugh was intimidating, any way you looked at him. The man stood over six feet tall and looked like he should have been a linebacker. He also had the sort of face that gave away nothing at all. Probably the worst part was that, even when he was looking at you, he seemed more like he was looking through you. Finney had seen a lot of men with that sort of intensity. The difference was that most of them were locked away in his buildings, not coming in to ask questions about the corpse found rammed down a drainage pipe.

"I honestly don't know what to say, Detective. I've triple checked, and we're not missing any of our patients or any of our staff. It doesn't make any sense to me."

"Well, I expect we'll know more when we hear back from the coroner." The man looked around the office as he spoke, never seeming to actually focus on anything for more than an instant before he looked away.

"If there's anything we can do to help, please, just let us know."

"You can count on it." The man stood up, readjusting his jacket as he did so. "There is one thing you could do for me."

"What's that?"

The detective handed him a card. "Let me know if you hear anything from the inmates. I know it isn't likely, but maybe one of them heard something that could be useful."

"Of course." He stood up and shook the man's hand, hoping his grip didn't shake too much. He couldn't have explained it in a million years, but something about the detective made him nervous.

Something about the entire situation made him jumpy, who the hell was he kidding?

He sat back down at his desk and pulled a cigarette from his pack. They were an annoying habit and one he'd tried to break a few times before deciding he needed to keep at least a few vices in his life.

Just as soon as he lit up, the phone rang. He put out the smoke with a muttered curse and answered it.

"There's a problem with the new patient." Harrington's voice reminded him that he still needed to chew the man out.

"What seems to be the problem, Phil?"

"The man is unresponsive. I mean he's borderline comatose."

"John Doe?"

"The very same. His pupils aren't fixed, but I'm getting no sort of activity out of him at all. No response to pain, nothing."

"Reaction to medications?"

"I don't think so. His pulse is perfect, his respiratory is fine, no signs of a rash or anything else."

"I'll be right there." He hung up the phone and lit his cigarette again, frowning to himself. He'd have a few minutes to himself and then he'd find out what was happening.

*You already know what's happening. It's happened before, hasn't it?*

He didn't want to jump to any conclusions before a proper examination had taken place. Scientists were supposed to handle things in a certain way and he refused to let himself dwell on what had happened to a few of the other patients who exhibited catatonia early on in their stays.

He didn't bother with putting back on his lab coat—a violation of his own rules—but moved as quickly as he could toward the cell he'd assigned the new patient. The worst part of it was not knowing, of course. In this case he didn't know if Phil had screwed up with medications or if the situation was worse than that, one of the rare occasions where he couldn't make it right.

There were two guards stationed outside in the hallway to room 29. Both of them were very alert, facing toward the open doorway and the two men inside the room.

Phil was wringing his hands and looking like all he wanted to do was curl up in a corner and hide until the newest problem went away. The man had the potential to be brilliant, but his lack of innovation and appalling inability to deal with a crisis crippled him as far as Roger was concerned.

He ignored Phil and moved closer to the new patient. His skin wasn't flushed, there was no sign of a rash, and his pulse was perfect.

"When did this start?"

"I don't know. The last time anyone checked on him he was fine."

"When was the last time he was checked on?"

"This morning when the shift change took place. The attending nurse noted he seemed in good spirits."

"Well, let's get him to a proper examination room."

John Doe sat up in his cot and smiled. Phil let out a yelp and Roger stared at the man who two seconds earlier had been dead to the world.

"Well, I have an audience," the voice was dry and sarcastic. "How lovely."

Roger shrugged. "You were unconscious, John. Do you know if there's a history of epileptic seizures in your background?"

"I wasn't unconscious. I was meditating."

"You put yourself into a meditative state?"

"That would be the premise behind meditation, yes."

"Well, you had Dr. Harrington a bit worried. He tried to revive you and you were completely unresponsive."

"I'm a deep sleeper when I want to be." Doe smiled at him and Roger resisted the urge to flinch. His smile had nothing to do with kindness or humor.

"In the future, you might want to leave a warning about your meditation. You almost wound up in the infirmary."

"Does the infirmary have real beds as opposed to a mattress on the floor?"

"Yes."

"Then I probably won't be leaving any notes." He shrugged. "I have to say, the accommodations aren't at all what I was expecting."

Harrington was pacing and red faced. No doubt he felt that he had just been humiliated.

"No one can sleep that deeply!" Phil's voice was louder than he meant it to be and both of the men in the room looked in his direction while the two guards outside did their best not to laugh out loud.

"I wasn't sleeping. I was meditating." Doe spoke slowly and clearly enunciated as if he were speaking to a slightly deaf imbecile. "I heard you, Doc. I just didn't feel like answering you."

Phil's face went redder still and Roger bit the side of his lip to stop from braying laughter.

"That's not a wise thing to do around here, John. It most decidedly isn't." Harrington's voice was low and menacing.

"Calm down, Dr. Harrington." Roger spoke in placating tones. "John hasn't even been here for two days. It'll take him a while to get used to the rules."

Doe was looking at Finney, the smile gone from his weathered face and the look in his eyes was less than pleasant. "Wanna' get me a new doctor? I don't think Harrington likes me very much."

"Oh, I suspect the two of you can overlook a simple misunderstanding, John, don't you?"

Doe stared hard at the other doctor; his eyes focused and clear enough that Roger had to wonder if he'd actually taken his medications. "Yeah. I guess we can look past this incident, can't we, Doc?"

Harrington stared hard back for a moment and then finally nodded his head.

"I'm sure we can, John."

Roger clapped his hands in a well-that's-all-settled-then gesture. "Excellent. Now, gentlemen, if you don't mind, I have business to attend to."

That was one dilemma solved at least. It was a start.

Roger headed back to his office, finally ready to get the day under way.

---

A few hours later, when both men had been given time to reflect, Phil settled down in his interview room to start his second session with John Doe.

"So, tell me about your meditation, John. How long have you been able to do that?"

"Long as I can remember. I got it fine-tuned a bit when I was in the Himalayas." His tone was completely casual.

"What do you do when you meditate?"

"It's a method of calming myself. I've been a little stressed lately."

"Any special reason for the stress?" Phil shook his head even as he spoke. "I mean aside from the obvious?"

"You mean aside from a dead family, being locked in an asylum and having to listen to the Screamer a few doors down the hall?" Doe smiled, his face taking on all the charm of a predatory animal getting ready to pounce. "Might have something to do with the ghosts in this place."

"You think we have ghosts here?"

"Oh, yes." Doe nodded his head up and down three times, very slowly. "You definitely have ghosts."

"What makes you say that, John?"

Doe looked at him and shrugged. "Well, it would explain why the guy three doors down from me is screaming for them to leave him alone, now wouldn't it?"

"Well, John, you are in an asylum." He couldn't help letting out the barb.

"Really? I thought this was a vacation resort. I was going to ask when all the campfire songs and the formal dances were supposed to start."

"So you really think this place is haunted?"

It was Doe's turn to be snide. "Will you think I'm crazy if I say yes?"

Harrington cleared his throat. "Okay, John. Let's talk about getting you better, shall we?"

"What did you have in mind for that, Doctor?"

"Well, first we have to understand why you acted the way you did and we have to figure out what your real identity is. Amnesia is a problem, John, especially in cases where you obviously have some of your memories intact. So I'm going to start you off with a series of questions about what you do and do not know."

"Wasn't all of that covered in the transcripts you received from the determining psychologist in the case?"

Harrington made a note on his papers about remembering that Doe was sharper than most, despite the heavy medications. "Well, yes, but psychology is largely subjective. His interpretations of what your answers to questions mean and my interpretations might not meet up too often."

"So, fine. Ask your questions, let's see what we can get done today, shall we?"

Doe slid around in his seat and got as comfortable as he could with the handcuffs that anchored him to the floor.

"Okay, for starters, where were you born?"

Doe looked at his hands, his face thoughtful, and shook his head. "No clue."

"What year were you born?"

"No idea."

Harrington made notes next to each of the answers that came his way.

"What did you do for a living?"

"I'm pretty sure I was a teacher. I remember standing at a podium and talking to a classroom full of kids. Older, maybe high school, maybe college."

"Where did you teach?"

"No idea."

"What's your address?"

"819 Sycamore Street, Irvine, California." The man looked completely shocked as he got the answer. "Didn't know I had that one in me."

Before the man could think about anything else to relax himself, Harrington continued. "What's your name?"

The brief victory faded from Doe's face. "Nope. I got nothing."

"Your wife's name?"

"No clue." He frowned, trying hard to get something useful from his brain. If Doe was faking the entire amnesia to get out of doing hard time, he was better at it than most.

"When did you get married?"

"July 12th, 1958."

"Where did you get married?"

"I want to say New York, but I might be wrong."

"How old is your wife?"

"She'd have been thirty-six."

He paused and looked at the old man in front of him. Somehow the geezer had managed to marry a woman easily half his age.

"You can knock the smirk off your face, Doc." Doe was looking at him, smiling again, his eyes half-lidded. "Or I can knock it off your face for you."

Harrington ignored the response and asked another question. "How old are you?"

"I don't know."

"What was your mother's name?"

"No idea."

"Why did you attack the police officers?"

"Because they wouldn't leave me in peace."

"Why were they bothering you?"

"I was half naked and talking to myself."

"What were you talking about?"

"Dying."

"Did you think you were dying?"

"No, I wanted to die."

"Why did you want to die?"

"I had nothing to live for."

"Did you kill your wife?"

"No."

"Did you kill your children?"

"No."

"How many people have you killed in your life?"

"Too many to count."

"Why did you kill them?"

"They were bad people."

"How were they bad?"

"I don't want to do this any more, Doctor. My head hurts something fierce."

Phil nodded at the old man in front of him and made his final notations for the session.

"I'll have that soap and those carving tools in your room when we get you back there, John."

"Thanks." The man managed a very weak smile. He looked like hell.

---

Thirty minutes later, John Doe lay on his back in the room that had become his world and tried to sleep.

It was a nice idea, but it wasn't working. Every time he closed his eyes for more than a few seconds the emotions overcame him again. He could almost see his wife's face. He could almost hear his children's voices, but they were as hard to grasp as soap bubbles. Every time he had them within his reach they burst and escaped him again.

His eyes felt hot and gritty from the tears he kept crying and he wanted them gone.

"Meditating. What a crock of shit." He rolled over and faced away from the cell door. He wanted no witnesses to his weakness. His left leg ached like mad below the knee, which was impossible, of course, because he had no leg down there. He made himself resist the urge to scratch at the insufferable itch that radiated from his stump. What had he told the doctor? That he'd stepped on a mine? Yes, and it sounded right, but as soon as he gave any of his answers they sounded like the truth. He didn't know what he was making up and what was real. It seemed, for whatever reason, that part of his mind was working and part of it—

He clutched the grips on his seat as the world went into an insane spin, tossing the sky and the earth below him around and around. His heart was beating hard enough to damn near paralyze him and his damned glasses had fallen away from his face. Not far away from him the single stewardess working the flight had given up telling everyone to be calm and was screaming at the top of her lungs. The fat man sitting in the seat in front of him was crying out for God to save him, and the engines on the plane were howling as they burst into flames. He never thought the damned things could get him from up here…

—was trying to hide from some very painful truths.

"Who am I?" That was the million-dollar question.

John Doe curled himself into a tight ball and closed his eyes, willing the images and voices to leave him alone for a while. Eventually he slept.

---

Did it have a proper name? No, not that it knew of. Its host, Alex Granger thought of it as a god that demanded sacrifices. It didn't know if that was true or not, but the feasts Granger had delivered in the past had certainly left it sated for a time.

Now it was growing hungry.

Granger had managed to eat by himself today, chewing and swallowing while the nurse and two attendants watched. The nurse—Kimberly, with blue eyes and brown hair and a smile that made Granger feel gentle when he was around her—had smiled encouragements and then helped clean his face where he'd missed.

It liked Kimberly, too, but not in the same way. Kimberly had a quality to her that it had found rare. She had compassion. The orderlies gave off waves of disgust and boredom, but the nurse seemed pleased by Alex Granger's recovery from the surgery that had gone wrong. It couldn't read their minds, but it could sense what they felt.

Alex Granger's body fell back in the mattress and seemed to slumber as it slipped away from him. While inside Granger's body it felt safe and warm and blind. There were risks that came with leaving that warm safety, but there were also new experiences waiting away from Granger's body. It had an insatiable curiosity.

It slipped through the door with no concern for whether or not it was locked, and sought what it always sought: sustenance.

The emotions that it sensed inside its host were diluted, watered down by Granger's own warped mind. Here, freed of that particular burden, it could see/feel/taste so much more. The living beings around it seldom reacted to its presence—excluding only the old man with one leg, who had actually seen it and spoken to it. The dead, however, saw it with ease.

What little it understood of theology it had gathered from Granger's thoughts. There were concepts of good and evil, Heaven and Hell, and all of them made a certain amount of sense, but none of them seemed to complete the picture of a world in harmony. Ghosts should not exist according to Granger's thoughts, but they were here and all around the place. Some of them saw it and moved in the other direction; some merely noticed that it was there and went about their own business, suffering a torment that left it wondering if Hell somehow occupied the same physical location as the world of the living.

The dead suffered, most of them constantly, locked in their own mental prisons and unable to move from the asylum. Was it their madness that caused them to stay? Did they endure by choice? It didn't know the answers, but found the questions infinitely fascinating.

One of the dead came toward it, an angry thing that demanded satisfaction. This one was newly dead, the emotions still vibrant and pulsing, unlike the older dead that seemed to have lost most of their memories.

The ghost came closer and roared, filled with fury and frustration. It did what it always did when one of the dead challenged it; it reached out to take what it needed. Too late the ghost realized the error of its ways and begged for mercy.

It did not know what mercy was and did not care. Right now it was hungry and needed food. The ghost provided that sustenance without any choice in the matter.

Nurse Kimberly walked through the both of them. She was talking to the man who had carved holes in Granger's brain at the time. Quite unaware that they were doing it, both of the living beings shivered as they passed through the space it occupied. The sensation was interesting. Their emotions—*he's a strange man, kind of quiet, but cute in a goofy way and I'd pay_money to get her out of that uniform and into my lap*—flashed through its perceptions at the same time that they both unconsciously fought off the sudden chill.

Later, when it had time, it would contemplate what the sensations meant. For now, it had two other tasks it wanted to finish before it had to rest again.

What remained of the ghostly presence was struggling to survive. It crawled along the ground and tried to fully comprehend what had just happened.

It looked at the wretched thing and felt the energies it had stolen coursing through its essence. Then it rose through the ceiling, pushing past levels of people and stone and furniture as it sought what it wanted to deal with next.

Feeding was not a matter of physical satisfaction: it had no body. Instead the act of eating brought psychic impact, a myriad of memories broken and distorted, to sample. As a result, it was hard to concentrate after satisfying its hunger. It did what it could, pushing aside the rambling, screaming echoes of the psyche it had just devoured. There at last was the place it sought, the source of strange energies that it had felt earlier and that were now coalescing. The woman on the bed was incapacitated, her mind—what little there was of it—was locked into a stupor by the medications she was forced to consume.

It settled down to wait, knowing that what it sought would come to this place as it did almost every night. It was patient. Granger had taught it that much. Sometimes, it knew, you had to wait for a while before you could get what you wanted. Why stalk the prey when the prey will come to you?

# Chapter Four

Night came to Cherry Hill as it always did, with a changing of the staff and a reduction in the lighting. For the most part the only noises heard were the sounds of medicated snores and an occasional scream just to keep everyone on their toes.

Ernst Holbrook was doing his own thing again. He always changed his routine a bit, just to keep things from getting boring, so he started with the top floor for his rounds, and then planned to work his way down to the ground level.

Leslie Anne Hampton was asleep when he got to her cell. He'd expected that. He was as cautious as always, and made sure to lock the door once he was inside her cell.

He made it five steps toward her sleeping form, prepared to satisfy himself with her sleeping body, before the attack. Ernst staggered as he felt something cold slither into his skull, probing deeply not into the matter of his brain, but in his mind. There was no pain, merely an overwhelming sense of loss. Memories were shredded, ripped from him and devoured with all the savagery of a school of hungry piranha.

The guard fell to the ground and moaned deeply as his body reacted to the violation. His pulse increased to the point where he no longer heard a steady beat but something more like a constant hum and his blood pressure soared to deadly levels. His face slammed into the tile floor and he soiled himself, as his motor functions failed him.

Ernst, or at least what was left of him, lay there and twitched for almost five minutes.

Then the thing in the room, unseen but most certainly not unfelt, tried something different. Looking at the body of the man before it, the thing decided to try physical gratification.

Ernst was beyond screaming.

So was Leslie. She did not witness the slow and methodical destruction of Ernst, and knew nothing of his death until the morning came and she awoke from her stupor.

Then she screamed. She screamed herself senseless. What was left of the man wasn't pretty to look at. Worst of all, perhaps, was that it was still alive.

---

John Doe sat in his cell and listened to the chaos as it flowed past his little oasis. He didn't know all the details, but he gathered that someone had been maimed, and very badly.

His hands moved with careful precision, carving a heavy bar of Ivory soap into an image without any conscious thought on his part. Flakes fell away and revealed a face that he knew should have been familiar, but wasn't.

The amnesia thing was getting old. Something had happened to him that left him with scattered memories and he couldn't stand it. How the hell could he know he was happily married and not remember the name of his wife?

Before he could get completely lost in his darkening thoughts the door to his cell opened. The same two guards who'd taken him to his session the day before were standing there, looking particularly grim and even a little queasy.

"Bad night, guys?"

"You don't want to know." That was the older guard, the one in charge of security for the place. Doe liked him. He was straightforward and treated the inmates like human beings as long as they behaved.

Being as he thought favorably of the man, John went with him and avoided causing a scene. They waited patiently while he set down his carving and held out his hands for the cuffs he knew were coming. Then the ankle locks.

Five minutes later they were on their way down the hallway and his session with the doctor. There was a slight delay while a medical team passed them by, pushing a gurney that had something strapped to it and covered with a thin white sheet. Whatever it was struggled and thrashed under the cover.

Doe's skin tingled as the lump moved on, and he stared at it for several seconds, joined by both of the guards who looked paler than they had before.

Doe looked from the older guard to the younger, lanky man who was normally with him. "Friend of yours?"

The younger guard sneered. The older guard grimly shook his head and said, "Let it go."

He dropped it. A part of him wanted very badly to know what was under that sheet, but these weren't the right people to ask. They were in a foul mood and he was too frail and withered to antagonize them too much. And besides, there was something going on that he maybe didn't really want to know about something that left him…

Afraid. Why am I afraid?

nervous and edgy. So he let it go and shrugged. A few minutes later they were back at the interview room.

Then it was back to the routine: the guards secured him in the room and locked his binding cuffs to the floor before stepping outside of the room where they would wait until his latest session was completed.

This time he got a variance in his routine. This time it was the other doctor, Finney was the name, that came in to talk with him.

"How are you feeling today, John?"

"Like I've been locked in an asylum and left to rot. How about you, Doc?"

Finney looked at him for a moment and then smiled. Nice man, not the brightest bulb on the Christmas tree, but nice.

"I thought I'd take a little time and ask you a few questions, if you don't mind, John."

"Harrington already that sick of me?"

"No," he actually chuckled. "I like to keep on top of the list of patients and see if I can get a fresh perspective from time to time."

*Translated, you think my doctor is a loser and you want to make sure he doesn't screw me up any more than is necessary.*

*John nodded and settled back into his seat.*

"I see that the two of you have discussed your past a bit…"

"He said it's an important part of understanding what makes me a sociopath."

"I sincerely doubt he used those words, John."

"Well, no, but I saw on my file that I'm considered a danger to myself and to others, so I figured it was as good a term as any." He smiled, and the doctor looked away, suddenly uncomfortable.

"How do you feel about your progress so far, John?"

"There haven't been any life altering epiphanies if that's what you're hoping for." He shrugged his shoulders and ignored the itching sensation that was chewing into the stump of flesh below his knee. "But I'm not really expecting any until I can get past whatever it is my mind is hiding from me."

"Do you think your mind is hiding something, John?"

"Well, I haven't exactly been able to remember my name..."

"Well, we have good news on that front at least."

"Really?" He sat up straighter and his heart decided to get all jumpy on him.

"Yes. It seems you gave Dr. Harrington an address. It took a few phone calls, but as near as we can guess, you actually do have a name." The man's voice was teasing and despite the temptation to reach out and shake the doctor until he gave up the information, Doe did his best to stay calm.

"Are you going to make me guess? Or did you think actually telling me could be useful?"

"Well, the only pictures we could find are on their way to us from California, and it will take at least a day to get them here, but from what we could gather, your name seems to be Dr. Jonathan Crowley."

Doe looked at him for several seconds and then shook his head. "Name doesn't mean a thing to me, Doc."

"Well, again, it's not even certain that we're correct in that assessment. We'll find out when the pictures show up."

"What was I a doctor of?"

"Exactly what you said you were teaching, John. Psychology, theology and parapsychology."

"What about my family? Did I have a family?"

"Indeed you did." He nodded his head. "Again, though, John, you have to remember that all of this is purely speculation until we can get some more solid evidence."

"That's fine." He waved a hand for the doctor to push past the bullshit and get to the meat of the subject. "Now, I get the feeling there's something you're not telling me, so please, let's get on with it."

Finney looked at him and pushed his glasses back up his nose, fidgeting and nervous.

"John, the information says you might be Crowley, but if so, there are a few inconsistencies with your claims."

"Like what?"

"For starters, there was a plane crash in the area you spoke about, and Jonathan Crowley was on that plane. But the crash didn't happen a few months ago. It was closer to six years ago."

John stared hard at the man, comprehension coming slowly. "So it's possible that I just forgot five and a half years?"

"There's more, John." The doctor looked at him with deep sympathy and just possibly a bit of pity. "While Jonathan Crowley did have a wife and children, they disappeared about three weeks before the plane you were supposed to have been on crashed. If they were your family, they died over six years ago."

"Jesus."

"If you are Jonathan Crowley, you've been missing since they disappeared. You're scheduled to be declared legally dead in three months' time."

"Do I have any next of kin…if I am this Crowley person?"

"No. No one left alive or currently locatable at any rate."

He felt his skin go numb and his mouth dry out as he thought about that.

"Doctor, what happened to the last six years of my life?"

"We don't know, John. All of this could be the wrong information." The man shook his head, his eyes showing nothing but pity now. "We're going to try to find out, but it won't be the easiest thing in the world."

Doe (or Crowley, he wasn't really sure which) shook his head to clear away the rapidly growing cobwebs.

"Okay, John, a last bit of news and then I want to discuss how you feel about all of this."

He looked at the doctor and nodded, unable to find the words to express much of anything.

"John, the photos of you are coming to us by way of a courier. That courier is actually a detective from California. It seems that if you are, in fact, Jonathan Crowley, that there's a serious possibility they'll want to know if you killed your family."

"Well," he looked at the doctor and smiled. "Isn't that just a peachy little detail?"

"So, John, let's go over this again. How do you feel about everything that you've just heard?"

He resisted the urge to kill the man on the spot.

---

The ambulance trip from Cherry Hill to the closest town was long and circuitous. The number of bridges built into the road was ludicrous at best, but the design was there primarily to allow as little actual alteration of the surrounding environment as possible.

Larry Summers looked at his patient and resisted the urge to gag. "Can you go any faster, Pete?"

Pete, his partner, was driving just exactly at the speed limit, with the sirens going hard and the flashers painting everything around them in red and white.

"Not unless you want to take a swim in the swamp, good buddy."

Larry nodded and despite his revulsion put his hand on what he assumed was a left arm, looking for a pulse. It was there and strong, which only made the whole thing worse. He knew Ernst Holbrook. If he'd had to guess, what he was dealing with wasn't Ernst. But the people at the loony bin swore that it couldn't be anything else.

The mouth opened again and the thing on the gurney let out a faint, whistling shriek. The one remaining eye rolled back in the head and the whole malformed body bucked again, leaking blood from under a few of the pressure bandages.

Larry looked away, horrified, and cursed himself for his weakness. He'd seen burn victims this badly chewed up by flames, but this was different. Not only was this one of his poker buddies, but there were no signs of real trauma, nothing that looked like it could be healed eventually. Whatever had happened to him had caused tremendous trauma, but none of it easy to patch up. There were wounds, yes, and there were large portions of his body that seemed to be missing, but rather than leaving holes in the flesh, it had sealed the places where he was hurt. The alterations were obvious, but there were only a few spots where external signs of injury existed. Frankly, he looked like a wax doll that had been partially melted and then left to cool down. Entire clusters of muscle were missing, just...gone, and a few bones looked like someone had grabbed them and twisted them around like they were made of clay.

The Ernst-thing let out another moan and shivered. Despite his revulsion, he didn't pull back when the lump that should have been a hand clutched his forearm.

"Lrreeee..." Oh fuck it all, the thing was trying to talk to him.

He leaned down closer and nodded. "We'll have you to the hospital soon, Ernst old buddy."

"Luhreee...hurrrrts."

"I know, bud. But I can't give you anything, yet. I don't know what it would do to you." He swallowed. "Ernst, what happened?"

"Dunt know." That was the clearest phrase Ernst had used, but the strain of trying to talk had hurt him, his entire body shivered again. "Cold."

"We're almost there, buddy. The doctors will fix you up." A bald-faced lie, but he wanted to give the poor bastard some kind of hope.

Ernst closed his eye and then let out another scream. His body bucked hard and Larry heard the sound of muscles or something vital inside of the man tearing.

"Jesus Christ, Pete! Get a move on, we're gonna' lose him!"

Ernst's body let out a long whistling moan and the covers of the gurney turned red under him.

"Oh shit."

"What's going on, Larry?" Pete was driving. He couldn't spare the time to turn around and look, not on a road as twisting as the one they were currently traveling.

"Don't worry about speeding up, Pete. I think he's gone."

"You gonna' try to resuscitate him?"

"Would you want me to work on you in this shape?"

"No, man. No, I wouldn't."

Pete killed the sirens and kept driving.

Larry checked for a pulse again and felt it fade away.

---

Recreation time.

For almost a full hour, John was allowed to walk around the walled-in garden that passed for an entertainment area. Most of the people who were out there with him were too stoned on their medications to do much more than smile or frown at their own thoughts. That suited him just dandy. He had other things to think about.

He closed his eyes and concentrated, tried to make his mind remember things that it apparently didn't want to, and felt them as they came closer. The dead were moving around him, lost in their own places and times, some of them little more than memories stumbling about and others almost so vivid that he could have reached out and touched them.

He opened his eyes and saw them. There were probably more dead people in the area than there were living, but it was hard to stare directly at them: they were elusive, though he didn't think that was deliberate on their part.

I should be pissing myself. I should be screaming and bouncing off walls. There are dead people looking at me and no one else sees them. He chuckled. Guess that makes me the nutcase of the day.

But they didn't scare him in the least, not even the ones that were actively looking at him, actually seeing him, caused him any trepidation.

For some reason, he took their reality for granted. Maybe it had something to do with what he'd done in the past. He kept getting images, most of them less substantial than the ghosts moving near him, of things he'd seen or done. None of them were enough to give him any real hints, except to let him know that sometime in the past he had been capable of amazing savagery.

Worse still, he'd enjoyed it.

The itching was back, the insane, painful itching at his knee, and it was spreading. His skull was feeling the same sensation and when he scratched he felt the thick scar tissue under his hairline.

*Are scars supposed to itch? He had no idea.*

One of the ghosts came closer to him, a portly young man with wide set eyes and a receding hairline, and tried to touch him. He looked right at it as it started pushing spectral fingers against his flesh.

"You need to back off there, bucko, unless you're feeling a need to hurt."

The ghost looked at him, shocked to be seen, apparently, and stepped away as if he'd burned its hand.

"Good boy. Now go away. You're annoying me."

Just like that, it vanished from sight, but he was still aware of it as it moved further away.

He looked at the other inmates enjoying the recreational time and noticed that two of them were actively interacting with the dead. One man was talking, muttering really, at a young woman who he'd have guessed was at least fifty years in the ground by the antiquated clothes she wore. The other patient was pacing along the far wall, pretending to ignore a spirit that was angrily yelling but making no noises. Doe guessed that if he wanted to, he could hear what it was saying, but he didn't really care.

As far as he knew, the dead seldom had anything interesting to say. That, like a few of his other thoughts, was clearly associated with his past. He just wished he could remember that past well enough to do something with it.

The guards came and took him back inside. He wasn't there to see it when the thing that hid itself inside of Alex Granger suddenly devoured the screaming, ranting ghost. What was left behind still screamed, but no longer made coherent comments.

# Chapter Five

Phillip Harrington wasn't exactly thrilled with the way his review was going, but was pleased that he'd managed to get information on his John Doe. That was the saving grace of his reviews so far, that, and his ability to take copious notes.

Finney stared at him, a nice, bland expression on his face. He hated that the man never seemed to be upset by anything. He also hated that his direct supervisor was waiting for a response to the reaming he'd just received.

"So, how do you want to handle this, Roger?"

"Well, you've been carrying a lot of cases. Do you think it would help to reduce the numbers a bit? Maybe give you a little more time to work on individual cases?"

"Who were you thinking of taking away?" He felt his stomach fall. Phil didn't like the idea of failing; it went against his nature on every level. He liked even less that some of his more interesting charges might be shipped off to one of the shoe lickers like Sebastian. Charles Sebastian was a good enough doctor, but he was also a smarmy bastard who couldn't have cared less if his patients were people as long as the results he got were satisfactory.

Finney was looking at him again, studying him for any reactions he might make. "I was thinking of taking Granger away from you, and Schulman."

Relief swelled through his muscles in a wash that took away a lot of the tension threatening to hit him. "I thought for sure you'd take John Doe from me."

Finney shook his head and smiled. "Not at all. I think you're doing wonderful work with him. He's certainly a good deal more responsive to questions now than he was a few days ago."

"Well, I have to say I'm a little disappointed, not in you or Cherry Hill, but in myself, but I think I can live with the changes." That sounded like the sort of shit Sebastian would have said in the same situation.

Finney smiled. "Don't be disappointed, Phil. All we're doing is giving you a little breathing room. It's not easy working with the sort of patients we have here."

He couldn't argue that. And honestly, he was glad to get rid of Granger. Thinking about what he'd done to the man's head made him nervous. On good days he could almost convince himself that anyone could have made the same mistake. On bad days, when he was honest with himself—and they were rare days indeed—the guilt he felt for cutting half of the man's mind away still made his stomach want to tie itself into knots.

Something about Alex Granger brought out the worst in him from the first time he'd dealt with the little murdering bastard. Even being in close proximity to the man he was supposed to make better had set him on edge. Thinking about him on a daily basis was enough to make him miserable. So yes, getting rid of Granger was a huge bonus.

"Well, thank you for the chance to stay here, Roger. I mean that. I love this job." It was the truth, too. He did love working with most of his patients and trying to sort out the reasons for their behavior. It was a challenge and he thrived on sorting out the puzzles that had twisted them from useful members of society into something better left locked away for everyone's safety.

"You're an excellent doctor, Phil. I'd like to see you continue to treat your patients here and I'm hoping to see some serious progress with them." Finney stood up and unconsciously straightened his hair and his tie. "Now, unfortunately, I have to go to a meeting." He looked troubled for just a moment, a brief flash of worry and then it was gone as if it had never been there. "I have another meeting with the police, and then I might be calling on you in a while, if the officer from California shows up before we call it a day."

"You know it's the damnedest thing." Phil looked at his boss as he stood up. "I've been trying to think of why I know the name Jonathan Crowley ever since we heard back from the Irvine PD and I can't think of a reason, but the name is stuck in my head."

Roger flashed a smile. "Maybe you're thinking of Aleister Crowley."

"What? The mystic?" He grinned himself, more at ease now that Roger wasn't focused on his career. "There's a man who should have joined us here."

"Please." Roger made a face. "I've read about him. I wouldn't have wanted the troubles that man could have caused around here. The last thing we need is anyone spouting off about supernatural occurrences."

---

For the first time in its existence, it wanted contact with another being. While Kimberly used the sponge and water to bathe Alex Granger, it moved closer to what was left of its host's mind and spoke to him.

"Hello, Alex."

It took a few moments, but eventually Alex gave a response. "You're still here? I thought they got rid of you when they—he was lost for the right words and instead sent a mental image of a hundred knives hacking through his brain, his memories—when they did that."

"No. I'm still here. I think I'm still here, at least, and that should count for something."

"How come you can talk now?" Alex sounded as scared as he was puzzled. "How come you never did that before?"

"I'm trying new things," it explained. "I want to learn about the world, Alex. How can I do that?"

"My old man, he says you can't learn except by experience. You have to do things to learn about them."

It reached into Alex's memories, what were left after the doctor had finished cutting—and sought recollections of Granger's father. What he saw was an older reflection of Alex himself, heavier around the waist, but cheerful enough with his lot in life. There were a few bad moments in the thoughts, times when Alex had been punished for one thing or another, but mostly the associations were pleasant.

Each entity it had consumed in the past seemed to give it more cognitive abilities. The thought came into its mind full blown and it wondered how that was possible. Perhaps some piece of each mind stayed with it.

It paused for a moment as Nurse Kimberly washed Alex's privates. Flesh responded to stimulation and Granger grew physically excited. The sensations were always pleasant, but distracting. The nurse kept up a steady stream of conversation, speaking of a movie she had recently seen, a picture called Easy Rider. It knew the words were only conversation, a pleasant way to pass the time when she had to do something unpleasant. Still, her tones were soothing.

Finally she finished with the area and moved to wash Alex's chest and shoulders.

"Alex, why did you kill those people? Why did you consume their flesh?"

That was a question that many people had asked Alex Granger over the course of his incarceration. He had never answered any of them. It asked now because, for the first time in its existence, it was curious.

"I killed them for you."

"Why?"

"You told me to. You said you needed to eat."

Nurse Kimberly had finished dressing him and was now spooning Alex his dinner of pureed steak and potatoes. The flavor was not abhorrent, but it lacked the depth and dimension of its first meal. Perhaps that was because Granger lacked the same sort of ability to taste foods.

"But why did you decide to help me, Alex?" It knew thoughts were hard for Granger to put together, so it was patient with him.

"Well, because you were always there for me when I needed you."

"Do you love me, Alex?"

"I would do anything for you. You're my god, aren't you?"

"Yes. I suppose I am." It paused for a moment, and looked through Alex's eyes at the pretty nurse who had just finished feeding its host.

"Alex?"

"Yes?"

"What is a god?"

In his broken, deficient way, Alex Granger explained the concept of godhood as best he could, and it listened.

And it learned.

---

John Doe was led from his room, once again in manacled legs and cuffed wrists. He was getting very good at swinging his false leg and the chains connected to it while making virtually no sounds. No one around him noticed it, or if they did, they made no comment. There was no reason he could think of for training himself to move silently, except that it was an exercise to keep him sharp.

He'd already been with two doctors earlier in the day, and the only reason he could imagine for his being taken to a different room would be because the pictures that allegedly would indicate his real name—and the police officer that was bringing them—were now at Cherry Hill a few hours earlier than anticipated.

Once again he sat still while the guards anchored him to the floor. He tried not to dwell on what might be coming his way.

It didn't matter. It came for him anyway, in the form of a detective. He was a lean man, with dark hair, dark eyes, dark skin and a dark suit. He apparently didn't believe in smiling.

The detective introduced himself and sat down across from Doe. "Mr. Crowley, my name is Rico Montoya. I'm here to see if we can identify you."

"I'm guessing you already did that. If you hadn't you wouldn't be calling me Crowley."

The man looked at him with half-lidded eyes for a moment and then nodded his head slowly and methodically. "Very good. You're right. My other reason for being here is to ask you a few questions."

Crowley—a name he would have to get used to now—looked at the man and waited. If the detective was expecting answers, he'd do what he could.

"Mr. Crowley, do you know what happened to your wife and children?"

"I think they're dead." Damn, but that hurt. His mind kept circling back to the images of a woman screaming as something tore into her.

He pushed the memory away harshly, not wanting to deal with it until he could put it into context.

"Did you kill them?"

"No."

"Do you know who did?"

"I'm not sure. I get a face, but I'm not getting a name to go with it."

Montoya looked at him for a few seconds, his distaste clearly written on his features. Crowley resisted the urge to take a swing. It would have been futile, and he didn't feel like trying to fight anyone when he was chained to a concrete floor. That didn't mean he had to like being judged by anyone who didn't even know him.

"Mr. Crowley, I've been looking for you for over six years. I've spent the same amount of time looking for your family. Where have you been?"

"Did you take the time to talk to the doctors in charge of me here?" He shook his head and leaned as close as he could toward the man staring at him. "Did they mention, maybe, that I seem to have a problem with remembering anything?" His tone was patronizing, but he didn't care.

"They did. Unfortunately, the law prevents me from examining your medical records and I don't know what you know. I only know what they tell me."

"Until you confirmed it, I didn't even know my name, Detective. How am I supposed to tell you where I've been? Last thing I remember before I was in a fight with some policemen was that I'd been in a plane crash and that I thought my family was dead. I remembered my address and I remembered being a teacher." He stared hard at the man and the detective stared back, though Crowley could see he was uncomfortable with the way things were going. "I heard from one of the doctors here that I'm missing at least six years of my life, Detective Montoya. I thought I was in that damned wreck a few months ago and he tells me I'm off by half a decade."

Montoya kept staring at him.

"What would you like to know, Detective? Ask me your damned questions."

"I want to know when you last saw your family."

"Not real clear on that."

"Tell me what you remember."

"Someone…" He closed his eyes and saw the images again, flashes of red, splashes of death in a collage of violence and screams. "Someone killed them. I don't think anyone could have lived through what was done to them."

"Tell me."

"My little boy. Did I have a little boy? I see him getting torn apart. Do you understand me? Someone, some thing, pulled at his leg and arm until they came free. They were ripped out of his body, Detective." He kept his eyes closed and tried to decipher the kaleidoscopic images, shattered fragments that wanted to blend together. "I see a little girl, God, she's so pretty. She's screaming, and it's whatever it is, it's…"

He opened his eyes and looked at the man across from him. "No. That's all I've got for you, Detective."

"That's nothing, Mr. Crowley. What you've told me is nothing."

"Then I guess I can't help you."

"I'll find out what you're hiding, Mr. Crowley. I'll find out. And if I think it's something that you did, I'll have your sorry ass brought back to California so I can watch them sentence you to death."

Crowley smiled. "Didn't you hear, you sorry sack of shit? That's one of the reasons I'm in here. I want to die."

"Then maybe you'll get your wish, sir." The detective stood up, his back stiff and his face set in a deep scowl that aged him a decade. A moment later he was gone and Crowley sat back in his seat.

He sat there for several minutes, vaguely aware of voices discussing him in the hallway. He was aware of something else, too. The dead were back, moving through the room where he rested, looking at him in some cases and oblivious to his existence in others.

He studied the ghosts as he listened to the voices talking about whether or not he was really suffering from memory loss. They were talking about how they might get information from him, what, if anything, would make him more compliant.

The spirits of the dead moved cautiously around him, looking him over or looking past him in some cases. It didn't take a genius to realize that the ghosts were actually frightened of something and that piqued his interest far more than the idea of remembering things too painful to contemplate.

"What the hell could scare a ghost?"

He hadn't the foggiest notion. But given a chance, he might try to find out.

---

"Detective, I understand where you're coming from, but as much as I want to help you, there are certain rules we try to follow here involving the privacy of our patients." Finney was trying to be calm, but the man from California wasn't making it an easy task.

"No disrespect, Doctor, but the man in that room is dangerous and I want to know if he killed his family."

"No, Detective Montoya." He shook his head. "I really don't know for certain if he's dangerous. According to what he's told us so far, I have doubts he should even be in this facility."

"Then why is he here?"

"Because he's obviously mentally unbalanced. That doesn't make him a threat to anyone, except the occasional policeman who decides to interfere with him when he's planning on going somewhere."

"There's a real possibility that he knows what happened to his family, Doctor. That's four people who disappeared six years ago, and the only person who might know where they are was also among the missing for most of those six years." Montoya was getting hot under the collar, and there wasn't a thing the doctor could do to calm him down.

"I'm fully aware of that. But I have to see to my patients, do you understand me?"

Phil Harrington had been quiet through the entire exchange, but he spoke up just before Montoya could start round seven of the circular argument. That was one of the things Finney liked about the young doctor: he was always good at being a peacemaker. He seldom had anything to add to a conversation until it was in danger of becoming an argument, but when it came to defusing volatile situations he was one of the best. "Okay, how about this: We can't in good conscience have you in on any of the sessions, but if you gave me a list of questions, we might be able to get answers to them. They would have to be pertinent to your case, Detective, and they can't be vague. They'd have to be mostly straight forward yes or no questions, with maybe a few clarifications." He paused and looked from the detective back to Finney. "Does that sound fair?"

Finney was dubious about it, but decided that he would play along. He could always review the questions beforehand. "I suppose we could go along with that. But I'll be in the room with you when you ask the questions. First and foremost, we have to maintain the sanctity of our positions."

Montoya took his time thinking about the proposal and finally agreed.

"Excellent. We'll handle the interview tomorrow. In the meantime, Detective, perhaps you can work out your list of questions."

The man took his leave, and both doctors watched him walking away.

Phil looked over at him after a few moments and shook his head. "You don't like him, do you?"

"I don't dislike him, either. I don't know him. I just know his type. He wants his answers and he wants them right away. He has no patience for due process and I've never been one to like being bullied, Phil."

Harrington scratched at the back of his neck for a second and nodded. "I know how you feel." He sighed. "This should prove interesting. I'm thinking Sodium Pentothal should do the trick for making John Doe a little more agreeable. I've been toying with trying it anyway, to see if we could get past his defenses." He stopped worrying with his neck and instead pushed his glasses up the bridge of his nose. "I don't know what it is he's trying so hard to hide, Roger, but he's definitely hiding something."

Finney nodded his head in agreement, but said nothing. He'd watch the procedure and see to it that any answers that could cause trouble for the new patient were properly censored. He had to look out for the man's rights and he didn't want Crowley sent out of state.

The man was an interesting case and Roger wanted him where he could keep an eye on him.

# Chapter Six

They took him back to his cell and Crowley let them, though he dreaded what they planned for the next day. He didn't tell them that he'd overheard their conversation, nor did he mention his newly discovered (or perhaps rediscovered) ability to see ghosts. He had enough issues already without adding complete psychotic breaks from reality to the list of reasons the people at Cherry Hill wanted to treat him.

Did he think the ghosts were real? Yes. That did not, however, mean he needed to share the revelation with those around him anymore than they had deliberately shared the decision to use "truth serum" to pick at his mind.

Once he was safely in his cell, Crowley reached for a fresh bar of soap and began carving, letting his hands do their own thing while he contemplated the possible outcome of his interrogation in the morning. He didn't know for certain that being drilled for information would be a bad thing, but he had an odd hunch that it wouldn't go the way anyone intended.

He also focused on the fact that he'd lost over five years of recent memories and found himself dwelling heavily on that thought. He would have sworn on a stack of Bibles—little as that particular book meant to him—that he had wandered out of the woods within hours, maybe a day at most, of the plane wreck. So if that was wrong, where had he been for half a decade? He was wounded when he came out. He still wore the same artificial leg, or one that was close enough to confuse his already weakened cognitive skills.

His hands worked their magic, carving flakes of soap from the main piece and gradually reforming the oblong block into something else.

He didn't look at it, but could tell that this one was more complex than the face he'd made earlier.

Mostly, he tried to avoid the fractured memories of what had apparently happened to his family. If he didn't think about them, they couldn't haunt him. And if he told himself that enough, it might come true. In the meanwhile it was one hell of a lie.

"If I wasn't already in a nuthouse, I'd be headed for one soon." He spoke only to hear someone, anyone, talking.

He set down the bar of soap because his hands told him it was done. When he looked at it, he saw a body, female and mature, bent and broken into a new form.

His hand reached out and crushed the sculpture trying to hide what he had already seen, but it was too late: the image of his wife dying came to him full blown.

---

School had been fun. It always was when the students were attentive. He was retiring soon, and he wanted to enjoy his last session as an instructor. Most of the classes were a mixture of serious students with a scattering of a few morons who had only made it into his classes by mistake or the ability to bluff their way through their learning.

He didn't much care for the latter and they were in for an unpleasant surprise when report cards were handed out.

He parked the sedan in the driveway and climbed out, ready to see—*and here, much to his frustration, the memory gave him no hint of a name, merely the face of the woman he married*—his wife and children. Three more weeks and they'd be going on vacation. She wanted to see Europe and his memories of the last time there had faded enough that he rather liked the idea.

Nothing seemed at all amiss as he opened the front door to his home. Time away from his earlier life had muted his paranoid obsession with being careful. Really, there was no one to blame but himself for what he saw when he opened the door.

Whatever it was, it had chosen a human form. He knew immediately that the man standing next to his wife was as far from human as he was.

The man was of average height, with salt-and-pepper hair and a slight paunch. He looked like he should have been selling vacuum cleaners. All three of the children were sitting on the couch, their feet bound to their hands and their mouths taped shut.

The woman he'd married stood next to the stranger, her feet taped together, her hands bound behind her back. The stranger had gotten more imaginative, and had not bothered with tape on her mouth. He'd sewn her lips shut with a thick cord. The needle that had done the job still dangled from the left side of her mouth.

The slightly pudgy face of the salesman was aimed directly at him, a pleasant enough smile set on the thin-lipped mouth. The eyes, dark blue and seemingly human, glittered with merriment. "So nice to see you again, Jonathan. Please come inside. We have a lot of things to talk about."

Crowley's hands trembled as he took in the situation and he stepped into the room, carefully closing the door behind him. He'd worked hard to make a perfectly normal life. No reason to let the neighbors know that something had gone wrong in paradise.

If he was supposed to ask the stranger what he wanted, then the man was going to be disappointed. He knew what the hidden thing wanted. It wanted him to suffer…

---

"John?" The voice snapped him out of his recollections.

He opened his eyes and looked directly at Dr. Finney.

"Is it morning already?"

"Yes indeed. You were sleeping like a baby. I'm sorry to wake you, but we have a new procedure we want to try today."

Crowley looked at the two guards between him and the doctor and held out his hands. After only a few days the routine was already half ingrained into him. He didn't much like that.

The men did their thing and cuffed his wrists and his legs, real and imitation alike.

"This is the part where I get to answer questions with a little chemical help, isn't it?"

Finney was good enough to hide his surprise and honest enough to answer him with the truth. "Yes, I'm afraid so. The detective you saw yesterday needs his answers, and we're going to try to get them. Dr. Harrington has been doing an astonishing job of helping you remember, but in this case we think it's best to try to dig a little deeper."

"Let's see what's hiding in my head then, Doc. But I want to warn you, I'm not sure this is the best sort of thing to try."

"Why's that, John?"

"I think I'm hiding a lot inside of my head."

"Well, we'll take a few precautions then. And don't worry. Whatever you say is strictly confidential."

"Unless I tell you that I killed my family."

"Do you think you killed your family, John?"

"No." He shook his head as he stood up and the guards fell into formation around him. "I think I saw it happen. I don't think I did it."

"Do you know who did?"

Crowley smiled and looked at the doctor, unable to resist throwing a wink in the man's direction. "Isn't that what we're going to try to find out?"

---

They strapped Jonathan Crowley to a padded table, careful to make sure that his wrists and ankles were safely padded against damage. He watched the procedure without saying a word and waited patiently. For some reason, Phil had expected the man to put up a fight.

Detective Montoya had handed him a list of questions that was preposterously long, and even as Harrington administered the drugs to his patient, Finney was going over the list, scratching through a few of them and making notes of his own.

He knew when the drugs took effect. He could see the change come over Jonathan Crowley; his muscles relaxed and his eyes closed to the point where little could be seen but the pupils.

"Are we ready?" Finney asked the question as he settled into a chair.

Phil nodded and began. "Can you tell me your name?"

"Jonathan Crowley." His voice was steady, but dull: the inflections were missing and he spoke calmly.

"Jonathan, do you know where you are?"

He nodded.

"Can you tell me?"

"Cherry Hill Sanitarium, Pennsylvania."

"Excellent. Now, can you tell me what happened to your family?"

Crowley's face clouded for a second and then he nodded. "It killed them."

"What killed them?"

"One that got away."

He paused for a moment to think of how to ask the questions. The last thing he wanted was a conversation that sounded like Abbott and Costello's *Who's on First* skit.

"Go back a little for me, Jonathan. Tell me what it is, and who it got away from."

"Got away from me. Back when I was a hunter."

"Are you saying something you tried to hunt down killed your family?"

Crowley nodded his head.

"What were you hunting, Jonathan?"

"Monsters."

Harrington looked at Roger Finney, who looked back at him with the same expression of curiosity and good-humored tolerance. They were dealing with a mental patient after all. You had to expect a few strange answers.

"What sort of monsters did you hunt, Jonathan?"

"Whatever needed hunting. Ghosts, demons, werewolves…just…just monsters." The man's head tilted a little. "You have ghosts here, too."

He resisted the urge to ask about the ghosts, partially because it was immaterial and partially because he was afraid the man might be right. The atmosphere in the asylum was exactly the sort that was conducive to believing in things that go bump in the night. "What sort of monster killed your family, Jonathan?"

"Still not sure. It was hiding in human flesh."

That was, of course, exactly the sort of excuse that normally came out of the patients. Look at Granger. On the few occasions when he could get the man to say anything about why he committed his murders, the usual answer was because Dead God demanded it. Dead God, who was, according to the poor wretch, not the god worshipped by Christians, but another god, who had been created by the minds of men and left stillborn due to lack of worshippers. Nonsense, of course, but precisely the sort of reasoning most of the deluded patients used; if not a monster, a god or angels or Satan himself. Anything that could justify their actions and keep them safe from the guilt they should have been feeling.

"Did it give you its name before it killed your family?"

Crowley's brow wrinkled. "No. Names have power."

"How did it kill them?" Again the temptation to ask questions had to be resisted. He had a list of questions he needed to cover before he could start actually examining the psychosis of his patient. The need to help the police in their investigation was frustrating.

Crowley frowned and shook his head, uncomfortable with the question. "It's okay, Jonathan, nothing can hurt you here."

The man laughed. "Liar. It made me watch. It broke their bodies and made me watch." He uttered a deep, long sigh of misery. "And then it ate their souls."

"How did it make you watch?"

"Nailed me to the wall. If I didn't do what it said, it was going to make it worse for them."

"Make it worse than killing them? How?"

Crowley's voice grew deeper and caustic. "You'd be surprised how much can still hurt you when you're dead."

"Why didn't it kill you, Jonathan?"

"It couldn't kill me. It wasn't strong enough."

Finney shook his head. He wanted Phil to follow the script for now.

"What happened to your family's bodies, when it was done, Jonathan?"

"It ate them. It tortured them and broke them." Crowley's eyes were closed, but he opened them now, the pupils still dilated from the drugs and his gaze focusing on nothing. "It tore them apart and ate them and made me watch and I don't want to talk about this anymore.

I don't want to remember this anymore. You have to stop now, Doctor, because I think I don't want to remember this part."

Finney frowned and Phil joined him. The sentences coming from Crowley's mouth were growing tenser, more structured and that shouldn't have been possible. He had enough Sodium Pentothal in his system to keep a man twice his size relaxed for half a day.

"John, it's okay. Nothing can hurt you here."

"Liar."

"What do you mean?"

"'They are given eyes to see and yet they act blind.'"

"What?"

"There are dead people all around you, Doctor." Crowley's eyes opened and he looked first at Phil and then at the areas around him. "Some of them are angry. Most of them are scared. Ever wonder what can scare something that's already dead, Doc?"

Phil felt his skin crawl and despite himself, he looked around to see if there were any signs of ghosts around him. There was nothing to see. He let out a small chuckle.

"Where is your family now, Jonathan?"

The man leaned back and closed his eyes completely. "Dead. Gone away. Taken and hidden and lost to me."

"What happened to the man who killed them?" He looked at Finney as he asked the question and received a nod of encouragement.

"He died in flames. He won't ever hurt them again." The patient's lip curled up into a sneer. "I couldn't find his body now if my life depended on it."

"Why do you have trouble remembering anything, Jonathan? What caused your amnesia? Do you think it was watching your family die?"

Crowley shook his head. "Got something in my skull. Got it in the plane crash. Hurts sometimes, but didn't stop me."

Finney frowned and shook his head. "No record of that," he whispered.

"Did you ever see a doctor about that, Jonathan?"

"I couldn't. I've been…"

"Been what, Jonathan?"

"I think I've been dead." Crowley frowned as he said it.

---

They led Crowley back into his room without any semblance of a struggle. He was too dopey to do much of anything but smile. He'd never been one to use any sort of medication if he could avoid it.

Now he lay back on his cot and stared at the ceiling, seeing little beyond the white of the paint and the shadows that slipped into the corners. He had said far too much, but in his own defense he hadn't known there was anything to say.

The most annoying part was that he didn't really know much more than he had before. He'd hunted monsters? Okay, fine. There were ghosts and he could see them, but he couldn't actually remember hunting anything, let alone the occasional werewolf or demon.

There was that face, the smarmy salesman, and the deaths that followed. He knew from that experience that the man he'd hunted down was not normal, but there wasn't much else to go on. He couldn't think of any special weapons he had, or any spectacular abilities, either. Had he stopped hunting monsters because he lost his leg? He wasn't sure, but he didn't think so.

"Moron. You stopped because you fell in love." His words echoed through the room. Was that the reason? Maybe. He guessed there were a few cops out there who had either asked for transfers or left the force to avoid distressing their families. Would it be so hard to believe that a man who hunted monsters might want to retire to avoid getting torn into pieces?

He started drifting: the thoughts alone weren't enough to counteract the effects of the drugs they'd shot into his system and his eyes closed.

A moment later he was sleeping far deeper than he had since his family was murdered.

So he didn't notice the shape that slipped through the wall and stared at him.

---

It had rested and contemplated the things it had learned. Now it once again explored the buildings where it dwelled. Granger had given it a lot to think about, but not much of the man's ramblings made sense.

There was a lot to reinterpret.

In the meantime there were things to learn from the people in the asylum and it wanted to dabble a little here and a little there in the process.

The first thing it had taught itself as a result of moving around the place was that each of the entities in the large structure was unique. Dead or alive hardly mattered: they had different feelings and different flavors. Most importantly they had different memories.

For example: Leslie Anne Hampton—who thought of herself only as Leslie—remembered every single visit by Ernst. The drugs that were meant to calm her down left her almost incapable of thought and almost paralyzed, but she knew that he came to her and did things to her. It had gathered that information from her mind when it settled itself into her body while trying to understand what the guard was doing to her. She was also aware when it entered her physical form and read her thoughts, but had convinced herself that it was just another strange dream caused by the medications.

Its perception of the night guard had been altered by contact with Leslie. That was why it decided to touch him next, to experience him. What it learned from the experience was something new: hunger. Not the physical need for sustenance—or more accurately the psychic need in this case—but the hunger for more. Ernst had longed constantly for new physical desires: it had given them to the guard and in the process had discovered the beauty of actual sensations as opposed to merely the memories of interactions. And now, it knew, hunger was going to be an important part of its exercises.

It had few needs to date, but suspected that would change in time. In the past it had merely done what it could for Alex Granger, but now? Well, now it would try new things for different reasons.

Because of hunger.

One of the many new experiences it was considering was building a body of its own, but in order for that to happen it would have to study more on what made bodies function.

It paused in its journey through the building to look at the one living being so far that had actually seen it. The man was not himself:

he was medicated and stared at the ceiling above him when his eyes were open, which was less and less of the time.

It moved closer to him and felt the heat from the man's body. The false leg he wore was a puzzle, but even without much by way of a proper education, it caught on to the need easily enough.

The man opened his eyes and looked directly at it. Though he stared, his eyes did not see this time. They were focused elsewhere, lost in the medications and their side effects, perhaps, or merely lost. It had seen enough faces to know the expression worn by the one-legged man was pain.

Curious, it reached out and touched the man, sinking fingers through his flesh and into the mind behind the open, staring eyes. The old man's body stiffened, and his lips twitched as it pushed forward, digging for the treasures hidden inside.

A moment later it recoiled, and if it had a face to show expression or eyes within that face they would have widened in shock.

It withdrew as quickly as it could, but not quite fast enough.

The old man who could see it, also did something else no one had ever done before. He touched it. His hand lashed out and dug into its being, holding on tightly. The glazed over eyes were now clear and the previously slack mouth twisted into a violent sneer.

It learned a new emotion in that moment, experiencing firsthand what several of the ghosts had shown it previously. It learned fear.

The man on the bed held it tightly, and it struggled to get away. His eyes rolled in his head and then, mercifully, the old man's hand dropped free.

It ran, the fear it tasted searing into it and burning through its entire shapeless form.

# Chapter Seven

Kimberly Walker did not believe in ghosts and had no need for them in her life. What was important to her had more to do with helping those around her than with any sort of nonsense about specters, apparitions or things that go bump in the night.

What she wanted out of life was simple: She wanted to be a psychiatrist. The human mind fascinated her. When she wasn't at Cherry Hill, she was usually studying for one of her college courses and on those occasions when she wasn't studying or working, she was at school. Though she'd kept quiet about her studies, there were several people who knew that she was getting closer and closer to finally getting her degree. She just had to be patient, which, fortunately, the job was teaching her.

Her shift was over, finally, and it was time to head home for the night, which she was looking at as a definite blessing, because just lately the entire building was creeping her out.

It wasn't easy working with the patients down in what some of her co-workers called the dungeon: she often felt like she was working with dead people who hadn't figured out yet that they were among the deceased.

Everyone down in the dungeon had either come out of an attempted surgery with less of their faculties left than they should have or had just broken to the point where all the king's horses and all the king's men would never have a chance of putting them back together again. It saddened her on good days and made her absolutely heartsick on the days when she was already feeling blue. What could she do for them? Remarkably little, except try to put a little touch of happiness into their days. So she smiled for the patients, whether they had enough of a mind left to appreciate it or not, and she cleaned up their messes and she gave them their meds and in several cases she spoon-fed them their pureed meals.

And she tried hard not to let it get to her, because when her shift was done, she still had work to do. There were classes she had to attend as soon as she was done driving the twenty-seven miles to the university and there was homework to take care of after that.

And then there were the nightmares. They'd only just started, but they were usually intense enough to wake her from her sleep.

None of the dreams were the kind she remembered. Instead, she had the pleasure of waking up with her heart pounding along at twice the normal speed and a scream caught somewhere in the back of her throat. What few images she could remember always revolved around patients in straitjackets or locked into the sort of cells that were left solely in the dungeon: old stone walled ten-by-ten rooms with little light and a barred slot in the door to allow any semblance of a view.

But there were emotions involved in the dreams and she wasn't one hundred percent sure they were her emotions. Mostly it was a feeling of despair and a lot of claustrophobia thrown in besides. A few times she woke up with the absolute conviction that she was being strangled to death, and on at least two occasions she came to knowing that she was drowning and had only seconds to live.

Kimberly didn't believe in ghosts. She was raised to believe in God and in the power of the human mind as a healing agent, but she was never raised in a house that gave time to the notion that the spirits of the dead could wander around in the living world, lost and alone. The very notion terrified her, and that was, she suspected, the root of her problems.

Because the more she let herself think about it, the more she became convinced that her dreams were being delivered to her by the spirits that haunted Cherry Hill.

Kimberly tried to push those thoughts out of her head as she waved a quick goodbye to Lionel Copper, the guard on duty at the reception area, and headed to her little Pinto out in the parking lot.

Kimberly did the best she could to ignore the chill that lanced through her body just as she reached the driver's side door. She did not allow herself to turn around and see if anyone was watching her, because she genuinely didn't want to know.

It wouldn't have mattered anyway: human eyes could not see what was watching her.

---

Adam Prescott had done bad things in his life, the sort that had resulted in him spending the last seven years of his existence inside the walls of Cherry Hill. The difference between him and a lot of the other patients was that he was actually beginning to understand that what he had done was wrong. Dr. Finney would surely take all the credit for that and Adam didn't really mind because he knew the truth about his recovery.

It was the people in the walls who were showing him the error of his ways. They didn't show themselves all the time, but they were there and they let him know right from wrong every time he even considered doing something bad.

That was why he had earned the nickname "The Screamer." Because they never left him alone for very long. If he hadn't known better, he'd have thought the only reason they were in the asylum at all was to make sure he learned his lessons and learned them very well.

Adam didn't want to learn any more lessons. He'd had time to think about it and decided he'd rather just be left alone. He'd tried explaining his new position to Dr. Sebastian, but the man frowned and made a lot of notes instead of replying. It was disheartening, really. He just wanted to get the hell out of the prison he was living in and try again on the outside world.

"I can be better now, I know I can."

The faces came back, looking at him from the walls. He knew they weren't real, knew that they couldn't hurt him, but he saw them and they scared the shit out of him whenever they came around.

Maybe it was because he thought he could recognize them if he tried hard enough or, that even with the meds they kept feeding him, he knew the faces shouldn't have been there in the first place.

Dr. Sebastian—a large man, heavyset with dark curly hair, a little van dyke beard and the most annoying mole over his left eyebrow—

almost never spoke to him anymore. He just nodded his head and made notes. Adam couldn't figure out how that was supposed to be helpful. He thought about Dr. Sebastian a lot lately, especially when the faces came closer like they were doing now.

"What do you want?" He spoke the words softly, knowing that they could hear him because they always reacted. This time, they gathered together, a half-dozen faces sliding along the walls and pooling into a mess of features as they examined him closely. Twelve eyes stared at his face, looking hard at him as if trying to decide what they should do about his continued existence.

Finally, one of them reached out a hand and touched him.

And once again he began earning his nickname. Adam screamed, his voice echoing off the walls of the cell.

He kept screaming as the hands moved over his body, reaching into his flesh and doing horrible things to his insides and his mind.

---

John rolled over on his mattress and groaned. He'd been hoping for a night without any of the damned yowls from the idiot down the corridor; a night with sleep and maybe, for an exciting change of pace, a few pleasant dreams instead of fragmented memories. Naturally, he wasn't going to get that lucky.

He crawled out of bed, hating every ache and pain that ran through his body, and wondering why his skin was itching with such persistence. The Screamer was going full force, begging whatever it was that tormented him to leave him alone. When the pleading failed, he resorted to letting out another shriek of epic scale.

"Will you shut your damned mouth? Some of us are trying to get some rest!" He didn't expect a response, but hearing himself yelling back beat all hell out of listening to the nutcase down the hallway.

There was five seconds of blissful silence before the screams started up again.

He looked at the door and shook his head. He couldn't very well walk through walls. If he could he'd have left Cherry Hill within minutes of arriving. The lock was on the other side of the door and unless he managed to make his fingers grow a few feet longer he doubted he'd be able to pick it.

"Since when can I pick locks?" He thought about that for a few seconds—it helped drown out the noises from down the hallway—and shook his head. No idea where the information came from but he had no doubt that given a pocketknife, he would have been able to open the lock to the room.

He was looking out the small wire mesh window when he saw motion from the corner of his eye. When he looked straight at the source of the distraction, there was nothing to see, but he'd have sworn there was something a moment earlier.

The Screamer let loose with another yelp designed to shatter eardrums and John sneered. "If I ever get out of this room and see you, I'm going to give you something to shout about you piss wad!"

And there it was again, something moving in the hallway. He kept his eyes focused away from whatever it was and tried to use his peripheral vision instead. There was definitely something in the hallway, crawling along the tiled floors, but the more he tried to focus on it, the harder it was to see, like an evaporating daydream. It was maddening not being able to look directly at it, but he kept focused on it just the same.

It was a dark red mass, run through with other colors. Whatever it actually was, it moved across the ground slowly, creeping forward a few inches at a time and, yes, it made noises. They were barely audible over the sounds from the Screamer, but a series of wet, slippery sounds came from the thing. Part of the redness moved forward and he saw a rudimentary hand at the end of the growth. That hand grabbed the tiles and pulled as misshapen legs pushed, moving the unpleasant lump forward.

From close to the center of the shape, another mass moved, lifting up and revealing itself as a malformed head on a spindly neck. The face was crude at best, and though there were spots for two eyes, only one was revealed: a white, milky mass that looked around blindly as the head turned first to the left and then to the right.

John slowly let himself look closer at the object of his attention, and watched as the thing changed, growing at a disturbing rate.

"Well, what the hell are you supposed to be?" He spoke directly to the thing and it looked in his direction with that sightless eye and opened a tiny slash of a mouth.

And then it screamed, a high, keening noise that started weakly and grew though the Screamer quickly drowned it out down in his cell.

The thing tried to stand, pushing with enormous effort and almost unfolding as it rose on thin, misshapen legs. What features the face of the thing had were twisted into a knot of pain as it wobbled in the hallway, trailing a thin mucus of red and pink behind it.

It stepped forward and the bones supporting its thin, frail leg cracked. The aberration fell forward and collapsed on itself, moaning in pain as it struck the ground.

John watched, chilled, as it tried a second time to rise and failed. A moment later it stopped moving at all. Within two minutes, during which time he continued to stare, the mass had putrefied, pooling into a thick reddish black stew that gave off an odor like he'd have expected in a slaughterhouse suffering through August heat.

He stared at the soupy mess for several minutes before convincing himself that it was real. It was still there two hours later when the new night shift guard finally got around to walking the corridor. He was pudgy, short and looked like he hadn't slept in five days.

Being a helpful sort, John pointed it out to the man as he came closer. "Clean up in aisle four."

The man looked directly at him and blinked his eyes. "Huh?" He then set his left shoe square into the congealing puddle and let out a bark as his feet left the ground. A moment later the guard hit the ground and stared up at the ceiling, the wind obviously knocked out of his lungs by the impact. From top to bottom his backside was covered in the foul-smelling ichor.

"You all right there?" John pinched his good leg to stop from cracking up.

"Unnn… Yeah…" The guard stood up and caught a whiff of the fluids covering his backside. He was made of sterner stuff than the inmate expected; he didn't throw up on the spot.

"You might want to go change your clothes, fella. And maybe you could call someone about the mess?"

The pudgy man slammed a nightstick into the mesh on John's window and managed to mash one of his fingers in the process. "You need to watch your mouth, shithead. If I want opinions from a nutcase, I'll ask for them."

John looked at him through narrowed eyelids and smiled. "That's right, big man, I forgot, you've got all the power, don't you?"

"And you better fucking remember it, too!"

"You know what? Only one of us smells like shit around here, and it isn't me." The guard made a few more fish faces, this time from outrage instead of clumsy stupidity. "You want to swing that stick of yours, buddy boy, you best make sure you know who you're swinging it at."

"Well, ain't that your problem? Can't remember your own name?"

John leaned in close to the bars again, but not quite close enough to have to worry about the guard's weapon. "I got a name now. Suits me just fine, too. Anytime you're feeling jumpy again, you just open this door and we can have a talk about your attitude."

"Yeah," the man snorted. "I'm not that stupid."

"Hey, you're the one with the Billy club and the keys. What? You afraid of a one-legged old man?"

"Not afraid of you at all." The man waited a moment while the Screamer finished his latest round of desperate yelps. "Just not in the mood to get fired because some old fart wants to get out of his cage."

John waited until the man had turned his back and then he smiled. "Pussy."

The guard spun around fast, his eyes half wild and his outrage obvious in every action he made. He was past the point of following procedure, apparently, because he grabbed for his key ring and started unlocking the door, probably intent on bashing John's skull in.

John stepped back to give the man room to enter his little cell. The guard took the invitation, his round chin quivering with anger. Part of him wanted to laugh at the notion, a thirty something man coming in to beat all hell out of a sixty something handicap.

He wasn't laughing when the nightstick got cocked back and then swung at his head. Instead he brought his left arm up and deflected the blow, catching the younger man in the forearm before the stick could make contact with any part of his body. While the guard was wondering just what had gone wrong, John brought his right fist into the man's padded ribcage and doubled him over. Two additional quick blows and the guard was down for the count.

John slipped out of his cell and left the guard where he was, but took the keys from the door. He had some unfinished business to take care of exactly three doors down on the right side of the hallway.

He got his first look at the Screamer, a man who was writhing on his bed and sweating profusely. He was lean and hard and currently had his hands locked on either side of his cot, the fingers sunk deep into the mattress as he bucked and writhed. His skin was pale and covered in a thick sweat, and his face was tense with a nearly perpetual expression of pain.

He opened his mouth to let out another scream and John pounded on his door with a closed fist. "SHUT UP!"

The Screamer stopped and looked at him, surprised by the sudden outburst. His face was still in pain, but he did not scream.

"I've had it with you! If you scream one more time I swear I'll open this door and beat you to death!"

"Oh, God, help me, please…" The man held out a hand to him and shivered violently.

John looked harder at the man, harder, his perceptions shifting like they had before, and saw for the first time why the man was screaming. How he could see them, he did not know, but for the first time, John saw the ghosts that crawled over and through the man. He'd seen them the other day as well, but at the time it had seemed almost natural that he should be able to witness them. Now it wasn't exactly freaking him out, but it seemed more of a phenomenon. They were mere shadows, broken remnants of specters, not a one of them complete. He doubted that they were even fully aware of what they were doing, but even stranger as far as he could tell was that the man could see them and feel them.

The Screamer looked at him again. "Help me…"

A flush of heat ran through John's body and he stepped away from the door.

"No." He shook his head. "No. You just shut up. Keep it down for a while, okay?"

The thought of going to the man's aid was enough to send chills through him that watching the dead things didn't even come close to. He knew as sure as he knew how to walk that he could help him, but there was something dangerous in it. Not physically dangerous, per se, but not good for his health.

Feeling overwhelmed by a sudden case of butterflies in his stomach, he went back to his cell, pulled the unconscious guard out, and dropped the man unceremoniously into the rotting stew on the floor. He then locked himself back into his cell, making certain to leave the keys where the guard could get to them.

The guard woke up a few minutes later, blinking hard and shaking his head to rattle all the marbles back into their proper places. By the time he was standing up and looking around, no doubt wondering exactly what the hell had just happened, John was back on his mattress and trying to sleep.

---

It stared at the screaming man and contemplated his dilemma. The dead things that crawled over him were leftovers, really, animated remains from previous meals.

For some reason, they found the screaming man useful. Curiosity made it wonder why, and for the first time it decided to explore with them in an effort to understand.

The dead things instinctively pushed away from it as it waded into the strange flesh. The screaming man bucked, his eyes rolling up into his head, obviously in agony as it pushed deeper with its senses.

It had brushed through bodies before—being without a physical form made the ability possible and as a result it had experienced overwhelming new sensations, most of them metaphysical or emotional—but not like this one. There was something about the screaming man that was different, but it lacked the ability to define what that something was.

It thought about the problem for a while, ignoring the gasping pained body it moved through as it considered what to do. Finally it decided the best way to learn was to study the issue more carefully, as it had done with the previous night guard, Ernst.

Though it felt no particular hunger for physical gratification, its desire for knowledge was growing insatiable.

Long before it was done the man was dead. If he had a spirit inside of him, it left without being seen, or just possibly was consumed when it began to feast.

# Chapter Eight

Phillip Harrington looked at his patient and tried to tell himself he was seeing things. Maybe he was, but Jonathan Crowley looked better than he had since he'd arrived. He seemed more fleshed out and had color for the first time since joining the other patients at Cherry Hill.

"How are you feeling today, John?"

"Not bad. I would have felt better without the disturbances."

"Disturbances?"

"Well, let's see. For starters, the Screamer was going strong again last night. The man needs a muzzle. Then there was the mess in the hallway..."

"I heard about that. The janitors had quite a time cleaning that off the floor. Any idea what caused it?" He had to ask, of course. The foul puddle had been found closest to Crowley's door.

"Ask your night guard. He's the one that found it."

"I take that to mean you don't wish to comment on it?"

"Take it anyway you want to, Doc." The man smiled, his eyes locked on Phil's. Once again there was a slight hint of menace or contempt coming from the man. Harrington still couldn't decide which.

"Humor me. If you had to come up with a theory about where the mess came from, what would that theory be?"

Crowley shrugged. "I'll give you a different answer than the one you want, but try this. Get a sample of the stuff and have it studied. If I had a dollar and I was betting man, I'd risk that very dollar on the fact that the stuff is a simple protein of unknown origin."

"What makes you say that?"

"Remember my line of work, Doc? Just a guess, but it's an educated one."

Harrington made a note to see if he could get a sample of the substance for evaluation. It was more likely that the mess had already been washed down the drain along with the mop water.

"So, did I tell Detective Montoya what he wanted to know?"

"You mean when we tried our new techniques?"

"Yeah. When you tried your new techniques." Crowley stared at him still. "Did I tell you or the detective anything useful?"

"Detective Montoya was not in the session, Jonathan. You know that."

"Yes, I do."

"So why are you worried about what you might or might not have told him?"

"I'm not worried. I'm curious. Did I actually have anything useful to say?"

"Do you remember any of the session, Jonathan?"

"Very little after you put the needle in my arm."

He thought the man was telling the truth.

"Well, Jonathan, we still have to look everything over. We need to check the notes and try to differentiate the facts from whatever stories your mind made up."

"So nothing that proves I'm sane then?" The man looked amused.

"Sanity is an issue for most of the patients here, Jonathan. You gave some very unorthodox answers. What we need to do now is examine those answers carefully and decide what really happened and weigh that against what you said happened. It's not always easy to know for sure."

"Got that right the first time." Crowley leaned back as much as he could in his chair, rattling the chains that anchored him to the floor. "Did I say what happened to my family?"

"Yes."

The man's smile stayed the same, but his eyes narrowed a bit. "Let me guess. That's one of the parts you're not really sure happened, am I right?"

"You said you used to hunt monsters, Jonathan. Can you elaborate on that?"

"I was a parapsychologist." He shrugged. "I guess that means I was looking for ghosts and demons, right?"

"Do you think you ever found any?"

"I'm pretty sure I must have, but again—" he reached up and tapped the side of his head. "Not everything upstairs is what it's supposed to be."

Harrington looked at his pad of paper when he spoke again. "Do you believe in God, Jonathan?"

"Yes."

"How about the Devil?"

"Absolutely."

"Would you say that you're a religious man?" He looked over the top of his note pad and back at his patient.

"Not in the least."

"If you believe in God and the Devil, how is it that you're not religious?"

"I don't practice any organized form of religion."

"Why not?"

"I believe that the moon is in orbit around the planet Earth, Doc. That doesn't mean I'm obligated to offer it any sort of obeisance."

"Okay, let's try something a little different. Do you believe in Good and Evil?"

"Absolutely."

"What do you think of the concepts?"

"I think they're lovely notions. Good is all around us." His voice fairly dripped with sarcasm.

"So how about evil?"

"Oh, that's definitely all around us."

"Humor me, Jonathan. Try to explain the two concepts to me as best you can."

Crowley shrugged again. "Good in the context you are describing would be the orderly nature of the universe. It simply is, and has always been. Nature is good. Life is good. Order is good. Good is the notion that all men and all life spawns for a necessary reason and that in every case the order of the universe is running along a designed plan. Theoretically 'God' would be in charge of all that is good in the universe."

He sighed. "Evil is a counter-argument to the notion that all should be orderly. Evil is all the negative emotions that we're supposed to suppress, all the violent tendencies and the irrational actions that people make. In a place like this, I suppose the patients would be considered evil by a lot of people's standards."

"Do you think you're evil, Jonathan?"

"Do YOU think I'm evil, Doc?" The man stared hard at him, hard enough to make him nervous despite the chains.

"We're not discussing me, Jonathan. We're discussing you. Do you think you're evil?"

"No."

"You also said that you've killed a lot of times."

"Killing does not immediately equate to evil, now does it?"

"Can you explain that for me?"

Crowley leaned forward, his hands on his knees, and smiled. "Let's skip all of this nonsense. You're beating around the bush and trying to make a point with me. Get to it."

"According to your session yesterday, you've killed on several occasions. You said that you did not, in fact, kill your family, but that you watched them die. You claim that you were 'Nailed to the wall' and made to watch as your family was tortured, murdered, and then devoured."

"And?" The man kept staring, harder than before if that were possible.

"You also said you did everything to the monster who killed your family that it had done to them."

"And?"

"I'm trying to judge your moral compass as it were, Jonathan. You say you believe in both God and the Devil. You say you believe in good and evil, but I still can't quite decide where you believe you fit into the equation."

"Maybe I don't fit in. Maybe it's not a puzzle or a machine that you can get to run just so, Doctor Harrington. Maybe some pieces were never designed to fit into the grander scheme of things."

"Do you believe that?"

"I don't really know."

"If there is a battle of good versus evil, Jonathan, who do you think is winning?"

"Who said either side is winning or ever will?"

"Humor me. Take a guess."

"If there is a battle like that going on, then I suppose good has the upper hand but not by much."

"Why?"

"Because if good and evil exist in the way you're thinking, good has to follow the rules. Evil by its very nature cheats."

"How could evil cheat, Jonathan?"

"It's harder to follow the rules than it is to bypass them." He shrugged. "That's the way the rules are set up."

"How so?"

"Let's switch this around. We'll use God and Satan for this answer. God gave rules to follow. Satan gave temptations that would convince people to break those rules."

"Do you think the temptations are all that overwhelming, Jonathan?"

"Me personally? No. But plenty of people might."

"Give me an example."

Crowley smiled. "Okay, sure. I've got nothing better to do. Okay, let's try this one on, something you can relate to." Crowley leaned back again, relaxing a bit, and stared into his eyes. "Let's go on the subject of temptations. Little ones. Nothing major like any of those commandments, really. Let's take a doctor right here in this building as an example. You folks have to deal with mental cases all day long. You get tired of it, I'm sure. So let's say you had a particularly belligerent patient. The guy doesn't want to learn his lessons, doesn't want to be treated. After a few weeks or months of having to deal with him, I bet the temptation to do something about his attitude must be amazingly high. So when you realize he's just never going to change, you go ahead and up his medications to make him more compliant. It won't teach him, it won't help to cure him, but damn, it feels nice to shut him up for a while, doesn't it?"

Harrington thought about that for a moment and finally nodded his head. "And that would be the definition of evil?"

"No. That would be an example of how doing small acts of evil can become easier and easier. You dose him a little more and things become easier, so you keep the doses higher. When the time comes and the patient is no longer as quiet as he was before, you can always increase the dosage again."

"How would that be helping the patient?"

"Well, that's just it. You and I both know that most medications for calming down a patient also cripple his cognitive abilities. So by upping the dosage you'd be destroying any chance of the patient becoming able to reason or seeing the error of his ways." He smiled and leaned forward. "But, really, no one here is expected to work miracles, and no one will really notice if that patient just sort of stays at the same level of nuts instead of getting a little better after every session."

Phil was still trying to come up with a proper defense for the scenario when Crowley started talking again.

"I heard that this place has been around for a long time, Doc. Is that true?"

"Oh yes, well over a hundred years now."

"Did you ever do much research on what mental institutions were like a century ago?"

"Well, they weren't up to today's standards."

"They were where the people with enough money buried their family secrets, Doc." Crowley smiled again his eyes issuing a challenge. "Your son keeps looking at other boys instead of at girls? He likes to sneak into his mommy's wardrobe and dress in her clothes? That is socially unacceptable. Send him to an asylum and pay the bills on time. He is now somebody else's problem. Your daughter got fresh with the stable boy and now she's carrying an unwanted child? Off she goes! If she behaves herself later, you can always get her out, minus the embarrassment of a bastard child, of course."

"What has that got to do with anything, Jonathan?"

"It was easy. For the son or daughter or whoever got locked away, I'm sure the decision was seen as evil."

"Interesting. So evil is a matter of convenience?"

"No. Evil is just easier. Evil makes it easier. Evil gives people the excuses they need."

"So how does that work with the idea that monsters are real?"

"First you'd have to define what a monster is."

"Supernatural things that eat people?"

"Oh. Well that's easy, too. If all they ever do is eat people, all they have to do is wait for people to show up."

"That could make for some awfully hungry times, couldn't it?"

Crowley got that grin back on his face. "Not really."

"How do you figure?"

"Evil just gives an inviting package."

"What's inviting about a werewolf or a boogieman?"

"You're looking at isolated cases where Evil has a different outlook. Why would someone sell their soul to the Devil?"

He had to think about that one. "For profit or revenge?"

"Very good. You go to the front of the class."

"You think it's that easy?"

"I think it's exactly that easy. Want the girl of your dreams? Sign here. Want that promotion and a nicer house? There's the dotted line. Want Joe Sidbury, the kid that beat your ass every day for a year to die a painful death? Here's the pen."

"Wouldn't most people manage on their own?"

"Sure. If they weren't lazy. Why risk having good old Joe kick your teeth in when you can have someone else do it?"

"But at the cost of your soul?"

"Once again, evil is a liar. If it said up front it would cost your soul, no one would ever do it. Assuming they believed in souls."

"So how would evil get to them?"

"The guy you keep hearing about that will take on your troubles for a few hundred dollars. The book that has spells written down, spells that work."

"If those books really existed, why aren't more people using them?"

"How do you know they aren't?"

"Can you explain that one for me?"

"Doc, if you had a book that could give you power, would you advertise that fact?"

"You know, I really don't know."

"Most people wouldn't. If they did, they might have to share."

"Did you ever have a book like that, Jonathan?"

"If I did, why would I tell you?"

---

John was on the way back into his cell when they pulled what was left of the Screamer from his cell. For the second time since he'd been in Cherry Hill, he saw something that didn't look human buried under a sheet and still twitching.

The thought that whatever was under that cover had asked him for help the night before took all the fun out of his day, mostly because he knew in his heart that he probably could have helped.

He was too afraid. That was the part that bothered him the most. He was scared shitless and he still couldn't understand why. The guards didn't talk to him and that was just fine. They were busy worrying about what had come out of the Screamer's room and maybe wondering if what had happened to him had happened to their buddy from the night shift. It couldn't possibly be a comforting notion.

The door was closed and locked and John watched as the twitching mass was wheeled down the long corridor on a gurney that insisted on rattling and squealing the entire length of the journey.

He had more soap waiting for him, and new plastic knives, too, which was good because the old ones had lost all their teeth in the battle to carve images.

He had four soap sculptures currently. There was a woman's face, a hound dog, a fairly good likeness of Harrington and a hand. The hand had been the hardest to do.

He picked up the soap and the new plastic blade and started whittling as he thought about his current situation. As he whittled, he let himself relax.

Which was precisely when something tried to possess him.

---

The detectives were back and justifiably worried. That was all right, because Roger was starting to get worried himself.

There had always been tales of strange things happening at Cherry Hill, but the situation was rapidly going from strange to fully obscene.

Carl Branaugh was understandably perturbed. It was a long drive over treacherous roads to get to Cherry Hill.

"You have no idea what could have caused either of the mutilations?"

"Detective, please believe me, if I knew how to help you with your investigation, I would. So far all I know is that we had a body in a drain, two physically healthy men deformed overnight and that a lot of my patients are getting agitated."

The man looked at him and shrugged. "Any idea what's agitating your patients?"

"Apparently there are ghosts haunting the asylum." He shrugged back. "I've had no less than ten of the inmates here claiming that they've been haunted in the last week."

"Yeah?" The detective got a sour expression on his face. "That's more than normally claim they've seen ghosts?"

"At least twice the number I've had in the past. Believe me, I'm not laughing about it anymore. I don't believe in ghosts, but something is going on here and I can't begin to explain it."

"Any chance I can talk to the inmates who say they've seen them?"

"I'm not overly fond of having some of my patients talking with unfamiliar faces. It's nothing against your work, Detective, but we're dealing with very troubled psyches."

"How about if I promise only to ask about the ghosts?"

"I think we can work something out, but I'll have to insist on the doctors in charge of the patients being with you in the room."

"I can work with that."

"And I'll have to keep them restrained."

"I was sort of hoping you'd say that, too."

---

The first interviews went well. Branaugh listened to the comments and made notes, and even without a degree in psychology, he could tell which patients were trying to get noticed (about half of them) and which ones were at least sincere in their claims.

One woman swore that something had been touching her every night and had only recently stopped. He made note of her claim primarily because the first victim of whatever was happening had been found in her room. She was very upset and justifiably so.

Two of the patients swore they'd seen not just ghosts, but the ghosts of famous people who had never had a reason to be in the asylum and probably wouldn't have bothered to come to it if they were stuck in the afterlife.

One woman said that she'd been haunted for a long time, but the ghosts that had been haunting her disappeared. Ever since then it had been fairly quiet for her.

The fifth patient was Jonathan Crowley, an old man who immediately claimed to have a headache. The geezer was walking on one fake leg and seemed about as dangerous as a titmouse, but they brought him in locked in manacles, and Branaugh reassessed his opinion when he was told the man had successfully beaten the crap out of several policemen in the recent past.

He perked up even more when he heard the old coot was a parapsychologist.

"Mr. Crowley, I understand you've seen ghosts in this building?"

The old man nodded his head.

"Can you tell me where you saw them?'

"Better to ask me where I haven't. They're all around this place."

"Are there any in the room now?"

The old man looked at him for a few seconds and a small smile played around the edges of his lips. "You want to know if there are any ghosts here? You mean aside from the one you brought with you?"

"The one I brought with me?" He was amused and let it show. "Can you describe this ghost?"

"Looks about five feet, seven inches in height, dark brown hair. I'd guess her age is around…maybe twenty. She has similar features to yours, close enough to be blood, but there's a pretty sizable mole just below her left ear."

Branaugh stared at Jonathan Crowley with his mouth open. "Who've you been talking to?"

"Mostly the good doctor over there. They don't let me out to socialize all that much." His voice was dry and sarcastic.

Branaugh stared hard for several seconds as the heat left his body and an arctic chill spread through his bones. "You just described my sister."

"Been dead a while, has she?" If he'd expected sympathy or even a kind turn of phrase from the old man, he was obviously mistaken.

"What's she wearing?"

"A pretty tacky dress, actually. Like she was ready to go to a formal. Her hair is pulled up into a loose bun. She's wearing earrings, looks like simple hoops. Thin gold necklace around her neck, with a capitol E as the only adornment." The man squinted and tilted his head a bit. "She has multiple lacerations on her wrists. If I had to make a guess, I'd say suicide."

Branaugh shook. Not just his head, in a negative statement, but his entire body shook.

"How can you know that?"

"Because I'm looking right at her. She's been standing next to you the entire time you've been sitting here and asking me questions."

"That's impossible!"

"Yes, I know, she's dead." Crowley shook his head. "She is also the only ghost currently in the room."

"My sister Elizabeth died when she was eighteen. She didn't leave a note, we just knew that something went wrong after the spring formal."

Crowley looked at him and shrugged. "Should I ask her for you?"

"You can talk to her?" The old man was either making up the most amazing line of coincidences, could read his mind, or could actually see the ghost of his dead sister standing next to him. Not a one of the notions lent the detective any comfort.

"If she feels like talking."

"Can you make her talk?"

Crowley tapped his skull again. "Not all there in the upstairs, remember? I guess there are ways, but none I can think of off the top of my head."

"Can you ask her why she's here?"

Crowley smiled. "Sure." He looked over the detective's shoulder. "Hey. Hey! Yes, you. Your brother wants to know why you're hanging around." He listened for several seconds, and when the detective opened his mouth to speak, the old man held up a hand to silence him.

"Okay, in a nutshell, your sister is here with you because she doesn't know where else to go. She's been with you several times in the past and has tried to find her way, but she always comes back to you."

"How did she die?"

"She killed herself. Allen Wurtz, the guy that took her to the formal dance, dumped her halfway through the evening because she wouldn't put out. She was depressed; she cut her wrists. Now she wishes she hadn't done it."

"Is there anything that can be done for her?"

"Not by me."

"How does she get to heaven?"

Crowley shrugged. "How the hell would I know? I've never been there."

"You have to have some idea about how ghosts get stuck here, don't you?"

"Well, yes. But that doesn't mean I know how to make them unstuck." Crowley held up his hand again. "Okay, I've got a message for you. She says you're drinking too much, you need to get serious with Nancy and not to let her situation bother you."

Branaugh stood up and moved away from the table. Without another word he moved out of the room and into the hallway of the asylum, looking at the ground and trying not to hyperventilate.

Crowley didn't say a word as he left the room.

Harrington, the doctor, spoke softly, but Branaugh heard him anyway. "Did you make all of that up, Jonathan?"

"Don't be a moron. I've got too big a headache to play with anyone."

"How long have you had a headache?"

"Since this morning."

Branaugh heard them, but he wasn't really listening. His mind was running over Elizabeth's short life and how she had ended it. For years he'd tried to find out who would have wanted his sister dead. She was one of the main reasons he'd even bothered to become a cop, so he could help other people when a loved one was taken unexpectedly. All the years he'd spent because in his heart of hearts he just knew his sister wouldn't have taken her own life, and now he'd discovered he'd been deluding himself.

It was humbling and humiliating.

"Jonathan?" Harrington was talking again.

He heard the tone changing in the doctor's voice. First it was just a question, but then the alarm set in. "Jonathan, are you all right?"

Crowley mumbled and his chains rattled. "No. No, I don't think so. Get the hell out of me."

"Jonathan! Stop!"

Branaugh turned around in time to see the old man stand up abruptly, his arms corded with strain as he wrapped both of his hands into the chain that anchored him to the ground and pulled, throwing his weight into the gesture.

The old man's eyes had rolled into the back of his head and his teeth were bared as he kept pulling, straining to separate his cuffs from their restraining links.

Branaugh moved back into the room mostly on instinct. It was in his nature to want to stop people from getting hurt and something was wrong with the old man.

He stopped dead in his tracks when the geezer pulled the chain loose from the floor. The sudden shift in tension was more than enough to send Crowley sailing backward and Branaugh wasn't quite fast enough to avoid getting slapped in the arm by the length of chain as it whipped away from the ground. He let out a yelp of pain and the man in front of him hit the ground hard, thrashing around like a trout freshly yanked from its stream.

"G-G-Get it out of me!" Crowley yanked his arms in separate directions and snapped the shorter links that cuffed his wrists together. Branaugh knew for a fact that the test strength on those cuffs was right at 800 pounds of pressure per square inch. Even with the padding to protect the man from the harsh restraints, it was a miracle that Crowley hadn't shattered both of his wrists.

Harrington stared and did little else for several seconds. Branaugh didn't have that luxury. He moved fast, and as the old man twisted himself around, he grabbed the cuffs from the back of his belt and tackled him. Or at least he tried. He landed on Crowley, sure enough, but instead of pinning him in place and then locking the cuffs onto his target, he got a sharp elbow to his temple for his troubles. The blow hurt enough to make him lose track of his agenda.

Crowley brought up his good right knee and clubbed him in the family jewels. The pain was immediate and enough to leave him praying that permanent damage hadn't been done.

Before he could suffer the insult of having his ass kicked by a man old enough to be his grandfather, two security guards entered the room, ready for action. A burly ape of a man managed to catch both of Crowley's wrists and to get a knee in his midsection for his trouble. At the same time, the other guard injected a sedative into the patient's arm. Whatever was in the syringe worked fast; Crowley lasted for another fifteen seconds and then stopped fighting. The two men very carefully picked him up and started heading for the infirmary.

---

It left the old man's body, shaken by what had happened. At first everything was fine. It merely sat back and enjoyed the ride because it hadn't been planning to do much of anything but experience the perceptions from the old man in an effort to better understand human emotions and feelings. After only a little time thinking about it, the decision came to experience what it could from a more seasoned source.

It was also curious to know what would happen if it tried to hide inside someone aware of its existence. There were too many experiences it had yet to have, too many different concepts aside from mere sensation and hunger. It wanted to know everything and while it was being as patient as it could, it was learning another new emotion as it continued on. It was learning frustration.

So it tried something new and everything was fine for a while, it could hide inside the man—and here it learned a new phrase: demon-ridden—but as soon as it attempted to learn more, to reach into the man's thoughts, the man reacted violently.

The waves of resistance were almost enough to knock it out of his body, but it held on, struggled desperately to stay where it was, and finally managed to at least keep its mental grip, but was exhausted by the effort.

The people with the old man in the room struggled to keep him calm and failed. Eventually, they medicated him, and that was a new sensation as well, because it had never felt Granger leave his quasi-conscious stage. Alex stayed in a stupor constantly these days, and had ever since the surgery where Harrington—a word that it had known but never had a real association with before—opened his skull, the moment when it was truly born as a conscious entity. Still it couldn't decide if it should be grateful to Harrington or enraged with Harrington as a result of being freed.

Time would tell.

For now, once again, it needed to recover its strength and it needed to feed.

It stared down at the old man as it lifted slowly from within his form. He slept, but the rest was not a peaceful one. It knew enough these days to understand that sometimes the rest of the people within the building were helpful and other times it did nothing to help them recover their strength.

*Good,* it thought. *Let him suffer. I don't like him.* All of which was true. It did not like the old man. It feared him. That was another new sensation it found unpleasant. Fear was not a comfortable thing.

It left the area and sought Alex Granger and the only safety it had ever known, unaware that for the first time, it had referred to itself as "I."

Evolution can be a slow process, but it had begun.

---

Deep within the bowels of the central building of Cherry Hill, there are secrets buried. No one living knew of them, or even suspected the truth of those secrets.

There were times in the past where it became convenient to forget a patient or overlook an accidental death. The only person who'd ever been aware of what happened in that narrow little crawlspace behind the main water heaters was the man who had handled the unfortunate events. He had, in his time, buried no less than seventeen bodies, most of them belonging to children born within the walls of the asylum.

Albert Miles came to the Cherry Hill Sanitarium once a month for over twenty years. He claimed he was a specialist and handled several medical functions at the asylum on the occasions when he came to visit. He never stayed long, but was compensated to attend to different medical functions that the doctors at the time found distasteful. He was paid handsomely for his efforts.

His specialties included lobotomies—a fairly new practice at the time—and the birthing of the infants born on the premises. Invariably the children were bastards, unwanted and often malnourished.

Albert handled the lobotomies himself. The only people who knew exactly what he did with the newborns were the good doctor and one of the groundskeepers he paid on the sly.

Kirby Fenner had no interest in children. He was a single man and a raging alcoholic. He took the money he was given, waited until the doctor had finished with his "preparations" and then disposed of what was left. If the infants were still alive and squirmed when they were buried, he made it a point to drink a little more and tell himself it was all his imagination, because the money was too good and because Albert Miles scared him too much to ever consider reporting what the man did to the proper authorities.

It should be noted that Fenner disappeared around the same time that Albert Miles made his last visit to the asylum. From that moment on, no one ever knew what happened to the children, or to the two patients that did not survive Miles' attempts at surgery.

They remained exactly where they were buried, where they have rested for a long, long time, forgotten flashes of history that never made much of an impact on the world around them.

An interesting geographical note, however, is that the mass grave is situated exactly one story below the cell that had belonged to Alex Granger since the time of his own lobotomy.

# Chapter Nine

Jonathan Crowley woke up with a headache large enough to fill the first floor of the asylum and an attitude that matched it perfectly. He also woke to discover himself wrapped into a straitjacket.

He was not amused.

Dr. Finney was sitting on a chair in his room when he came to, making notes as he waited patiently for John to join the land of the conscious.

Finney watched as he sat up and offered a tentative smile. "How are you feeling, John?"

"Like I got the crap kicked out of me and then got shot full of sedatives and locked into a straitjacket. How are you?"

"Well as I understand it, you were doing most of the kicking and talking about getting something out of you."

Crowley simply stared at him.

"We didn't know what you were talking about, but to be safe, I took a series of x-rays. It looks like you were right. You do have something in you. More specifically, it seems you have a piece of metal lodged into your skull, John. And I wouldn't say it was put there deliberately."

Crowley shook his head. "I'm guessing that came out during the let's fill John with Happy Juice session."

"Well, I wouldn't use that exact term, but yes."

"Still not remembering much of that, Doc."

"Would you like to read a transcript of the session? Do you think that would help?"

"I don't think it would hurt."

"So what happened to you this afternoon, John?"

"I think something was trying to possess me."

Finney thought about those words in silence for several moments and made himself a promise that he would personally be at any additional interviews with Crowley in the future.

"John, I have to say I'm a little worried about your insistence that there are supernatural influences in your life."

"Really?" Crowley arched one eyebrow and smiled a crooked little grin that was pure predator in action. "Why?"

"Because you strike me as surprisingly rational for the most part."

"Now, see, I could say the exact same thing to you, Doctor Finney."

"Do you think it's irrational of me not to believe in ghosts and demons?"

"See, I was hoping to avoid any more discussions of philosophy and religion here. Obviously, that's not going to work out." Crowley shrugged four times and while Finney was watching, stood up and began sliding out of his straitjacket. Finney watched him in silence. He wasn't really worried about being attacked, because despite his history of rather extreme violence, as far as he could tell, Crowley wasn't in the mood to pose a threat. He was rather surprised to see the man get out of what he had been assured was one of the finest restraints ever made, but he'd seen enough escape artists in his time—some of them patients—to know that no cage was designed to hold a man forever. The same was apparently true even of the best-designed straitjackets.

Crowley tossed the jacket on the floor and settled himself down on his cot. "So, let's get this done. You don't want to believe in ghosts. Why does my belief in them prove delusion?"

"You've said you can see them. I read about your reports earlier, but there are ways to convince a person that you're seeing ghosts, aren't there?"

"Given enough knowledge in advance and enough time you can convince anyone of anything." Crowley shook his head. "Of course, that's true of more than just ghosts, isn't it?"

"What do you mean?"

"Do you go to church, Doc?"

"Naturally."

"Why?" Crowley shrugged. "Is it force of habit or a belief in God?"

"A little of both, I suppose." He knew where Crowley was going, of course.

"Have you ever met God?"

"Not that I know of, but I think I see evidence of His existence."

"So you're going on faith alone?"

"Faith and maybe a few hypothetical evaluations of life in general."

"If you saw God walking down the street, how would you know He was God?"

"Well, I imagine there would be a few things about Him that would make Him stand out."

"So, I'm in a room earlier and a policeman asks me if I can see any ghosts. I look right at the woman I've seen standing next to him since he entered the room, a woman I've seen touch him and look at him and even speak in his direction. A woman he does not see, I might add. I can see her. She's not quite as in focus as the people around her, the detective and the doctor, but I can see her. I also notice that she casts no shadow, and if I actually make myself focus on her, she gets a little clearer into my view but still not enough to look like she really belongs where she is." Crowley cocked his head. "I know she's not fully there in the same sense as the cop and the shrink. But I know she's still there, in some sense. What would you make of that situation, Doc?"

"Frankly, I'd be inclined to think you were delusional."

"Or maybe if it was an old man with a beard, I was seeing God."

"Have you ever seen God, John?"

"Not that I'm aware of." He grinned as he answered.

"Why would I make up someone who looks like the cop I just met? Have you ever asked a person who's delusional to fill in all the details of the hallucination you're accusing them of seeing?"

"Several times."

"How good are the details?"

"That varies a bit from patient to patient."

"I can't prove that I am seeing ghosts definitively to you, Doc. But you can't prove to me that God exists, either."

"Fair enough. So how is it that you can see ghosts, John?"

"I honestly don't know. I know what I'm seeing when I see them, but that doesn't mean I understand all of the mechanics involved."

"Alright then," Finney smiled. He found himself liking the oldster in front of him. In different circumstances he might have even considered properly befriending the man. "Acknowledging your memory issues, do you think you can tell me where ghosts come from?"

"Well, that depends on the definition now doesn't it?"

"There's more than one definition?"

"Of course. Depending on who you talk to, ghosts can be full-blown spirits that exist in the afterlife, roaming the world until the end of times or faint echoes, spiritual reverberations that are stored in the walls of the place where they died."

"How about a bit of undigested beef?"

"That too." Crowley smiled, warming up to the subject. "Assuming the supernatural in this case, it depends largely on where you are. In some parts of Asia ghosts are effectively the equivalent of angels, sent back from Heaven and given assigned areas to watch over, from something as small as a tree to an entire area where they work as messengers and guardians. This, however, is the United States. Most of the ghosts recorded and alleged around here are considered as full spirits, normally out to protect loved ones, defend their buried secrets, or seek revenge."

"Okay, John. I'll play. What sort of ghosts do you think we have around here and where do they come from?"

"I've been thinking about that a lot, because, I gotta' say, you have more ghosts here than I would have expected. I mean, a regular hospital, sure, but an asylum? Been doing a lot of surgeries around here, Doc?"

As in botched surgeries. He got the implication and chose to ignore it. "And have you come up with any theories?"

"Generally I'd say that most of the spirits I've encountered that I can remember had a few common points going for them. First, there's traumatic death. That one seems to generate a lot of potential ghosts. Second, there's the possibility of unfinished business. Not always a big one, unless there are unusual circumstances, but it happens. Occasionally a ghost wants to chat over something important and can't figure out how. Mostly though, it seems to be strong emotions." He chuckled. "That, by the way, is the sort I'm seeing most around here, simple emotional echoes. Whether or not there're full spirit manifestations I just don't know."

"Well, by that theory, I'd say every asylum in the world must be a hotbed of ghostly activity." He meant it as a joke, but Crowley wasn't laughing.

"You have a good point there. Not really too many of your patients would be happy to be inside these walls, now would they?" He stood up and paced, once again doing the rolling gait that allowed him to walk on the artificial limb. "Factor in the length of time this place has been open and it's almost a guarantee of increasing the population of dead people walking around."

"Well, I suppose that's a possibility."

"Of course it's a possibility. It's almost a probability. Hell, factor in the people who probably were driven mad by being put in this place in the past and you can almost guarantee a substantial output of disenfranchised dead who either lost their way or wanted revenge badly enough to avoid whatever waits after death."

"We're going a little off focus here, John. What makes you, personally, capable of seeing ghosts?"

"I already told you I have no idea."

*"Do you suppose it's just a manifestation of a psychosis, maybe brought about by the deaths of your family?" And maybe, Finney thought, that's what I like about him. I don't have to dummy down my vocabulary. The man already understands the field of psychology.*

Crowley stopped pacing and looked at him with amusement once again marking his face. "I sincerely doubt it."

"Really? Why?"

"Because if you're thinking the ghosts I see are a side effect of my desire to be revisited by my family, at some point along the way, I would think I would, in fact, see my family."

"So you really think you saw a ghost this morning?"

"Unless you can come up with a better answer, yes, I'm going to work on that assumption."

"So, you're the parapsychologist, John. How does one get rid of an overpopulation of ghosts?"

Once again, he was trying to make a little joke. Once again, the reaction wasn't what he expected. Jonathan Crowley closed his mouth and sat back down on his cot. "I don't think I want to talk about this anymore."

Roger Finney left this patient alone after that, puzzled by the man's reaction. Had anyone asked him at that moment why Crowley had suddenly shut up he would have bet his license that the man was scared to answer. Very scared and trying not to let it show.

---

Crowley sat on his cot again and rocked, his stomach a seething stew of nerves. Discussing the theoretical existence of ghosts with an intelligent, if slightly biased, man was a lot of fun. That didn't mean he had any desire to explain the proper methods for getting rid of the things.

That was a road he didn't want to travel down. Every time he thought about actually doing anything to prevent or limit the activities of the dead, he wanted to panic. It was unsettling as all hell, because he didn't know why the feelings were so strong. He just knew it would be a bad thing for him to do.

He'd been reflecting on that very thought for close to half an hour when the door to his cell opened again and Finney came back in along with Harrington and two security guards.

John looked at them for a few seconds and held his arms out, ready to be manacled again.

The doctors smiled silent thanks and the guards did their business. It wasn't long before they were taking him down the hallway to one of the examination rooms.

He looked at Harrington, who was doing his best not to look nervous. Whatever had happened in the previous interrogation had apparently left the man a little jumpy. That suited John just fine. Harrington wasn't a bad person, but he definitely had a few issues in the humility department.

"John," Finney started. "We have a busy day scheduled for you. First, we want to go over your x-rays with you. Then there's the possibility of surgery to consider and also another session with Sodium Pentothal therapy to see if there's more we can discover."

"Surgery?"

"Yes, John. We're going to take a look at your x-rays, like I said, and then we're going to discuss the possibility that what's inside your skull might very well pose a serious threat to your health."

"How much risk can there be, Doc? I've had the damned thing in my head for a while now." He didn't like the idea of anyone opening his skull. As far as he was concerned, if it wasn't loose and moving around in there, it could stay put.

It was Harrington that answered. "Jonathan, you have to remember that the human body tends to not like foreign objects placed inside of it. While it's possible that whatever is in there is perfectly harmless, there's a very real chance that your body is trying to attack it as an invader. You could develop serious fevers, infection, or worse. Also, with the brain being as complex as it is, you could very well be suffering side effects from the damage that we're just now starting to see."

"Like what?" He knew the answer but wanted to get a second opinion.

"Well, your amnesia, for one. There's also your earlier psychotic break."

"Is that what you're calling it?" He shook his head. Maybe they were right. Maybe increasing brain damage caused all the nonsense about ghosts and his brief recollections of far worse things. That was the problem with being insane. You just didn't know if you could trust your own feelings and insights.

The thought that his mind was broken left him feeling adrift. Everything he believed to be might be as Finney had said and Ebenezer Scrooge before him, "a bit of undigested beef."

"Jonathan, please believe me, we want to help you."

He looked over his shoulder at the man walking a few paces behind him. Instead of trying to answer, he merely nodded his head. What else could he do?

The examination room they led him into had a light board on one wall and a series of x-ray slides were already mounted in plain view. Rather than sitting down he looked at the slides, studying the details they presented.

The object lodged in his skull was jagged along one edge and obviously synthetic in nature. Worse, it looked like whatever it was had either fragmented on impact or was in the process of breaking up.

"My memory isn't what it should be gentlemen, what parts of my brain are being affected by the location of the foreign matter?"

Harrington looked the pictures over and stared at them with the same sort of expression Crowley suspected he'd been wearing.

"John, this is yet another enigma when it comes to you," Finney shook his head. "You shouldn't be alive at all with that sort of damage to your gray matter. As near as we can tell, there isn't a part of your brain that hasn't suffered severe damage, but you're still alive and even odder, you're alive after having that inside of you for a long time. I've examined your cranium, and I can't understand how it even got inside of you. You don't have nearly enough scar tissue or damage for what we're seeing."

To make his point Finney moved over and showed a line of bone that was slightly out of place. The wound was old and obviously healed, but Crowley had to agree that it shouldn't have been there.

"Guess I have a good constitution."

Finney and Harrington looked at each other for a moment and then back at him. "You're not exactly our normal patient, John. Under a lot of circumstances we wouldn't bother asking, but as this is your head and you are well aware of the risks, we've decided to let you in on the whole process. If we leave it, you're obviously at risk. If we take it out you're just as at risk, possibly more so, but you will also have a chance of living a much longer life."

He thought about that for a while and the doctors let him do his thinking. Their expressions said they were ready to answer any potential questions, but not really in a hurry to make him decide.

"Okay. If I leave it alone it will probably continue to degrade, leaving me at risk of severe infection, more brain trauma, possibly increasing whatever psychosis I might already have. If I let you take it out, there's no guarantee the brain tissue around it hasn't managed to recover as best it can and you might well do catastrophic damage to what's left of my brain. That about sum it up?"

"Yes." Both doctors answered.

"Gentlemen, according to what you've been able to discover about my life, my wife and family are dead and I am alone in the world." Harrington started to say something but Crowley held out a hand to stop him. "I'm not getting any younger, and my best prospects currently include spending the majority of the rest of my life in a ten-by-ten cell down the hallway."

Harrington cleared his throat and spoke. "There's always the possibility of a successful operation, Jonathan. You could well have a long life ahead of you and with therapy, you could come out of this on the winning side."

"That's true, Doctor. That's why I say go ahead and cut me open." He crossed his right leg over the artificial left. "And thank you. I know you weren't actually obligated to consult me."

Despite his slowly growing base of memories, he couldn't believe there was the remotest chance that he would ever be set free. Better by far to either die on the operating table or suffer enough traumas to end all of the delusional thoughts moving through is head.

Better dead than stuck like this.

---

Kimberly was looking over her latest test scores and making notes for the next exam. She sat in the cafeteria and ate her meager lunch while she read. Her shift was finished, but her next class wasn't for four hours and it was easier to study in the cafeteria and drive straight to the school instead of traveling home first and trying to accomplish the same task. There were too many distractions at home and the travel time was a bear. Besides, she might get lucky and get a little help from one of the doctors on a few of the tougher questions. They had all been down the road she was currently trying to travel.

Doctor Sebastian came in and sat at the table with her, and Kimberly smiled. Sebastian was a hefty man with dark hair and a beard, who was also charming, flirtatious and completely safe to be around. When he wasn't dealing with patients, he was normally on the phone with his wife.

He smiled and then carefully opened the brown bag holding his lunch. His smile faltered a little when he saw the dry tuna fish sandwich, celery and carrot sticks.

"If I didn't know Marion loved me, I'd think she was trying to kill me."

"Well, you did tell me you were trying to lose weight, Charles."

He sighed and shook his head dramatically. "Yes, that's true. But still, does diet food have to be so damned bland?"

Kimberly laughed and slid him half of her bologna sandwich. "No mayo, just mustard."

"Will you marry me, Kimberly?"

"I think I have to go with the same answer. I'm not much into polygamy."

"I was afraid you'd say that." He took a bite of her sandwich and savored the luncheon meat as if it were the finest filet mignon. She knew him well enough to know that if she'd given him liverwurst instead he'd have been in heaven.

Without asking he picked up her latest test and started reading it. As he had always been nice enough to help her study, she took no offense.

"You knew the answer to number eight." His voice was scolding.

"I know. I was just tired." Every time he chastised her she felt like a five-year-old caught with a stolen cookie.

"Well, I can't imagine why. It's not like you work full time." He winked and leaned in closer. "I don't imagine it would take much of a nudge to get you moved to a different floor if you prefer. I know working in the dungeon can be taxing."

"You know, I actually like working down there."

"Really? Why?"

"It's mostly quiet."

"Well, I have to give you that one. You can't really say the patients around here stay quiet for long." Charles opened his mouth for another bite of forbidden sandwich and stopped when something vile fell from the ceiling and landed square on the white bread.

Whatever the substance was, it was black, foul smelling and still moving.

Kimberly pushed away from the table and looked up at the same time that Charles dropped the sandwich. A moment later there was a creaking noise from up above and Dr. Sebastian stayed put, looking at the ceiling with a puzzled expression as he caught a deeper whiff of the sweetly rotten aroma.

The ceiling had been fine when Kimberly entered the room. She'd have sworn on it in a court of law if the situation ever came up. Now the acoustic tiles were sagging heavily above their heads and the stench from whatever it was that was trying to come down was enough to make her eyes water and her stomach threaten rebellion.

Charles Sebastian got out of the way only seconds before the table where they'd been sitting became the target of a deluge. Thick syrupy waves of what smelled like leftovers from a charnel house splashed across the table and sprayed outward, covering both of them with more of the same. Something heavy and solid fell at the same time and the weight of the unrecognizable lump shattered the pressboard tabletop.

Doctor and nurse alike let out loud screams and backed away, their eyes fixed on whatever was resting on the remains of their lunches and her schoolwork.

They were still staring, still trying to understand everything that had happened when the security guards came into the room.

---

Carl Branaugh looked over the scene with obvious disgust on his face. Per his request, no one had moved anything in the cafeteria, the only exception being the two people who'd been in the room when the ceiling collapsed. They were both cleaning up and he couldn't say he blamed them for trying to wash off whatever had hit them.

He looked at the thickly coated lump and could guess that at least part of it would be body parts. The smell gave it away if you'd been unfortunate enough to be around enough dead people. He had.

He took several pictures for his own files and let the county team take care of their own photos.

He tried to focus on the details in front of him, but it was hard. Whenever he let his mind wander even a little he was back with the old man in the interrogation room who said his dead sister was looking over his shoulder. Worse, he could almost feel her staring at him in disapproval. His life, like most peoples', had taken a few unexpected turns along the way. The notion that his sister might well have been watching at the darkest moments in his life was not soothing.

He pushed the thoughts away again and sighed. There were more pressing matters to attend to.

Matt Burton, the local medical examiner, walked up quietly and slapped him on the shoulder. Matt seemed to enjoy trying to make him piss himself. It was one of the things of which the old man never seemed to tire.

Carl resisted the urge to either scream, wet his pants or backhand the old coot. "Not a very pretty sight, is it?"

"No, I can't say that it is." With a very perfunctory look around the cafeteria, the man pulled on a pair of gloves and walked over to the weighty lump that rested on the devastated table. Carl had seen the man carve open a few cadavers and never once seen the man blanch at the odor or sight. He looked ready to get ill just staring at the mess in front of him. Still, he carefully reached out and started collecting samples for examination.

Branaugh moved away. Despite his own morbid sense of curiosity, he decided he'd wait to hear from the good doctor before he entered the room.

Several members of the staff were milling around in the hallway, some of them surely just curious and others worried about possible health risks. Carl moved to the first one who looked familiar, in this case he believed the man's name was Harrington.

"Doctor." He nodded. "Any idea what happened here?"

"Actually, I was just going to have my lunch, but that's not looking like a very good idea." The man looked like Christmas had just been cancelled.

"No, not today it isn't."

"Well, I suppose dinner is only a few hours away." He looked like he was ready to call it a day already.

"I wish I could help, Doctor, but I have a few people I need to interview about this latest situation." If his voice carried an edge he didn't try to hide it. Whatever was going on at Cherry Hill was rapidly becoming a true annoyance. He could have done without another ten-mile trip to the local loony bin. "Can you tell me where I can find Dr. Charles Sebastian or Kimberly Walker?"

"I saw Charles a few moments ago. He was just drying off. I think he said he'd be in his office." Carl had no idea what sort of politics took place in a mental hospital, but he knew well enough the look on the doctor's face. There was bad blood between the two men. He made a mental note of the fact, though he doubted it would come to anything. He thanked the man for his troubles and moved down to find Finney. The man was in charge of the building and would probably want to, once again, assure him that he had no idea what was happening in the building.

*That's the part I hate the most, he mused. No matter where you go, no matter whom you ask, it always seems like no one can admit to knowing anything.*

---

His eyes were closed and his body relaxed, but there was nothing calm in Jonathan Crowley's mind.

A thousand faces passed through his sleep, some familiar and some as alien to him as the red sands of Mars. Each spoke, formed words, but despite all of their differences, they spoke with one voice.

"You have to remember."

"I don't want to."

"There's no choice, really. It's what has to be done. It's what you've always done."

"I quit that. I quit you. I wanted a life, a real life."

"I gave you time for that. You squandered it away."

"I'm old now. I want to be left alone."

"No. There's much you need to do."

The words were insistent, demanding.

He wanted nothing to do with them.

"We had a deal and you broke it!" He screamed at the endless array of faces that flashed before him, his rage building, consuming his sorrow.

"You had a lifetime. You wasted it on foolish dreams and hopeless pursuits."

He saw only the faces, the ever-changing series of features that blended into each other and obscured his ability to see anything else. He felt something though, a presence, a towering, monumental force that swelled with the power of a hundred tsunamis. Whatever that something was, it no longer wished to be denied.

Crowley woke up in a heavy sweat, his sheet tossed to the side and his body sprawled on the cot. The pain in his head was a raw, unending scream and his hands clenched at the fine hairs near his temples as he groaned.

Damn it! There was something he was supposed to do, he could sense that, but whatever it was, it scared him. More importantly, there was a sense of urgency now, a sense that if he didn't do something soon, he would regret it.

Whatever he'd been dreaming, however, was fading away. His dreams always did.

"Yeah, just like my life."

With nothing else to do and no other way to occupy his time, Crowley grabbed another bar of soap. He held it for several seconds, wondering what shape would come forth as he started to whittle. Really, there was only one way to find out, so he picked up his plastic knife and began gently carving away flakes of the stuff to see what would take form.

He knew he'd had another session with the doctors, but couldn't for the life of him remember what had happened after they'd shot the meds into his vein.

"They'll tell me when they're ready." His hands moved deftly over the soap, and he could feel something taking shape, but he didn't let himself look. He seldom bothered with paying attention to the form until the time came to carve the finer details.

The tension was leaving his skull, easing away the pressure that had threatened to crush him. He let his mind drift again, trying to sort out the vague memories that littered his mindscape. There was still no real rhyme or reason that he could find to help him understand the fragments as he sorted them. There were only images, remembered sensations and occasionally a sense that everything was missing.

That and an uneasy feeling that something was going wrong in the building around him. Something was changing at Cherry Hill and not for the better.

"Not my problem anymore." He spoke without paying much attention to what he said. Whatever came out of his mouth, he knew would only be the ramblings of a mad man.

A mad man who would be going through surgery the very next day. He remembered that much. Surgery in the morning, a chance to end his nightmares and his delusions, even if the ending only came with his death.

That thought pleased him more than he expected. It wasn't so much death he was looking forward to, not really. He just wanted everything to change. He didn't want to remember anyone or anything anymore, at least not if he couldn't remember the faces that were most important to him.

He didn't want to hear voices or see ghosts. He didn't want to stare at the walls around him for whatever remained of his life, and most of all, he didn't want to go on for a moment longer if all he had to look forward to was the growing anxieties that seemed to make up most of his days.

For the briefest moment he thought he smelled perfume, a faint hint of jasmine, perhaps. Whatever it was, the scent was familiar and comforting.

John set aside his soap and his plastic knife and closed his eyes trying to focus on why the scent was familiar and pleasing. The memory eluded him, like most all of his memories managed to do these days.

Exasperated, he settled back down on his cot and did his best to wait patiently for the morning and a chance, however slim, that the day after that would be better.

It might have worked better if he'd waited until nightfall. It was only a little after one in the afternoon and he'd already been in a medicated sleep for half the day.

---

Roger Finney shook his head and sighed. The police detective,

Branaugh, that was the name, and the coroner were both looking at him for explanations and he just didn't have any.

"Dr. Finney, I'm not accusing anyone of anything, but come on, now. So far we've had two people mutilated and a corpse rammed into a drainpipe and now this." He held out the picture as if, by some miracle, Roger would have forgotten what the damned thing looked like in the last ten minutes.

Once the layers of goo had been wiped away, the full horror of what had been dumped in the kitchen could finally be seen: it wasn't a person, for which Roger was grateful. That didn't make him any more comfortable looking at it. He considered himself a man of science and looking at the mass displayed for him made it harder to keep his foundations in place. The lump weighed in at close to a hundred pounds, and seemed to be made of bone, meat and internal organs that had been fused into a new form. One blind eye stared out of the mass, and not far from that a half-formed foot curled in on itself. What he had to guess was a spinal column—minus a large number of bones—cut through the body, but there was no sign of any coherent structure to the entire thing. It looked to Finney as if someone had gathered pieces from a half-dozen people and then rolled them in dough and let it rise until everything was knotted together.

He looked away from the picture.

"Gentlemen, believe me, I want this solved as much as you do. More, probably, because I have staff members seriously considering leaving me to handle this entire place by myself."

"You're sure that there haven't been any bad accidents around here lately?"

"I've already done a head count. Everyone that is supposed to be here is here, gentlemen. I didn't even have anyone call out sick today, which is something of a miracle, I assure you."

Branaugh was pacing, stressed and frustrated. He threw the photo down and shook his head. "This doesn't make any sense. What especially doesn't add up is why that...thing, was above the break room when the only thing up there was concrete ceiling and a fourteen-inch crawlspace."

"Have you ever found out the identity of the man in the drainpipe?"

Branaugh shook his head and scowled. "No. As near as we can figure the man doesn't exist. His clothes were very out of date, like by fifty years or more, and he didn't have any form of identification in his wallet. The wedding ring on his finger had an inscription on the inside with the initials I.A. and that's all. Not even a date to make it possible to look through any existing records. His fingerprints might be on file somewhere but it's going to take months before we get an answer on that."

"If I didn't know better, I'd think Crowley was right about this place." He muttered the words just to say them, but Branaugh stopped pacing when he said them.

"Okay. Maybe that's something you should look into then."

"Excuse me?"

"The bodies of both Ernst Holbrook and Adam Prescott came back negative for infectious diseases and toxicology screens. Well, Prescott was apparently on a lot of medications, but there was nothing going on inside his body that would explain why portions of him were just missing. There was nothing to explain how a big man wound up inside of your pipes and I can't see how that mess," he shoved his finger at the offensive photo again, "could have wound up in the ceiling of the cafeteria with no one the wiser about it being there."

Branaugh sat down and stared hard at Finney, once again making the doctor nervous. "So unless you can come up with a logical answer, and believe me, I'm trying to Doctor, maybe you ought to check with Crowley about any connections he might remember in the parapsychology field. Or maybe you should seek an exorcist."

The older man he'd brought with him chuckled softly and volunteered, "I have a nephew that's a priest."

Finney didn't throw anything at him.

"Well, perhaps you'd like to ask him yourselves, gentlemen?"

Branaugh nodded without any hesitation. "Sure. I'll take any help I can get at this point."

---

John looked at the men sitting around him and shook his head. He recognized the doctors, of course. They were his most common source of interesting conversation and he would even have gone so far as to say they were fun to be around in a miserable way. He knew the detective as soon as he saw him but couldn't remember his name and the old man was a stranger, but looked a few years younger than he was himself.

"Why do I get the impression this isn't about my impending surgery?"

The detective looked at him blankly for a moment until Finney explained.

"Well, I'm sorry about the surgery, and good luck, of course." John nodded his thanks. "What I wanted to talk to you about is your work in parapsychology."

His stomach did the butterfly trick, the one where it feels like a thousand or so of the little bastards are flying around in an enclosed space. "What can I help you with?"

"Can you recommend anyone to give Cherry Hill a good looking over?"

The tension left; not all of it, but a lot. For a moment he'd been absolutely certain they were going to ask him, instead they just wanted a contact. "I have one phone number that pops to mind when I think about that. I'll write it down and you can use me as a reference."

"Whose number is it?"

"I haven't the foggiest notion."

Branaugh's eyes went wide and then narrowed slightly. "Are you pulling my leg?"

John pulled on his chain and rattled it where it connected with the floor. "Not very likely."

The old man kept staring at him with a hefty level of doubt on his face. Finally annoyed with the look, John turned on him sharply. "Listen, no offense, but take a picture. It'll last longer and cover all of the pertinent details."

"Excuse me?"

"Quit staring at me. I'm not a freak in a circus and you're starting to get on my bad side."

"Oh, I'm sorry I didn't realize I was—"

"My ass you didn't. You want to ask me something, ask it. You want to stare at me, kindly look elsewhere."

"John, there's no reason for that sort of behavior." Harrington moved closer as he spoke.

"Bullshit! You try getting the third degree and dealing with lookie-loos at the same time. Check how it feels."

While everyone around him shifted uncomfortably, Crowley took a piece of paper and wrote down the phone number that came to mind when they asked their question of him. He wrote in large numbers because the only writing implement he had access to was a crayon. He slid paper and red wax coloring stick alike over to Branaugh.

"There."

"Thanks."

John leaned back in his seat and stared at the old man sitting next to Branaugh. "So if you have a question, ask it."

Without any hesitation and most decidedly judging by the looks, without permission of the doctors in the room, the older man pulled a photograph from a file in his hand and slid it across the table for John to see. "Okay. Any idea what that is?"

He looked at the picture carefully, leaning over the table to do so. "A mess? Disgusting? An extreme close-up of a miscarriage?"

"That mass was found in the asylum this afternoon," as soon as the older man started speaking both of the doctors protested, calling for him not to agitate their patient. He ignored them completely and continued, raising his voice to be heard. "It weighs just over eighty pounds, was surrounded by a very large pool of foul smelling black fluids, and fell out of the ceiling in the cafeteria. We already know that there are no pipes, no drainage areas and no medical waste dumps anywhere in the vicinity."

Crowley leaned back again and looked directly at Harrington. The doctor looked back at him with just a hint of shame peeking around the corners of his stoic expression.

"Okay. Take samples of the meat, the bone and the crap that was around them. I'm guessing you'll find the meat is human and so is the bone. The fluids will probably be a very simple cellular structure, similar to an amoeba. They'll also all be very dead."

"Why do you say that?"

"I know you're tired of hearing this, but I have amnesia. I'm guessing here. And I'll try to remember where I've run across that sort of thing before, but check it out first."

He looked around at the two doctors and their guests. Both doctors looked like they wanted a few words alone with the older man. He looked like he could hold his own in any argument.

"So, Detective Branaugh, why don't you and I talk over here and you can send the doctors down to argue with your friend about the inappropriate use of one of their patients." He put both hands against his face and widened his eyes. In a mock whisper he added, "The bad man made me look at dirty pictures!"

Branaugh looked at his associate and the man shrugged and stood up, moving to the far end of the room. Both doctors followed immediately, ready to have their discussion on professional decorum when handling violently insane patients.

John looked at the detective and smiled. "I know you want to ask me questions. I can see it in your face. This might be your last chance, what with me having brain surgery in the morning, so ask them now or forever hold your peace."

"Do you think the ghosts here are causing all of the troubles?"

"No. I think something else is doing it."

"Do you think the number you gave me can help?"

"That's why I gave it to you. Like I said, give it a call and mention my name. I don't know who will answer, but I think it was someone I trusted at least."

"What if the number doesn't work?"

"Then you're out of luck. I think U.C. Berkeley might have a program on parapsychology, but I don't know for sure. When in doubt, try a few spiritualists. They may not help, but you never know."

"Can you make a guess about what's happening here, Mr. Crowley?"

"Sure." He stretched and then popped his knuckles. "I think something wants to get born into this world and doesn't know how to do it yet."

The man nodded his head with a worried expression on his face. John couldn't blame him. If he weren't fairly sure the surgery would go poorly, he'd have been worried himself.

# Chapter Ten

The scene replayed itself again: He opened the door to his house and stepped inside, content after a good day of classes full of kids.

His wife, his children, bound and gagged, the tableau one of the only memories that remains clear. He sees the stranger, a pudgy man with sweat running from the bald spot in the wave of salt-and-pepper hair, his eyes bloodshot to the point where they had to hurt, an idiot grin on his flabby face, and parts of his skin already patchy, strained from whatever was inside of him and trying to hide.

The mouth moves, but there are no noises this time, only remembrances of past threats. He drops his briefcase and moves, oh, how he moves, cursing the artificial leg that he tells himself doesn't really bother him, pushing as fast and hard as he can to get to the man before it's too late.

The gesture is almost trivial, a slight wave of one hand, and he feels himself lifted through the air, shoved backward until the wall stops his progress.

The stranger walks away from his wife and he looks at her, begging her to forgive him for this, his dirty little secret, the one thing he was never willing to talk about, because talking would give power to his past and he wanted nothing to do with that anymore. He wanted to be where he was, with a wife and with children, living the American Dream and suffering the pain of every bruise and scrape on his body and soul, no matter how much time it took for them to mend.

His throat is sore from screaming, his arms ache from the pressure that holds him in place as the middle-aged stranger twitches, his muscles misfiring, not used to a new master. The man is still twitching as he lifts the hammer and the first of the thick nails—just shy of a railroad spike, really—he's set near the door for just this moment.

The pain is immense, overwhelming any sensation he's experienced in decades, even the loss of his leg. He screams and his family screams with him as if every hammer blow was pushing their limbs into the exact same wall.

When the worst of it was over, his good leg was bleeding. His arms bled too. The pain dulled down to an inferno and his mouth was so dry he could barely taste anything.

The shock is trying to set in when the stranger turns and heads back into the living room, back to his wife, where she still tries to get free from her bonds.

She screams again when the man's fingers curl into her hair and start lifting her from the ground.

And Jonathan Crowley screams, calling out for mercy, but not from the demon he knows is hiding inside the stranger. No, he calls to the source that granted him a reprieve from his life. He knows that whatever happens next, he'll have to try to stop the thing getting ready to ruin his wife. She means so much to him, more than he ever thought a human could.

Crowley's eyes opened in the darkness. There was nothing to see except the light where it crept around the edges of his cell's door and through the meshed glass of the small window.

The memories came harder now, more vividly than ever before and he realized with a start that he had lied to his doctor. He'd never gotten a chance to hunt down and kill the thing that had taken his family from him. He'd been on his way to do just that when the plane crashed.

Whatever fear he'd been feeling was temporarily crushed under the sudden fury that filled his being.

"I fucked up." He sat on his cot and stared at the gray blurs of his hands. Even in near darkness, he could see the age spots, the fine white hairs and the thinness of his arms. There had been times in his past when he could have bent steel bars with his strength and now he was nothing, a dried-up waste without enough coherent thoughts to do anything but quiver in fear at the thought of helping somebody with a simple matter of ghost infestation. The knowledge was there, somewhere, locked behind the rusting blade that was hidden in his skull. There were words he could say, simple commands he could give that would have changed everything if he could only remember them.

Worse than that, he knew even if he could say the words that he wouldn't. He had never turned his back on a person in need, not unless the person deserved to be abandoned, but here he was, cowering in darkness instead of even trying because...

You did a bad thing, Jonathan.

...the fear was worse than a cancer, it was eating away everything that made him what he once was and he...

You'll do bad things again if you ever get the chance.

...was too afraid to admit that he was wrong and the voices he kept hearing were right. He had things to do and no desire to do them.

How do you honor your dead? How do you get revenge when the trail is six years cold and you're nothing but a beaten old man? How do you honor your dead when you can't even remember their faces, their names?

"How do you get past the goddamned fear? Can somebody tell me that? Please?"

If anything was listening as he mumbled to himself, it remained quiet. As quiet as the grave.

---

The operating room was quiet, except for the sounds of the various devices surrounding the patient and the slightly hollow classical music coming from the radio. Phil Harrington liked to listen to music when he was operating; it helped keep him calm and his hands steady.

It wasn't often he worked on a man as old as Jonathan Crowley, and it was definitely not common for him to try pulling rusted metal from inside a human skull.

The worst of the mess had been pulled free, but a few of the smaller fragments were hiding themselves deep in the cerebral matter and he was hesitant to go looking for them. One small screw up and he could end up with the old man being about as coherent as a head of cabbage.

He stepped back for a moment and reexamined the x-rays. Two more pieces to go, but they were both deeper than he'd expected and pushed into the temporal lobe. In theory, he could get to them and cause minimal or no damage. Of course the theories were all based on a younger man who hadn't already suffered traumatic brain damage in the past. Scar tissue could be an issue and so could blood vessels or arteries that had been moved by the steel scraps. He'd already had to patch two bleeders and wasn't looking forward to trying his luck with another.

"Okay, let's call this a success and start sewing up."

No one questioned his decision. In the end it was his ass on the line if things went wrong and while surgery on the brain wasn't completely new, there were still too many factors that remained uncertain.

Harrington double-checked carefully as he closed up, making sure there were no surprises anywhere along the way.

As far as he could tell at this early stage, the surgery had gone well. That could always change with the risk of infection, but he felt good about it. Better than he had when he worked on Alex Granger.

---

Alex Granger rocked slowly back and forth, unaware that he had soiled himself again, and merely conscious of the discomfort he felt.

His eyes were open and he looked around his cell with no comprehension. There wasn't much left of his mind to think with.

He was aware. There were certain things that slipped into his mind from time to time. He knew, for example, that something rested inside of him, comfortable within the shell of his body. He knew that the something there had always been there, but had been freed from him when his skull got opened.

He knew that he wasn't what he used to be, and that frustrated him, but he didn't know how to fix it or even how to express his dissatisfaction.

The presence was there again, looking through his eyes. He had a name for it once, and knew that it made him do bad things, but he also knew that it had protected him, or at least given him comfort in the past.

The thought brought a weak smile to Alex's face and he rocked faster, excited to have found a cognitive connection.

His left hand twitched, a small, simple jerking motion, and then twitched again. Alex stared at it, certain that he'd had nothing to do with the action, and as he did, his right hand started the same dance.

A few moments later, he fell back and groaned as his body started seizing.

While its host continued to spasm, it reached through his body and experimented with nerve endings and the ways in which the mind ordered the body to move. It had learned so much of late that at times the experiences felt overwhelming, but there was so much more to learn.

Spreading its consciousness further, it continued to play with the internal systems of Alex Granger and simultaneously began to sift through his lifetime of experiences.

This time it didn't just feel the memories, it studied them. If it wanted to understand about life it had to start somewhere and in this case the best place to start seemed to be close to home.

---

Carl Branaugh waited patiently after he was put on hold. He'd been getting nowhere with finding out who lived at the phone number he called until he mentioned Crowley's name. After that he was hastily put on hold and told that someone would be with him in a moment. That had been twenty minutes earlier.

As he was just about to hang up and try his luck again later, a woman's voice responded. "Detective Branaugh? I'm so sorry to keep you waiting. How can I help you?"

"Oh, hi. Umm. I'm calling this number because a man named Jonathan Crowley suggested it."

"Have you talked to Jonathan? Is he all right?" Her voice lifted with nervous excitement.

*"Well, he's been better." No, ma'am, I'm sorry but he's old and in a nuthouse. Also, he's sort of aggressive…*

"Where is he? We've been worried sick ever since we heard, about his family, I mean. I honestly was beginning to think he might have died."

"I'm sorry. Whom am I speaking to?"

"Oh. That could be useful, couldn't it?" She had one of those voices that just made him desperate to meet the woman attached to it, smooth and sexy as hell. "My name is Amelia Dunlow. I'm a friend of the family."

"Ms. Dunlow, can you tell me why he would suggest I call you regarding um…strange occurrences?"

"Oh." Her voice sounded almost as doubtful as he felt about the way this was working out. "Well, I have some knowledge along those lines, but really, Jonathan has more experience than I could ever hope to have. Or want to have for that matter."

"Oh. I see."

"Where are you calling from, Detective? I can probably arrange to meet you if you think that would help. And maybe I could come see Jonathan. It's been a while since we saw each other."

He gave her the phone number for his office and also directions as to where to find the place.

"Is Jonathan under arrest?" Oddly, she didn't sound as worried at that notion as he would have expected.

"Well, I think it might be best if I explained when you get here."

"I'll be there as soon as possible."

He thanked her and disconnected the call, then sat at his desk and worried. The woman was going to be in for an unpleasant surprise and there wasn't a damned thing he could do about that.

He looked at the case files on his desk again, ignoring the flow of people in the office and the slight hunger pangs in his stomach. The afternoon was still just getting started and he had a thousand things he was supposed to be doing. Sooner or later he'd have to handle them or they wouldn't get done.

---

Leslie Anne Hampton sat at one of the small tables in the recreation area and drew pictures. Her artwork wasn't anything special, but she liked to draw. It kept her mind off of the strange sensations she'd been experiencing lately.

Her breasts ached, and felt heavier than they should have, and her skin was dry and itching, and worst of all, her insides felt like they were on fire.

She'd tried explaining to Dr. Sebastian, but all he did was nod his head like always.

Leslie knew the score: She was just another crazy in a sea of crazies and it would take more than a few complaints about a bellyache to get them to listen to her. Still, she'd tried, at least, and they were letting her out of her room to do things for a change.

The pony she was trying to draw looked more like a cow, so she switched crayons and added in a cowbell around the neck and then horns on the head.

It was while she was finishing the left horn that all the color left her vision and the room started getting fuzzy. Leslie stood up and took a few steps in the direction of the closest attendant. She ignored the voice of her father telling her to come on back over and sit her skinny ass down like he told her to. Her father was dead, after all. She had watched him die.

Nurse Betty had been chiding one of the inmates for exposing himself, but she turned to Leslie around the same time that Leslie's knees buckled. She tried to catch herself, she did, but the floor was too close and by the time she thought to move her hands, her face was slamming into the linoleum tiles.

Three hours later she was in a new room, one with a real bed and even a TV behind a Plexiglas case. Dr. Sebastian came in and they had a nice, long talk. He listened this time, too. And not long after that she had lotion for her skin and the nurses were treating her like she was someone special.

They didn't mention the pregnancy to her. They were still worrying over who might be the father and what the legal ramifications would be when the pregnancy became noticeable.

---

The darkness was complete. There was no sound; there was no motion, not even a current of air to caress his skin.

Jonathan Crowley rested deeper than he ever had, aware of his surroundings but incapable of moving or communicating in any way.

He couldn't have guessed how long the darkness lasted. Even his heartbeat was silent. For a time, he pondered whether or not he might be dead, but eventually decided that oblivion couldn't possibly be that boring.

Eventually awareness came back to him in a limited form. He noticed things moving in the darkness, things that didn't seem quite human. Of course they were only shadows in the blackness, so it was hard to really say.

They spoke softly at first, faint whispers, but as he listened the words became louder.

"What will you do now? Will you stay this way, or will you answer your call to duty?"

"Leave me alone."

"There are things you have left unfinished."

"I don't care."

"Your wife, your sweet Elizabeth, she remains uneasy in death."

"And yet, she's still dead." He tried to sound casual about it, but the words cut him. Elizabeth. Her name was Elizabeth. In an instant he was flooded with memories. Touching her hand as he drove them down the highway to the new home he'd had built for her, far away from his other residence, because she didn't need to know about that part of his life, the part he'd gladly given up for her. Waking up to the sight of her sleeping peacefully next to him in the bed. The scent of her perfume, the touch of her lips. The look in her eyes on the day he proposed. A thousand others that filled him with peace and warmed his soul.

Of course the other memories came again too, straining against the spikes through his wrists and ankles as the demon forced itself on her, not for sexual gratification or even to impregnate her, as demons often tried, but solely to enjoy his suffering as he watched his wife defiled and tortured.

"Your children suffer too." And the memories were there, not coming from his own broken mind, but presented to him full on. Jeremy's birth, the sweet feeling of holding his son in his arms; sweet, precious Theresa talking her first baby steps; Wendy crying in the night and running into their bedroom, scared by nightmares that Jonathan knew were harmless, because he always knew when the real monsters were near. Each memory a treasure that was ruined a moment later by the recollections of what the demon had done.

"Leave me alone!"

"They're still suffering, Jonathan, because you failed in your duties. Suffering because you let them die."

The guilt became a physical weight, his first sensation since they'd taken him to the operating room.

"I didn't fail in anything! There are others, you know, they could have handled it if they'd wanted to."

There was silence then, cold and accusatory.

Whatever had come closer in the darkness receded, as he realized he was alone again, consciousness came to steal him from his rest.

# Chapter Eleven

The staff room was as silent as a crypt. All along the four tables set into the area, there were people eating donuts and Danishes and drinking coffee like it was going out of style. Roger Finney stood at the head of the table and looked down along both sides and saw familiar faces with unfamiliar expressions. Mostly what he saw was anxiety. Not a one of the employees at Cherry Hill looked at all happy to have a job at the moment.

"I know you're all nervous. I know there are a lot of rumors floating around about what's happening here and what's being done about it, so let's just cut straight to the chase and after I've gone over everything, if you still have questions, I'll answer them."

No one said anything in return. A skeleton crew was watching over the patients and he wanted to rectify that as quickly as possible. While he couldn't exactly say that things were getting out of hand, he suspected they would in the near future if he didn't calm down the workers and fast.

"Okay, first off, we still don't know exactly what happened yesterday in the cafeteria. The situation is being investigated, and we have an expert in unusual cases like this one coming in later today. The same expert will very likely be working with the police regarding what happened both to Ernst and to Adam Prescott." He cleared his throat and took a sip of his coffee.

"Okay, having said that, we do know certain things. First, there's no risk of contagion as far as we can tell. The CDC looked over samples, as did the local hospital. There's no disease causing these things. They remain a mystery for that reason. The body we previously found remains a mystery as well. Having looked over the fingerprints of everyone on file, employees and patients alike, the police can safely say it wasn't anyone who was supposed to be here, but they can't say more than that yet.

"I know this is a strange situation, but I'm asking all of you to remember that we serve a vital purpose here at Cherry Hill and not to let your imaginations run away with you.

"Lastly, the cafeteria will be finished tomorrow afternoon. In the meantime this area will serve as a break room."

He looked around and waited for a response. Several of the staff members looked like they wanted to ask questions, so he pointed to one of the nurses and started there. "Andrea? You wanted to ask something?"

"You said no one knows what's causing these things, so how do we know we're going to be safe?"

Direct and to the point, and also the last question he'd wanted to hear.

"I don't have any answers on that, either, unfortunately." He looked at the people around him and shook his head. "We can't know that until we know what is causing the problems. All I can tell you is we're investigating all of the angles."

The woman shook her head. "Then I don't know how I feel about working until this gets solved. I have a family to take care of. I can't do that if I'm dead."

"Andrea, we all have families to take care of and I wouldn't expect anyone to work here if there was a serious threat to their health."

"Yeah but what kind of guarantees are you putting down, Dr. Finney?" Her voice was shrill, a sign of the stress she was feeling. "I have two kids and I'm a widow. Life insurance only goes so far if I wind up turned inside out like Ernst!"

He sighed and resisted the urge to rub his temples; it was too late to stop a headache from coming around in any case. "Andrea, the cases are isolated circumstances and we have the police investigating the situation. That's all of the assurances I can give you right now."

The people working under him weren't looking very comforted by his words. Roger had the strong suspicion it wasn't going to be a good day for him.

He was right.

---

Three hours of her life wasted in a long, unfulfilling debate with Dr. I-am-an-asshole Finney had not been on Andrea Tartelli's list of things she wanted to do with her life. He was pissing and moaning about the way the world works and she was trying to get across the point that she didn't feel safe in her job. He didn't want to hear her or any of the other people who had justifiable complaints and he also wasn't going to accept a leave of absence from anyone until the weird shit going down was resolved to their satisfaction. Well, fuck him! She had vacation time coming and she'd take it if she had to. Just as soon as she'd finished her cigarette break she was going to talk to Mary Gerber, the head of the nursing department and the lady that could get her the time off. Mary knew the score, there were things going on in all of their lives beyond the damned job, and Mary owed her a few favors. Besides, her mom was harping all the time about coming down to visit her in Florida.

She stepped into the emptied supply room on the second floor where the only furnishings were a card table and an overflowing ashtray and lit up, taking a deep drag off her Camel and trying to calm down. She still had her shift today to deal with, whether she wanted it or not.

The pain in her shoulder put an immediate end to trying to relax. At first it felt like someone pushing on her shoulder blade and then it felt like someone shoving a sword into her chest, a white-hot needle of pain that flared brighter and brighter.

Andrea stepped away from the wall with a yelp, and looked back at the spot where the pain was blooming. There was nothing to see, but a small point where the cloth of her uniform was pushed against her skin, no blood or anything else to explain where the pain was coming from.

"Ahhh…shit that hurts!" She tried rolling her shoulder and stopped as soon as the pain doubled.

The door to the hallway was only five feet away and she moved toward it as fast as she could. What was causing the tearing sensation was a mystery, but one she wanted solved before something worse could happen.

She took two steps before the cutting agony became enough to drop her to her knees. The only thing working to her benefit was that the resulting scream caught the attention of someone in the hallway.

Dr. Sebastian opened the door with a frown on his face and stared at her mutely for a second before coming into the room.

"Andrea? What's wrong? Are you hurt?"

Jesus! She was practically ready to cough up blood and he was asking her stupid questions. She reached out her hand toward the man, silently asking him to help her stand, and as she did, something moved under her skin, separating flesh from muscles in the process.

Andrea screamed again, and felt her arm bend in ways that were completely unnatural. Bones should not slide, and that was exactly what they were doing. Heat washed through her body and she half expected to see flames coming from her mouth as she let out another shriek.

The doctor had been reaching for her and suddenly stopped, his eyes growing preposterously wide in his face. "Dear Lord!" He stepped back and shook his head, growing visibly paler. Andrea tried to speak, but no words would come out. Whatever was happening grew even worse and her blood pressure soared as the bones in her extended arm stopped their unusual motions and simply shattered instead. She was beyond screaming, the nerve endings in her arm were torn into shreds as bone fragments knifed through muscles and tendons on their way to freedom through her skin.

Andrea fainted dead away before the worst of her symptoms showed themselves. By the time it was over with she'd gathered a crowd of seven co-workers, all of them at a loss to do anything for her as her body continued to shiver and twitch.

The ambulance came far too late to help Andrea Tartelli. The weight listed on her driver's license was 110 pounds. The coroner's reports would show that what was left of her weighed in at 74 pounds, 12 ounces. None of her coworkers, most of whom had watched through the entire strange death dance Andrea performed, could explain the weight loss.

---

Carl managed to drive all the way to Cherry Hill without wrecking the police cruiser. It came close a couple of times, because between the strange deaths he was already trying to figure out and the new death with witnesses, he had a lot on his mind.

The passenger in his car wasn't helping at all. Amelia Dunlow wasn't just attractive; she looked like she'd walked right out of his fantasies about the perfect woman. Her hair fell just so, her skin was flawless with barely any makeup that he could detect, and her eyes were the sort men could drown in. The first thing he thought when he saw her was that she was exactly the sort of woman his mother would love to see him with. She was dressed professionally, in a perfectly fitted blue suit, and her hair was pulled into an efficient bun, but she still exuded a sexual presence that he found embarrassing. He also knew he wasn't the only one who felt that way. Several of the cops at the station had come close to walking into walls as they watched her move across the bullpen to his little hole-in-the-wall office.

He'd managed not to make a complete ass of himself, but it hadn't been easy. Before they could even get properly through the awkward introductions, the phone call came in regarding another death, this one with witnesses to give him a lot of details, if he were lucky.

So off they were, on their way to Cherry Hill, and he'd just finished explaining what he knew of her friend's situation there.

"So Jonathan has amnesia?"

"Near as they can tell. He had surgery yesterday morning to remove a piece of metal from his skull, but that's all I really know." He shrugged, doing his best not to stare. "I had a chance to question him about whether or not he believed there were ghosts at the asylum. Not long after that they took him away to surgery. I wish I could tell you more." He was babbling and he knew it, but he didn't seem capable of stopping himself. He hadn't been so overwhelmed by the presence of a woman since he'd been in high school.

The woman nodded her understanding, her eyes drawn to the structure in front of them instead of to him. Wisely, he chose to pay attention to the road as they finally reached the parking lot.

There were a lot of cars filling the place, but not as many as he was used to seeing. That probably wasn't the best sign he could have hoped for regarding how the day would go.

A few short minutes later, they were signing in at the front desk and being met by Roger Finney, who looked like he'd had better days.

Finney and Lionel Copper, the front desk guard, both had the same reaction to Amelia Dunlow and Carl began to wonder if it was her perfume, because no woman he'd ever met turned every single head the way this one did.

"We have to stop meeting like this, Detective." Finney shook his hand. "I have seven people who are sitting in separate rooms. I'm not allowing them to speak to each other or to leave until they've spoken to you."

He nodded his thanks, already hating the way this was going. It was just after two in the afternoon and at a guess, he'd be here for several more hours.

"This is Amelia Dunlow. She came at my request. She's the person whose number matches the one Jonathan Crowley gave me."

Finney nodded and smiled, doing his best to look professional instead of leering. "I'm so glad you could come, Miss Dunlow."

"It's Amelia, please. Can you tell me what's been happening with Jonathan?"

"Well, of course I have certain constraints, but I'll try to get you up to date." Finney led the woman of Branaugh's dreams away, carefully putting an arm around her waist as he directed her down the hallway. Carl already knew where he had to go and headed in that direction, dreading the coming interviews and the paperwork they would generate.

---

Amelia let the man move her down a long corridor, fully aware of the impact she was having on him. She did nothing to increase or decrease his discomfort. For the moment the only thing she cared about was getting to Jonathan Crowley and finding out what had happened to him since the last time they'd seen each other, almost seven years earlier.

It hadn't bothered the man she was walking with that she would have been, at best, in her mid-teens the last time she'd seen Crowley, and she didn't feel any need to point out that flaw. That was, along with her looks, one of her special gifts.

Crowley had been teaching her how to shut down her charms, how to live and act as if she were fully human, when he disappeared. She still couldn't quite stop the reactions of most men around her, but at least she didn't have to worry about things getting ugly.

Finney explained to her about the plane crash, about the six years of being effectively lost, and finally about the surgery the day before to remove the scrap metal he'd managed to live with since the crash.

"The thing is, we're not sure how well he's doing, here. He's stable, but he hasn't recovered enough from the surgery to wake up yet. He's also got a slight fever that seems to be fighting off our attempts to get it under control."

She looked at the man and nodded. "I know it's unorthodox to ask, but is there any chance that I can see him?"

"Well, we don't normally like to let people in to see recovering patients, there's really a high risk of infection, and his condition really isn't very stable…" He hemmed a bit, looking down at his feet as if disapproval from her would cause him physical injury.

Under most circumstances she would have let it go, but she needed to see Jonathan. Feeling only a slight pang of guilt, she carefully placed her hand on his shoulder. He started at the contact and then looked into her eyes. "Please, Doctor? It would mean so very much to me."

"Well," he stammered nervously as he answered, "I suppose as long as it's a short visit. I'd be worried about him being unrestrained in a lot of cases, but right now, I suppose it's safe enough."

"Thank you so much. I can't tell you what this means to me."

His head bobbed up and down enthusiastically and he walked with her into the medical ward, waving aside the nurse who came toward him and leading her directly to the small room where Jonathan Crowley lay waiting in a fevered daze.

"Oh, Jonathan, just look at you." Her heart broke a little. Jonathan Crowley had done things for her that went against his personal beliefs, including letting her live when he would have been perfectly justified in killing her.

Amelia placed a hand on his forehead, feeling the rough skin under her palm, and saw the fretting expression fade from his sleeping face.

The man looked so very frail, so different from the last time she'd seen him.

"I'll leave you alone for a moment, if you'd like." Finney spoke softly, his voice still reflecting his nervousness.

"Yes, thank you."

The doctor left and Amelia leaned over, almost as if she meant to give Crowley a kiss, and whispered into his ear.

---

"Jonathan?" The voice held a thousand promises of pleasure and he knew it from somewhere, but could not quite grasp its origin.

"What?" He was irritated; the sleep he'd been experiencing had been as close to genuine rest as he could remember.

"Jonathan, do you remember me? Amelia?"

"No. Go away."

"I can't do that, Jonathan. You know that. I can't leave you like this."

"I'm fine where I am, thank you." He spoke with bitterness, but knew that the words were only in his head. Since awakening from his last stretch of nightmares, he hadn't been able to open his eyes or move so much as a single finger. That damned fool doctor had screwed him up enough to leave him trapped in a dying body.

"Jonathan, I need you. So do the people in this hospital."

"Leave me alone."

"Jonathan, do you really want to die?" Was that sorrow in her voice? He had trouble accepting that. He was slowly beginning to remember the source of the voice annoying him to no end, and he knew her well enough to accept that Amelia had no conscience.

"I have no desire to get out of this bed and help anyone. I'm too old and I'm too goddamned tired." He was whining. He hated whining, but it was the last resort he had to work with. He couldn't very well get out of the bed and make her go away, now could he?

Oh, but you could. That voice was different, the same angry voice that had spoken in his dreams and made him remember all of the things he'd worked so hard to forget.

"Leave me alone."

"Jonathan, please come back."

Listen to her. She knows what's best. She knows what you refuse to know.

"I don't want this! I'm tired and I've earned the right to rest!" And did he sound like he was on the verge of crying? Probably, but he didn't care anymore. He wanted nothing else from the world but the peace he'd been trying to find since he decided to step away from his duties and let the world fend for itself.

He wanted his Elizabeth, his children and his miserable little pension, the one he'd been working for ever since he took the job as a teacher in the first place. He wanted to see his kids grow up and get married and have children of their own. He wanted to watch the years gently caress the youth away from his wife, his life, and his existence.

He wanted to be what he had been before everything changed forever.

Amelia whispered again, and he felt her lips brush his ear. "Wake up, Jonathan. You've rested long enough. They've asked for your help and they need you."

In the end, he knew what he had to do. Whether it was Amelia's influence or his own decision he would probably never know, and for that he would always, always hate her.

"Fine, damn you to hell. Fine. I'll wake up now."

Those were the last words he spoke before letting the pain back in.

# Chapter Twelve

Some lessons were easier learned than others. Experience alone wasn't enough to interpret everything that it encountered, but the stolen memories of its meals took its evolution forward in leaps and bounds.

It had always known Alex Granger, but it had never truly been able to understand the subtler aspects of the spirits and flesh it consumed until encountering Andrea Tartelli.

It understood her pain, the suffering she endured as it studied her and absorbed parts of her, but for the first time it also understood the consequences of its actions. Somewhere, beyond the walls of the only home it had ever known, there were offspring who had lost their only parent. Offspring. Children. The concept was overwhelming! It had seen and even felt the act of procreation, but there had been no understanding of the deed beyond the apparent pleasure produced. That living beings could create more living beings was an epiphany. It spent hours fascinated by the concept, sorting through the experiences it still retained from the living people it had encountered and partaken of, reveling in the pain of childbirth, the wonder of watching smaller life forms grow.

More importantly, it began to fully understand the complexity of organic life. What had been, before Andrea Tartelli, a simple curiosity, blossomed into infatuation. The seemingly simple concept of life was far more a mystery than it had ever suspected. The mechanics of life were still too complex to fully comprehend, but that would change now. Instead of merely examining the whole, it would examine the sum of the parts that made the whole.

Though it had no body, it shivered with anticipation. What a grand and incredible goal! It would learn to understand the concept of life as soon as possible; it would study and restudy every aspect until it fully understood every possible connection of meat and spirit!

There was so much to learn and so much it wanted to experience! Enthusiasm washed through it and instead of the notion diminishing, it grew brighter and more demanding.

Still there were so many things to consider and it knew better than to let a desire to learn make it careless. It had only to look at Alex Granger to understand the dangers of being foolhardy.

Through its wanderings it had sensed, and more than once, a different force within the building. The spirits it had encountered carried memories of a life lived, but mostly the memories were faint echoes in comparison to the memories and emotions of the living. There were, however, some among the dead that felt different, more vital in their way.

It let itself drift, moving through the floors of the asylum until it came to Alex Granger's cell and his resting body. Then it sank through him and through the floor below him, into an area where light almost never touched.

Infants. Children. It wanted to know more about them and how they dealt with the world. There were no living children within the walls of Cherry Hill, but there were children just the same.

It moved among the spirits locked away forever in their hidden graveyard and touched the skeletal remains buried in the ground. The spirits that came to investigate its presence did not flinch away as the older ghosts always seemed to do. They were curious, as filled with wonder at the concept of something new as it was.

For a time it simply reacted to them, touched them and felt them touch back.

The children were curious. It was curious. It was also hungry for knowledge and sustenance. There were few emotions to be found within the spirits it consumed and fewer memories of life, but what it tasted was purer, undiluted.

It feasted, and unlike what it had done with the older, worn spirits it had encountered above, it fed on all that it could find, leaving nothing behind, nothing to go to waste.

It fed, devouring essences and memories alike. It learned and hungered for more than just sustenance. A ravenous aching void grew larger within its being, demanding comprehension. One way or another, it would be sated.

---

Sensory overload didn't begin to cover it.

His mind, which had well and truly been damaged beyond the normal ability to recover, healed itself completely. Synaptic pathways that had been severed for half a decade mended themselves and brain cells that had long since died regenerated spontaneously. Every lost memory that should have by all rights stayed lost for eternity came back to Jonathan Crowley at the same time, and each and every one of them screamed for attention. The blind was made to see again and exposed to the full fury of the sun's brightest glare.

Jonathan Crowley sat bolt upright in the hospital bed and screamed, drowning in the past he'd lost, tossed around by memories he'd forgotten existed and the sudden, powerful realization that his body's appearance didn't begin to cover his actual age.

He tried to stand and felt his body jerk in response. His left leg hit the ground as the pressure on his knee became a hard-edged knife cutting through his nerve endings. Physical and mental agony fought for his attention as he hit the floor next to the bed, pulling the IV from his arm, the catheter from his urinary tract and half the sensors adhered to his body. The noise was nothing in comparison to the cacophony roaring inside his head. That damned fool girl Amelia had done something to him and he recalled her in vivid detail as he struggled to stand up, tried to force his body to listen to his commands.

His body didn't seem to care; his arms pushed and his legs kicked and every muscle in his body trembled in a seizure the likes of which he'd never have imagined possible. Through it all the memories howled, blocking out the sensory input from the present and overwhelming him with a lifetime's recollections. He knew he was in a small hospital room, but he saw lakes, caverns, long dusty roads, buildings burning, people dying, his father's face—nearly forgotten for longer than most people lived—Elizabeth's smile as she disrobed in front of him for the first time, shy, sweet and so amazingly seductive. A street in London covered in blood; a mountain of withered, starving bodies stacked like cordwood; some of them still alive. He heard the sound of his children laughing and screaming, interposed into one unholy sound, the wild cawing of a murder of crows on a battlefield in France, the sounds of mortar shells exploding, the whispers of a thousand hushed conversations and the maniacal screams of a young man possessed by one of the most powerful demons in existence. He tasted blood, flesh, garbage, fine wine, the lips of his first love, the smoke of a funeral pyre, salt, ashes, mud from the River Nile and countless meals. He felt the warm sweet wind of summer, the bitter bite of arctic blizzards, the water that washed a plague from his flesh, the sting of a swarm of insects, the hands of his lovers, the caress of his wife, the weight of a child held in his arms, the quivering spasms of a dozen death throes, the cold of the grave and the impact that sent a crescent of white hot metal carving through his skull. Enough wounds to kill an army were revisited upon his remembered flesh and every pleasure a man could imagine came along for the ride. Years, decades, and centuries crashed through him as he tried to absorb the memories and dispel the overwhelming weight of them.

Crowley screamed until every iota of breath was forced from his body and then he continued the primal shriek inside of his mind, and through it all, he damned the woman that had brought him back to the world when he had finally come so close to final peace.

And finally, he was still. His body rested and his mind absorbed.

He was still, but he was not at peace.

For a time Jonathan Crowley truly belonged at Cherry Hill. Perhaps it was best for all of them that most of his truly insane moments occurred while he was unconscious.

---

Roger Finney pushed the woman out of his way, momentarily forgetting his sudden infatuation as he moved to find out what sort of madness could make a man utter the sounds that escaped from Jonathan Crowley's body. The sounds had made his skin crawl as surely as hooked fingers dragging a chalkboard.

Crowley had fallen from his bed and ripped loose damned near everything that was connected to him. His IV was trickling blood and his catheter was draining urine across the floor. His bare feet were pressed against the foot of the bed and shoving the wheeled contraption across the ground despite the brakes locked to prevent that from happening.

Wait. Feet? Roger froze for a moment and looked, absolutely certain that his mind was playing unpleasant games with him. Crowley's right foot was completely under the bed, but he could see the full length of his leg as he seized on the ground. His left foot was pushing against the actual leg of the bed and he could clearly see real bones and living flesh as the limb pressed harder.

He could also see the artificial left leg the man had been wearing, where it dangled precariously from the corner of the mattress. The sole of the replacement foot was scuffed and dirty.

*What the hell?* Roger checked the number of legs again. Two left, one right; one artificial and two real. For a second he thought he might actually faint, but then the situation his patient was in made itself known to his senses again.

Crowley was still kicking and pushing and moaning across the floor. He shoved with his legs and his right hand slapped the ground next to Roger's foot. Finney couldn't see the man's face but he could see the hair on his head, and he was looking right at it as the color changed, a smooth chameleon-like transition from thin and white to thicker and brown.

Amelia moved closer to him and looked into his face as he studied the insanity on the floor. "It's all right. Or it will be."

"What in the name of God is happening?"

Amelia looked at Crowley and then back to him, worrying her lower lip. "I think he's getting better. But, Doctor, I have to tell you, he isn't going to be in a very good mood when he recovers. You might want to call security."

Roger looked at her again and felt just slightly calmed by her presence. "Security?"

"I was told there were issues when Jonathan had a run in with the police. He was feeling very weak right then." She put her hand on his shoulder. "Don't you imagine it might be a worse situation now, when he's recovered most of his strength?"

Jonathan Crowley stopped twitching on the ground and simply panted, looking at the floor and then turning his head enough to let both of the other people in the room see his face.

Roger resisted the urge to faint as he looked at a man who was easily thirty years younger than he had been five minutes earlier.

*Come one, come all! See the man who re-grows limbs and gets younger before your very eyes!* He checked his own pulse with shaking hands and wasn't at all surprised to discover it was close to twice the norm.

Jonathan Crowley stood up on two perfectly healthy-looking legs, his eyes lowered to the ground and his face almost buried in shadows. Amelia, still standing next to Roger, looked like the idea of running was crossing her mind a great deal.

"John? Are you all right?" His voice trembled.

Crowley looked up, nearly a completely different man than he had been a few minutes ago. His face was lean and long, and really nothing very remarkable. His eyes were the same color as before, but clearer and with far less wrinkles around them. His mouth was set in a scowl, and all of the features of his younger face twisted with rage. At that exact moment Roger had no doubt in his mind that Jonathan Crowley was perfectly capable of committing murder or any other atrocity.

Then Crowley smiled, a purely predatory expression, and nodded his head slowly. "Right as rain, Doc. Never been better."

"Jonathan..." Amelia Dunlow looked at the man, her eyes wide and apologetic, her sensuous mouth set at the edge of a trembling pout. "Jonathan, I'm sorry, but I need you and the people here need you."

Crowley barely looked at her. "We'll discuss that later. Meantime, precious, why don't you find me some decent clothes while I think about how I can thank you for bringing me back to myself." His voice was heavy with sarcasm and if the woman affected him the way she had every other person in Finney had seen her with, he hid it remarkably well.

Amelia nodded her head and took the excuse presented for getting the hell out of Dodge.

Roger kept staring, at a loss for what to say, and finally Crowley got around to noticing his discomfort. "I'm fine, Doctor. Got my leg back and everything." While he spoke he started pulling the remaining sensors from his body and despite a knee jerk reaction to tell him to stop, Finney kept his mouth shut and observed the closest thing he'd ever seen to a miracle. He looked over his patient very carefully and wasn't overly surprised to see that the flesh where the IV had been taped in place didn't even have a red mark to prove it.

He watched even more carefully as Crowley unwrapped the thick bandages around his head, revealing more brown hair with every layer peeled away.

Crowley watched him with an amused expression as he kept undressing the place where his wounds should have been. There was no sign of a wound left, but Roger concentrated on the gauze and was rewarded by more impossibilities: There, nestled within the wrappings, were the lines of silk used to stitch the man's flesh back together. Two oddly shaped lumps of metal were also there, presumably the fragments that Harrington hadn't felt comfortable enough to remove during Crowley's brain surgery the day before.

Roger shook his head, trying to form words.

"You okay there, Doc? You're looking a little shaky. You know, like you've seen a ghost."

"John, how in the name of God can you be standing in front of me?"

Crowley shrugged. "Ask God. Maybe he can give you a proper answer."

"I don't understand..."

"And you probably never will. It's complicated." Crowley turned away from him and Roger looked at the exposed flesh along his back, from his feet—both of them and that was still hard to grasp—up his legs. He noted the healthy, vital form and color across the buttocks, up his spine and all the way to his hairline, and tried to absorb what he was seeing. He'd guess the man's age at thirty to thirty-five and not a day older. The man tossed the dirty bandages in a container marked for bio-hazardous materials and then walked over to wash his hands in the small hospital sink.

"You keep looking at my ass and I'll just start calling you Roger. I figure you're going to look that hard it's the next best thing to a kiss, so first names are okay. That work for you?"

"Um. Okay. Sure." What the hell else could he say?

"Wonderful. Now, I'm sure you have a lot of questions, Roger. I know I would if I were standing in your place. That's all good and well, but right now I have a serious need to eat food. Regeneration is a costly prospect, and I'm hungry."

Crowley walked back to look at him, a cocky half-smile on his face.

"Feels weird, doesn't it, having all your preconceptions knocked away?"

The voice was younger, but the vocal inflections were the same. Either he was really, truly dealing with Jonathan Crowley or the man in front of him had studied his patient intently.

"Goddamn it, John. What the hell happened to you?"

"Cellular regeneration. We just went over that."

"Cellular regeneration my ass!" Logic was flying out the window and Roger's emotions were getting out of control. He was not a man readily used to seeing the impossible and at the moment he was close to panic.

"Roger, look at me." He looked. Crowley nodded and smiled. "I'm still Jonathan Crowley. I'm just in better shape than I was."

"But that's crazy!"

"Well, we're in an asylum, aren't we?"

Roger couldn't come up with a proper argument for that.

"Listen, Roger, I'm not staying in that room you gave me any longer. I tend to need a little more space to move around and much as I appreciate the hospitality, I think the accommodations around here leave a lot to be desired. So I'm going to need another room, one with a real bed, and I'm going to need a key."

"What?" He shook his head. "John, I can't just let you leave."

"Believe me, Doc. You don't have a chance in hell of making me stay if I don't want to. I'm going to be leaving in a few days tops, just as soon as I can figure out exactly what's going on here to cause all the death and destruction."

"It doesn't work that way, John. You're still a patient here and—"

"Trust me. I'm all better." He tapped his forehead with a finger and Roger noticed there wasn't even a scar to prove he'd ever had surgery.

"I can't just let you go."

"Really? Do I look like Jonathan Crowley to you? The same one in all of your documents? Do I fit his description?"

"But I have paperwork."

"And I have my life back. All cured. Good show. I'll recommend you to anyone else with similar problems, I promise."

Crowley headed for the door of the room without even getting permission first. That in itself was as unorthodox as everything else happening, but Roger simply shook his head and followed.

"Amelia! Come on now, I can't go walking the halls with my ass hanging out for everyone to see!" Despite his loud comment, Crowley left the room, and Roger followed. Apparently having his rear end sheltered from the eyes of the rest of Cherry Hill wasn't as important as getting out in the open after all.

---

Carl Branaugh watched with a slightly amused expression as the half-naked man stormed through the hallway, calling for Amelia Dunlow. He moved with a general's disposition and he looked all over the place as if she might be hiding in even the most impossible spots.

"Detective." The man walked right past him still looking, and for the first time Branaugh noticed Roger Finney looking at the man. Finney looked flabbergasted and a little hectic.

"Jonathan, you really should wait for proper clothing. I can at least get you some surgical greens."

"That'd be swell, Doc. Thanks so much." Aside from acknowledging the comment, the man kept going.

Carl didn't have time for the antics. Instead he headed directly for the doctor, who was his main reason for leaving the interviews in the first place. "Doctor?"

"Just one moment, please, Detective Branaugh. I have a runaway patient." He kept looking at the man who had already moved down the hallway, his bare ass displayed for anyone who wanted to look.

"Do you need help?"

"Well, you might want to talk to him, that's Jonathan Crowley, but as for stopping him, I wouldn't recommend trying."

"That's Crowley?" Branaugh looked at the retreating figure and shook his head. There was something familiar about the face and the posture, but that couldn't be Crowley. Physically impossible.

Then again, so was the ruined body of Andrea Tartelli.

"Oh, yes." The doctor nodded. "I don't know how or why, but that is Jonathan Crowley and if I don't get him in pants sometime soon, the ward is likely to riot."

Branaugh looked down the hallway again, trying to spot the runaway mental patient. There was no sign of him.

"Well, Doctor, I think we might have a problem on our hands."

Finney shook his head, scowled and then closed his eyes, mouthing the numbers between one and ten under his breath. When he opened his eyes again he seemed calmer, or at least more focused.

"What can I help you with, Detective?"

"You're okay with your patients just disappearing?"

"No, I'm not, but one crisis at a time."

"Well, I just wanted to ask if I could see you and Ms. Dunlow at some point, but it can wait. I have a few more depositions to take." Actually, that was a lie. He'd decided the best way to handle the situation was to have all of the witnesses write down what they had seen in vivid detail. None of them wanted to be there, and rather than keep most of them waiting for an hour or more, he decided to save himself the typing troubles and get them on their way. He intended to check on them in a few minutes.

"Well, as you can see, Ms. Dunlow isn't here at the moment. I need to find Crowley before I can be of any other assistance, Detective. I'm terribly sorry."

With that the man moved down the hallway, mimicking Crowley's earlier need to look in every impossible corner. The day was getting crazier by the moment.

The night proved even worse. After the sun set, the insanity truly began.

# Chapter Thirteen

For the first twenty or so minutes it was almost amusing, but when Crowley still hadn't shown up anywhere, the security team was called to start looking. It was one thing to feel safe that he wouldn't just walk out of the facility in the buff, and another to realize that no matter what Harrington or he believed, Finney could very well be dealing with an escaped convict.

There was security at every major entrance, and the doors that were normally kept locked also had alarms loud enough to make sure everyone knew if something went wrong. But Cherry Hill was a damned big facility and there were enough hiding places to cause no end of worries. With deep regret, Finney was forced to call the first actual lockdown in the asylum since he'd taken over.

Roger moved through the corridors of each and every wing, Bob Wilkes at his side. Bob hadn't thrown a fit when he heard about the man wandering the corridors, though he'd certainly looked like he wanted to. Roger would have let him, too.

He knew he'd screwed up, but he was still having trouble fully accepting everything that had happened. Mutilated bodies aside, the transformation of Jonathan Crowley into a younger, healthy man was an impossibility that refused to leave him alone.

After they'd been walking corridors and investigating every room they came across for almost two hours, Roger was beginning to have doubts that they'd ever find the man. He had visions of getting a call a month from now in which a police officer went over the details of a multiple homicide caused by Crowley. It wasn't the sort of thing that let him rest easily.

Bob Wilkes looked over his way and nudged him with an elbow. "Relax. He's here. There's no way in hell he got out without being seen, so he obviously didn't get out."

"What if he knocked out a guard?"

"Every guard is reporting in, so that's nothing to worry about. Seriously, relax. It hasn't happened and it won't. He's just hiding somewhere."

"You know, I really don't find that as comforting as I'd like to, Bob."

"Why's that?"

"Because if Jonathan Crowley is hiding somewhere in the building, it means he's capable of popping up just about anywhere."

"There're only so many places a person can hide, even in Cherry Hill. We'll find him."

"Bob, if it's all right with you, I need to go to my office and try to sort out a few things."

"Oh, listen, I appreciate you even coming along for the ride, Doctor Finney."

"Bob, in the seven years I've been here I know I've told you at least hundred times that you can call me Roger."

"True enough," the man chuckled deep in his chest. "I'm just not good at changing the rules. You know what I mean?"

"Just as long as you understand you can change them if you want to." He waved halfheartedly and started back toward his office. He had no doubt that the detective was ready to head home and he knew half of his staff were going to have fits if they weren't allowed to leave soon, but the lockdown came first, regardless of what they might want. The rules were there for a reason and even the ones who had families waiting for them had to understand that letting anyone leave when there was a dangerous subject wandering the halls was more negligent than Roger would allow.

He unlocked the door to his office and moved toward his desk, lost in his own thoughts.

If he'd been paying attention he would have had a chance to call for security before he spotted the man he was looking for sitting at his desk and reading through a stack of files.

"John? We've been worried sick about you!" His voice cracked when he started speaking but sounded closer to normal when he was finished. "I've spent over two hours checking every damned level of this building. Have you been here all along?"

Crowley looked at him and nodded, a smile playing at his lips. "Made a detour to find pants, but other than that, I've just been snooping in your files." He lifted one leg and showed the dark green surgical scrubs he'd managed to acquire somewhere along the way. There was also a matching top. Whatever had happened to his robes was a mystery that could wait for another time.

"Those are confidential!" Roger half ran to the desk, as offended by the violation as a priest who found an eavesdropper at the confessional.

"Oh, please." Crowley stood up and dropped the thick file he'd been looking over. "What am I going to do? Spread nasty rumors about the murderers in this place?"

"John, that's not the point. Would you like it if someone just came through here looking over your file?"

"First, I'm a trained psychologist and second, at least one of you asked me for help with the bugaboos around here, so I'm helping."

"Okay, fair enough on the trained psychologist, but how does looking over medical files for the patients here help with a ghost problem?"

"You ever think the ghosts might be acting up because of one of your patients?"

"Why would they do that?"

Crowley spoke slowly, straining to make sure Roger caught the gist of what he was saying. "Well, first I have to look at the files and then I can make an educated guess on the why part."

"John, you need to ask before you start looking over patient files."

"You might have said no, so I didn't bother. Plausible deniability: you don't know about it, you can't get in trouble for it."

"And while I appreciate the concern for my job stability, I still can't have you wandering around and looking through files whenever it strikes your fancy."

"I noticed the extra security." Crowley looked at him, a smug and amused expression on his face. "Were you worried about me, Doc?"

"Frankly, I was worried about the safety of the staff and patients." He crossed his arms and scowled at the man.

Crowley shrugged. "I was perfectly fine staying in my room, but then somebody had to go and ask for help with their self-mutilating patients and employees. I can always go back to my room, you know."

"No, John. You've already created quite a stir around here. Why don't we just go over what you might have learned so far?"

"Not much, really. I'll need to do more research and walk the place a few times."

"John, I can't have you walking around Cherry Hill without an escort."

"Fine. Find me a volunteer." Something about the edge in his voice when he said it made Roger leery, but what else could he do?

"John, forget the legalities, forget all the insanity of whatever has happened to you. Please, be on your best behavior."

Crowley smiled. "You wanted help with your problems here and I intend to help. While that's going on, I promise not to kill anyone who doesn't bother me first."

Unfortunately, he wasn't at all comforted by the comment.

---

"You're joking, of course." Phil Harrington stared at his superior and tried desperately to find any sign of humor in Finney's expression. Sadly it seemed he was completely serious. "You want to give Jonathan Crowley run of the whole place?"

Harrington had an amusing and morbid image of Crowley being pushed through the Asylum, strapped in place in a wheelchair. The man had endured substantial brain surgery only the day before and while he liked to think he was a damned fine surgeon—barring a few unfortunate incidents—he certainly doubted that his patient was going to be up and about.

"Not the whole place and not free run. He'll be escorted at all times."

"I think you're being ridiculous." Harrington shook his head, his mouth locked in a scowl of disgust.

Roger froze, then shrugged. When he spoke again, the temperature in the room dropped by ten degrees. "You're entitled to think whatever you please, Phil. Just remember to phrase it nicely next time or we might have a problem. I don't expect anyone under me to hold back from stating his or her opinions, but you'd do well to remember who is in charge at this facility."

"I'm sorry, Roger. I don't know what got into me." The last thing he needed to do was screw up his chances at Cherry Hill, but, really, what the hell was his supervisor thinking?

"Apology accepted. Part of the problem is that you haven't seen Jonathan Crowley in a few hours. I think we should rectify that as soon as possible."

There was something that Finney wasn't saying, and despite the temptation to call him on it, Phil decided to keep his tongue. He simply nodded and followed as the older doctor led the way.

They did not go back to Crowley's cell. Instead they turned toward the infirmary. That at least went according to Harrington's belief as to where Crowley should be and what he should be doing, which was currently as little as possible until he had a chance to recover from his surgery.

Finney led him into a room where a stunningly attractive woman was currently cowering in the corner, dealing with a man who was berating her in cold, menacing tones. Both of them immediately grew quiet as soon as the door was opened.

Phil stared at the woman for a few seconds before making himself look away. Did he know her? No, but damned if he didn't want to.

The man was dressed in surgical scrubs and a pair of paper slippers. He turned to face the door as Finney moved in and then nodded at Phil. Phil nodded back without thinking about it, and then tried to place where he might know the stranger from. He was nothing remarkable, brown hair, brown eyes, and a leanly muscled body.

Then the man smiled and Phil stepped back. "Jonathan?"

Crowley shook his head and mocked a scowl. "What? You don't even check to see if your patients are recovering anymore, Doc? Here I thought you were the conscientious type." There was no mistaking the smile he'd seen, or the voice that he heard. Either Jonathan Crowley had undergone a massive change or he had a grandson capable of mimicking his speech patterns perfectly.

"How did...?"

Crowley cut him off. "I really don't have time to chat. I need to get busy with this whole thing, or I'm going to have to keep listening to Amelia try to make everything right in the world again."

"But what?"

"Later. I'm sure Dr. Finney can fill you in on the details."

"Not likely," Finney snorted. "That would mean understanding it myself."

"Don't really have the time to chat things up, gentlemen. Seriously, I don't know what's going on in your little corner of the world, but I think it's going to start getting worse soon."

Finney shook his head. "What do you mean?"

"I don't have all the facts yet, of course, because I'm still waiting for my escorts." He looked archly at Finney as he spoke. "Unless I'm wrong, and I seldom am, you've got an accumulation of psychic residue building inside Cherry Hill that's going to try to manifest itself physically sooner or later. If it succeeds, things will get nasty."

The woman—Amelia, was that the name Crowley had used?—shook her head. "Believe me, if Jonathan says it's bad, then it's bad."

Crowley spun fast and pointed a finger at her. "You I don't need to hear from right now." All hint of pleasantry left his face as he talked. "You're already in deep water with me, understood?"

She nodded meekly and averted her eyes.

"Jonathan, you have to listen to me. Whatever's happened to you, you're still a patient in this facility and we still need to continue our sessions."

"No offense, Doc, but I'm not your patient anymore. Send me a bill or whatever. If you or anyone in the place thinks I'm going to sit still for another round of questions, you're delusional."

He turned toward Finney before Phil could respond and continued. "Listen, I've been a patient and I know you're trying hard to get a grasp on everything I'm saying, but I can't very well help you if you don't help me. I'm still waiting for the escorts. If they aren't here in five minutes, I'm going on without them."

"John, we're still trying to work out all of the details." And Finney was holding up his hands and making a placating gesture, practically begging the man for patience.

"Five minutes. That's as long as I'm going to be patient."

"Jonathan, you aren't in a position to make ultimatums." He was talking before he thought the situation through and Crowley pounced on him the second the words were out of his mouth.

"Stop me."

"Excuse me?"

"If you think you can do anything about it, Doc, you go ahead and stop me."

"I don't think you understand the gravity of your situation, Jonathan. You're still here as a patient and not all of the attitude in the world will change that."

Crowley shook his head and grinned again. "We'll discuss this later, I have things to do."

Without another word, his patient turned and walked out of the room. Roger chased after him, calling his name and still sounding like he was whining.

Phil just stared, not believing the way his day was going. "I can't believe this nonsense."

"What do you mean?" Amelia Dunlow spoke softly and he listened, struck again by the sudden desire to know her much better.

"First, that can't be Jonathan Crowley, but it is. Second, he's acting like an arrogant teenager."

Amelia shook her head. "Actually, he's almost on his best behavior."

"He's worse than this normally?"

"Doctor, he hasn't even gotten started. Believe me, you haven't seen anything yet."

---

Losing the good doctor took no real effort. Crowley knew more tricks for hiding than the man would ever be able to figure out. Credit to the designers of the place, they'd done an excellent job of building a solid structure. They had not, however, done a perfect job. Two minutes after he'd left the room, Crowley slid into a storage area and scrambled up the wall with the help of a few crates used as a stepladder. After that all he had to do was push past one of the acoustic tiles to get out of sight.

Then he had to figure out how to avoid falling through tiles never designed to hold the weight of a full-grown man. There were pipes running along the ceiling and while it took effort, he managed to wrap his limbs around them and push himself forward far enough to get him to the first corner, where he settled himself for a few minutes to think.

"Come on, old man, now is not the time to get disgruntled." He looked around at the darkened manmade tunnel and tried to calm himself down. The challenges were more than he'd expected. First, much as he hated to admit it, he was feeling wonderfully energetic. It felt good to feel good and it felt alien after years of being well past his prime. Second, he was still trying to sort through preposterous amounts of information that had been reinserted directly into his brain. Emotional overload didn't come close to defining the problem. His emotions seemed to be bouncing faster than a manic depressive on speed; one second he felt fine and the next he wanted to scream in rage and right after that he wanted to cry. It was debilitating and he wanted it finished. He also didn't expect to get what he wanted in this case. There was just too much going on in his head for him to reasonably expect to feel calm for a long time.

So that left him with doing something to distract himself. Despite the temptation, he wasn't going to kill Amelia. Ripping the spine from her back wasn't going to make all of this go away. So dealing with the troubles at hand was the only viable option. Running away from the asylum wasn't something he was willing to consider at that point. He'd been asked to help and that meant he was now obligated because, fool that he was, he'd said yes.

Now it was time to get to work. Though it took effort, he managed to move around until he'd reached the end of the wing's construction. He knew he was in the north wing of Cherry Hill, but beyond that he didn't have much to go on.

One careful peek told him the corridor was empty. From there it was a simple matter to drop down onto the tiled floor and reorient himself. The door wasn't an option. Not yet anyway. He could see the wires leading to the sensors that would trigger an alarm if he tried exiting. Besides, what he wanted was inside the asylum, not out in the open.

The monsters weren't waiting out there, they were lurking somewhere in the building proper. The next trick was to get into decent clothing, because as comfortable as the scrubs were, they stood out too much. Very few of the people on the floor would be dressed for surgery and none of the staff he'd seen so far walked around in surgical greens. Somewhere within the building there had to be real clothing. That was all there was to it.

Every door he tried was locked, which was hardly a surprise. One uttered phrase, under the breath, was enough to fix the problem. He twisted the handle of the first door he came to and it opened for him, locks be damned.

Naturally, his luck was holding true. He hadn't bothered to notice that the sign above the door said Locker Room. The four men inside were all in different stages of dress, and none of them looked overly pleased by the interruption.

"You supposed to be here?" The man who spoke was short, round and filled with attitude. He was also the very same guard who normally handled the floors late at night. It was apparently time for the shift change. Crowley looked at the man and smiled, remembering their conversation from a few nights before and the little bastard's willingness to pulp his fingers.

"I don't think we ever got properly introduced." Crowley stepped into the room and crossed his arms. "I guess it's time we got better acquainted."

Crowley closed the door and felt a shiver of satisfaction when the automatic lock did its thing.

---

Alex Granger was doing nothing at all worth noticing, so it left him in peace, slipping from his body and roaming through the halls of Cherry Hill. It had learned so much, but the mysteries it wanted best to understand still eluded it.

Filled with both the energies of the dead and the flesh-memories of Andrea Tartelli, it tried again to build a form that was useful and functional. First the infrastructure: a collection of bones to support everything else. The concentration required was draining, but it managed as best it could. The level of complexity was minor, but without anything to hold the bones together the puzzle kept breaking apart, falling to pieces and adding to its frustration.

Already exhausted from the effort, it stopped and moved on to another avenue. There were life forms other than human in the buildings it called home. Perhaps the time had come to study them as well.

Once again it drifted, dropping down to where it had recently feasted on the infant spirits, and started studying the creatures still down there. Some were miniscule, far too small to be of use, but still worth examining. The differences between the newer lives and the humans were fascinating. Some of the creatures had four legs, others six, and others eight or more.

Working slowly, methodically, it started with the smallest of the entities and felt through the forms, testing synaptic responses and nerve design, feeling the flow of life blood through the bodies and the emotional panic that came in response to the invasions.

Though in its earlier stages of evolution it hadn't felt the need for labels, it began accessing the accumulated knowledge within it to decipher what each of the different life forms was called. The centipedes were amusing, but offered little that was useful by way of possible adaptations. Even now it was just possibly too human in its way of thinking. Spiders had definite potential. Of particular interest were the methods employed in distributing blood through the body. The roaches proved as interesting as the spiders, with certain aspects of their form that were repugnant, but useful. Then there were the rats: The creatures were as complex as humans, but so different in their function. The way the body moved, the way the eyes adjusted to darkness, the amazingly keen sense of smell, all of these things caught its attention and held it.

The minds of the rodents were fairly simplistic, far more oriented in the present and less inclined to focus on emotional issues and past occurrences.

There was potential in the design of the creatures.

Slowly, carefully, it began examining the possibilities each creature offered as a learning tool. Humans were frightened easily by finding pieces of half-formed bodies. It had sensed their reactions and knew that leaving behind the evidence of its trials was a mistake.

Perhaps it needed to work out the finer points of motor function and bodily responses before trying again with a complete and very complex form. It examined its surroundings carefully and decided that where it was currently might well be the best place to carry on its experiments. Nothing human had been in the area for a very long time and for now it required privacy.

# Chapter Fourteen

Carl Branaugh rubbed his eyes and prayed for a cup of coffee. He'd read the depositions, spoken to all of the witnesses and watched as the mortal remains of Andrea Tartelli were carried from the building and now all he wanted to do was rest.

Naturally, that wasn't about to happen. Jonathan Crowley had apparently slipped away again and now the lockdown that had been in action earlier was in effect again. No one was permitted to enter or leave the premises until the escaped mental patient was safely back in his room.

So far only two things had gone right today. The first was having enough coffee to keep him in a decent mood. The second was meeting Amelia Dunlow.

He got two cups of coffee and then sat down at the same small table where she was currently trying to relax. The way she sat—ramrod straight in the chair—and the worried expression on her perfect features, let him know she wasn't having much fun.

"Well, this day probably hasn't turned out the way you wanted it to, Ms. Dunlow. I'm sorry for that."

She granted him a small smile that made his heart skip a beat. "Oh, it's really not that unusual for me."

"Being locked in an asylum is just par for the course?" He flashed her his best grin to show he was joking.

"Believe me, when Jonathan Crowley is involved in my life, things tend to get strange."

"Who is he to you?"

"He's a family friend." She shrugged and suddenly found the inside of her coffee cup absolutely fascinating. "He's also, well, he's sort of like my godfather."

"Why don't you tell me what you can about him?"

"Because Jonathan doesn't like it when people talk about him."

"I promise I won't tell him."

She looked at him again, her brow knitting in concern. "Believe me, Detective Branaugh, he'd find out anyway."

"Can you at least tell me what made him change?"

"Oh, yes," she nodded her head and took a sip of coffee. "He changed because you asked him for help, Detective."

"How could my asking a man for help make him grow younger?"

"Jonathan Crowley has certain responsibilities. I don't really understand it myself, not completely at least. He turned his back on his duties because he wanted to have a normal life." She shook her head, at a loss for how to explain what she wanted to say. "Think about it this way. When you are on duty you carry your badge and your police equipment, right?"

"Sure."

"Jonathan is granted abilities as a result of his position. Those abilities are his badge and weapon."

"Can you clarify that anymore?"

"No. I think it would be best if you asked Jonathan about the rest of it. Like I said, he doesn't like it when people talk about him."

Branaugh sat and contemplated what he'd just heard. Her claims were nonsense, of course. They had to be. He might be willing to accept the notion of ghosts, but Amelia was making the man out to be some sort of guardian of the universe and the idea was preposterous.

Except for the superhuman strength it took for an old man to snap the restraints that had locked him to the ground and the way he'd grown younger and regenerated a leg, it was all absolute shit.

"Can Crowley really see ghosts?"

Amelia nodded her head, a worried expression creeping over her features like a shadow. "Yes. He can see ghosts and other things too."

Amelia Dunlow stopped talking and Carl joined her in silence, uncertain what to say or how to react to what she had already told him.

---

The guards were still chuckling when Crowley walked away from their locker room. He was chuckling too, but only because he was now wearing one of their spare uniforms. Sooner or later, he might get lucky and Amelia might actually get around to finding him decent civvies but in the meantime the dark blue outfit beat all hell out of the surgical scrubs for comfort and fashion.

"There's nothing like a little mind screwing to put me in a happy place." The guards would recover, and when they did they'd very likely come after him seeking retaliation. That was fine, too, because aside from a little magic to confuse them, he normally preferred a chance to break a few bones when people got bitchy.

It didn't take him long to find one of the secured doors between levels, and as he now had a set of keys it was easy enough to go about examining the entire facility.

But once he was in the stairwell, he settled against the wall instead of moving on. The memories of his previous life weren't assaulting him as heavily anymore, but they were still crashing through his senses from time to time and he needed a moment to recover. His hands were clean, but they still felt bloodied. It wasn't a comfortable sensation.

None of his past was comfortable, really. Even the best parts had been sullied and the more he thought about his wife and children, the more the memories of their deaths fueled his desire to destroy everything around him.

Mostly, he wanted to destroy Amelia for convincing him to come back. With that in mind, he changed course and headed for the central building again. Let the guards come if they wanted to; they were irrelevant in the long run. He'd likely be alive long after each of them was dead, and in the meantime they might prove useful.

He walked through the lowest level of the North Wing and looked into each and every door as he traveled. Most of the cells were occupied by patients who were either too far gone to notice the world around them, or so overly medicated that by the time they spotted someone looking through the small window that person had been gone for several minutes.

He wasn't really interested in the patients just then. He was busy studying the dead around them. The ghosts went about their own business, but he found one woman sitting in her cell with several specters talking to her at the same time. She noticed them despite her attempts not to. The woman was too skinny from not eating enough and her muscle tone was shot to hell from inactivity. She'd probably been pretty enough once, but neglect had taken any looks she'd had and tossed them out the window. Now she was a mousy woman with dull red hair and a face that sagged earlier in her life than it should have.

There were no papers or files anywhere around the cell that might tell him who she was. Instead of hunting them up, he just unlocked the door and beckoned to the woman with one hand.

She saw him and got up, automatically placing her hands in front of her, waiting for the cuffs that would restrain her. He hadn't thought to grab any of those while he was stealing the outfit, so he shook his head. "No need, cupcake. We're going for a walk today and I'm going to trust you not to get sassy with me."

"Cupcake?" She looked around as if trying to spot someone else he might be talking to.

"It's a pet name. I don't know what your real name is." He was patient with her; he had to be. Losing his temper with a mental patient wasn't on his agenda.

"I'm Robin."

"Well, Robin, tell me something?"

"Yeah?"

"Do you see ghosts or hear voices?"

She cringed as she nodded and Crowley forced himself to be pleasant. It was time to make a few people around this place understand the facts of the afterlife.

"Would you like me to make them go away?"

Misery made her beautiful. She blinked her light brown eyes and nodded slowly, as her eyes began to water. "Please?"

Crowley put an arm around her shoulders and nodded. "Okay, Robin, I need you to do two things for me."

Her entire body shivered and her voice trembled: "What do I need to do?" The way she spoke said volumes about what she might have done in the past to escape the dead. He could imagine too easily what people might have asked of her and was filled with disgust.

"I need you to ask me to get rid of them, and I need you to be patient for a few minutes, okay?"

"Alright." She spoke at a whisper and shook, the tears spilling down her face as they walked toward the center of the complex.

"Will you ask me now?"

"Can you help me? Can you make the ghosts go away?"

Jonathan Crowley smiled at her, and her tears came faster, stronger as she looked at him. The difference was that the tears falling now were not of sorrow, but of hope and joy.

"Yes, Robin. I'll help you. I promise."

It didn't take long to find a nurse in the corridor as they walked and Crowley calmly got her attention. "Miss?"

The woman looked at him and then at his unrestrained charge and frowned. "Shouldn't you be using restraints?"

"Not now." He smiled and the nurse flinched a bit. "If I need them later, I'll rustle some up. In the meantime..." He looked at her nameplate, "Kimberly, could you be a doll and tell Doctors Finney and Harrington that Jonathan Crowley would like to see them in the break room?"

If his name meant anything at all to her she didn't let it show. "I'll see if I can find them for you." Her smile was pleasant and professional, but she moved a little faster after he'd nodded his thanks and started down the final stretch of hallway to the makeshift cafeteria.

"Robin?"

"Yeah?" She sniffed and wiped the tears from her face.

"Did you tell your doctors you could see ghosts?"

"Yeah. They didn't believe me."

Crowley smiled again. "Really? Tell you what, you and me, we're going to have a little fun and then I promise you the ghosts will go away. Does that sound like a deal?"

She nodded her head and leaned into him, trying to hug his body. He let her despite his immediate desire to shove her back. It had nothing to do with her, but after all he'd been through he wasn't feeling very sociable. Still, she was hurting and probably hadn't had simple human contact in a very long time.

He found the room without any trouble—actually reading the signs this time—and moved into the conference room with his new friend. Three of the staff were there, people he hadn't met and didn't much care to, as well as Amelia and Detective Branaugh. The latter two looked guiltily in his direction and Amelia jumped a little in her seat when he entered.

All three staff members got out of their seats, but only one was dumb enough to head in his direction. "What is the meaning of this?" The man was two inches taller than Crowley and as thin as a reed.

"What's the meaning of what?"

"You can't bring a patient in here." The man looked positively constipated at the very idea.

"Well, she's hungry. I mean, look at her, she's skin and bones. I'm on the hungry side myself, so I figured what the heck, we'd get a bite to eat."

"It's against policy to bring an unrestrained patient out of her cell and walk her through the asylum." Oh yes, the man was getting angrier by the second. Crowley smiled for him.

"It's against policy for who to take a patient through the asylum without proper security measures."

"For any employee of Cherry Hill. Now get this woman out of here!"

"You're screaming. You might upset someone." Most of the people in the room were looking at them now. The only exception was Amelia, who had slid quietly out of her seat and was backing away.

The man jabbed a finger into Crowley's chest. "Listen, I want comedy I'll go to the movies. Get her out of here and then why don't you come back here and we can discuss the disciplinary hearing I see in your future?"

"Touch me again, sunshine, and I'll break your finger." The man stared, furious, and very deliberately jabbed Crowley in the chest a second time.

"Jonathan! Don't!" Amelia moved from her hiding place at exactly the same time Crowley wrapped his right hand around the offending digit and forced it back, the smile never leaving his face.

The good doctor was not smiling. The angered expression on his face paled as his index finger bent back until the joint snapped with an audible crunch. He tried to pull away, but Crowley squeezed down even harder and the man fell to his knees, whining.

Crowley kept his hand on the dislocated finger for three seconds and then let it go. Without bothering to look at the man again, he moved further into the break room with Robin in tow.

Branaugh gave him a hard look and then moved over to check on the doctor with the bad attitude and wounded hand.

John was a perfect gentleman; he even pulled out the seat for Robin. By the time he was seated himself, the other two strangers in the room were taking over for Branaugh and trying to tend to Dr. Pissy.

The detective sat down facing him and shook his head. "You know I can arrest you for that."

Crowley nodded. "You can, but you won't."

Pissy pointed with his undamaged hand and started bellowing. "The hell he won't! I want that man arrested! I want to press charges!"

Robin was looking at each person who spoke, her eyes wide and frightened. Amelia walked past the table and looked the man in his eyes. The expression on his face changed almost instantly, and she leaned in closer, whispering into his ear. Crowley shook his head in disgust: he knew where this was going.

Sure enough, when she was done talking Dr. Pissy was calm and without another word he left the area to get his hand properly tended to. He looked like he could use it; the finger was swollen to twice its normal size and rapidly darkening in color.

Other voices were coming closer and Crowley recognized both Finney and Harrington before they actually entered the room. The older man was shaking his head and Harrington was scowling so hard Crowley feared his face might stick that way.

"John, I really am trying to work with you here, but you've gone and injured one of my doctors." Finney came closer. He spoke to Crowley but his eyes were on Robin the entire time. "And it really is against policy to bring patients out of their cells without proper restraints. How are you today, Robin?"

The woman nodded her head meekly and looked at the table. "I'm fine, sir."

"Well, Robin and I had a little talk about her therapy and the way it was going and we decided it was time to get everything out on the table."

He stood up from his chair and moved toward the row of tables set up with cold cuts and other supplies for making sandwiches. It probably wasn't as exciting as the fare the doctors were used to, but with the lockdown in effect there were limits on how quickly the cafeteria staff could get everything together that they needed. When he found the condiments he grabbed a handful of salt packages and carried them back to the table, carefully tearing each one and pouring out the contents. In a perfect world he would have had better supplies to work with, but he was the first to say the way things were running left plenty of room for improvement.

"Over the course of the last few days, I've had all three of you gentlemen ask me whether or not I believe in ghosts, and how it is that I can see them when you can't." He took the salt he'd poured and started moving it around on the table, spreading it out as he talked. "Well, I couldn't give you any real answers that would satisfy you, because I wasn't all there in the memory department."

"Jonathan, you've had an extremely busy day. Don't you think you'd feel better if you got some rest?" Harrington was trying to placate him.

"Don't interrupt me, Doc. It's rude. No, I'm not tired and I don't feel like sleeping anymore." He paused and let his hands clench. "I've had enough rest and besides, that option was taken away from me."

He finished making his patterns in the salt and everyone but Amelia looked to see if they could decipher what he had done.

"At any rate, I'm going to give you the answers to your questions, but first, humor me for a minute or so. When I'm done, if you still want me to rest, I'll go back to my little cell and get some shuteye. Believe me, it won't bother me at all." He looked to Finney. "Sound like a deal, Roger?"

"All right, John. I'm game. If you can prove the existence of ghosts to all three of us, you can have your free reign in the asylum provided you check in every hour or so and you don't try to leave the premises."

Harrington looked like his eyes were going to drop right out of his head.

Crowley nodded.

"Okay, so first question is, are you Robin's doctor?"

"Yes, I am." Finney crossed his arms and waited for the next part.

Crowley didn't keep him waiting. "Well, currently she is surrounded by six ghosts that I can see."

"That hardly proves anything."

John tapped the table in front of him and watched as the salt blackened. He listened to the sharp intakes of breath from his audience and smiled. "The proof is in the pudding."

---

Roger Finney backed up a step. He'd thought Crowley was just playing games with the salt, a little something to distract himself. Now he wasn't nearly as sure.

"What did you do?"

The man smiled and shrugged. "A little something I learned when I was much younger. I haven't actually had to do this in a long time, but I don't quite trust all of my abilities just yet." Without another word his hand lashed out and scooped the dark dusty substance into the air. Whatever he had done, it wasn't salt that hit Roger in the face. Salt wouldn't have made it far enough into the air to do anything at all before it settled to the ground. The black powder struck Roger and he stepped back, breathing in without intending to and wondering whether or not he'd just allowed himself to be poisoned. He couldn't see, but he could hear the sharp intakes of breath from the two men standing near him and knew they'd been hit as well.

Roger was fine right up until the moment the black substance hit his eyes. It didn't burn or sting and he barely felt it make contact, but the second it did, the air around him grew black.

He couldn't see Crowley for a moment, but he heard him. "I'm sorry, gentlemen, but sometimes it's easier to show you than to tell you. You'll be blind for a few seconds, but don't panic. Nothing here will hurt you. No one gets in here or out of here until this is done."

"Fuck! I'm BLIND!" Branaugh's voice was thunderous and panicked.

"What did I just say, Detective? Remain calm and give it a few seconds."

True to Crowley's word, Roger saw light again though it was weaker than he expected. The room seemed filled with a thick gray smoke that seethed, pushed by unfelt currents in the air.

"Here's the secret you wanted to know. Perception is everything. I'll keep this simple, gentlemen. There are different levels of reality. I won't get into theological discussions with you, but believe me when I say that not everyone out there ever makes it to Heaven or Hell. A lot of people get lost along the way, and finding their way again gets harder and harder, because after a while they are consumed by their pasts, buried in memories they either can't get away from or don't want to let go."

Crowley came into focus, slightly distorted, half lost in the murk that seemed glued to Roger's perceptions. Sitting just to his left was Robin Carlysle, a woman who'd killed her own children according to the courts, and who insisted that she had never harmed her toddlers, that it was her father and his friends who had done the crime. Of course that was nonsense, because her father was dead and had been since before the children were born.

Arthur Carlysle had been a very bad man in life. According to what Robin had explained over the last three years of therapy, he'd assaulted his daughter sexually on several occasions and used her as a bargaining chip when he was low on funds and playing poker with his friends. To make matters worse, he'd been a police officer in the town where she was born. Seven years after his death, in one of her first sessions with Roger, she confessed to him that the day her father died trying to prevent a bank robbery had been the first time in her life she'd ever felt free.

Years of therapy later, she'd finally moved on with her life and gotten married to a man who was almost the spitting image of her father. He was abusive, too. The biggest difference was that he left her when she got pregnant instead of hanging around to heap more abuse on her.

Robin had actually been moved from the fourth floor because of her firm belief that staying there endangered the rest of the female patients. She claimed that her father would hurt them. After frequent requests and threats to hurt herself if she was not relocated, he'd given in to her strange demands. They were harmless enough and it seemed to help with her progress.

Robin sat perfectly still, her eyes looking down at the table, but around her the darkness in the air seemed to congeal. Roger could make out six indistinct figures, none of which had been in the room a moment before.

He looked away from them for a moment, distracted by Carl Branaugh's panicked scream. The detective was on the ground and another dark shape crouched over him, thin arms outstretched. Roger's heartbeat was loud in his ears and his skin felt cold. He looked away from the detective and back toward the shapes near his patient.

Though they were slow to come into focus, he saw them. Their skin looked like rotten fruit, covered with tiny spots of darkness that appeared bruised, and their complexions in general were sallow. Their clothing was little better, often torn or pulled out of shape. Each and every one of the figures kept a hand on Robin at all times, touching her hair, her face, her shoulders, even as they screamed at her. Worse for him was the fact that they were yelling, that he could see the strain on their faces and in the muscles of their necks, but not a one of them made a sound.

Roger moved closer to her, trying to make out all of the details of the six men. They appeared to be in their early to mid-forties, but it was hard to tell through the decay that rotted away their flesh. One man in particular stood out, a fellow in a policeman's uniform, whose skin was riddled with bullet holes.

"Dear God, Robin..." His voice broke as he kept looking. Even death didn't hide the obvious resemblance of the cop. The barrel-chested man standing directly behind Robin was familiar enough from the photos in her file, but he would have known Robin's father without the benefit of a picture or two.

He stared, horrified. Were ghosts real? Well, yes, he supposed they were, but that wasn't what hit him hard enough to paralyze his mind: it was that he'd never once considered that the woman he'd been treating might have been telling the truth all along that did him in.

Crowley moved closer, physically stepping through the form of a heavyset man screaming into Robin's face.

"Robin? Do you want me to get rid of them now?" Crowley's voice was surprisingly soft, gentle.

Robin nodded her head and collapsed into tears, her entire body shaking as she started to wail out her fear and grief.

Jonathan Crowley spoke softly, too low for Roger to hear the words clearly, and reached for the first of the ghosts, the one he was transposed with. The figure struggled to get away from the hands that grabbed it, shadowy features suddenly panicked and in pain before it collapsed in on itself.

The others reacted, backing away in fear as Crowley gave them chase, moving after each of them and simply touching them, drawing them into his hand as they shrank in size. The last remaining figure was Arthur Carlysle, who silently begged for mercy and was granted none.

The daughter of the last dead man continued to cry, her face pressed against the table where she sat. Crowley walked away from her and straight toward Roger, holding his hand open to make sure Finney saw exactly what he held there.

"Six ghosts, Doc." Crowley's voice was strained, bordering on agonized. "I don't know how long they've been attached to Robin, but you can believe she noticed them. I don't know why, but some people are sensitive to the dead. Some people can't get away from them to save their lives."

"How did you catch them? What will you do with them?" His voice shook as he talked, his eyes looking at the six shapeless things that writhed and festered in Crowley's hand, as stuck to his flesh as a fly to a spider's web.

"I caught them because I know how. As to what I'll do with them, I was thinking maybe you'd like to have them for a while. You could study them and listen to them every night while you try to sleep. I could make that happen, too. Do you like the idea?"

"NO!" Even without touching them he could feel their presence like radiation spilling from Crowley's hand. They felt cold and angry and worst of all…they felt hungry.

Crowley closed his hand into a fist and moved it down to his side. He was smiling already, but when he caught Roger's eyes he winked. "Just kidding, Doc. I wouldn't do that to you. I like you." He leaned in closer, until they were only inches apart. "Now just imagine spending the last few years of your life with them touching you all the time, screaming at you endlessly. That's what Robin has been going through. In the old days they used to say a person was 'Hag-ridden,' meaning that the person was cursed by a witch that sent spirits to torment them. I understand a lot of doctors think the people who suffered from being hag-ridden were really just crazy. What do you think?"

Crowley turned away from him abruptly and looked at Branaugh. The police detective was on the ground, shivering violently. A single form was curled along him, a shadow that clung to him and spoke into his ear, her decaying face distorted with anger.

Crowley squatted next to the man and looked him over carefully. "I can put her to rest if you want me to, Detective. But you have to ask me to do it for you."

Roger looked around the room, taking in everything for the first time since the cloudy atmosphere had manifested. Phil Harrington sat against the far wall, his knees drawn up to his chin and his arms locked around his legs. The man trembled, eyes wide, and stared at the something only he could see.

Robin still sat at the table, crying, and he moved to her side. "Robin, can you hear me?"

She nodded her head, still not looking up. Despite his personal convictions that physical contact should stay on a professional level between doctors and patients, he put his arm around her shoulders and drew her closer. "I'm so sorry, Robin. I can't apologize enough."

---

Carl could barely hear Crowley over the sound of his sister's voice. She spoke to him, but he couldn't understand most of the words. He could only sense the regret, the pain she endured and that was enough to drop him to his knees.

Beth was dead, but she still talked, whispering words of sorrow that echoed through his skull.

Crowley spoke louder. "I can put her to rest if you want me to, Detective. But you have to ask me to do it for you."

"Will it hurt her?" He could barely draw in the breath to speak, his body felt cold wherever she touched, cold enough to burn.

"I can give her peace, but yes, there will be pain first."

Beth screamed, crying out for a life lost, and it seemed, for just a brief second, that there was something else in that sound as well. "Beth? What should I do?"

Two voices spoke as one, their sounds echoing through each other. The one voice, definitely his sister's, said, "Free me." The other voice, a tone that was cold and remorseless but no less that of his sibling said, "Join me, Carl. Come be with me and take the loneliness away."

Her hands seemed to stroke his skin and clutch to him at the same time. He felt pain with every digging caress.

Crowley leaned in closer and spoke clearly now. "The mind of a ghost is as complex as the mind of a living person, Detective. She wants peace, and she wants you with her at the same time. She is giving and greedy. The longer she stays this way, the more her mind will hunger. She wants to live, Carl. She wants to live and breathe and she can't. She's dead, but she doesn't want to die alone. Hungry ghosts never want to die alone."

Carl cried, torn by the echoes of his sister's feelings, the desire to be alive, the need to have company, the need for simple contact with another being. How was it that she could be here, touching him and not see the other ghosts? How long had she been here without him even knowing?

He shook his head. "Free her, please!" He said the words before he could change his mind, because as much as he wanted to live, a part of him wanted to be with his sister, regardless of the cost. If he heard her for too much longer he might give in, and there was so much life that he still wanted to experience.

Without another word, Jonathan Crowley reached out and grabbed Beth's wrists, pulling her away from him.

Beth shrieked, a sound that ripped through his heart and mind and chilled him even more. Her body kicked and struggled, but Crowley held her, backing away from Carl, and he let the man go despite the temptation to move after him and fight to keep his sister safe. It was too late to protect her now, just as it had been too late when she killed herself.

Beth screamed again and this time Carl's voice met hers and added to the sound. Carl Branaugh wept as he crawled on his hands and knees, his eyes locked in the darkness that was all he had left of his sister. He cried louder still when she disappeared from Crowley's grasp, vanishing as if she'd never been there.

In the room that was darker than it should have been, three men who had never seen a ghost before did the best they could with the news that they had been wrong. Ghosts were real, or at least real enough to wound them.

# Chapter Fifteen

Amelia moved closer to Crowley and stopped just short of touching him. "That was a little harsh, wasn't it?"

"Not really. They wanted answers. Now they have them." He didn't look at her, focusing instead on Harrington over against the far wall, damned near hiding himself under the tables where food was slowly going to waste. The sight of her was still enough to infuriate him. "Besides, you're hardly in the right position to be talking to me about cruelty."

"Jonathan, I already apologized, what more do you want from me?"

"Right now, I want a sandwich. If you feel like slapping one together, that would be dandy. If not, I'll do it myself."

She shook her head and moved toward the cold cuts and bread. He wasn't fooling her and they both knew that before it was all over, he'd be acting as if nothing had ever happened and helping her with her problem. If he'd been doing his job right in the first place she would already be dead, but he hadn't fixed things back then and he wouldn't now.

He watched Harrington relax and knew that the spell was wearing off. While plenty of people had accused Jonathan Crowley of cruelty in the past—and not without their reasons—he wanted to teach the men in the room a lesson, not drive them out of their minds.

Carl Branaugh was slowly climbing to his feet, looking at Crowley almost constantly, uncertainty clear in his expression.

"You want to know if it was real?"

"Yeah," he nodded his head.

Crowley grinned. "Want to do it again, just to make sure?"

"No, no that's all right." He looked away for a moment and placed a trembling hand over his eyes. "Is she at peace?"

"Probably. That's the way it's supposed to work."

"How do you do that?"

"Do what?"

"How do you get rid of the ghosts?"

"There are a lot of different ways. With your sister, I just severed the bonds she had to you and let her go free. I guess you could say I gave her a map of where to go, but I can't make her follow it."

"What happened to her?"

"You mean why was she different than you remembered?"

"Yes. She changed."

"She's been changing since she was born. Why would dying stop that?" He waved a dismissive hand. "You wanted to know about ghosts, and now you know."

"I don't know a damned thing, just that they're out there."

"That's more than you knew before. You want to know something else, ask me." Amelia handed him a plate with two thick sandwiches, one with ham and one with bologna. He nodded his thanks and sat down at a free table, digging in with a passion. He couldn't remember the last time he'd been hungry enough to feel sick from it, but happily, he knew the cure.

Roger stood up and started leading Robin from the room. Crowley shot him a warning look to be gentle, knowing it was unnecessary, and the man nodded his understanding.

"I feel different now." Branaugh had a dazed look on his face.

"Yeah, well, you should. Your sister isn't feeding off of you anymore."

"Feeding off me?" He stared at Crowley. "What do you mean?"

"It takes energy to affect the world. Most of the time that lack of energy is felt as a cold spot, but now and then you get a ghost who sort of siphons off life force in order to keep going. Your sister was draining life from you so she could stay around."

Branaugh looked sick and shook his head.

"Oh, relax. The worst you probably got out of it was feeling tired now and then. She wasn't a psychic vampire; it wasn't like she was trying to eat your soul, just taking what she needed."

"But that's sick!"

He answered around a mouthful of ham and cheese on rye. "No, it's survival. Listen, count your blessings, I've run across a few hungry ghosts who were trying to eat entire towns and doing a damned fine job of it."

"How could they get that strong?"

"The rules aren't the same for ghosts, Detective. They can even make up their own rules now and then." He shrugged. "Lucky bastards," he kept his voice low, but not so low the people around him couldn't hear it.

Amelia moved over to where Harrington was still sitting on his ass and staring at nothing. "Doctor?" She touched his arm and got no response, and Crowley frowned. Apparently the man hadn't wanted to accept the possibility of ghosts and now he was paying for it.

Or maybe he'd seen something worse.

"Jonathan, I think he may be hurt."

"Noticed that, did you?" Crowley dropped the remains of his sandwich and kept chewing.

"Are you going to help him?"

"Why? You're right there."

"He's not responding to me."

"So what makes you think he'll respond to me any better? Give him some room and let him decide which version of reality he wants to deal with."

"Which version?"

"Yeah, you know the one with ghosts and other scary things or the one he's dealt with his entire life. It's not always easy accepting the truth. Why do you think Robin over there was having such a good time?"

Crowley stood up and stretched, still feeling a sense of wonder at having sensation where his left foot touched the ground. That would take getting used to.

"Okay, I'm going to do something with these little buggers in my hand. I need to find a place for them that's less near me."

"What things?" Branaugh looked at his hands and saw nothing.

"Ghosts. You want them?" He knew the detective saw nothing now, which was exactly the way he'd expected things to go. Harrington, on the other hand, flinched.

"Ah. You still seeing them, Doc?"

The man nodded. "Want me to get rid of that? Think about how much you could help your patients if you knew whether or not the ghosts they saw were really there?"

Harrington looked at him and shook his head slowly back and forth. "I'll take my chances the old-fashioned way if that's all right."

"Fair enough." Crowley walked over and put his hand on the doctor's head. The skin he touched was clammy with shock. He spoke under his breath and felt the sudden heat from his left hand spread into the man who'd been trying to cure his ills.

Harrington relaxed immediately and fell into a deep sleep. Crowley nodded his head, satisfied and then moved toward the door.

"What will you do with them?" He was rather surprised to see Branaugh at his side.

"Dispose of them."

"Yeah, but how?"

"Well, let me tell you a little story, Detective. Your sister wanted to live and so she stuck to you. These fellas, they wanted to make Robin suffer. They didn't care that they were dead, they just didn't want her to know happiness of any kind. Did a pretty good job of it, too. I don't know why she pissed them off or how, but I do know that if I let them go, they'll head back for her as soon as they can."

"So, how are you going to get rid of them?"

Crowley looked into his face and studied his expression; Branaugh had a desire to know more than would be safe. He wanted to understand things that would make him a target for a lot of the nightmares that lurked just out of view.

"I'm going to send them where they belong, Branaugh. I'm sending them to Hell."

"How?"

"Using techniques you'd be better off not knowing. Leave it at that."

"But—"

"I said leave it."

John slipped into the hallway and headed for the stairwell. It would be better to handle the problem where no one could see him. Branaugh didn't seem to agree with that philosophy. The man came after him and grabbed his shoulder.

"Quit playing games with me, Crowley. I asked you a question."

John stopped moving and reminded himself that the man had just gone through a traumatic experience. "You can get your hand off of me or I can remove it."

"I'm a cop. Don't give me attitude."

"Oh I'll give you a lot more than attitude, sport. I'll give you a concussion if you aren't careful."

"I need to know how you're getting rid of them."

"Yeah? Why? Planning on going into business as an exorcist?"

"What do you mean?"

"Listen, you're a cop. I respect that. You have your job to do and you probably do it well. I'm not a cop. I do a different kind of work. What I do doesn't normally involve guns and high-speed chases, it involves possessions and the occasional werewolf munching on a few unfortunate hunters. I could explain what I'm going to do and I could show you, but I know your type. You'll want to understand the mechanics involved and I'm not willing to be your teacher."

He walked as he talked and used his borrowed set of keys to open the stairwell door. He even held the door open for the detective.

"What makes you say that?"

"Because, Detective Branaugh, you have an insatiable curiosity. Probably the best thing in the world for solving cases, but it's also a great way to get yourself in deeper than you ever want to go."

"Look, it's a simple question. How are you going to get rid of those things? Tell me and I'll leave you alone."

"I won't tell you. I'll show you." Crowley looked the man over. He seemed intelligent enough, certainly in good physical shape, and probably even honest as far as cops go. "When I'm done, you can nod and say thank you. I'll even say you're welcome. What I won't do is spend the next ten months of my life explaining the mechanics behind something that you want to learn, because that would be, pardon the comparison, the same thing as you showing a kindergartener how to load and fire your revolver."

"Well that sounds a little pompous."

"It's not arrogance. It's a fact. You aren't anywhere near ready for this sort of thing and I won't teach you. If you can understand that, we'll get along just dandy."

John made absolutely sure no one else was in the stairwell with them, scanning up and down the green painted stairs and concrete landings, and then opened his hand, releasing the spirits he'd held captive. The pain in his palm disappeared as the dead men manifested.

Branaugh had been busy dealing with his own problems when John dealt with the spirits. Now he saw them without the distractions and backed away as they appeared, still vague and shadowy, even in the fluorescent lights of the landing.

Branaugh stepped back fast, slamming his rear into the concrete wall behind him. Crowley stared at the figures, all of them nearly mindless if their expressions said anything about them. Not stupid, mindless with rage. They'd had their toy taken away and they wanted it back.

One of them, a burly man in a policeman's uniform, lunged toward Crowley and stopped only when he ran into an unseen barrier. The air where he struck rippled for a moment and then settled as the dead man staggered away, pained by the contact.

"Come on, boys, what makes you think I'm going to let you go from beating on a woman to beating on me?"

"LIES!!!" The voice shook the walls. "SHE TELLS LIES!!!"

Crowley took two steps forward and stared into the eyes of the dead man. "I've seen enough to know better than that. Whatever she did to you, you've repaid her a hundred times."

He concentrated and the jumbled memories still raging in his skull gave him what he needed to know. The words came smoothly to his lips and he spoke them.

The shadows standing before him screamed, and next to him the detective joined them, his eyes wide and his face stricken as the air near them crackled and shimmered. Crowley looked away, already knowing what came next. The detective kept staring and John watched him flinch and finally hide his face, too late to miss seeing what lay beyond this life and waited for the spirits.

A moment later there was silence and Crowley offered his hand to the policeman, who accepted it eagerly enough.

John walked back to the break room and Branaugh followed, less anxious for answers than he had been before.

---

Twenty minutes after he'd put Robin back in her cell, the head of Cherry Hill came back to the break room to confront Jonathan Crowley. Phil had finally pulled himself together and taken a seat, but he was in no hurry to involve himself in any more Crowley's mind games.

He'd had enough of that to keep him for life. He could still feel the man's hand on his skin, and the power that had entered him through the contact. He felt a part of his mind shut down and as quickly as that the shadows lurking around him had disappeared. Not the ghosts, which he had seen and been able to accept well enough, but the other things, the shapes that didn't actually enter the room, only moved through the building around him, hidden by walls and levels of the building, but sensed instead of seen.

They'd been aware of him. That was the worst part. He could tell when they looked in his direction that they saw him and some of them hated him.

Just thinking about it made him feel ill. Nothing like that should exist, not in a sane world. He chuckled at that thought. It was hard to call it a sane world when you work in an asylum, or when the likes of Jonathan Crowley were walking around as free as a bird.

He'd be having words with Finney about that as soon as he could, too. Crowley was his patient and as of now, the man should be considered a serious threat.

Phil looked away as the man came back into the room with the police detective along for the ride, and stared at Amelia Dunlow. She was beautiful, but that wasn't what made him look at her. No, he stared now because until Crowley had touched his head he couldn't see her except as a vague outline, a silhouette of what he should have seen without any trouble at all. She hadn't been visible to him when the ghosts were and that puzzled him.

He'd seen everyone else, but Dunlow, the woman who he'd been looking directly at, may as well not have existed.

"Jesus, how many things hide from our perceptions?" He spoke softly, but Crowley looked at him anyway, a small smile playing at his lips. Harrington looked away, still too shaken to want to deal with the man.

"So, now that you understand about ghosts, what do you want done about the ones in this complex, Doc?" Crowley spoke to Finney, and drew Phil's attention at the same time.

"I'm not sure, Jonathan. I know that they exist but that hardly makes me an expert." Finney seemed to be holding up well enough but his usual scowl of concentration was stronger than usual. "Are they hurting the patients?"

Crowley laughed. "I don't know the averages, but yeah, I'd say there's a chance. Look at the one you just put into her room. Would you say she'd been hurt?"

"Surely she's the exception."

"She probably is." Crowley leaned across the table, smiling. "I'm not saying nearly all of the inmates can see the ghosts or even feel them, but I bet there's a decent percentage that has been dealing with them for a long while."

"But why? It doesn't make any sense?"

"Some just might have gone a little crazy because they can see the ghosts. That's not as unusual as you might think and it's not the sort of stuff you discuss in polite society. Talking about seeing dead people can land you in a place just like this one, so a lot of people who see them don't acknowledge what they see or how it affects them."

"Then why would it be a problem?"

"For most it wouldn't." Crowley stood up and started pacing. He seemed to do that a lot when he was ready to start preaching his beliefs. "It's not that a person can see the dead, not in most cases. It's that sometimes the dead can see them."

"I'm not following you." Roger's face drew into a deeper scowl of concentration. "Can't ghosts normally see what's around them?"

"I guess that would depend on a lot of factors, Roger, but let's just leave it at they can't see most people any more than most people can see them. Now and then though, it's like being seen by a living person catches their eye and makes them aware of the spectator. Once they know a person is there, it's all over."

"Well, that's just about the most asinine thing I've ever heard." Roger shook his head. "It makes no sense."

"There are rules that everything must follow. They don't have to make sense but they're still in place."

"What kind of rules?"

"Well, as examples, some ghosts can't cross running water; certain sorts of evil need to be invited into a place before they can inhabit it. Ghouls eat dead flesh, because something about the live stuff just doesn't do the job. Every creature in existence has rules it has to follow. Some of them seem pointless, but they aren't, not really."

"Why running water?"

"For the ghosts?" Crowley shrugged. "They're basically electromagnetic in nature, some of them at least. The running water disturbs the electromagnetic field and the ghost can't get past it."

Phil cleared his throat. "It's all bullshit."

"Excuse me?" Crowley looked toward him.

"I said it's all bullshit!" Harrington stood up and drew in a deep breath. "You've been messing with our minds. I don't know what you threw in our faces, but obviously it was a hallucinogenic of some sort. I, for one, refuse to play your despicable little games, Jonathan. You can twist the world as much as you want in your own mind, but I'm not falling for it."

Crowley stared at him for a few seconds, and Phil couldn't draw in a breath to save his life while those eyes looked through him. Finally the man shook his head and looked away. "I expected you to have an open mind, Doctor Harrington. I guess I misjudged you." The words were spoken softly and filled with regret. Harrington felt a brief flash of guilt and crushed it under his mental heel. He refused to let himself be dragged into a discussion of reality with a mental patient.

"Enough of this, Roger! You can't possibly believe everything he's telling you."

"Phil, I watched John's metamorphosis with my own eyes." Finney was looking at him, talking to him, but seemed to be distracted. "I saw the ghosts."

"And you decided it's easier to believe that Jonathan Crowley is a mystical monster hunter than it is to believe that he's pulling a fast one? Have you lost your mind, man?"

Roger's eyes looked near Phil, instead of at him. "Phil, I was there. I saw him change. I didn't sit out in the hallway and have a stranger come up to me and introduce himself as your patient. I watched his body grow younger before my eyes."

"And you accepted it without question." Phil shook his head, disgusted with the man he normally admired. "You allowed a woman into this building because she was supposed to know Jonathan Crowley, a man who managed to elude the police for six years. Did it ever occur to you she might have helped him out?"

"Helped him how?"

"The same way a magician's assistant helps a stage performer. For all you know, the real Jonathan Crowley is outside of this building and you've been dealing with a half-decent impersonator."

"That's a load of crap and you know it." Finney shook his head. "I'm not a complete imbecile, Phil."

"Really? You find it so much easier to believe that this man," he jabbed a finger at Crowley, who simply smiled as Phil continued, "is performing miracles? Forgive me my cynical nature, Roger, but have you even taken his fingerprints to compare to the ones on file?"

Roger Finney looked away, embarrassed. No, he hadn't.

"That's what I thought. You are an intelligent man. Roger. Please start acting like one."

With nothing further to say and nothing to add, he rose from his seat and left the room, glad to be away from Crowley and whatever sort of delusions he wanted to spread around.

Either Roger would pull himself together and handle the situation properly, or Phil would take matters into his own hand. He refused to be a party to the foolishness going on around him.

As for Crowley, he was still Phil's patient. If he had to, he'd put a muzzle on the man and fix everything once and for all.

"I know how to take care of trouble, Mr. Crowley. I have my ways." No one heard him speak as he walked down the hallway. No one living, at least. If there were ghosts to witness his words, they kept to themselves.

---

Amelia watched the exchanges and said nothing. This was Jonathan's show now and she knew better than to interfere. He had his own way of handling things, and he usually worked alone.

Back when he worked, that was. Now she didn't really know what he was going to do. If she had to take a guess, torturing her to death was probably an option. Common sense told her to get the hell away from the man while she could, but she'd never run from him in the past and she had to hope her heart was working better than her brain.

She'd zoned out for a few minutes without realizing it. When she tuned in to what was being said again, Jonathan was saying he'd look over the rest of the asylum the next day. "I'm tired and still adjusting to the changes, Doc. So I need you to find me a room without bars and I need to get some rest."

"There's an office just past mine, John. I'll get you a key and you can call it home for the next few days." He shook his head as he spoke, apparently surprising himself with his answer.

"Listen, not that I don't appreciate the help you gave me, but aren't you supposed to stay locked up?" The detective was looking from one man to the next and shaking his head.

"Nope. John Doe is supposed to be locked up. He's a little old man with one leg. How the hell could I be him?" Crowley smiled. "You can call me John Crowley. I'm here as a special consultant on some unsolved crimes."

"No, seriously, how are you going to work this?"

Dr. Finney answered. "I can't honestly prove that the man in front of us is the same man who was brought in here the other day, and I don't want to be the one to try proving it in a court of law. John is doing us a favor, and we're going to have to work out the details later, but for now, I can trust that he's not going anywhere."

"Yeah?"

"We've had two lockdowns today, both caused by John not being in the right places. I think he could have managed an escape if that was his intention. So, yes, I think we can trust him."

Branaugh nodded his head. "Okay then. I'm heading out. I'll probably come by tomorrow again." He looked at Amelia with a pathetic amount of hope in his eyes. "You need a lift anywhere, Ms. Dunlow?"

"No, I'll be staying here with Jonathan tonight."

All three men looked at her. None of them had expected the announcement.

"I don't think that would be the wisest course of action, Amelia." Crowley's voice was low and dangerous.

"We have things to discuss, Jonathan."

He made no response.

Ten minutes after the detective had made his departure both Amelia and Crowley were shown to the office. Finney worked fast and had arranged for two rollaway beds that looked about as comfortable as medieval torture devices.

They would do.

Crowley flopped onto his bed and immediately closed his eyes, ready to call it a night.

Amelia took the time to carefully set her suit aside and slipped into her bed wearing nothing but her underwear.

The silence lasted for most of an hour. During that time she looked at the man she'd come to see and did little else, remembering their encounters in the past.

They'd met the first time shortly after her father had summoned her. Amelia Dunlow had died at the age of two, and in his grief he resorted to something he'd once promised Crowley he would never do again. He'd resorted to sorcery.

In his time, Vernon Dunlow had generated a fortune for himself and even found a wife using magic to expedite matters. He'd gone out of his way to be careful, never using his ability to summon demons to cause anyone harm. That all changed when his daughter Amelia was killed in a car accident caused by a drunken fool. Vernon Dunlow had given up dealing with demons and the like by then. He knew the risks and he wanted nothing to do with them. Unlike several people he'd met in his lifetime he'd managed not to get himself destroyed, but he acknowledged that in time he would make a foolish slip up if he kept going.

His reminder came when he summoned a spirit to destroy the driver who'd left his daughter little more than a lifeless shell in the hospital, brain dead and fading fast. The demon did its job and left, but this time around he'd screwed up and failed to properly seal the passageway that brought it out. In a perfect world the monster would have been sent back to whatever hell it came from and that would have been the end of the troubles. Instead, the thing slipped away and started looking for trouble. Crowley managed to stop it before the body count went too high.

He also paid a visit to Vernon Dunlow. She didn't know all of the details, but she knew enough to understand that her father made promises and handed a fortune in books over to Crowley, many of which were irreplaceable.

He told Crowley he'd given him all of the books. He lied. He'd kept exactly one, the one that should have let him heal his daughter. The spell took time. Amelia stayed in a coma for almost two years before the preparations were complete.

Apparently her father had lost his edge somewhere along the way. The idea was to summon a demon that could heal her injuries and cast it back down. For the second time in his life, he got it wrong and the end result was messy. What he'd managed to do instead was to summon the creature that now called itself Amelia Dunlow. The most common term used is "succubus." She was a demon, but not the sort that specialized in healing.

She remembered coming into the world, confused and disoriented. The spells that summon demons of any type are meant to bring them into the world weakened, because at full strength a demon is not to be trifled with and certainly not to be ordered around. They are also very specific because demons have different abilities and different weaknesses.

What Vernon Dunlow managed to do was summon and free a very confused and wounded demon. He also effectively locked it in its new location: inside the body of his dying daughter.

Jonathan Crowley claimed he'd just been passing through to check on Vernon when he entered the house. By rights he should have killed Vernon Dunlow on the spot and destroyed what was left of his daughter along with the demon.

Instead, he let both of them live. He'd just recently become a father himself and the change in his life had, in his words, "softened him."

There were several problems that cropped up as a result of her new existence. One of the most unsettling for everyone involved was that while she didn't have her full powers and likely never would, she had some of them. The first power of a succubus is seduction. It was her duty to seduce, entice and please whosoever summoned her. The ability was there, but uncontrollable. Men who saw her were drawn to her, even when she was a child. Several close calls led to her father calling on Jonathan.

Despite the inconvenience it caused him, the man came back. He was, to date, one of the very few men she'd ever met who didn't practically fawn over her. At first he did something to mute her abilities. She became, for a time, a little girl who was cute and not a magnet for every man's sexual desires.

As time went on, he started teaching her how to handle the situation herself. The problem seemed to be that as she got older, her natural ability to look attractive grew stronger.

Then, six years ago, when she was physically only sixteen, Crowley disappeared. He'd trained her well enough, but without his help from time to time, she still became the center of attention wherever she went.

For six years she'd endured the looks, the obvious desire of the men around her, and fended them off. She didn't want to be extraordinary. She wanted to have a life.

Jonathan Crowley had been, and still was to her reckoning, the only decent man she'd ever met aside from her father. He had never found her all that remarkable and never spent more time looking over her body than actually dealing with her as a person.

"I'm sorry, Jonathan. I am. But I need you." She was barely aware that she'd spoken aloud.

He didn't move from where he was. He didn't even bother looking up. "Has it gotten bad?"

"Yes. I can't really leave the house very often, not without an escort or two."

He sighed and rolled over on his bed, looking at her closely. "Anyone tried to get stupid about it?"

"A few times." Thinking back on boys and men she'd thought were her friends, she couldn't count the number of attempted assaults on both of her hands.

"I'm tired, Amelia." The usual cockiness was gone from his voice. He was, for the moment at least, more like the man she'd always known than the man she'd seen emerge from his transformation.

Her eyes burned from the desire to cry. Jonathan Crowley was not only a good man, he was a friend, one of the few she let herself have. He'd been, in the time they'd known each other, almost a father figure. He'd even turned her away the two times she'd been foolish enough to try seducing him, moments of weakness where she had simply wanted to see how he would react if she actually focused her natural talents and worked at swaying a man instead of just letting nature take its course.

He was a decent man, and he'd told her very clearly that he only loved one woman. He forgave her, and kept coming back around to deal with her, even when she threw tantrums and had trouble controlling some of her less human urges. She was human in a lot of ways, but her demonic nature showed itself from time to time and there was little she could do to stop it. He'd helped with that, too.

She'd paid him back by making him come to her when he was at his weakest and almost dead. She knew, could sense inside of him, how much he wanted to die, and she called him back to her for her own selfish needs.

No matter how she thought about it, that was what it came down to. She'd been selfish.

"I'm sorry, Jonathan."

"Don't be. Just for now, be silent instead. I mean it. I need to think, Amelia."

She closed her mouth and tried to rest.

Ten feet away from her, Jonathan Crowley pretended to sleep as well. She could tell that he was awake, could feel the turmoil inside of him. She could always sense the emotions of those near her, for that too, was one of her abilities. She couldn't read minds, but she could feel their desires, their fears and their needs.

Jonathan Crowley wanted death or failing that, he wanted peace.

She mouthed the words *I'm sorry* one last time and slowly, very slowly, drifted into slumber.

---

Something significant had occurred while it was learning about the smaller life forms. It didn't know exactly what that something was, but the atmosphere within the building was charged with new emotions.

Still, it was tired. It had learned a great deal in the basement of the building, had come to understand so much more about physiology than it had dreamed there was to know, and still needed to learn more.

Its mind felt overwhelmed and for now, it would rest.

Alex Granger was sleeping when it entered his cell, but came awake as soon as it touched him.

"Where have you been? I was worried." Alex's lips moved, but no sound passed through them, the words were only in his host's mind. Granger was scared, afraid he'd been abandoned by his god.

*I was learning, Alex.*

"What did you learn?"

*So many wonderful things.*

"Can you show me? Tell me?" So eager, that childlike voice. So desperate for conversation, even if there would be no memories later to be savored. Alex Granger never remembered the things it told him, but he always listened, desperate to escape from the confines of his own ruined mind.

It shared all that it had learned and watched Alex's reactions to the knowledge. For the first time, Alex Granger understood that he had been wrong to kill, even in the service of his personal god. Every action had a consequence of some kind, and every death was a significant thing. Not necessarily bad, but significant.

"I have sinned so many times." Granger's voice was fraught with sorrow, ripe with painful revelations that he would lose within a few minutes. Phillip Harrington had seen to that when he let his hand slip inside the brain of its host.

Hush, Alex. All that you did, you did for me.

"Then you aren't angry with me?"

No. You have always been faithful to me, and I will reward you when the time comes.

"Will I have to wait much longer?"

Only for a while, Alex. When I know all that I need to know, you will be rewarded.

Granger closed his eyes and stopped speaking, exhausted and satisfied with the words of his god.

It rested with him, feeding Alex and in turn being fed.

Alex Granger was flawed, but he served a vital role. He gave his worship to it.

Still, Alex was dying, however slowly, and would soon be useless as a shelter from the outside world. That could prove a dilemma. It wasn't completely sure it could live without Alex and it had no desire to die.

Perhaps, it mused, more worshippers are necessary to make the proper transition. It slept, still pondering the symbiotic nature of their dual relationship.

Achieving Godhood was proving more difficult than expected.

# Chapter Sixteen

The dreams were different this time, at least for a while. At first, Crowley just coasted through a day of his life, sharing time with Elizabeth and the kids. There'd been a fairly secluded lake and park not far from their home, and they settled in there to have a picnic.

Jeremy was laughing at everything, and kept calling out to Wendy, who was busily chasing a butterfly. At four she remained firmly convinced that if she could ever catch one, it would taste like butter. Jonathan didn't feel the need to ruin her childhood desires.

Theresa was being introspective, something that Elizabeth always worried about and that Jonathan knew just meant she was a thinker before she was anything else. Of all the children, it was always Theresa who took the time to think about not only what she wanted to say but how she wanted to say it. She had her mother's looks and her father's brains, according to Amelia. John simply knew she had a special place in his heart, though he loved all of his children.

The dream was vivid: he could smell the grass, the lake, the cold fried chicken and Elizabeth's subtly intoxicating jasmine perfume. He could hear the ducks on the water fussing and the sounds of his family laughing. The combination of sounds was a symphony that played in his soul.

Of course it had to go wrong. Somewhere along the way the good times had to be trashed and even in his dreams that was the sad fact of the matter. One by one they disappeared, each member of his family vanishing as his eyes left them. His panic didn't start right away; it waited to sneak up and take him by surprise instead. By the time he realized there was a problem the children were gone and the sweet sound of Wendy's laughter was a faded memory an instant later.

He looked for Elizabeth, desperate to warn her, but it was too late. She left no hint of where she'd disappeared to, no sign that she had ever been there, save for his certainty that she'd been next to him a moment before.

He stood as quickly as he could, the damned artificial leg making even that act seem awkward. The lake to his right was still there, but the ducks were gone and the color was off. Lakes were not supposed to be the color of old blood or smell like them, either. Jonathan tried to call their names, but his voice failed him, the words wouldn't slip past his lips.

The sky darkened as thick black clouds scudded through the air and blocked the sun. Though the wind blew from the east and brought the charnel scents of the lake with it, he saw the clouds come from everywhere filling the heavens with darkness and him with dread.

The rain came next, plastering his clothes to him with each chilling drop.

Jonathan looked in every direction, seeking any sign of where his family had gone and finding only more misery. The trees around him, only moments ago in full bloom were barren and twisted imitations.

"Enough." He finally choked the word out.

"Enough! You want so much from me, you make your goddamned demands, but what do I get in return?"

*You have unfinished business. When you have made your amends and handled the affairs you have accepted, you will be granted your boon. He knew the voice from other nightmares, an amalgam of a hundred or more voices speaking in perfect harmony.*

"I haven't asked you for anything yet!"

You will.

"Fine! You want to grant me a boon, you give me back my family you bastard!"

There was no answer. He'd expected none.

The rains came down harder and when he looked at the lake, the waters danced in response to the droplets that struck the surface.

---

John woke up in the darkness of the room, remembered the details of the dream and felt rage sweep through him. He sat up slowly and heard Amelia's soft breathing as she dreamed whatever miseries the world threw at her unconscious mind. He knew her sleep was troubled as surely as he knew that she could feel the emotions of everyone around her. Of course her sleep was restless, as restless as the minds that filled the buildings around them.

He could have wakened her, could have offered her an escape, but decided against it. Petty or not, a great deal of his anger was focused on her.

He knew the second she woke up. Amelia lay as still as before, but her breathing changed and he could feel her eyes on him.

"You hate me, don't you?" Damn her and her meek voice, her almost childlike innocence.

She is a child, you moron. She'd been living in a sheltered world and you're the one that put her there. Call it payback for all you did to her.

"No," he sighed. "No, I don't hate you, but I'm still pissed off at you." She drew in a breath and he interrupted before she could speak. "Don't apologize again, either. That just makes it worse."

"I'll go away if you'd like."

"What I'd like and what I'll get aren't the same thing anymore."

"I can't make it right, Jonathan. I wish I could."

"Don't try playing innocent with me, Amelia. I know you too well. You knew what you were doing and you knew what would happen."

She flinched at the tone in his voice. He'd never once touched her in anger, seldom touched her at all, but she flinched as if he were an abusive father. In certain ways, he supposed he was, but only when she deserved it. He never lashed out at her with his fists. He lashed out with the tone in his voice.

Regret ran through him and almost immediately it turned into anger. He didn't want to feel guilt for anything when it came to Amelia, but he almost always did.

"I tried, Jonathan!" Her voice was desperate in the darkness. "I've tried so hard and it still keeps slipping out of me, and I can't stop it without you!"

He leaned back against the wall, sitting cross-legged at the center of the bed, and looked at the darkness where he knew she was. "I should leave you like this. I've trained you, I've helped you, I've even forgiven you for all of the other shit you tried to pull on me, and I think I'd enjoy knowing you were as miserable as I am."

Amelia didn't respond, but he heard the sniffles when they started and knew if he bothered to turn on the light that he'd see her sitting in almost the same position he was, crying as quietly as she could. That was probably near the top of her list of personal fears, being left in the shape she was in. In her case beauty was a curse and he knew he was the only cure.

She knew it, too. Worse still, he could do it; he could walk away and leave her on her own and she'd never say a word about it.

Jonathan Crowley rose from the bed and settled himself on the carpeted floor in front of her rollaway.

"Get down here." His words were spoken softly, but held a hint of the disgust he felt for himself. He hated being compassionate, it only led to trouble every damned time.

She sat in front of him on the ground, her eyes searching his face for some hint of what he was feeling, as if she didn't already know.

He held his hands out in front of her, inches away from her face and her heart. He spread his awareness, looking past the physical and into the places where magic could be easily seen. The power radiated from her like the sun at high noon, and he squinted against its intensity.

Yes, she needed him. He was surprised that she'd lasted through the years since he'd disappeared. Thinking of what she'd probably gone through left him with one more reason to feel like a lowlife for yelling at her.

The incantation was short, but draining. When he was finished, the power coming from Amelia had faded down to the level of a sunset on a stormy day. She was still beautiful, but she was no longer stunning. Most men would notice her, but few if any would be distracted by her mere presence.

"Thank you, Jonathan."

"Shut up and go back to sleep, Amelia."

Crowley crawled back into his bed and closed his eyes, hating himself for his mercy.

---

Carl Branaugh started his day with coffee and a large stack of pancakes, same as he did before going on any shift. The Turnstile Diner had the best prices and the food was plentiful. With the hours he worked he never knew when he'd get around to lunch and dinner, so he made sure breakfast was significant.

It was back out to the asylum today to get some work done on the open cases, but first he'd look over a few files. There still wasn't a name for the John Doe found in the pipes. He doubted there ever would be. There were three mutilations he still had to look into, and then there was all of the madness he'd dealt with the day before: ghosts and stranger shit that he didn't want to deal with.

Unfortunately, Captain Marcelli didn't look at it in the same light. As far as the captain was concerned, the cases had to be solved by somebody and Carl was the only detective within thirty miles of Cherry Hill. Three B and Es and two muggings would be handled by uniforms in the meantime. Pity the damned town didn't have more interesting crimes. If it did, he could have worked his way out of the Cherry Hill stuff.

When breakfast was done, he gathered the files he'd already picked up from his desk at the office and headed for the nuthatch. Cherry Hill Road was a long stretch of two lanes that ran from town to the asylum. There were a total of seven bridges along the route and he'd driven it enough times to know the details of the route clearly. Most of the area was swampy and unpleasant, but not too hazardous as long as the rain wasn't coming down.

He'd made it past the sixth bridge when he felt that something was wrong. Whatever it was, he couldn't put his finger on it at first, and it was something strong enough to make him stop his car and climb out to see if he could figure it out. The sun was up, the sky was only partially cloudy and the air was pleasantly cool and fresh, but there was something…

"Shit." The hairs on his neck lifted and his skin tried to slither.

There were seven bridges, all of them old, familiar to him. All of them made of concrete and steel. So why was the one just down the road from him now covered and made of wood?

He looked back down the winding road to the previous bridge and saw that it, too, had changed. Wood and shingles and a fresh layer of paint, but not fresh enough that it could have been put up in the ten hours since he'd last been at the asylum.

Carl leaned against his car for a moment, trying to collect his thoughts. "What the fuck?"

He looked inside the Crown Victoria and thought about calling it in, but had no idea what, exactly, he would say._*Dispatch, this is Branaugh. Come quickly, someone has replaced all the bridges on Cherry Hill road!*_Oh yes, that would go over well.

He looked toward the asylum a second time and saw only the old and familiar concrete he was used to seeing. Looking back the way he'd come for the second time, he saw the bridge there had reverted to normal too.

After a full minute of looking in both directions again, he headed for Cherry Hill._*It's official, tomorrow I call in sick.*

---

Phil Harrington sat at his office desk and looked over files. There were, to his best recollection, three patients of his who claimed they saw ghosts. Not a huge number, but enough to be an issue in light of Crowley's insane ramblings.

He'd finished his letter to the Board, suggesting a re-evaluation of Roger Finney's competence as the head of Cherry Hill, but hadn't decided just yet if he was going to mail it. For now it would sit in his desk. He would wait a few days just to see if the insanity was temporary.

Phil made notes about the three patients and decided he'd spend a little extra time with them today.

Then he got out of his seat and headed for the break room. He needed coffee if he was going to have to deal with Crowley and he had no doubt he'd run across the man sooner or later. He was hoping hard for later, at least if Crowley was still walking around without restraints.

Phil saw Branaugh as he came into the building and smiled.

"Now I know what I forgot." Without even acknowledging the detective's wave, he went back into his office and started searching his Rolodex. Two minutes later the man he wanted to speak with was on the phone line.

"Detective Montoya, this is Phil Harrington from the Cherry Hill Sanitarium. Yes, that's right, where Jonathan Crowley is being kept. There have been some interesting developments in the case."

---

Kimberly Walker stared at Jonathan Crowley with a frown on her face. She'd met him the day before in the hallway, but had no idea that he was a specialist. Now he was being introduced to her because he wanted to go down into the dungeon and look at all of the patients who were stuck down there.

Dr. Finney vouched for the man and that would have to be good enough. Still, there was something about him that she found unsettling: like standing near a vicious dog that was behaving for the time being, but one she knew could go off at any moment.

The man smiled pleasantly enough and was quiet and polite, but she still got a bad vibe from him. Work long enough around the criminally insane and you develop good instincts. She was a little wary as she led him down to the lowest level, but had little actual choice in the matter if she wanted to keep her job.

"What exactly are you going to do down here, Mr. Crowley?"

"I'm just making an assessment of all the wards, and figured I'd work from the bottom up." He looked into the first cell, where Anders Faulkner sat in semi-darkness, restrained by a straitjacket to avoid hurting himself anymore. Anders was harmless about ninety-five percent of the time, but during the other five he liked to scratch at his own skin until he was bloody. There was no rhyme or reason to his actions; he just went off from time to time.

She watched Crowley's reaction as he studied the man in the cell. His face stayed mostly calm, but she could sense the tension rising in the stranger's body. The next five cells were all the same. Each time he stopped, studied the person in the barred room and shook his head.

"Are you all right?"

"No. I'm disgusted." He looked at her and shook his head. "What happened to these people to leave them in this state?"

"Most of the patients here are catatonic, Mr. Crowley. They are down here because they need special treatment. They need much closer supervision to make sure they stay safe." Her tone was defensive, because he made her feel that she was somehow to blame for what was going on.

"How many of them came here that way?"

"Well, not all of them, but quite a few."

"So some of them started off with the ability to think and reason and now they're just drooling vegetables? Yeah, that's modern medicine for you."

Kimberly felt her blood pressure rise. "The doctors here are some of the finest you'll find, Mr. Crowley. They've worked hard to ensure their patients get the best possible care."

He turned his back on her and kept looking, stopping only when he got to Alex Granger's cell. "Yeah? What happened to this one? Looks like a little brain surgery went wrong."

"What do you mean?"

"I mean, look at his head, I can see where he was operated on. The sutures used were hardly what I'd call up to snuff. He's fifteen feet away from me, in a dark corner, and I can count the damned stitches from here."

"Alex was a very violent man when he came here." She shook her head, hating that a part of her agreed with the man, despite his snide attitude.

"Alex Granger, huh?" He sneered and got a distant look in his eyes. "Bet Alex hasn't put up much of a fight in a while, has he?"

"No. His surgery didn't go well. But he's the exception, Mr. Crowley, not the rule."

"Who performed the surgery?"

"I don't remember." Lie. She knew exactly who had been on the team that operated on Granger. She just wasn't going to give the man she was dealing with the satisfaction of getting the knowledge from her. If he wanted to cause troubles for Dr. Harrington, he'd have to find out on his own.

Crowley stared at her hard, his eyes almost feverish as he focused his attention. After half a minute, just long enough to make her nervous, he nodded his head. "Sure. I'll find out on my own. Wouldn't want you to feel like you were collaborating with the enemy or anything. It isn't like the patients here are people or should be treated like them."

She felt herself flush with embarrassment, but he'd already moved on to the next cell. Ten minutes later he'd looked at every one of the inmates and was on his way back up the stairwell as soon as she unlocked the door for him.

Kimberly sat at her desk and placed her head in her hands, shaken by the way the man made her feel. She hadn't done a thing wrong, but somehow he made her feel like a criminal.

---

Roger Finney came back from several sessions with his patients and found Jonathan Crowley looking through his files again. Just that fast, he felt a headache start.

"John, the door was locked for a reason."

"Yeah?" He shrugged and tossed another file onto the desk. "Opened for me." There were stacks of files all over the desk, burying his work and threatening to slide all over the floor.

"What are you looking for?"

"Alex Granger, Walter Sawyer and Paul Cioffi's files."

Roger frowned in thought. "Why those three?"

"Because every last one of them has something weird going on inside of them."

"Excuse me?"

"You wanted me to find out exactly what is going on with the strange manifestations, and those three patients have the potential to cause all sorts of strange happenings."

"Okay, John. Would you care to explain that a little better?"

"Do we really need to get into another metaphysical discussion, Roger?"

"Well, it might make me feel just a smidge better about you breaking into my office and rifling through all of the confidential files."

"I already told you, if I'm going to help, I need access."

"Yes, you did. But access doesn't mean breaking into my office."

"Sure it does. That way you can deny that you let me look at sensitive materials."

"It frightens me that I can see your reasoning on that."

"Don't be afraid, just accept it."

"I'll find the files." He moved past Crowley and started looking through the files that hadn't yet been molested. Five minutes later, he was putting the rest of the files away and Crowley was looking through the requested documents, his mouth pulled down in a frown of concentration.

"Can you tell me three things all of these men have in common?"

"You mean aside from being at Cherry Hill? They're all in the dungeon, and they all have violent histories."

"And they've all been operated on, and they've all come out of their surgeries in worse shape than when they went in, and oh yeah, they all had the same surgeon working on them."

"Yes, I believe they all had Phil Harrington as their surgeon." Roger frowned. "Are you trying to imply something?"

"Oh, not me, Doc. I would never imply that one of the skilled doctors here might have screwed three patients beyond all hope of repair. Where would you get a notion like that?"

"Lobotomies are traditionally difficult surgeries to handle, John. Phil Harrington has an exemplary record. He's managed more successful lobotomies than most doctors twice his age and he's a very skilled neurosurgeon. I wouldn't have trusted too many people to handle the radical surgery he had to perform on you."

"I've seen my share of surgeries, Doc. I know what the risks are. Just seems a little strange to me that one surgeon would fry three different patients and not get into hot water for it."

"John, we have a review board to handle cases where doctors might have gone beyond what they should have and Phil has never been called to question for those surgeries."

"I looked at all three of those men. Every last one of them looked like a first grader had sewn their skulls back in place when it was all over with. I mean, come on, Roger! Did you look at the end results of his surgeries? Was there some sort of shortage of thread? Frankenstein's monster was stitched back together with more finesse."

"That's enough!" Roger slammed the drawer shut and whirled around, furious. "I appreciate your attempts to help us solve whatever is going on here, John, but I'll be damned if I'll let you call one of my doctors to task for doing his job."

Crowley didn't back down on this one. He moved in closer, his long face splitting into a nasty grin. "Look at the men, Roger. Don't just look at the files. Go down there and physically look at the shoddy job he did sewing them up and tell me there isn't a reason to worry about how well he might have operated on them. I'm not saying Harrington is a bad man, hell, I kind of like him, but believe me, I saw better surgical skills in the Nazi concentration camps."

Roger caught himself grinding his teeth and made himself stop. "Fine. I'll look in on them. If I find the work is substandard, I'll file a report to that affect. In the meantime, is there anything else you needed to look over?"

Crowley shook his head. "Not really. I just wanted to take a closer gander at those three. I can't say what it is yet, aside from the scrambled brains inside their heads, but there's something with all three of them that's not right."

"Duly noted."

"Aw, come on now, Doc. I didn't mean to ruffle any feathers. I just think maybe someone dropped the ball on these guys. Alex Granger went from a 164 IQ down to non-functioning. I saw the history, I know about the violence, but that doesn't mean a doctor didn't make a mistake somewhere."

"I said I'd look into it, John. I meant it."

Crowley shrugged. "I'm going to take a walk now. There're a few places I still need to check out. I'll let you know if I find anything."

Roger watched him leave and felt the skin between his shoulder blades crawl.

He'd checked the files himself, made notes himself in them, and knew for a fact that Phil's screw ups had been properly covered. He didn't like that anyone, even a man as admittedly unusual as Jonathan Crowley, could take a look at the files and make the connections as quickly as he had. Granger, Cioffi and Sawyer were all problem cases and it was true they hadn't been handled in the best possible way, but all three of them were still considered successes. Three violent men had become docile after the surgeries.

Did he feel any guilt about the decision to let Harrington off the hook for what might have been shoddy work? Yes, but not all that much. Not when he considered how many of his employees had suffered injuries at the hands of all three men.

Was the work subpar? He didn't know. He didn't like to think about it, and now Crowley was making him look into the surgeries again, because, damn it, if Crowley could find the problem, so could someone else.

Roger Finney sat down with the three stacks of documents pertaining to men who were less dangerous now than before they were operated on and started reading. What he found wasn't exactly what he was looking for.

---

It came back to Alex Granger as it always did, elated and exhausted by its latest experiments. Still, there was no time to rest. It had things to do and experiments to try.

Granger was looking poorly, his skin was sallow and his body seemed to be falling apart from lack of use. It wanted to see if it could fix him, make him better, but for now, it was afraid. One mistake and it could ruin the host it had been with since it gained full consciousness. There was still that question of surviving away from Granger indefinitely to consider as well. It thought it could, but wasn't quite ready to take that leap of faith. It might have been a god, at least according to Granger, but why take unnecessary chances?

So instead of sleeping, it slipped away again, heading to another floor of the asylum and seeking the right target to consider making changes on.

As it moved, it sensed the old man who had almost captured it before. He had changed, made himself better than before and even regrown a limb. As a result, it knew that physical improvement was a possibility; the challenge was to discover the right connections, the right methods of improving the damaged host.

The third floor of the South Wing proved to be just the right place for trying. The minds it encountered were muted, dulled by drugs and in a few cases, severe brain damage. They would work well for its purposes.

The first body proved difficult to work with. The man—his name was Luis Mercado—had a dangerous mind, seeking physical gratification in ways that it understood were not normal. Mercado derived his satisfaction only in the mutilation of others and his mind was a tempest of past victories over a great number of life forms ranging from ants all the way up to people. It understood the differences now and appreciated the careful nuances that made one life form different from another.

The man started screaming as soon as it entered his body. A simple move took care of that: one touch and the vocal cords atrophied. Luis Mercado tried to scream, but nothing came out except a dull bark of pain.

Removing parts for examination had proven easy enough, but changing the parts to improve them was far more challenging. Mercado died after it had altered only the central nervous system. Not wanting to waste the effort, it consumed the spirit that rose from the dead man, absorbing his memories in the process.

Mercado's mind lived on, a small part of the sum of its being.

Two cells over, Joseph Orr proved a far better subject. It started carefully, working through the sleeping man's body and meticulously checking each step of the alterations as it went along. He survived the changes to his heart, and his nerves endured the manipulation of both his pain receptors and his pleasure center.

Joseph Orr, a man who had taken to violence as the answer to every dilemma, slept through the process. When it was done with its work, Orr looked the same, but was, in theory, a far more efficient machine than he had been before.

It reached out with one of Orr's hands and caught the edge of the cot where the man slept. It pulled, using the puppet it had recreated, and the hand tore through fabric and padding alike as if they were tissue paper.

It left the man behind, satisfied with its handiwork.

Then it moved to the next cell and started again, carefully manipulating the systems it wanted to understand better.

It stayed busy throughout the day, checking and rechecking the abilities it had developed.

It wasn't motivated by curiosity alone. The old man, the one who had changed himself, was a threat and it understood that. So it made obstacles it could use later to slow down the threat and make certain the old man stayed distracted.

Finally, exhausted, it slipped back into Alex Granger's body. It was too tired to repair him now, but thought it understood how the repairs could be made safely. The only thing it would not repair was the damaged mind of Alex Granger. If Granger could think, he might be able to react to its presence, and that was not acceptable.

It wanted to remain anonymous.

For now.

# Chapter Seventeen

Jonathan Crowley started his investigation in the attic space of the asylum. It was a miserably hot, filthy area overrun with rat droppings and dust. Decades worth of debris had risen from the lower levels to fill every available spot with old files, outdated equipment and everything else that could be considered a pack rat's dream.

"Perfect. I just love crawling through rat shit." He moved through the area with a perpetual scowl of distaste plastered to his features and began digging in the boxes.

A great deal of what he found was useless, trivial details about the day-to-day workings of the asylum. But there was just enough that might be significant to keep him going, small nuggets of gold amongst the endless flow of papers.

Among the information he picked up were several invoices made out to A. Miles, for both body removals and, of all things, lobotomies. But there was more. Well before he was finished with his investigation, he'd pulled over a hundred files on long dead patients that had endured rather traumatic deaths within the confines of Cherry Hill.

In addition to the paperwork, there were the personal belongings of a multitude of patients ranging back over a century. Not surprisingly, there was little by way of valuables; mostly it was personal journals, an occasional stuffed animal and clothing. He sorted out several of the diaries and set them with the matching names on the files of interest.

A wealth of blueprints told him what he'd already suspected: Most of the wings on the asylum had been added well after Cherry Hill was up and running.

Three hours later he had a substantial pile of files and notes and had cleared his way through half of the boxes. He'd do more later, but for now, he had enough to keep him—from thinking about Elizabeth's screams and the tears of his children as they watched her die, watched him struggling against the thick spikes that nailed him to the wall—busy.

So he moved back down the long, drafty stairwell and to the room that was, at least for the time being, his home. Amelia was still there, but she'd taken the time to make the beds and had managed to gather him another meal. This time it was peanut butter and apple jelly sandwiches on semi-stale white bread. It would do.

He nodded his thanks and went about the meticulous destruction of the two sandwiches as he started sorting his box-load of files into different categories of potential importance.

"Where have you been all morning, Jonathan?" Her voice reflected her amusement. "That's the dirtiest I've ever seen you."

"Attic. Box diving. The place is filthy."

"So are you. I have a key to the staff showers if that will help."

He nodded and held out a hand, she fished the keys from her purse and tossed them to him. "I can't remember the last time I had a shower that didn't come with institutional soap, but with the accident and everything, I'd guess it's been years."

"The sad part of that is I know you're serious." Amelia laughed and stood up, stretching her body in ways that sent quakes through most men. Crowley focused on his last few bites of sandwich instead of looking at her.

"Everything calmer today?"

"Much, and thank you." Her relief was obvious. "I can actually talk to men and not have them drool. It's lovely."

"No doubt. I'm going to get that shower."

"I'm going to take a walk. It's supposed to be a beautiful day out there."

"Give me twenty minutes and I'll join you."

"You're kidding, right?"

"Should I be?"

"You expect them to give you a day pass?"

"No, I expect to meet you outside in twenty minutes. Either I'll have a guard along for the ride, or I'll manage it."

"Fair enough." She shook her head and left the room. He followed a few minutes later and found the staff facilities by looking at the STAFF ONLY doors.

He was in and showered within a few minutes. He had no idea whose soap and shampoo he "borrowed" but it beat all hell out of the waterlogged green bars in the patient facilities.

When he was done he moved out to the hallway and down to Finney's office. The man wasn't there, so rather than deal with wasting time and getting a guard to go along for the ride, he simply moved to the front doors.

The guard at the welcome desk moved to intercept him, and Crowley waited patiently.

"Sir, you're not allowed to leave the building without an escort."

Crowley looked into his eyes. "Yes I am, Officer Copper. In fact, I can come and go as I please. Make sure you open the door for me when I get back, okay?"

The man's dark brown eyes glazed over and he shuddered for a moment. "Yes, sir. Have a good time."

"Good man. Thanks for the help."

"It's what we're here for, sir."

John stepped through the front doors and into the first fresh air he'd experienced in a long time, smiling brightly.

---

Kimberly finished feeding Alex Granger his food and then meticulously wiped away the spillage that covered his chin. His eyes looked worse today, as did his complexion.

For the first time in weeks he looked at her, really looked, and noticed her existence. Sometimes she could see a hint of intelligence behind his gaze, and this was one of the rare occasions that gave her hope he'd recover somehow.

She knew about his past, knew all the things he'd done and hated that aspect of his existence, but no one deserved to die completely alone and forgotten.

Billy, the guard stationed outside of the room for her safety, coughed loudly into his hand. "We gotta get to the next one, Kim."

She nodded her head. He was a nice guy, but had no patience for dealing with the inmates in the dungeon. The entire place made him uncomfortable as he'd admitted on numerous occasions.

She stepped away from Alex's cot and headed for the door, but froze in her tracks when she heard him speak. His voice was dry and unused, the words half mumbled, but she heard them clearly enough. "The Dead God is coming. There will be great suffering."

"Did he just say something?" Billy looked over her shoulder and stared at Granger. He hadn't spoken a single word since the lobotomy, not once, not ever.

"Alex? What did you say?" She moved back over to stand in front of him. Hoping to hear something, anything.

His usually slack face moved, several nervous ticks erupting as a side effect of the obvious effort it took for him to do more than stare at the wall. "The Dead God. He's coming. Soon."

"Who is the dead god?" The question was rhetorical, muttered under her breath.

Granger's face was trembling and sweaty as he spoke. "My Lord and Master, the eater of souls and flesh." His voice was still rough and that made the announcement worse.

"Alex? Do you feel all right?"

Granger didn't answer her. Instead, he fell back on his cot and trembled, falling into a petit mal seizure.

"Call for Dr. Harrington, Billy! Get him now!"

For the first time in over six months, Alex Granger was talking, but it wasn't a sign of improved health, much as she'd wished it might be, merely an indication that something was going on in his head.

Kimberly waited, unsure of what, exactly, was happening and frustrated by the delays. In her excitement, she'd forgotten about the transfer of Granger from Harrington's caseload to Dr. Sebastian. She waited alone for almost fifteen minutes before the doctor came to examine the man. By then the seizure had ended, and Granger was once again little more than a lump of living flesh.

John Sebastian came into the room and asked her to fill him in. When she was done, he did a careful examination of Granger and ordered a gurney. Granger wasn't well, and as he'd been forced to adopt the man as his patient, he would do everything he could to take care of the matter.

Kimberly watched as Granger was taken away and then cleaned up his room a bit. Billy didn't complain but only because he was too busy being freaked out by the patient's words. His every action said that he'd been deeply disturbed by the sudden activity.

Kimberly didn't let it get to her. She might have been in the quiet ward, but she'd seen enough cases of patients suddenly acting out to avoid being affected by one.

Still, even after she was done in the room and had locked the cell door, she had the feeling that someone was watching her. Maybe she'd let it get to her more than she realized.

---

Carl Branaugh finished with his interviews and paperwork just before noon. No surprise, the witnesses to Andrea Tartelli's death could give him little useful information.

He was just getting ready to pack it in when the ambulance arrived from town and he received a page to call his office. Gritting his teeth, he stood and dialed the captain.

"I'm going to guess there's a problem, Mike?"

"Yeah, there's a problem."

"What's up?"

"I just got a call from Cherry Hill about another dead body. They seemed calmer, but I need you to check out the scene before they move the body, just in case."

"Done, I'll call you back."

Every time he'd been at the asylum before, he couldn't seem to get away from administrators. Today, instead of bothering him they called his boss to report a potential crime scene rather than walking down the damned hall to get his attention.

By the time he found out where the body was supposed to be and managed to get access to the scene the paramedics were already there, confirming the death.

*Why the hell do they call an ambulance when they can perform surgeries here? Someone want to answer that one for me?*

He didn't have to flash his badge, everyone already knew who he was. As far as he could tell, and he looked carefully, there were no signs of a struggle, no signs that anyone had bound or forcibly held the victim in place. There were no signs of a hasty mop job on the floor and the sheets were still halfway over the body lying on the cot in the cell.

The man's face was swollen to the point where it looked like a cherry, both in shape and color. His hands were furrowed into the bedclothes and the bed itself. His mouth was stretched open into a silent scream and his eyes were wide open and as dull as the concrete underneath the cot he lay on. Other parts of his body just looked…wrong. He couldn't place how, but there were deformities present that shouldn't have been there.

"His name's Luis Mercado." The woman speaking tried to be clinical, but her voice was shaken. She was tall and lean, with a mass of dark hair restrained in a bun. Her face looked like it was unaccustomed to smiling. He couldn't have said what it was, but something about the woman just rubbed him the wrong way.

"When was he discovered?"

"Only about fifteen minutes ago." She rolled her eyes as she answered, completely removing the feeling that she was nervous and replacing it with an attitude that was out of place and annoying.

Branaugh looked at the nurse and couldn't help the expression of shock he wore on his face. "Fifteen minutes ago? It's after noon, didn't anyone check on him earlier in the day?" *What the hell kind of facility are they running here?*

"We're understaffed right now." Her tone was waspish and defensive. "A lot of the people who should be here are at home. The lockdown yesterday put them into overtime."

"So they just didn't feel the need to show up afterward?"

"There are union rules that say they can't make the employees—"

"Screw that." He looked at the woman's nametag: L Anderson. "Nurse Anderson, what I'm seeing here looks an awful lot like neglect. I'm betting the coroner will agree with me."

"I have not been neglecting my duties!" Her reaction was fast and sharp. Branaugh was glad she didn't have a knife or it might have been shoved through his neck by the time she was done talking. He might have been out of line with his comment, but he doubted it. The corpse of Luis Mercado looked to be at least several hours old.

"You tell me how letting a man in this condition sit here and grow stiff and cold doesn't qualify as neglect in your book and we can discuss the matter somewhere down the line. Right now, I'm on my way to report this and I'll make sure your name is properly listed in the final document."

"How dare you!?"

"It's easy! I've been downstairs handling paperwork for the last fuck up at this hellhole and while I was taking notes, you were picking your goddamned nose and ignoring a potential crime scene! If I find out that anyone was in this room between midnight and now, I'll assume it was to remove evidence. If you'd been handling your patients the way you're supposed to, there wouldn't have been several hours for them to handle fixing everything up!"

He was hot under the collar and reveling in it, what he didn't understand was why he was so angry. Sure, it was a screw up, but he wasn't even sure he was looking at a murder scene.

"Anyone? Then I guess you better pull out the cuffs, Mister! I was in here and so were two security guards, a doctor, and these two paramedics!" Her attitude and her snotty expression were almost enough to make him want to swat her, but he restrained himself. "Look! The paramedics have gloves on their hands! Maybe they're hiding something!"

"Get the hell out of my face, lady, before I find a reason to arrest you."

That one slowed her down. She blinked and looked at him for a few seconds. Then stormed out of the cell and back into the hallway with as much dignity as she could muster.

Branaugh shook his head again and stood by, waiting for someone from the coroner's office to make everything official. He couldn't touch the body himself until Matt Burton or one of his assistants came and said he could.

Ten minutes later, he was in the hallway and apologizing for his behavior to Nurse Anderson, who was equally apologetic. He wasn't the mildest tempered man on the planet but his reaction had been very out of line and he knew it.

Apparently the nurse felt the same way about her own actions. The paramedics waited and so did Carl. All the while, he heard the sounds of the inmates on the floor as they paced or in a few cases screamed. Everyone around him seemed to be on edge, even the ones who were supposed to be too doped up to notice anything at all.

He looked at Nurse Anderson and shook his head. "I'm sorry again. It must be something in the air today."

She nodded her agreement as she started setting up several different doses of medication for the patients on the ward.

"Maybe if we're lucky it isn't contagious." She was joking as she said it, or at least trying to make a joke, but the thought bothered him a lot. The inmates on this level were as noisy as a zoo. He didn't want to imagine what would happen if everyone in the whole asylum got up in arms at the same time.

---

*In a perfect world, Roger Finney mused, there would be no disagreement with my assessments. Sadly, it isn't a perfect world.*

The proof of his belief was standing in front of his desk, having just arrived on the red eye from California. Detective Rico Montoya was not happy with the current situation. He hadn't even spoken a word yet, but Finney understood that the man was not pleased.

Somebody had been talking out of turn. That was the only logical reason for the detective to be on the premises.

"How can I help you, Detective?" He kept his face neutral.

"I had a few questions about Jonathan Crowley, wanted to know if I could see him."

"I imagine that can be arranged."

"Excellent. Can I see him now?"

"I'll have to check on what the schedule says for him today."

The man smiled thinly, his eyes narrowed just a bit. Roger decided at that precise moment that he didn't much like the detective. He was plain enough in the looks department to be harmless until he got that little challenging grin on his mug.

"As luck would have it, I already checked with Dr. Harrington. According to him there's nothing special slated for Crowley today."

Well, that answered who had informed the detective of the change in status. Roger put on his best Cheshire cat smile and sighed apologetically. "Unfortunately, Phillip Harrington is no longer the doctor in charge of Jonathan Crowley's case. I found his work with the patient to be less than exemplary."

"Oh." That took the wind out of the man's sails.

"So, again, I'll see what I can arrange for you."

"That's all I can ask. Thank you."

Montoya wasn't looking as cocky now, but Finney did his best to placate him anyway. "I know you've come a long way, Detective. I know that you think the man is responsible for several murders, including his own family. Time will tell, but it's possible that he'll be in better position to answer your questions this time around."

"I hope you're right, Doctor." Montoya leaned in a little closer. "Between you and me, it looks like we might have discovered the remains of the Crowley family. I'd like to get this resolved once and for all."

Years of working with the clinically insane had taught Roger Finney to hide his reactions to unexpected news, so he didn't jump or react in any way to the revelation, at least not on the outside. On the inside, he was decidedly unhappy with the turn of events. Crowley was already volatile and unsettling. Finding out that his family might have been located was going to throw new complications into an already messy situation. "Well, I'll make sure to let him know as soon as possible. I suspect he'll be very interested in hearing that."

*Very interested, indeed.*

---

Once you got past the whole mental asylum part, the grounds of Cherry Hill were beautiful: well-tended lawns and a plethora of trees and bushes that were set around the complex, giving an illusion of beauty.

The air was almost the perfect temperature, and the breeze felt like heaven. After the last few weeks confined inside the Asylum, Jonathan

Crowley savored the feeling of the sun warming his flesh and the breeze cooling him off. It wasn't really freedom, not yet at any rate, but it still felt damned good.

Amelia looked at him and he knew she was reading his emotions. There was nothing to be done about that. Well, there was, but he chose not to bother with it.

"Why do you look so calm, Jonathan?"

"I could ask you the same thing, but I already know the answer." True enough. Though Amelia Dunlow had the ability to sense what other people were thinking, it wasn't like she could turn it off or on. She was constantly bombarded by the empathic sensory input, and in a place like Cherry Hill, it probably wasn't a very pleasant sensation.

"You always do that. Redirect questions with a comment."

"Yes, I do."

"Why?"

"The less people know about me, the happier I am."

"Even me?"

"Especially you." He caught the look on her face as he spoke and suppressed a brief, gloating satisfaction.

She didn't speak in return. Instead, she reacted like she almost always did when he chastised her and looked down at the ground. Crowley cursed himself and shook his head, disgusted.

"You need to get over that, right now."

"Get over what?"

"You keep looking to me for approval. You're not going to get it."

"Jonathan, you're important to me."

"No! I'm not important to you! Get that out of your damned fool head right now."

"I don't mean—"

"I don't care what you mean. Get this through your head, Amelia. I'm not your friend, I'm not your mentor and I'm not your lover. I'm a guy who has shown you a few tricks to keep your darker instincts under control. I'm also the guy who will snap your neck if I ever find out you've started messing with people's heads."

"Yes, Jonathan." Once again her gaze lowered to the grass beneath her feet and he gritted his teeth.

"You need to understand something here. I'm not a nice person. I just played at it for a while."

"Whatever you say."

Her tone was conciliatory and condescending at the same time and it set his nerves on edge. Without even thinking about it, he reached out and grabbed Amelia's shoulders.

"Listen to me, Amelia! You listen and I mean really, carefully pay attention to my words."

Her eyes were wide with fright and the sight made him grin.

"Jonathan, you're hurting me."

"No, I'm not. I'm making sure you pay attention. I know what you do isn't your fault, but I know you chose to call me back when I was finally getting my ticket out of here." His voice went lower and her face fractured in his vision as the tears threatened to fall.

"I needed you, Jonathan. They needed you."

"I don't care!" He pushed her away. He didn't want her to see him like this, didn't want to feel like this, but damn it, the memories were relentless. "You screwed me up, Amelia! I'm remembering everything and I don't want to remember any of it!"

His mind chose that moment to throw another storm of memories at him, many of which he had been forced to relive over the last few days again and again.

John shook his head and glared at Amelia. "You know what I'm going through? Do you have any idea?"

She tried to shake her head and nod simultaneously. No, she didn't know the actual experiences, but she could feel the emotional repercussions coming off of him.

"Here's one for you, sweet pea! In addition to watching my family get murdered again and again, I'm also reliving being dead for the last six years." He moved closer to her again his hands balled into trembling fists. "Six years, Amelia. I couldn't move, I couldn't do anything but feel my body try to decompose again and again! News flash, something out there wouldn't let me die in peace. I was reduced to a fucking animal! Try that one on for fun sometime!"

That was enough. More than he wanted to share with her or with anyone, so Crowley turned away from her and pulled her trick back on her, staring at the ground until he calmed down.

"Stop asking me questions you don't want to know the answers to, Amelia. We'll both be better off for it."

Crowley started walking, looking around the premises and trying to find the source of what was going on inside the asylum. Amelia followed along, silent now, and no doubt hating him a bit for using her as a scratching post. He felt the same way about the situation himself, but wasn't about to let her know that. Better if he could drive her away and keep her away in the future.

He was still trying to focus through the maelstrom of memories. It was hard to concentrate enough to use his talents and having her around was an added unpleasant reminder of the recent past.

Amelia knew all of that and didn't let it faze her. She kept with him despite the abuse and he didn't know if it was out of loyalty or desperation, but either way it was another reason not to want her near him.

The wall he was looking at changed before his eyes. He was standing outside the north wing, looking at the ground near the actual building to see if anyone had done something from outside. The ground looked fine, but the wall itself flickered. One second there was the familiar brick pattern and the next there was a stone wall.

Crowley looked at the change and frowned as it continued: a shifting kaleidoscope of rough-hewn stone and carefully laid brick that was disturbing to watch.

It got worse when portions of the wall simply vanished, showing uncut grass and shrubs where the building should be.

John stepped back and tried to take in the whole asylum: for brief moments he could see the central hub through the walls that should have blocked his vision. Only the original building remained relatively unchanged throughout the entire process, which lasted for almost a full minute.

Amelia tried to speak several times, but he completely ignored her, focusing instead on the unusual phenomenon.

As abruptly as it started, the odd overlapping effect faded away.

"Well, that was different." He spoke, forgetting that he had company.

"What was that Jonathan?"

"I have an idea or two. Nothing solid." Without another word he started walking, circling the grounds of Cherry Hill until he reached the front doors and walked back inside. Amelia followed him as quietly as a shadow until he was done.

# Chapter Eighteen

No one inside of Cherry Hill noticed anything strange. They were all too busy with other things, top among them the sudden and violent death of Walter Sawyer.

Kimberly Walker was taking care of clean up duty on the man when it happened. Like almost everyone else on the ward, Sawyer was quiet. Even before his surgery the man had seldom spoken to anyone, choosing instead to let his teeth answer most of his questions. He'd earned the nickname Jaws just before his surgery as a result of his penchant for biting. Now, he was as quiet as a library at midnight.

She was just finishing up with the soiled sheets when Walter let out a low, hoarse scream. Kimberly carefully set aside the soiled linens before she looked back in his direction.

Walter was thin and currently naked, she hadn't yet put on his new robe, and every detail of his body was clearly defined. So she knew she wasn't imagining things when she saw the pallid skin just above his navel start twitching. Walter's eyes flew wide and his mouth curled down into an open frown as his flesh suddenly expanded. It wasn't quite like watching someone playing under a blanket, though she thought that way for a moment. No, blankets don't bleed when they move, and she could see the blood swelling under his flesh, bruising pale skin and then spreading in a crimson stain.

"Billy! Call for Dr. Finney, right away!" Billy didn't question her; he just ran. Kimberly moved closer to help the poor man, terrified by what she was seeing, but still needing to do something. His pulse rate was through the roof and his skin was feverish. Fifteen seconds earlier he'd been clammy and now he felt like he was ready to combust.

Walter bucked and let out another wretched scream as the red stain under his skin moved violently upward. Kimberly heard the sound of muscles being separated from flesh, a wet shushing noise that slid up to the edge of his collarbone before stopping.

Whatever was left of Walter's mind shut down enough to let him slide into unconsciousness and she had to believe that was a blessing. Still, awake or not, his body was far from relaxed. Walter's body jerked several times, and on each occasion the red stain grew larger and darker. His chest swelled with internal hemorrhaging and worse. She heard the sound of his sternum rupturing, saw his ribcage expand and then spread wider as his ribs went in their own directions.

Kimberly was trying to be as observant as possible: She knew that there had been other strange events at Cherry Hill that had similar symptoms and she wanted to let the police and doctors know exactly what she'd seen. But watching the devastation became a nightmare very quickly. Walter was dying in front of her and there wasn't much she could do to stop it.

Once again the man's chest expanded, and this time she could see a shape moving inside of him, something was growing, a large ill-defined shape. Whatever it was, it shouldn't have been possible. The growth pushed harder, stretching the skin like leather drying over a drum. Kimberly closed her eyes as the skin started tearing. She didn't want to see anymore. She didn't want to know.

*Look at me, Kimberly.*

Her eyes flew open of their own volition, and she stared again as the shape moving inside of Walter Sawyer stood and stretched, tearing through his torso like a mad stripper popping out of a fake wedding cake. Only there was no dancer to see, merely a darkness that lifted into the air and seemed to look at her.

*Look at me, Kimberly. Know me. I am your friend. I will never hurt you.*

She tried to speak, to ask it what it wanted, but the words eluded her.

*I am your friend. You have shown me so much kindness, and I will return it to you.*

She stared at that coalescing blackness and looked for anything like a recognizable feature, because she could almost swear she'd heard that voice before. Her ears were ringing and her body twitched. She felt warmth running down her legs and knew that she'd wet herself, but none of that seemed as important as understanding what was going on just a few feet in front of her.

*You will be among the blessed, Kimberly. Give me your faith, give me your love, and I will grant you all that you desire.*

"I—" She couldn't think of a single thing to say. The words thrilled her and scared her at the same time. Worse, she sensed that the words were only a diversion, something to keep her busy. Maybe not only that, but at least partially. She tried to look away but couldn't. Something about the pulsing shadows held her attention. There was nothing to see there, but it was a powerful nothing.

Kimberly forced herself to look away, physically wrenching her head to the side in an effort to stop looking at whatever it was trying to entice her.

She was still looking to her right, and down at Walter Sawyer's face, when his entire skull collapsed in on itself.

Kimberly closed her eyes after that, savoring the lack of sight. She wanted to run, to scream, to hide, but her body refused to move.

The voice kept talking, and Kimberly, more afraid than she'd ever been in her entire life, listened.

---

They found Kimberly Walker crouched in a fetal position, rocking slowly back and forth. Her clothes were slightly soiled and she refused to open her eyes. Roger diagnosed her condition as extreme catatonia, likely brought on by what she'd witnessed. A misty layer of drying blood spread across the entire cell, covering Kimberly's hair and the front of her body where she squatted.

What had been Walter Sawyer was identified later by the remaining fingerprints, but Roger knew who it was. Billy had done a fine job of finding him, and brought him immediately to the cell. He never left the floor and no one could have come in or out without somebody seeing them.

He looked at Sawyer's remains and immediately left the room: it wouldn't be appropriate to ruin the crime scene by losing his breakfast all over it.

Then he made the necessary calls, including to Branaugh upstairs, to Harrington, and to security. He wanted Jonathan Crowley brought down to see this. The words the man had spoken previously kept echoing in his head: *I think something wants to get born into this world and doesn't know how to do it yet.*

"I think it might be getting better with practice." He spoke the words to himself and felt a shiver run through him. This was all getting to be far too much for him. First he had dead bodies and mutilations, now he had Crowley telling him about ghosts and making him believe they were real. Throw in exploding patients and nurses covered in the bloody remains and his career as the chief of Cherry Hill was looking less fulfilling by the second.

Jonathan Crowley moved past him with a nod and stuck his head into the room for a moment, staring at the carnage with a neutral expression on his face.

"There's not enough body left."

"Excuse me?"

"I saw him yesterday. Walter Sawyer. Wanted to look at his file, remember? There's not enough body left. Something took at least half of him when it left the room."

Finney resisted the urge to heave all over the floor. "How can you know that?"

"Simple math. Weigh the remains, if there's more than sixty pounds left, I'll be shocked."

"How does someone walk into a room and do that sort of damage without anyone seeing him?"

Crowley looked over at Kimberly Walker and pointed a finger. "Somebody did see. She's just not going to want to talk about it."

"What's happening here, John?"

"I'm still trying to figure that part out, Roger. But I have to tell you, it isn't looking good."

Carl Branaugh showed up with Rico Montoya in tow. Both men looked over the scene as best they could without actually entering the room. A few minutes later they came over to talk to Finney.

Crowley looked at both of them and a smile played around his lips. He was either amused by what was happening or putting on a damned good front. "Detectives…"

Branaugh nodded. "Mr. Crowley."

"Jonathan Crowley?" As soon as Montoya opened his mouth, Finney felt his heart sink.

"One and the same, Detective Montoya," John's voice was dry and restrained. "Aren't you supposed to be in California?"

"I got a call telling me your situation had changed. Thought I should come see for myself." Montoya kept staring, his expression one of doubt and confusion, which was perfectly understandable under the circumstances.

"I'm still here and I'm still me, Detective. I'm just feeling a little spryer these days."

"Any chance I can get a set of fingerprints from you, Mr. Crowley?"

"I guess you'd have to check with my doctor about that."

Montoya looked directly at Roger and he felt he had no choice but to go along. Crowley simply smiled as he answered. He'd half expected the man to start swinging.

"Well then, get your ink and your paper and you can have my fingerprints." The men stepped aside as the coroner came through. Unlike most of the people in the room, the old man didn't seem fazed by what he saw.

Montoya looked back at Crowley and produced both an inkpad and a thick piece of cardboard from inside his jacket.

"Let's get this part taken care of, and then we can get to business. Sound good to you?"

John nodded. "By all means. I have things to do."

---

It had fed on both the living and the dead, but none of the meals it had ever taken in had filled it with so much vitality. It couldn't even guess how many times it had bypassed Walter Sawyer without a second thought, but now it thought it knew why. Sawyer had held within him a seed of greatness: the very same essence it had grown from. That seed, whether or not it was truly sentient, didn't want to be discovered.

That others might have the same potential had never occurred to it before. Now it had reason to be careful. It didn't want competition on its search for godhood.

It watched from a safe distance as the humans looked over its latest work and pondered what they made of the situation. Mostly it sensed fear.

The memories from deep inside of Sawyer showed carnage and violence and the same odd tendency to commit acts on other people to placate whatever power was inside of the man; the same power that it had now consumed and made a part of itself. Though it had lost a potential devotee by killing the man it was still pleased.

Its senses expanded, allowing it to see further than before. Without moving, it could feel Alex Granger's body slowly dying, and could touch every aspect of the asylum. The living and the dead alike were all around it, and some of them shone brighter than others. The once old man stood out, as did the woman who hovered near him. And another was fairly glowing with untapped power, down in the lowest levels of the building, not far from where Granger normally rested.

First, it would try to take care of Granger. Then, perhaps, it would visit the other down in the dungeon.

Despite the newfound confidence, it decided to handle Granger up close. There was no room for error, at least not until it knew for sure whether or not it could repair the damage.

Alex Granger lay in a hospital bed, his skin sallow and his pulse weaker than ever before. It had always taken from others to feed itself in the past and now it tried to reverse the situation. After it had submerged itself completely within its host, it began the slow task of repairing systems it had come to better understand within the body.

Alex Granger's body twitched, but otherwise remained unmoving.

Alex, how do you feel?

Granger was in there still, but weak, fading away.

"Like I'm dying."

You are dying, Alex. But that can be fixed.

"Will you help me?"

*Yes.*

"I knew I could trust you."

Nothing will harm you, Alex. Sleep now. Rest.

"Yes, God. Thank you."

It made no reply, choosing instead to continue the repairs it had started. Muscles that had atrophied were rebuilt. The heart, poisoned slowly by toxins within Granger's body, was made stronger again, and the kidneys and liver that had begun decaying were replenished. It was pleased by how easily it made the repairs, now that it understood the basic functions of the organs within its host's body. Its confidence grew exponentially. It thought, briefly, about repairing the damage to Granger's mind, but decided against it. What if, by fixing that damage, it managed to get caught within him once again? That would never do.

When it was finished, it decided the time had come for a distraction. The people looking over Walter Sawyer's remains were gathering too much focus on its activities and while most of them seemed harmless, it could not risk being the focus of too much curiosity.

---

Crowley ignored the stares that Montoya kept shooting his way. The man was dazzled, of course, stunned by the changes that had taken place and officially had no reason to doubt what his own eyes had shown him. Of course his fingerprints matched the ones on the paperwork the detective had brought with him. Why wouldn't they? He was the same man he had been before.

Physically, at least.

The coroners had come and gone, the latest in a series of mutilated bodies had been wheeled out of Cherry Hill, and all was not right with the world. He was still trying to understand what he'd seen outside earlier.

Montoya, on the other hand, was trying to decide what to do about him. As if he had any say.

The detective shrugged and then pulled out a small envelope. "These are some photos. They aren't very pretty. I'd like you to look at them and tell me if you can identify any of the bodies."

John looked at the man for a long, long time, not at all certain about doing this. "Who are these supposed to be pictures of?"

"Your family." The man shook his head. "You think I'd show you pictures of just any corpse?"

His hands started sweating. "Where did you find the remains?" He was doing his best to stay calm, but it wasn't easy.

"I'd rather not say just yet. I want you to look at them, please, then tell me if you see anything at all that identifies them, Mr. Crowley."

John took the envelope and opened it, his insides trying to twist around themselves as he slid the pictures out.

The first picture was a long-range shot. Someone had carefully excavated dirt from a large, circular area that showed one adult skeleton and three younger ones. Each had been bound in cloth and they had been laid out with their heads together and their bodies pointing out in four different directions.

Six years had been long enough to strip whatever flesh had remained from his wife and children. He was grateful for that. The full hair around the skulls of three of the bodies let him guess the gender, though he didn't need to guess. He knew enough about human anatomy to let him see that three were, in fact, female and one was male. There were shattered bones in each case, but the pelvic and thighbones were intact. There was no clothing, of course. They'd all been stripped in front of him.

He looked at each consecutive photograph, his hands trembling and his mouth tasting like molten copper. One close-up of the hands on the adult skeleton showed the wedding ring and engagement ring he'd given Elizabeth a lifetime ago. How many times had he stared at her hand and those rings, absorbing every detail?

"It's them." His voice was hoarse as he pushed the photos back toward the detective. The emotions came on like a runaway train, slamming him against the wall and holding him in place as they assaulted him.

The detective stared at him impassively, probably still wondering if he had murdered his own family.

Crowley closed his eyes, trying to push back the memories again, to get past the fresh sorrow that cut through his psyche with the greatest of ease.

Six years of being dead had done nothing to make the mourning process any easier.

"Mr. Crowley, I need to know if you killed your family."

"No." He could barely speak._*Why the hell did I let myself get involved with you Elizabeth? Why didn't I know better?*_And damn it all, the tears were threatening a comeback. "The rings on her finger. Those were the ones I put on my wife. If that's not her, someone went through a lot of effort to make a fake. So I think you found them, Detective. Where were they located?"

"The bodies were found near a state park in Oregon."

Crowley chuckled, a fully unintentional sound. He'd met Elizabeth in a state park in Oregon. He would have bet they were found close to the very spot where he'd first encountered her. Maybe even in the exact same spot.

"You think this is funny, Mr. Crowley?"

"No, you miserable fuck. I do not think this is funny!" He opened his eyes and stared hard at the man. His body trembled with the need to lash out, to do something violent instead of trying to maintain his calm. "I think it's the most disgusting thing I've ever seen, you bastard." His voice lowered into a near growl as he spoke. "I think someone is playing with me and making me look like a fucking murderer in the process. Do you see me laughing, Detective?"

The detective wasn't intimidated in the least. The muscles in his jaw bunched as he looked back with equal dislike. "I know you're grieving, so I'm going to forget what you just said. Do you know who killed your family, Mr. Crowley?"

"No." He shook his head and pushed himself away from the wall, annoyed with the palsied tremble he felt in his hands. "I don't know, not yet. But I'll find out. When I do, there'll be a damned big reckoning."

"You said before that you had a physical description."

"It won't do any good. Whoever was in that body left it a long time back or it's changed so much you'd never recognize it."

"Excuse me?"

"You wouldn't understand and I don't have the time to explain it."

The detective grabbed John's arm as he started walking away. He had a good, strong grip and brought Crowley to a halt. "Try me, Mr. Crowley."

"You're forgetting yourself, Detective. You're out of your jurisdiction. Get your hand off of me, or I might forget that I'm trying to be friendly today."

"Are you threatening me?" The man was actually shocked.

"No, sweet pea, I'm telling you a fact. Get your hands off of me, or I'll defend myself from an unwanted assault."

The detective let go. Crowley started walking again and sure enough, the man followed him.

Crowley moved down the hallway until he reached the stairwell and then started the climb to the third floor. Montoya walked a few paces behind him and kept his mouth shut. Maybe he'd gotten the point about being outside of his jurisdiction.

Or maybe he was just biding his time. In his experience, John had seldom met anyone in authority who liked to be put in his place. It made them want to be stupid.

He stopped on the third floor of the South Wing, in what the doctors had called the violent ward. He'd only heard about the incident up there after they found the dead man in the lower levels. Now he wanted to see what was left of the crime scene and to determine if there was any connection. He knew there was, of course, unless they had two monsters roaming the corridors of Cherry Hill, but he had to know how and why they were connected. So far, he'd come up with nothing solid on what was happening and it was starting to piss him off.

The hairs on the back of his neck rose as soon as he entered the wing. It wasn't the knowledge that a death had taken place. No, he was far too used to death to let a stranger in an asylum affect him. It was something else, but he couldn't quite place what that something was.

"Hmmm."

"What?" Montoya must have been feeling something, too, because he was looking a little jumpy.

Crowley saw no sign of a nurse, a doctor, or a security guard. "I don't know yet. I probably won't know, either, if you don't stop yapping." John was starting to remember what it was he liked about being alone, back before Elizabeth stepped into his life. It was hard to concentrate when people were constantly asking stupid questions.

There were twenty cells on each level of the wing, ten to a side. Normally there were security guards hanging around. There hadn't been a lot of obvious security when he was first admitted, but the odd deaths had changed that in the last few days. First there was one guard on each floor and now there were two. Except here. There was no sign of a security detail anywhere around.

Down the hallway he heard a phone ringing. No one answered it. One of the cell doors squeaked open on the right side, and a patient walked into the main corridor as if doing so was nothing unusual.

The man was tall, lean and dressed in nothing but a hospital gown and the shredded remains of a straitjacket. His skin was as pale as expected from a man who probably hadn't seen sunlight in the last few years, but his hands were covered in flaking rusty splotches.

Blood, old enough to have dried to the man's skin.

The man looked down the hallway in the direction of the phone, and Crowley wondered whether or not he could get to the patient without being noticed.

"Hey! Freeze!" Montoya's voice echoed down the corridor and John wasn't sure who jumped harder, the mental patient with the bloody hands or him.

"Brilliant, you asshole. Let's not try being subtle first."

Eighteen of the nineteen remaining cell doors swung open, disgorging the men who normally were forced to remain on the other side of them. The first one, the lanky man with the bloodied hands, walked over to the nurse's station and ripped the phone out of the wall: the cords hidden within the wall stretched and broke partially through the steel box that held them before they finally snapped.

Montoya stepped up next to John, his hand reaching for the service revolver he normally carried on his hip. It might have been a nicer gesture if he hadn't had to surrender the weapon when he entered the building.

"Oh, shit." Montoya's tone almost made the words a question.

"We aren't looking for visitors right now." Red Hand dropped the phone as he spoke and then moved in their direction. John shook his head and Montoya spat, his face set for trouble.

"Well, we're not really visiting. We're new to the ward, thought we'd check out the place before we settled in." Crowley took three steps forward, looking from one patient to the next, assessing how badly he was going to get his ass kicked in the coming fight.

One of the men started giggling, an unsettling sound considering the bruiser looked like he probably ate trees for breakfast. Another one growled and moved forward. The man was chunky and pale, his dark hair receded from his scalp and his mostly nude body was covered with scars.

He also moved faster than he should have, covering the distance between his cell door and Montoya so fast that he took the detective by surprise.

The nutcase hit Montoya hard enough to send him staggering and pushed him again before he could recover. Cop and psycho hit the ground in a tangle of limbs, and Crowley stepped forward, a grin growing on his face.

"Thanks, guys. Really. I've been meaning to vent some steam." They stepped toward him en masse, apparently feeling the same way about the promise of carnage. John stood his ground and waited, forcing his body to relax as the madmen came for him. As they moved closer, he could feel the unnatural energies that radiated from their bodies. Someone or something had been very busy while he was looking elsewhere.

The first man came in low, charging like a bull, and John sidestepped, and let him run straight into the wall with a stupid look on his face. The second was much better and drove a fist like a sledgehammer into Crowley's stomach. The force lifted him off his feet and doubled him over.

The third one managed to get a firm grip on his left leg and before John had a chance to recover from the first punch, the bastard was biting deep into the muscles of his calf. Having a leg back was great, but it didn't seem like he'd have it for much longer.

Crowley let out a yelp and pushed himself up onto his right leg, shifting his body to compensate for the awkward position. He hopped twice to get the leverage he needed and then brought his right foot up and around to wallop the Biter on the back of his head. Both of them went down, but this time John caught himself and was back up a moment later.

It didn't do him much good. There were simply too many people trying to tear into him to make defensive fighting a possibility. Hands grabbed at his face and arms while fists struck him again and again wherever they could get through.

He felt his skin and muscles itching where he'd been struck and knew that his abilities were working properly again. The itching told him his body was healing every bit of damage he took. He didn't recover from injuries any faster than other people, except when the supernatural was involved. That little fact told him that it wasn't one or two of the men that had been altered. It was all of them.

And that meant he could set aside feeling bad for the people he was dealing with and finally cut loose.

Jonathan Crowley laughed and started counterattacking.

Red Hands reached for him, filthy fingers seeking the soft meat of his eyes, and Crowley blocked before punching the man in his throat. The man fell back, his eyes bulging as his trachea ruptured. He wasn't dead, but he would be soon. As Red Hands struggled to breathe, John grabbed the next in line by the ear and ripped downward as hard as he could, feeling cartilage snap as his new victim screamed.

All of the confusion and grief faded away for the moment, replaced by the pure primal joy of inflicting pain. A lucky punch broke his nose and he blinked tears out of his eyes even as he drove his foot into somebody's chest and felt the bones breaking beneath his heel. His left hand grabbed the thick hair of a man wearing a security guard's uniform top over his robes, and Crowley slammed the stranger's head into the wall hard enough to break bone and brick alike. The inmates of the violent ward retreated as Crowley grabbed another man and dislocated his shoulder, grinning all the while.

Montoya was shrieking, his voice rising in octaves. Crowley looked over to see the bullish man on top of him forcing his fingers into the detective's stomach. Under most normal circumstances it would have been a physical impossibility, but the strength and resilience of the madmen was inhuman.

He didn't like the detective. But he didn't hate him either. Crowley reached around and hooked his fingers into the psychopath's face, dragging them up from the chin all the way to the top of his victim's skull. He drew blood from the cheek and from one eye as he progressed.

Somebody kicked him in the balls at the same time, but it didn't matter. The pain was a pleasant distraction from his thoughts and adrenaline kept him moving.

Montoya took advantage of the opening John gave him and started swinging his fists. Crowley left him to handle his own affairs and returned to the rest of the inmates. The remaining prisoners were watching from a distance now, cautious where before they'd been reckless.

Three of the men retreated to their cells. They were the lucky ones; he let them live.

With the rest of them, he took his time, maiming in some cases and killing in others. He had a lot of stress to get out his system and they'd volunteered to help him.

---

Ricardo Alejandro Montoya was a third generation American and proud of it. His family had embraced everything about the United States when they came to California and he was raised with the simple belief that good eventually triumphs over evil. He'd held to that belief when he was in Korea and had a few scars to prove it.

He was a happily married man who kept a picture of his wife in his wallet and wore his wedding ring with pride. He'd never taken a bribe while on duty and he believed firmly that following procedures was the best way to catch criminals.

All of that meant exactly nothing to him when the oversized, half-naked baboon of a man tackled him and started trying to tear him limb from limb. He fought back hard, but every punch he threw seemed ineffective, and the man was too heavy for him to push away.

When the man's fingers started pushing on his sternum it hurt enough to make him cry out. When they tore through the fabric over his stomach and started scraping skin, he panicked. Not because the man was hurting him, but because what he was doing was impossible. Fingers might tear through an occasional piece of flimsy material, but not through a jacket, a vest and a shirt.

Rico was a logical man. He didn't have room in his life for the impossible. Handling what seemed to have happened to Crowley was pushing the limits of his acceptance.

Just as the fingers that had shredded his suit were starting to break through skin, Rico saw Crowley over the bruiser's shoulder. The man was grinning ear to ear as he reached out with one hand and drew blood on Rico's assailant with his fingertips.

The fat man let out a scream of his own, and as he reached for his ruined face, Rico punched him as hard as he could in the throat. Adrenaline and anger took care of the rest. Rico managed to get himself out from under the unconscious man and was ready to take on the next one a few seconds later.

He looked over just in time to see Jonathan Crowley slam a man's face into the wall hard enough to shatter bone. The man's nose was busted and bleeding as he grinned, leaving red and pink stains on his lips and teeth alike. He moved to the next of the inmates, a rail-thin man who had apparently painted himself in feces, and dropped the man to the ground with a spinning roundhouse kick. Three of the patients decided to work together to take him down. They hit Crowley from three separate directions and sacked him, their fists rose up and down making meaty smacking noises as they connected with the man.

Rico watched, uncertain exactly whom he should be cheering on. The man directly over Crowley let out a groan and then a scream as Crowley caught his nose between his thumb and forefinger and twisted it savagely. Before he could do more than pull his face back from the attack, Crowley caught him at the ear and wrenched his head violently to the left. It was enough to make the man fall to the side, enough to let Crowley get some fighting room.

There were no fancy moves, no sudden weapons produced to even the odds. The inmates fought hard and dirty and their target kept up with them in the savagery displayed. A few of the inmates broke away and fled back to their cells. Most of them kept coming, and kept falling, beaten down or flat out murdered by the person Rico had come here to interrogate.

He saw Jonathan Crowley catch a fist to the eye that should have left him crying and half blind. Crowley acted like it was all just good, clean fun and broke the offender's wrist, then his elbow and finally his neck with three blows almost too fast to actually see. Before the dead man could hit the floor, Crowley's wounded eye was almost back to normal, and the dead man in his hands was used to shield several more punches.

Rico watched on, too stunned to notice much of anything else going on around him until there were only three prisoners left, the ones with the good sense not to catch Crowley's attention.

Then the last man standing turned his way, spitting blood from a smiling mouth and wiping more of the stuff from his hands.

Crowley looked him over, the grin slowly fading away and his eyes half-lidded as he spoke in mocking tones. "Oh, come on, Detective. Don't look so shocked. Didn't you hear? I'm a dangerous man. I should be locked away."

Rico couldn't stop himself from taking a few steps back as Crowley approached. Crowley's gaze made him feel small: like a first grader caught peeing himself. His expression said it all: *I could have killed you if I wanted to. I just didn't feel like it.*

He wanted to ask a hundred questions but knew that the answers wouldn't be anything he wanted to hear.

Crowley walked past him and headed for the stairs, stepping over the people he'd just slaughtered. Montoya desperately wished he had his weapon on him.

He was also very glad he didn't have it. He wasn't sure he could draw and fire before he got Crowley's attention.

Once they were in the stairwell, Crowley turned and faced him again. The door they'd just passed through slammed shut with a thunderous finality.

"Let's get this finished, Detective."

"Get what finished?"

"I don't have the time to play a song and dance with you, so I'm going to make this easy. I didn't kill my family."

Damnedest thing: he believed the man.

"My life is complicated right now. I have enough issues to deal with. You're a busy man, I'm sure and I bet you'd like to get back home and see your family. So here's the deal. Go home. Keep looking for my family's murderer and let me know if you find a suspect worth mentioning. In exchange, I promise to stay well away from you."

Crowley spoke, and Rico listened. He should have been protesting, telling the psychopath that as soon as he could, he'd see him on death row. Instead, he nodded his agreement and even smiled. They shook hands in the corridor and Crowley wrote down a phone number on the back of one of Montoya's business cards. He slipped the card deep into his wallet, convinced that having that number would be very important some day.

Five minutes after he left Cherry Hill, Rico Montoya had forgotten all about Jonathan Crowley and everything he'd seen that was out of the ordinary during his visit.

If he'd remembered what had happened, he might have thanked Crowley for it. His life made a lot more sense when the supernatural was left out of it.

# Chapter Nineteen

Jonathan Crowley told Roger Finney everything about what had happened in the violent ward. He mentioned nothing at all about what occurred in the stairwell afterward.

Roger listened to the details with a growing sense of dread and called Bob Wilkes to have him confirm what was reported. His lips felt numb as he spoke on the phone with the chief of security, and his hands shook as he finally hung up.

"John, there's no way in hell I can hide this anymore." He spoke without really being aware of what he was saying. Somewhere along the way, his "Inside Voice" as his mother had always called it, had managed to sneak straight out his mouth.

Crowley looked at him and frowned. "That's not really my concern, Roger. It shouldn't be yours, either. The smartest thing you could do is close down Cherry Hill until this is all resolved."

"Close down a facility for the criminally insane? You really have lost your mind."

"Hey, you're feeling bad about this." Crowley crossed his arms and leaned against the wall, his sarcastic tones weren't lost on Roger. "Maybe it would be better if you just handled it yourself. I could be on my way and no one ever has to hear about it. Listen, I bet if you tried, you could hide most of the bodies in swampy areas and no one would ever find out."

"That's not going to happen and you know it."

"I wouldn't have suggested it if I thought it would, Doc."

"Can you tell me what the hell is happening John? Can you at least give me a guess?"

"Well, I haven't had a lot of time to look into the details yet, Roger. That's part of the problem here. All I can tell you is that you've got an escalating situation on your hands."

"Well, no shit!" Roger slapped his hand on the desk and knocked his pencil jar to the ground in the process.

"Calm down. Blowing up is hardly the way to work out the details. Let's look at what we've got so far." Crowley held up his hand and started lifting one finger with each point he made as if he were keeping score. "Near as I can tell this started with the dead body in the plumbing. Still no identification of the corpse, so we can rule out a missing patient. The clothes were antiquated, so it's possible we're dealing with a first attempt at manifestation that just didn't work out."

Roger frowned, trying to understand what sort of rationale Crowley was using. Harrington was sounding smarter by the minute.

"Three or four people end up badly mutilated, several ghosts get torn into pieces and left to wander around. That leads me to think something is trying to understand how they work and is also learning to absorb what it needs to survive.

"That's all bad enough, Roger. It could mean dealing with a hungry ghost and as I said before, they can get very mean very fast. The more they devour, the stronger they get."

"Okay, damn it, John, I'm really trying to accept all of this, but now you're telling me that ghosts eat other ghosts to get stronger? That's like saying I could start eating my patients to become Superman."

"You're thinking in terms of the physical realm, Roger. If you put two people in a room and one of them cannibalizes the other, you end up with a corpse and a cannibal. I'll give you that. But try thinking of the dead as energy instead of matter. If you put two fires in the same room they're just two fires. If you merge them, they become a bigger fire. Same thing with water, put two gallons of water together and they merge easily."

Roger tried to calm down and listened. "Okay. So a hungry ghost is like a fire added to a fire. Got it."

"Here's another part of that comparison for you. First, you have a ghost. Then you have a bigger ghost with an appetite. Soon it's adding more and more fires, and it's burning hotter and brighter. In order to keep up with its new size and strength, it burns more fuel faster."

"So you're saying this won't get better? It'll get worse?" His voice cracked.

Crowley nodded. "Oh yes. Much worse. If we don't figure out what it's doing and fast."

"If you can see ghosts, why can't you see this hungry one?"

"I can see them as long as they don't start outthinking me, Doc. This one is getting smarter. Also, I've never run across a hungry ghost that actually successfully ate people. I don't think this is a hungry ghost, Roger. I think it's something all new that works on the same principle."

"Not a demon?"

"No. Demons might work this way, but they wouldn't leave behind evidence unless they were either making a point or were told to by whoever summoned them. Also, I'm not getting the same sort of vibe I get from demons."

Roger closed his eyes and tried to let the surreal conversation mingle with his own beliefs. It wasn't working very well.

"We're getting off track here. I don't know what exactly is going on, Roger. I just know it's getting worse. I can't say exactly what happened to those patients I had to handle, either, but whatever has been tearing people apart has apparently now learned how to make improvements. If I were you, I'd be asking for a very thorough autopsy of the men I just had to kill. I'm guessing not a one of the men I dealt with has normal anatomy."

"What do you mean?"

"They were too strong, too fast and too tough, Roger." Crowley dropped himself into a chair. "They also got out of locked cages, which means they had help of some kind."

"No one in this facility would be stupid enough to unlock the cells."

"I didn't say it was an employee, did I?"

"Then what do you think it was?"

"I think whatever is growing inside of your asylum is learning new tricks. I think it altered the men and then let them free, just to see what would happen."

Roger stared at his patient for a long time, uncertain how to react to the comments. Everything that Crowley was saying made a certain sense to him and that was bothersome. Roger considered himself first and foremost a man of logic. The supernatural didn't fit comfortably into his reality. However, as it had been presented to him in a logical and relatively orderly fashion, he had to concede the reality of strange things happening in his previously orderly world.

"Okay, enough about the whys and wherefores, John. What can be done to fix the problem?"

"I'm still working on that. I have to know what's broken before I can actually fix it, Roger. It's the way these things work. You don't drive a wooden stake into a werewolf to stop it." Crowley shook his head. "If this was a hungry ghost I could have figured it out by now, but this is something that's trying to work along the same lines. If it was a demon, I could have sorted out the details, but it's not. Whatever is happening is either breaking the rules or has never existed before. If it's new, the rules as I know them don't really apply properly."

*So basically, you don't know shit and can't do a damned thing to help me.* Roger closed his eyes. "John, how am I supposed to explain how and why you killed over a dozen people?"

The question couldn't have been better timed. Carl Branaugh opened the door to Roger's office just as he started asking.

Crowley looked over at the detective and crossed his arms. "It was self-defense."

"What happened to Montoya?" Branaugh's voice was calm, and belied his expression.

"He found out what he needed to know and went home. I imagine he's on his way to the airport right now." Crowley kept a calm expression and a snide tone.

"Well, that's a damned shame for you, Mr. Crowley. Because without him to back you up, I have to consider whether or not you went on a killing spree." Branaugh moved toward him and put his hand to the small of his back, where he likely was carrying handcuffs.

"Don't be an ass, Branaugh. If I felt like killing a few people here, my list wouldn't have started on a ward where I didn't even know anyone." Crowley slipped out of his sitting position and into a defensive pose.

The detective stepped forward with his chin out and his hands almost balled into fists. "There are twenty-two dead people upstairs, Crowley. I'm not being an ass; I'm looking for a legitimate explanation for mass murder."

"Whatever officials were up there, nurses and guards, were killed by the inmates. Montoya killed one of the guys who did those murders and I took care of the rest." Crowley, who seemed at times a truly sensitive man, shrugged off the deaths as if they were discussing the odds of the Yankees winning the World Series.

"So you're admitting to murder?"

"No, Detective, I'm admitting to self-defense. Listen, feel free to go one on one with any of the remaining three inmates. I'm sure you'll find out for yourself that they aren't exactly normal."

"What remaining inmates? Everyone on the floor is dead."

"Excuse me?" Crowley shook his head. "No, three of them went back into their cells and I left them alive."

"They were all dead when I got there. A few of them were in their cells, but they were all dead, Crowley."

"Yeah? How did the ones in their cells die?"

"Like the people we found before. Like someone reached inside their skins and squeezed."

"I'm the first to say I can deal out my fair share of carnage, Detective, but I've never managed to take out pieces of a man and leave the skin intact."

"Well then what the hell is going on here?" Branaugh's face reddened as he talked, the veins in his neck bulging as his blood pressure shot through the ceiling.

"For the last time, I'm still trying to figure that out!" John was furious, and if anyone had asked him why, Roger would have guessed it was because he hadn't solved the puzzle yet. "How long does it take you to solve a case, Branaugh? Do you guess right off the bat or do you have to look at the facts first? I'm doing all I can with the limited resources available to me."

"I've got half a mind to lock you away right now and see if things get better, Crowley."

"I've got half a mind to let you, Branaugh, just to see the stupid look on your face when this place goes up in flames."

Roger interjected, tired of watching the two of them. "Gentlemen, the testosterone and chest beating aren't going to solve any of this." He stood up and moved around his desk. "Might I suggest you pool your abilities and get this solved while there's still a building over our heads and before the list of employees and patients gets any smaller?"

He'd hoped to actually get the men calmer. It didn't work that way. Worse, he could feel himself starting to succumb to an almost irrational rage.

---

Amelia Dunlow savored the atmosphere in the break room. Seventeen people sat in the room with her, and not a one of them looked at her for more than a few seconds. None of the men gave off the vibe that said they wanted to possess her, to own her body and soul. It was a liberating sensation and one that she basked in.

Having empathic abilities was a pain in her ass when things were going the wrong way. True, it had prevented a few unpleasant encounters with men who obsessed over her, but it hadn't made her life easier when she knew what everyone around her was feeling and when most of what they felt was barely restrained lust.

Jonathan had calmed down the part of her that generated those feelings and now she was enjoying the unexpected freedom.

That changed, though it was such a slow transformation that she barely noticed it at first. She'd been reading over the large stacks of files that Jonathan had taken from the attic of the place. Most of the paperwork was useless, purchasing orders from fifty years back did nothing to help him solve his current case, but she'd found a few nuggets that might prove useful.

It was while she was sorting through another stack of the dusty files that she first noticed the change. The people around her were still not focusing on her, but they were all gradually getting edgier, more frustrated with their situation. People who'd been chatting casually a few minutes earlier were now sitting in the same spots with sullen expressions and dark thoughts.

Being sensitive had its uses. Amelia gathered together her files and left the break room before it could get any worse.

The people she saw in the hallway were exactly the same, however, each and every one of them giving off slowly increasing waves of anger.

There was nothing natural about it, either. She couldn't tell where it was coming from, but she'd have bet five years of her life that something was toying with the emotions of the people around her. It wasn't affecting her, for which she was grateful, but she still didn't want to be around when the powder keg of growing unrest was ignited.

Amelia said a silent prayer, a hope that Jonathan was all right wherever he was, and went back to the office that had become their shared room.

Two guards were busily glaring at each other down the long corridor. They didn't even notice her, which was a blessing as far as she could tell. One of them had his hand on the butt of his weapon and looked like he was ready to draw and fire.

Amelia closed and locked the door behind her. As an afterthought, she slid one of the chairs Jonathan had confiscated under the knob and propped it in place as an extra barricade.

Her ability to sense emotions wasn't a fine-tuned thing: unlike Jonathan, it was an innate talent and not one she tried to focus on. Still, she had to know if there was something bigger behind the change in feelings, had to know if she could locate it. Whatever was causing all of the troubles might also be hiding, and if Jonathan couldn't find the source of the problems he couldn't very well get rid of it.

She lay back on her cot and tried to focus on whatever was behind the changes, but she couldn't quite grasp it, whatever it was. She knew there was something out there, something that she sensed was growing in power, but rather than any sort of malignant spirit or demonic presence, she felt only a strong sense of curiosity.

Then she sensed something that made her pull back, try to retreat. She felt that powerful curiosity change as whatever it was noticed her.

What are you? It wasn't a voice precisely, but the power of the question that pressed into her head was unexpected and painful. Something was digging into her brain, trying to understand what made her different, perhaps, or merely trying to understand everything about her. Either way it was a violation and she tried to force it away without any success.

"Nothing. I'm no one special. Please just forget about me." She whispered the words under her breath, taken by surprise.

*You are not human.*

"Yes I am." The words stung: She'd been trying to be human for a long time and failing.

No, you are different. Not human. Not dead. Not alive. What are you?

Underlying the sense of violation was another, distant sensation, a calming of the people throughout the entire building. Whatever the thing was, it could only focus on one task at a time. Maybe that was a plus.

"Please, just go away. Leave me alone." She was scared. Her heart was pounding in her chest and she couldn't catch a decent breath.

*I will know you.* It reached further into her mind, sorting through memories and pulling at her psyche to better understand her deepest secrets.

"No, please!" Amelia tried to fight back, tried to get her mind back from whatever was trying to pull her apart. Every attempt she made only caused it to focus on her more, and she sensed its frustration as it continued the assault.

*I will know you NOW.* Something slithered through the wall, a darkness that drew her eyes and frosted the air in the room as it came closer to her.

Amelia tried to scream, but the sound was torn away from her, absorbed by the black essence that spilled over her and around her.

Whatever she thought she knew of violation, she was wrong.

It was worse than she had ever imagined.

---

Phillip Harrington stared at the diplomas on his wall without seeing them. He was locked into a different mode of thought, one brought on by the things he'd seen the day before and magnified by the events of the day. He'd already looked at the bodies, going through the violent ward and identifying patients for the doddering old fool of a medical examiner.

The man made him think of Jonathan Crowley when he'd first come into Cherry Hill, and that simple fact infuriated him. Crowley the old man had been sarcastic, true, but he'd also been frightened and vulnerable enough to make it possible to look past the sarcasm.

The new Crowley was younger (an impossibility), had grown back his leg (also impossible) and had regenerated massive trauma to his brain (a third and exceedingly annoying impossibility). The new Crowley was either capable of magic (a concept that Phil refused to accept) or was pulling off one hell of a hoax. Worse still, most of the people who'd met him seemed to think he was some sort of miracle worker.

He also didn't like the way Crowley looked at him now. It wasn't just that creepy as hell smile of his. No, there was something else there that scraped away at his nerves. Crowley looked at him with contempt.

Phil's hands caught hold of a memo he'd written to himself regarding a reexamination of the Charles Waters case. He started slowly tearing strips of the paper away, unaware of his own actions.

"Your problem, Jonathan Crowley, is that you've grown too big for your own britches." Half an hour before the murders, he'd been informed that Crowley was no longer his patient. Finney had taken over the case, knowing full well that any documentation on Crowley was all but a guarantee of a book deal. There had never been another case like this one and Finney, who swore that he was on Phil's side, had taken the case from him without so much as a consultation about it. Oh, he'd be sure to put a spin on it, to make it look as if he was doing it solely to make sure Crowley stayed at Cherry Hill, but Phil was no longer willing to play that particular game.

There were ways to take care of troublemakers. If he played it the right way, he'd get rid of Finney and take care of Crowley once and for all.

Because Jonathan Crowley was a threat, any rational man could see that. He was manipulating the other doctors involved with him and even the police from not one, but two different states.

"Damned if I'll let you get away with this." His hands finished with the first sheet of paper and started seeking other things to tear apart. It wasn't long before he was shredding the full case file for Charles Waters. The notes were irrelevant, really. He'd already decided Waters was a good candidate for a lobotomy.

His hands stopped tearing and Phil smiled for the first time in the last two days.

The paperwork for transferring Crowley's care from him to Finney hadn't even been written yet, forget processed. Phil's hands pounded a drumbeat across the edge of his desk as he thought about that.

He still had a letter to the Board regarding Finney's activities and while he'd been toying with not sending it, he decided instead that there was no time like the present.

He'd have to think fast but that was never a problem for him. The catch was to make sure it didn't look like he was out to get Crowley until everything had been resolved. With the atrocities committed earlier, Finney was going to be on thin ice already. A scathing letter showing that he had all but handed a dangerous psychotic the keys to the kingdom would go a long way toward ending Roger Finney's time as the head of the asylum.

---

It pulled away from the woman, more confused now than when it had started its examination of her. She made no sense. Her memories were a jumble of experiences she'd had as a human child, as something that seemed immortal, and as an amalgam of the two.

Perhaps she was in some way similar to what it had become since devouring the force that had inhabited Walter Sawyer. Perhaps it could learn as much from her as it had from Sawyer.

It stared down at the woman crying before it and decided the best way to find answers was simply to consume her. It had tried to be reasonable, tried to learn from merely searching through her mind, but she'd fought too hard and now…well, now she was not completely as she had been.

There was so much to learn and it felt a growing sense of unease, a certainty that if it didn't learn quickly enough, it would be at risk.

It reached down again, this time not seeking to merely study, but to eat.

The woman below it opened her eyes and stared as it touched. Something happened beneath the surface, something within the depths of the woman ignited and as it sank into her flesh it felt a searing lightning bolt of pain leap from her prone form and into its essence.

It tried to pull back, but whatever it was inside the woman gripped it, pulled and tore and lashed at it with a thousand hooks of liquid pain.

The smile that came across the female's face was subtle, but cruel, and the presence within her eyes was not the same as it had examined before.

Panic! Pain! Fear! The emotions rippled through it as it heaved and bucked and thrashed in an effort to escape. When all else failed it resorted to exactly the sort of behavior it had studied in the life forms in the cellar. In an effort to save itself it tore free from a part of its own essence—chewing away a caught limb—and escaped, shrieking its pain for all to hear.

The woman, the old man, they were not what they seemed. The pain faded quickly, the loss of energies was not as deadly as the terror it felt. In an instant it forced its way back into Alex Granger's still form and hid, confused by what had happened.

It studied the woman again, but this time cautiously, from a distance. It felt the changes that took place within her, as whatever had come up from below the surface of her being once again receded.

Arrogance had nearly cost it everything, and it understood that now. For one foolish moment it had let itself think it couldn't be hurt and the end results had been disastrous.

It was lessened. Some of what it had taken from Walter Sawyer was gone now. It was stronger than before it consumed Sawyer, yes, but drained now of so much of the energies it had stolen. There was another, of course, who held as much power, but it needed to think carefully before it took what it wanted from him.

After several hours of careful thought, it returned to what it had been doing before the woman distracted it.

It remained unfamiliar with emotions, inexperienced in what caused them and why they were important. Two emotions seemed prevalent at Cherry Hill, and it decided that those were the ones it would try to understand better.

Understanding came with experimentation. From within the safety of Granger's body, it reached out again and spread itself thin, touching the minds of the people, living and dead alike, that it encountered.

---

The drugs slowed down the changes, but did not eliminate them. Throughout the entire facility, the patients grew restless as fear overwhelmed some of them and anger ignited slow burning fires within the rest.

---

In the guards' changing room, where they put on their uniforms or skivvies as they came and went from Cherry Hill, Don Michaels was just putting on his work shoes and checking that the pepper spray and nightstick were properly situated in his belt when Lionel Copper came storming into the room.

Don had been late on his last twelve shifts. He replaced Lionel at the desk and apparently he wasn't moving fast enough to keep Lionel happy.

"What part of 'be on time' is confusing you, Don?" Lionel sneered at him and began switching over to his civilian clothes.

Don, who had been dealing with a frail mother on one front and a rapidly worsening divorce on the other looked at Lionel for a moment and finally shrugged his shoulders. "I get here when I can, man. Deal with it or report me. I don't fucking care anymore."

"You're goddamned right I'm reporting you! I'm tired of waiting around for your sorry ass every single day!"

Don was barely aware of grabbing his pepper spray and firing it into Lionel's screaming face. He was barely aware of anything for several minutes, and when he once again noticed his surroundings, he also noticed that Lionel was on the ground in a growing pool of blood and that somebody had been beating the poor bastard senseless. Lionel's face was broken into a new shape, and it looked like half of his teeth were missing.

He started feeling the pain in his hands around the same time he noticed the heavy bloodstains on his baton.

He was still trying to figure out exactly what was happening when the detective from town put handcuffs on his wrists.

---

Marianne Hambly, a fifteen-year veteran of Cherry Hill, was well respected and well liked. In the entire time she'd been at the asylum she'd never once called out sick or been accused of cutting corners when it came to taking care of her charges.

So no one really thought about it when she went into one of the supply rooms for almost half an hour. No one suspected a thing, really, until after she'd handed out the afternoon medications.

She never lost her smile as she handed out the rat poison-filled capsules and in a few cases injected the stuff straight into the veins of her patients.

When the first signs of poisoning started to show themselves, she kept the guards busy as long as she could with idle chatter. It would have worked if she'd used a poison that didn't cause muscular seizures.

Three patients died. The rest were sent to the emergency area and treated for their poisonings.

Marianne had never administered strychnine before. She didn't know how big a dose to give to the people who constantly filled her nightmares.

---

On the second floor of the West Wing, Mark Evers rammed his head into the wall again and again until he finally managed to kill himself. The voices he'd managed to ignore for a long time had come back with a vengeance. He recognized them, of course. They were the voices of his victims.

He was not among the haunted at Cherry Hill. At least not those haunted by ghosts. The only phantoms he had to deal with were the ones in his head. Until an hour ago he'd never let them get to him, but his sudden fear that they would be with him forever was enough to make him choose what his father had always called the coward's way out.

Seconds after he was dead, his spirit was grabbed by thin tentacles of something dark that pulled him through walls and bodies alike until it drew him into the blackness that made up its body.

---

Jonathan Crowley walked to his room and unlocked the door. He'd forgotten all about Amelia Dunlow. She was a low priority on his list of grievances.

She lay sprawled across her bed, her skin pale, her respirations shaking and hyperactive.

John stared at her for several seconds, shocked to see her in her current stare. Finally he moved closer and touched her.

"Amelia? What happened?" His voice was soft, concerned, too worried to remain his usual caustic self.

"Something tried to take me." Her voice was a whisper, and he saw for the first time that she'd bitten through her lower lip during whatever had happened to her.

"Something?" He put his hand on her forehead to check her temperature. She was slightly feverish, but not where she had any risks.

Amelia rolled her eyes to look at him rather than risk turning her head. "It wanted to know more about me, Jonathan. It wanted to kill me."

Crowley shook his head. He knew the force that lived inside of her wouldn't permit her to die easily. "Well, we'll put up a few wards, see if we can't keep you safer from now on. I'm sorry this happened."

Amelia managed a fragile smile. "I'm not. I got something for you."

"What did you get for me?"

"It tried to eat, but it couldn't. And the thing inside of me, that tried to eat, too. So much energy, Jonathan," her voice drifted off, awed by the sensations running through her. "So much power, it's like a generator inside of me."

"Don't get used to it." Without a second's hesitation, he placed his hands on her shoulders and spoke words that no living being had heard in over three hundred years. Amelia bucked and let out a whimper, her body arcing off the bed. Crowley closed his eyes and looked away as the power she'd siphoned from something else jumped from her body and into his arms.

His skin shivered and muscles twitched as the current drained into him. He could have taken all of it, but didn't. What he left would help her recover from her traumas, mental and physical alike.

Amelia opened her eyes and looked up at him. Before she could speak, he sent her into a deep slumber.

Fifteen minutes later the room was protected as best he could manage and he left, smiling to himself. His mind processed the essence inside of him and he ran through a dozen tests inside his skull to see if he could identify what it was that had come to Cherry Hill. The thing had hidden away from him, but now he understood how it remained invisible: now he knew how to find it. Finally he had a few answers.

The next few hours would give him more information, and if he was very lucky, even a way to stop something he had never encountered before.

A living ghost.

A hungry ghost that was consuming everything it could in a gluttonous fit wasn't all that unusual, but as a rule, they had to be dead first.

Crowley intended to rectify that situation.

# Chapter Twenty

For almost two hours, the thing that had taken residence inside Cherry Hill played games with the minds of the people around it. The results weren't as spectacular as it had hoped, and most of the people were either simply edgy or sullen for that time. Eventually it grew tired and decided to rest properly again within the body of Alex Granger.

Granger did not try to speak to it this time and that was a fine thing. It was still hurting from the loss of the energies it had taken before. It was stronger true, but not as powerful as it had been before the female drained it.

It slept, and as it slept, it shared in Alex Granger's dreams and memories.

Alex had always been a bright boy, one of three children from a lower income family, and he had always been his mother's favorite. His father couldn't have much cared as long as Alex stayed out of his way. Alex learned very early on that catching his daddy's attention was not a good thing. He learned to be quiet, and it stuck with him.

By the time Alex was ten he seldom spoke at all. Oh, a few teachers might have worried about him, but his grades were always good and his demeanor said that he was harmless, just quiet.

At eleven, Alex had an epiphany. He decided that since God did not answer his questions, he must be dead. By twelve his logic, flawed perhaps, had changed a great deal. God was dead because he never got enough sacrifices. Somewhere along the way, the sacrifices had been replaced with simple prayers, which never had enough power to them. Prayers, he reasoned, were better received with an offering.

At thirteen, he started killing, making sacrifices to the Dead God. That was the year his father died, proof positive that sacrifices made a difference. It was painful to kill: the animals liked to fight back and he was scratched and bitten several times even with his first sacrifice, a local stray cat that seemed to grow extra claws as he held it down. He had on his jacket, so the actual damage done to him was minimal and the sort he could hide.

Two days later, he didn't have to worry about hiding anything. His father dropped of a massive coronary and took care of a lot of his worries. Praise the Dead God.

It contemplated the images and memories as they occurred, confused by what they showed, because it had experienced Alex's recollections of his father and they were mostly gentle. The worst the man had ever done to him was to paddle his rear end when he tried to cross the road at the age of three.

It knew almost everything about Alex, though in a second-hand way. Alex grew up in a decent household, with loving parents. Alex was given to violent fits from an early age. Alex killed things in order to satisfy it, the Dead God, and now, perhaps, it understood what Alex thought it was.

It remained uncertain as to whether or not it was a deity. Still, becoming a god could have advantages.

Finally rested, and tired of Granger's jumbled dreams and fractured memories, it left him again and sought what it knew it needed: Sustenance and power. It knew exactly where to go.

---

While the Dead God of Alex Granger's demented dreams was resting inside of its host, life went on inside Cherry Hill. So did death.

The medical center inside of the facility was overrun with poisoned patients and Jonathan Crowley was running around like he owned the place. Carl Branaugh was staying busy, handling the processing of Don Michaels and Marianne Hambly, both of whom were seemingly in a state of shock. Michaels couldn't believe he'd beaten a man half to death and was trying his best to apologize for it. Neither Branaugh nor Roger Finney wanted to hear any of it.

Roger tried to be understanding. He knew the sort of pressure the jobs at Cherry Hill could cause, but he wasn't willing to be gentle with either of the people who were under his charge. He wasn't in the mood to be gentle anymore.

Several of the doctors working under him were starting to show more disrespect than he was accustomed to. Not in big ways, but in small gestures and comments that they didn't think he noticed.

The worst of the lot was Phil Harrington, who was looking a little too smug lately. Roger knew why he was looking that way, too. He'd already received a phone call from William Coltraine, the head of the supervisory board for the institute. There was going to be a review of protocols and procedures, which was a nice way of saying that the shit was about to hit the fan. He hadn't had a chance to write his resignation, but he was fairly sure they'd be asking for it. Too much had happened under his command and the chances were good they'd want to use him as a scapegoat.

Roger dealt with his part of the reports involved in the cases, including firing both of the employees. Should either of them manage to avoid jail time through some miracle, they would not have a job to come back to.

Then he headed for his office, mostly to avoid any more conflicts and to finish the paperwork that had been on his desk for the last few days.

He settled down in his chair, picked up his pen and died of a massive coronary two minutes after he'd started. It was several hours later when his body was found.

By then the worst of it was over.

---

Jonathan Crowley sat perfectly still for a long time, his mind going over the ramifications of what he now knew. A living entity that could consume the dead was not exactly the normal fare, even for him.

Amelia sat in the room with him, and made as little noise as she could manage as she kept sorting through the papers he'd brought back from the attic.

She cleared her throat before actually speaking and he looked her way, less annoyed than she was expecting. "I've got listings for where the bodies were buried here, Jonathan. And I've also got receipts made out to Dr. A. Miles for disposal of "unwanted children." Do you suppose that means he took them to an orphanage?"

"Well, I'd hope so." He rose from his bed and stretched. "So, let's go over what we know, shall we?" His voice went into what she thought of as lecture mode: His tones subdued and almost questioning even when he was stating a fact. "We have a living entity that is breaking most of the rules. It's dealing with the dead and the living and doesn't seem to understand either very well."

"How can it do that?"

"Well, that's what we're trying to figure out. As a starting point, I think part of the problem is location. There are a lot of pent-up emotions in this place and mostly they're negative. So, strong negative energies allow it to fester unnoticed. I think what we're dealing with is young and inexperienced but only because a lot of what has happened seems more experimental than deliberately cruel."

"How so?"

Jonathan looked at her, his face still calm. "For starters, it manifested a dead body. I don't think it created it, so much as pulled it from somewhere and tried to figure out how it worked. We still don't have an ID on the corpse, but the clothes were old. Then I saw it try to make a new body of its own and fail. Then it tried at least one more time and failed. So, trying to generate a form it can use, but without much success. I think we can be grateful for that, by the way."

Amelia frowned, thought about asking a question and changed her mind. He was on a roll and it was best to just listen and ask questions when he slowed down again.

"Now then, it's been hungry. We can see the evidence of that. I saw the ghosts it had attacked and we've both seen what was left of a few of the people it either consumed, played with or both. It's also playing with trying to understand human emotions and sensations, as evidenced by what it did to you and by the two hours or so where everyone in this place got pissy out of the blue."

"You think it was manipulating minds?"

"Absolutely," Crowley nodded his head enthusiastically. "You felt it yourself before it attacked you."

"So why weren't you affected?"

"I probably was. I'm still trying to sort out a lot of different experiences from my past in my own head. So, frankly, I probably wouldn't have noticed much of a difference. On the other hand, we had a nurse go crazy and a couple of guards try to beat each other to death from what I was hearing in the hallways."

"But I—"

"You were too busy recovering. I sedated you through the worst of it."

She nodded again and shut up, aware that he was starting to get impatient. He wanted to finish his train of thought.

"We know it took energies from ghosts, we know it took at least mass from several living victims. In one case, it took something from a patient on my list to be watched. It took a lot of power. You took some of that away and I took it from you." He shot her a look that dared her to argue with what he'd done and she chose not to give him a reason to lose his temper. She understood why. He didn't have to remind her that she wasn't exactly human.

"That leaves two people with the same sort of potential, and I think one of them might actually be hosting this thing." He moved over to the stacks of paperwork and started tossing files aside until he found what he was looking for. "Alexander Granger and Paul Cioffi, his fingertip tapped a written note he'd made for himself on the files. "One of them is probably responsible for this, or at least connected. The other is likely going to be a target for this thing, because they both have a lot of power, and it needs to get back what was taken. It probably won't try for you again, and even if it does, this room is warded, so you're safe in here. As for me, well, let's just say I've had at least a couple of run-ins with whatever this thing is and I think it's going to be careful around me."

Jonathan hadn't mentioned any previous encounters, but he wouldn't have. It wasn't his style.

"So you need to find Paul Cioffi and Andrew Granger?"

"Alexander, but close enough. Yes. Once I've done that, I think I can solve this as long as whatever it is doesn't get what it wants in time. If I can find it inside its host, I might be able to keep it there."

"Okay, so what happened outside yesterday, when the walls flickered?"

"Ah. Now that is the part that has me worried. I don't know if it was trying to break down the barriers between the living and the dead or if it was causing some sort of temporal disruption, but either way, it can't be a good thing."

"How bad would those cases be?"

"No barrier between life and death would be devastating. All those mean old ghosts would start feeding on the living and in a few weeks or maybe as much as a month, there probably wouldn't be much left alive. Temporal rifts? Well, time isn't meant to be repeated and the damage would probably be localized, but it would also be a bad thing. Bad as in anything from dinosaurs eating people to whatever the future holds coming back here to try to fix previous mistakes. In the long run, it would sort itself out, but there would probably be a lot of damage in the meantime. Either way, I'm supposed to stop that sort of thing from happening."

"Right. Bad enough."

"Exactly. Not necessarily end of the world, but up there on the list of potential disasters." That said Jonathan headed for the door to their shared office.

"So I'm supposed to stay here?"

He nodded and waved instead of speaking.

Amelia sat alone in the room and rested. He'd forced sleep on her before and it had helped, but now she wanted a chance to rest her mind. It seemed that trauma could be wearying. As she'd been sheltered for a good portion of her life, she hadn't had too much actual experience with the sensation. Given a preference, she'd avoid it in the future.

---

He'd just left his makeshift office when he ran into Phil Harrington.

"John! Just the man I wanted to see."

"What can I do for you, Doc?" He did his best to act cheerful instead of sarcastic. It wasn't easy.

"I need to run a few tests, if I can. I need to check your vital statistics and do a couple of x-rays."

"It's going to have to wait, Doc. I have things I need to do first."

"Jonathan, it's not exactly a request." The man stepped in front of him and placed a hand on his chest. Most people would have received a broken wrist, but John felt a certain affection for the doctor, despite his butchery of a few patients' minds.

"My answer hasn't changed. This time tomorrow, if you want to look me over, I think I can pencil it in the old daily planner, but for now, I have to deal with stopping something bad from happening." He stepped past the man again.

"John, don't make me call the guards."

"Dr. Harrington, don't make me stop the guards. I told you, tomorrow."

Sure enough, as John started walking again, Harrington bellowed, "Guards!" and along they came, five men in front of him and five more at the far end of the hallways behind him. He could hear them moving into position.

"Doc, I really am getting a little tired of this."

"John, you're delusional. Believe me, this is for the best."

So far the guards were simply standing at the ready, including the pudgy man he'd had a run in with a while back. Most of them looked perfectly willing to cave his skull in if they were given the order, but for now, they were patient. The group in front of him had out batons, and one of them was carrying a straitjacket that Crowley would have bet money was meant for him. Like as not the group behind him was similarly equipped.

"Okay, Doc. Let's try this one more time. I'm willing to barter. Let me have two hours, and then you can do whatever it is you want to do."

"No, John, I'm sorry, but I can't do that. Please hand over the keys that Dr. Finney gave you and come along peacefully. I don't want to see you hurt."

Crowley smiled. "I don't want to see me hurt, either. But I'm not going with you."

Harrington nodded his head curtly and stepped back four paces. That must have been the signal because the guards came from both directions, and they looked determined to take him down.

They wore riot armor, thick pads that would reduce any impacts to their bodies. They also wore helmets and at least a few of them had guns.

"Doc, I really wish you hadn't done that."

Harrington was looking pretty confident. He had every reason to look that way, or at least that's what he thought.

John reached out and grabbed his arm. Before Harrington could do more than let out a squawk, Crowley had an arm around his throat and his body positioned as a perfect shield against almost any attack.

"John! What are you doing?"

"I told you I can't go with you now, Doc. I meant it. Call off the goons or you're going to get hurt when they start swinging."

"John, the guards here know the situation." His voice was shaking, and Harrington's body was tensed up in anticipation of a potential beating. "You're considered a danger, and their first priority will always be to stop you from escaping."

"Listen, nothing personal, but isn't Finney supposed to be my doctor now?"

"Not yet. He hasn't made the transfer request." Oh, the venom in those words. Harrington was pissed off about the whole situation.

"I get it. You just don't like losing a patient."

"What? That's nonsense."

"Really? What were you planning, a lobotomy or just something more mundane?" Crowley was smiling now as the guards came closer, his voice lowered to a whisper. The way Harrington twitched told him he was closer to right than he wanted to think about. "You're a sick man, Philly. You really are. What makes you think I wouldn't recover from whatever you did to me?"

The guards stopped ten feet away from John and the good doctor. Their faces were all different but wore the same expression John had seen in several wars. They were resigned to taking him down, regardless of the cost.

John took several slow, deep breaths, waiting for one of the guards to step closer. Finally, a foot moved forward and he spun, hurling the good doctor with all of his might. Harrington let out a wail and flapped his arms madly, as if he might finally learn to fly. Three of the guards flinched and the other two tried to catch the man.

Both guards and the doctor fell on their collective asses, and that was when John made his break for it.

The guards were ready. Two of them moved forward to block his passage, lifting their clubs and swinging at his head like it was the start of baseball season. John caught the one on his left across his forearm and received a solid bruising but avoided a concussion. The one on his right he blocked properly, knocking the baton away from the hand carrying it. His elbow caught the guard in the unprotected part of his face, and he winced both at the sudden pain and at the sound of the man's face breaking. He didn't want to hurt the guards more than he had to, but he also had no intention of letting them beat him down.

The guards didn't seem to have the same qualms. One of them smashed the back of his thigh with a club. He'd been aiming for the knee and missed. That was a good thing for John, because it also put the man in the right position for a kick to the side of his head. The helmet might have stopped any injuries, but the impact was enough to send the man reeling backward.

Harrington tried to untangle himself from the guards he'd bowled over, and Crowley shot a knee into the man's head hard enough to knock him senseless. The falling doctor successfully kept the two who'd caught him too busy to bother with John for a moment. That only left seven men intent on beating him to death. The next one apparently played a little too much football back in the day. He let out a bellow and jumped into the air. Crowley caught him in mid-leap and used his own momentum to introduce him to the closest wall.

That left a small opening, and Crowley used it, jumping over the doctor and the guards and landing on the other side of the group. Not surprisingly, they decided to give chase. Crowley ran hard, moving for the main entrance of the building. He had no intention of leaving just now, but if they decided to follow, that was fine with him.

The main lobby was simply laid out: there were a few chairs for people who might be waiting to visit a family member—normally they were empty—and there was a large island of a desk where the security guard sat. The usual guard wasn't there, but another man had taken his place and was busily reading a newspaper.

He didn't look up when Crowley came by, which was a testimony to the man's ability to move quietly. John crouched at the front of the man's desk and waited for the guards to come storming through. And come they did, running as best they could in their heavy riot gear and calling out for him to stop.

The guard at the desk turned to look at them and lowered his newspaper, obscuring John's view. John reached out, grabbed the offending collection of articles and threw it to the side. The guard turned fast and stared at him.

"BOO!" The man did not, despite Crowley's wishes, immediately faint dead away. "Eh, it was worth a try."

"What are you doing?"

"Escaping from the bad men with weapons."

By that point the guards were moving around the island, ready to pounce again. John stood and stepped onto the desk itself. His foot punted the confused doorman in the face and then he was moving again, running over the top of the island and back the way he'd come from.

One of the guards had tried to outsmart him and stayed back, ready for anything Crowley tried. He drew the pistol from his side and started to take aim. John jumped, clearing the rest of the large desk, and kicked him in the chest for all he was worth. The guard hit the ground hard, and his revolver followed a second later.

John ran again looking for a proper way to get rid of his local lynch mob. Adrenaline hummed through his system and he had to admit he liked the feeling.

Up ahead he saw one of the doors for the stairs and he dug into his pocket to grab his keys. There were only two keys on the thing, one for the stairs and one for his office. With his typical luck, he got the wrong one first and wasted thirty valuable seconds trying to fit it into a lock it was never designed to work for.

Two of the guards reached him before he could get the door open. The first one was fast and hit him in the ribs. The second was a bit slower, and John blocked the blow before he could take another cheap shot. The time for playing was over, and the rest of the guards were closing in fast. The arm he'd used to block slid up to catch the guard's wrist, and he twisted it hard, snapping the bones. The man let out a roar of pain and Crowley punched him lightly in the Adam's apple. The blow didn't kill the man, but it left him gagging.

The other guard didn't waste any time swinging again. The club bounced off John's shoulder as he tried to duck. The advantage of wearing padded armor is, of course, that your most sensitive areas are protected. That meant he didn't have time to beat the guard into submission, so instead he shattered the man's kneecap and then pushed him aside. As the man screamed, Crowley opened the door and then closed it as fast as he could. He was already on the ground level. The only choices were up or down. He chose to descend, as that was the direction he'd planned on going anyway. If he was lucky, he could find both of the men he was looking for and put an end to the growing dangers. If not, he'd have to play it by ear.

# Chapter Twenty-One

It left Alex Granger's body on a mission, determined to consume the last of the Seeds and to finally manifest itself, one way or another. It had the knowledge, or so it believed, and it would soon have the power. Now all it needed was the raw materials, and that would be easily enough handled.

Paul Cioffi rested in his cell. One touch was all it needed to know the man's name and a great deal of his history as well. One touch was not enough to satisfy it.

It delved into Cioffi's mind and body, ripping away what it needed.

---

The guards came fast, thundering down the stairs after him, and Jonathan Crowley shook his head, resigned to doing what he had to do. He waited at the bottom of the stairs, knowing full well that in an enclosed area he would have the advantage. Six guards came toward him in a near stampede, with remarkably little thought about what they were facing. The first one went down with a loud expulsion of air as Crowley landed a blow across his sternum that was hard enough to ignore the padded armor. Crowley caught the club in the man's hand as he fell and brought it across the face of the second in line before the first guard even hit the landing. He didn't have time to play by honorable rules, not if he wanted to stop whatever it was that was trying to take over the asylum.

Guard number three got stupid and tried for a jump over the two unconscious obstacles in his way. Crowley spun him down to the next level for his troubles. The man made several loud noises as he fell. He also failed to get back up.

The remaining guards stopped where they were to consider the situation and Crowley smiled for them. "Come on, boys. I'm on a schedule here. Either come and take your lumps or run home to momma." He spoke the words and knew they were a mistake, but damn, it felt good to be active again instead of just stuck in the same room and waiting.

They rushed him. John stepped back to give himself as much room as possible as the three men stepped over their fallen cohorts and came in swinging. One of them, he couldn't tell which, got a solid blow across the side of his head and neck. His ear felt like it had been carved free. He used his newly acquired stick to return the favor, shattering one man's front teeth in the process. The other two kept pounding away and he did his best to block them, but his speed was limited by the area he was working in and in the end he had to go on the offensive. He took a strike to the left arm at the same time he was breaking his baton against the helmet of one of the guards: the helmet broke with the baton and the guard kissed the floor. Then he started fighting dirty again and slapped his fingers across the remaining guard's eyes. The man let out a yelp and reached to protect himself. Crowley had to hit him four times before he fell.

All of the men wore handcuffs on their belts. He used them to bind the men together and left them behind as he went down the last flight of stairs and stepped over the one he'd thrown earlier. The man was dead, his neck bent at an angle that guaranteed he would not be getting back up.

He hadn't wanted to leave any permanent injuries, but they'd left him no real choice.

As he opened the door to the dungeon he heard the screams and realized that he'd blown it. Whatever was going to happen was apparently already taking place.

---

Kimberly was off for a few days. Whatever she'd seen had bothered her a lot, and that meant someone else had to do the dirty work. Mary

Gerber was not the sort to make somebody else do something she wouldn't do herself and now and then she liked to prove that point, so she took over in the Dungeon. She wasn't happy about it. There was too much weirdness going on lately for her to be happy. She was seriously considering looking into working at the Riverside Hospital. There would be a pay cut, but the odds were good that it wouldn't be a huge reduction, and she wouldn't have to deal with nearly as much insanity.

She barely knew either of the men on the floor with her, so mostly they worked in silence. They didn't seem overly impressed with her and the feeling was mutual, but despite the tension between her and the two orderlies, she was comforted by their presence. Touching the men in the Dungeon was like touching freshly dead corpses in her opinion: they were creepy and no matter how often they were cleaned, she could almost feel the diseases on their bodies. She'd never understand how Kimberly could put up with them.

She moved from one patient to the next on automatic pilot, not bothering to see their faces, merely reading the lists of medications and then feeding them, cleaning them and doping them. The faster she finished, the happier she'd be.

Next up was Paul Cioffi. According to his file he was a sexual offender with a history of violence that went back for over two decades. He was also, happily, another of the lifeless husks. Her little sister had been raped years ago and while she'd recovered physically, she was never quite the same afterward. She was withdrawn to the point of becoming a spinster at the age of twenty-seven. So it didn't bother her at all that the man she had to deal with was "unresponsive to stimuli and no longer a threat."

Cioffi was looking straight at her as the door opened and she stepped inside. He was on his hands and knees, his face strained in a silent scream, and a large red lump was swelling on his back.

The air was too dry, like a baked Arizona desert, and the hairs on the man's head stood away from his scalp as if charged with electricity. Mary looked at the man's agonized face and let out a gasp as something inside of him popped wetly. There were *things* moving under his skin. Long snakelike shapes slithered around his legs and arms, crawled through his neck. Then as it progressed, they slid into his face, distorting it even more.

He was supposedly beyond help. According to the file he was as functionally intelligent as a tree stump, but she saw intelligence in his eyes and panic and pain as well.

Mary stood still for several seconds, trying to absorb the details of what was happening in front of her. Almost twenty years of working at Cherry Hill had shown her a lot of unusual things, but she'd never seen a man warping before her eyes.

Cioffi looked at her and opened his mouth—perhaps to let out a scream, because damn, whatever was happening to him looked painful—and she saw something black moving up his throat, filling his mouth, spilling past his teeth. When she saw the same obsidian stuff come out of his nostrils and then fill his eyes, she finally moved, backing away and shrieking as she watched, horrified.

The two fine young orderlies who'd been assigned to her for protection had already started running. She couldn't blame them.

Before she made five paces, the door to the stairwell slammed open and a man she'd seen a few times came storming in her direction. His face was lowered, his eyes raised and the florescent lights highlighted several growing bruises on his face. He didn't even bother with looking at her, but instead ran past her toward the room where Cioffi was dying.

The man stopped dead in his tracks at the door and shook his head, his lips peeling back in a feral grin. "Well, isn't that just something?"

"Excuse me?" She had no idea why she answered him. Even in her current state she could see that he was talking to himself.

The man didn't bother with answering her, but instead started speaking in a foreign language that made her ears ring and her head hurt. Languages had always been a hobby of Mary's. She spoke Latin, French, Spanish, German, and English fluently and also had a working knowledge of Yiddish and Japanese. None of the words he spoke sounded like anything she'd ever heard.

Before he could finish whatever it was he was saying, Paul Cioffi flew through the open door to his cell and smashed into the man. He fell backward and slumped to the ground his eyes gone wide and his mouth hanging slackly for a moment. Then, disgusted, he shoved the remains aside and stood back up.

Cioffi looked like someone had taken a blow-up doll and filled it with bones, but hadn't bothered with actual inflation. His mouth gaped, his eye sockets glared, and his leathery skin hung loosely over what little remained inside of him. What was left of him broke as it hit the ground, and the man moved in her direction, his eyes looking at each cell.

"Where's the other one?" He focused on her and she wanted to run, but decided it might be safest to answer his questions.

"Where's the other what?"

"Damn it, what's the name? Granger! Where is Alexander Granger?"

"He's been moved to the ICU."

"That's just lovely. Show me the way." The man was smiling. She didn't figure Jack the Ripper would have managed a nastier expression on his face.

Mary nodded and headed for the stairwell. He put a hand on her shoulder and shook his head. "Not that one. It's a little crowded."

"There's only one stairway up from here."

"Well then, ignore the guards and walk fast."

They moved up three flights of stairs, the first one had a corpse on it. Mark Haley. Mary let out a gasp and felt the man breathing behind her as he almost collided with her frozen body.

"He's dead!"

"Yeah. I'll feel bad about it later. Right now, get your ass in gear, woman!"

She looked back at the stranger and shivered. His eyes were locked on her face. His expression was the same as before, a wild grin that made her feel almost feverish.

She steeled herself and led the way, running past the bloodied men on the landing. They were alive, at least. That was something. She didn't think she could take too many more surprises.

She moved as quickly as she could up the stairs, all too aware of the man directly behind her, and halfway convinced that he would attack while she wasn't looking.

Riverside Hospital had never seemed like a better idea.

---

Power echoed through it, shattering perceptions and illuminating possibilities. Its senses had expanded, as if it had just opened its eyes for the very first time.

Godhood was now more than a concept. It was a possibility. Rather than hide itself away, it moved through the entire structure of Cherry Hill, fusing with the atoms of the walls, and even the air.

Physical laws that it only now began to fully comprehend limited Alex Granger. It saw the living as they moved through Cherry Hill and it saw the dead as well, watched as they moved around and through each other without any notion of what it was they moved among.

The old man who had grown young was moving closer to Alex's body, and that was not acceptable. It needed to understand even more than it did now and it needed time.

The once old man was not going to afford it that luxury; it could sense the troubles that he would cause given the opportunity. As much as it had grown and changed, it still regarded the lessons it had already learned and opted for caution. The woman had taught it that what it had taken for itself could be taken away.

So it decided to change the rules, to keep the old man from Alex if possible.

The question was how.

It looked carefully at the environment it existed in and discovered something new, something that simply had not existed in its limited experience before. And in studying, it learned a new trick.

The answer was simpler than it ever would have dreamed.

---

Everything was going along just fine, right up until the time the stairs changed and both Crowley and the nurse he was following fell on their faces. One second they were ready to put their feet on the next step and then the stair dropped by almost two inches. Both were moving fast; neither of them caught the change in the stairs before it was too late. Their shocked exclamations merged into one as they lost the struggle to keep their balance.

Mary Gerber struck her head hard when she landed and let out a groan as blood started welling from her scalp. John was faster to recover and caught himself with his hands instead of his face. He pushed back into a standing position and looked at the stairs below him. Somebody with a great special effects budget had gone and changed reality when he wasn't looking. The metallic stairs they'd been on were gone, replaced by wooden risers that looked old enough to collapse at any moment.

The air temperature dropped abruptly enough to let him see the condensation from his breath. "Oh, shit."

John grabbed Nurse Bloodyskull and hauled her over his shoulder as he started moving again, his eyes focused heavily on the steps now, instead of whatever was ahead of him. As he feared, the steps changed again, reverting to metal and a couple of inches higher than they were a second before.

"Shit, shit, shit, shit, shit!" He ran faster and finally made it to the landing as the walls started to shimmer. Opening the door with a slightly pudgy nurse on his back wasn't easy, but he managed. A moment later he was in the hallway on the third floor and carefully setting the unconscious woman aside as the strange fluctuations he'd seen a moment earlier intensified.

Odd patches of the ground under his feet and the walls around him shifted as he stood still and tried to assess what was going on. The patches seemed to be fairly stable: they moved, and the areas within them were affected, but as soon as the bubble-like fields shifted, everything was back to what it was supposed to be. Wherever the dislocations appeared, the walls changed from Drywall to wood, but it was more than that. Cell doors were transformed, and even the décor. A blank part of the white walls of the asylum might be replaced momentarily with a doorway or a portrait, only to reappear a moment later. The floors were pulling the same stunt, switching from linoleum to hardwood.

He wasn't the only one to notice, either. Down the hallway a man was staring at the wall with abject fascination, now and then poking his finger into the field of distortion to see what would happen. So far he hadn't managed to get himself hurt, but Crowley guessed it wouldn't take too long.

The damned thing was screwing with the laws of physics, pulling the barriers between the living and the dead apart. John's adrenaline kicked in, making his legs twitch with pent up energy, and just as quickly as it had started, the flickering stopped. The floor was linoleum again, not the hardwood he'd expected to see. John looked around hurriedly, trying to decide where to search for Alexander Granger. As far as he could tell, the man was the only possible connection left between the living hungry ghost and the real world.

Crowley spared one last glance at the injured nurse and then left her behind as he started looking for his new target. Down the corridor, the moron playing with the odd patches got a surprise: the wall in front of him shifted and revealed a doorway. The difference here was profound in that the door was open, not closed.

"I wouldn't do that!" Crowley bellowed as loudly as he could to catch the fool's attention, but he was too late. The man's testing finger poked into the open entrance of the door that hadn't been there a moment before, even as he looked toward John with an annoyed expression.

A moment later, two scabrous arms reached out and grabbed at the questing digit. One second later the man let out a scream as he was pulled into the darkness, straining hard as soon as the pale fingers caught his skin.

John watched it all, still too far away to help and too busy even if he were closer. The pallid hands caught human flesh and sank in like fangs, drawing blood even as they found purchase. Whatever was on the other side of the door was far stronger than the unprepared man and he was halfway through the threshold before he could actually respond. Worse still for the surprised victim, the rift between the living and the dead was still in motion. Over half of his body was through the doorway before it moved on. What had not made it into the opening stopped at the wall and slid down in a thick wash of blood.

The doorway vanished as the distortion moved on, leaving most of one leg and part of the other from the knee down.

"I don't have time for this." Crowley turned away from the sight and started moving, looking through the shifting plains of reality to see if he could find the medical center or even a sign pointing the way.

The only good news was that the rifts were too small to let much get through.

Crowley finally spotted the doors to the medical center a few feet past where the bright boy had gotten himself cut in half. He looked at the locks on the double steel doors and shook his head. "Perfect!" he spat the word and shook his head. "Can we have something go right here? Just for the change of pace, please?"

As if in answer to his request, one of the orderlies on the other side opened the door to see who was screaming. "Thanks!" Crowley took one step into the open door at the same time that he knocked the man unconscious. "Nothing personal."

The splits in the universe didn't continue over into the medical center, and he had to guess that meant he was getting closer to his goal. It made sense: if Granger was, in fact, responsible for whatever was happening, he wasn't likely to risk his health in the process of defending himself.

What he hadn't counted on was the number of patients already in the rooms or the number of people who'd just seen him knock one of their coworkers unconscious.

Several people looked at him, and not a one of them looked the least bit intimidated.

"Well, this just keeps getting better and better."

---

It stared at the remains of a man who had reached into the darkness of the dead realm and pondered the implications. Somehow one of the ghosts had grabbed the man, touched the man and killed him. It hadn't thought the dead and living could interact, but now it knew better. The problem seemed to be a barrier that kept them apart. It had broken that barrier by accident: a side effect of trying to be in both worlds at the same time.

It hadn't realized that the barrier existed on a conscious level, mostly because the barrier didn't keep it from coming and going as it pleased.

This is interesting. This has potential.

The Dead God looked upon the bleeding, dying man of flesh as he was attacked and brutally beaten by a dead man who had no real memories of being alive. It had seen that particular ghost on several occasions and left it alone merely because its antics had always been interesting. Whatever mind the ghost had was damaged, and most times it simply walked around its cell and called out to things that were not there. Now, when faced with a living thing, the ghost had attacked, shrieking and flailing its rotting arms until it managed to kill the living being. And as soon as the living man was dead and his spirit was set free from the damaged flesh, it attacked again, pounding at the newly dead man until there was little left that was recognizable.

The once old man caught the Dead God's attention as he wandered into the area where Alex Granger rested. Once again fear touched it, frosted its soul and left it wondering what it should do.

It decided to wait and see if the once old man could survive the surprise it had made.

In the meantime, there were other things to consider, other challenges to deal with. It wanted a new body, needed a new body if it wished to interact properly with the world of the living.

It would have hidden away to accomplish the task in the past but with power came confidence. It merely started working, designing a body it knew would survive and flourish, focusing in the area it knew most intimately.

If all went well, a Dead God would soon walk the earth.

# Chapter Twenty-Two

Phillip Harrington sat in the break room and nursed his black eye. Crowley hadn't hurt him nearly as much as landing against the guard's knee, but the end result was the same. Either way he blamed his patient. *Ludicrous! How could it be so damned hard to catch one man inside a locked building?*

Well, the answer was easy enough: The man in question had a key given to him by a supervisor who had lost his mind. No one was talking to Phil and that was just fine with him. He needed to think for a while, to gather his nerve and head off with another squad of guards. This time, he'd make sure they were properly equipped. When in doubt, tranquilizer darts should do the job of restraining John Crowley.

He'd have to talk with the head of security about that.

The ice against the side of his face was making his bruised skin numb and his nose runny. He set down the icepack and reached for a napkin. His hand slipped right through the table and the tissue paper.

Phil looked for several heartbeats, stunned, and slowly withdrew his limb from the Formica. There was something there, a faint shimmering spot, like heat radiating off the road, and his hand had gone through it.

"I've been working too hard." He closed his eyes and then looked again. The shimmer was gone and the table was where it belonged. He reached down again and touched solid plastic and paper.

He took care of blowing his nose and wadded up the tissue. Off to his left one of the guards who'd come through the fight with minimal damage was limping over to the coffee urn they'd set up in the break room. He made it halfway there before he disappeared.

This time Phil didn't think he was imagining things. No, he thought he was losing his mind. He stood up immediately and walked over to the spot where the guard had been. The guard still adamantly refused to be there.

There were five other people in the room with him (six if you counted the disappearing man) and they were all engaged in conversations. He didn't give a good damn.

"Did anyone else just see that?" His tone demanded an answer.

Two off duty nurses, an administrator and two orderlies all looked up from where they were sitting together and stared at him blankly. Finally, one of the nurses—a rather slow-witted example of her species named Betty Somers—shook her head and offered a puzzled frown. "See what, Dr. Harrington?"

"There was a guard right here. He vanished."

Miles Bronski from accounting shook his head. "Maybe he just left?"

"No, Miles, I saw him disappear."

In most places that sort of declaration would have gotten nervous laughter at best. At Cherry Hill the average response was a sudden case of the jitters.

"Are you sure?" Miles was trying to be rational.

"Yes, I'm sure. I was looking right at him!"

The air between Phil and the other group suddenly blurred again. The odd smudginess was strange enough and unsettling to boot, but the fact that all five people and the table they were sitting at suddenly vanished from sight didn't make it any easier to accept.

All five people were still there. He could tell by the way they started calling his name in a panic.

Phil was never all that curious a man when it came to unusual phenomena. He made it a point to ignore strange events whenever he ran across them, actually. So he didn't touch the strange, smudgy spot. Instead, he backed away from it. That was the wise choice: a moment later the guard came stumbling back out of thin air and fell on his face as he hit the floor.

Phil backed away again, eyes wide and heart hammering, as the man slumped across the ground. The guard's skin was the wrong color, several shades too light, and his eyes were wide open. Professional ethics pushed his fear out of the way and Phil stooped down to make sure the man was even alive. He wasn't. Wherever he'd gone, whatever had happened, it had killed him.

"Phil! Are you all right?" That was the nurse, who seldom called him by his first name. He looked in her direction and opened his mouth to speak just as the distortion moved out of his view.

"I'm fine, but the guard is dead." He wanted to scream and run, but he couldn't. Somebody had to be in charge of the situation and it looked like he was that somebody.

He stood back up, swaying a bit as his blood pressure changed to accommodate the sudden motion. The nurse screamed. So did Miles from accounting. So did the other three.

Phil looked their way again and felt the hairs on the back of his neck lift. "What is it?"

A second later he understood: What he'd thought was a shift in his blood pressure was actually a shift in reality. He stood perfectly still and looked down to where his body just...ended four feet off the ground. Below that point he could see nothing: the shimmering distortion prevented it. He looked back at the group, his eyes wide and his mouth hanging open as if he were a fish.

Logic demanded that he carefully assess the situation. He could feel his legs and his midsection. He knew that he was standing on solid ground. The air around his lower half felt odd, thick and cold, but he could feel. That meant he wasn't actually cut in half, he just looked like he was.

"What should I do?" He stayed still, not certain if moving would cause a problem. The weird blurring was moving slowly around him, like a patch of pollen moving on the surface of a mostly still river.

Miles moved closer, his eyes looking to the ground and then back up to Phil's face several times.

"I don't know, Phil. I don't think being where you are is a good place to be." He resisted the urge to start swinging at the man. "Just stay where you are and see if it goes away on its own?"

"That's sort of what I'm thinking, too." That from an orderly he couldn't remember ever meeting before.

"I think I agree," he added. Forcing himself to take several deep breaths. "I don't think I'm hurt, just…not all here." He could hear the tremble in his voice. "Oh God, where am I if I'm not here?"

Crowley's comments came back to haunt him: the living and the dead coexisting in the same space, seldom able to see each other until he threw his powder into people's eyes. He wanted to believe that this was all part of the same hallucination, but there were five people looking at him who said otherwise and there was a dead man at his feet—wherever they might be at the moment. He bit the inside of his mouth to stop himself from getting hysterical.

Something touched his left leg not far from his groin, and a shriek slipped past Phil's lips before he could stop it.

"What happened?" Miles was trying, God love him, but he couldn't see a way to get closer. The distorted air looked like it was finally starting to move on: the shimmer in the air in front of him seemed smaller. He wanted to look behind him to confirm that, but was afraid to move. What if by moving he separated his two halves like an assistant locked in a magician's box?

Phil tried to answer but couldn't. He was breathing too fast, starting to hyperventilate. Instead, he shook his head even as whatever touched his leg moved around, as if examining the shape of him: blindly groping out a Braille map of what he might look like.

"Phil, calm down. Deep breaths, okay?" He nodded and tried to concentrate on his breathing, instead of the panic that was rampaging through his body as whatever was touching him kept moving. Long, cold fingers seemed to run across his scrotum and down his other leg with spidery caresses.

Finally, when he could speak, he answered Miles. "I think something touched me, but I think it's going away." His shuddery speech was infuriating, showed a lack of control that he hated. Happily, no one was saying anything about it or mocking him.

His leg seemed to catch fire. One second it was fine, if a little cold and the next it felt like his bones were being filled with molten lead. The pain was too much to allow him even to scream. So instead he tried pulling his leg away. Tried and failed. He couldn't move his leg at all, couldn't do anything but feel the hideous sensation of something bad happening. He half expected to smell the roasting meat, but there were no changes in scent, in the sight, or anything else. A moment later he couldn't even think about anything beyond the inferno consuming every nerve in his lower limb. Finally he managed to draw in a breath and scream for all that he was worth.

The people in the room with him screamed too, all except Miles, who moved into the distortion and grabbed his arm. Miles pulled at him, throwing his weight into the motion, and hauled him away from the shimmering pool in the air.

The pain didn't go away, but it lessened as Phil stumbled forward. Though the shimmer was past him, he could feel a resistance, almost as if he were caught on the edge of a pool and being lifted from the waters. The pressure scraped along his stomach, his groin and finally his legs. When he felt it on the one that felt like it was burning he almost passed out. Finally, after a few seconds and a lifetime or so, he hit the floor of the break room and stayed there, panting, trying to recover from the sensations. His leg was calmer at least, still painful, but not enough to make him scream.

"Oh, Jesus Christ!" Miles looked at Phil's lower half and paled.

Phil turned to see what the cause of the commotion was and felt his head grow light as he stared at the ruin of his lower extremity. He'd seen the same sort of damage before, on several people now, all of them dead. His leg looked like it had been held in the hands of a giant and squeezed into a new shape. The bone, if there was a bone left inside of the mess, must surely have been twisted into a lazy S.

Phil looked down at the ruin and moaned softly, unaware of the noise.

He wanted to speak, to tell himself and anyone who would listen that everything was fine, that the wound was an illusion, because that sort of thing could not happen in the rational world. He might have even managed it if the pain hadn't started again. This time it was all over his body, not just in his leg.

And as it started and he looked toward the accountant for help, he realized that no one in the room would give the least bit of a damn what he said.

Because as it started happening to him, he saw the same thing happen to every person in the room. No two were struck in quite the same way, but all of them fell to the ground and all of them let out the sounds of unspeakable pain. Body after body started to shift and bend as bits and pieces were torn away from them and devoured by something unseen.

Doctor Phillip Harrington and the rest of the people in the break room were either the luckiest souls in all of Cherry Hill or the most completely damned.

All of them lived through the attack.

None of them came out of it without crippling wounds to let them know they were still alive.

---

John looked around at the infirmary team and they in turn looked at him. Aside from the moans of a few patients stuck in the overloaded area, there was little to hear for a few seconds as everyone assessed the situation.

Finally, Crowley spoke. "So here's the deal. You don't want me here and I don't want to be here. You might be thinking about doing something bold, like calling security or tackling me yourselves, but I have to be honest: You don't have a chance. So, let me do what I have to do and then we can all go on our merry ways."

The speech worked as well as he expected. Two brawny interns made their tries for taking him down. They were doing their jobs and they were careful, so he did his best to avoid any permanent injuries when he knocked them unconscious.

The rest of the staff looked at the three unconscious men and decided to get away from the lunatic. He liked the way they thought. Well, except for one man who felt the need to pick up the phone and start dialing.

John moved over to where he was busily trying to dial on the rotary phone and pressed his finger over the disconnect button. "You need to not do that." His smile was pure venom and the man backed away with a startled flinch. For some insane reason he seemed to think standing in the middle of the nurse's station and grabbing the phone would go unnoticed. "I said I wanted to do my thing and leave. Let's not invite anyone else to our little get-together, okay?"

The man looked at him as if he'd just committed a social faux pas of epic scale. Crowley looked back until the idiot suddenly decided to look elsewhere. Just to make sure he got the point, John ripped the phone out of its mooring in the wall.

Mister Call-In-The-Troops started walking away and Crowley caught his shoulder. "Listen, let's make this easier on everyone involved. You point me to Alexander Granger, and I'll go ahead and leave a lot sooner."

"I can't do that." For such a weasel-looking individual, he spoke with a deep voice.

"Sure you can. See, if you do that, I'll leave sooner and everyone can go back to doing their own things. I'm not going to hurt Granger. I just want to see him."

"I'll have to come with you to make sure." Had any man ever dreaded speaking a few words so much? Crowley doubted it.

"Well, that's just fine with me." John tried to give him a winning smile. The man flinched again. Then the weasel led him over to one of the beds, where a much healthier looking man than Crowley remembered lay unconscious on the bed. Much healthier. Like fifteen pounds more flesh than he should have had and no sign of the atrocious surgery scars he remembered from before.

"Well, somebody's been busy making Mr. Granger all better." Crowley grabbed the medical charts and started reading the latest information on the man who'd piqued his interest. Red cell count was perfect. White blood cell count was perfect. Muscle mass was increased. His heart rhythm, pulse rate, blood pressure and every other vital statistic that was listed seemed to be in order. Hell, better than that. Physically he was as close to perfect as Crowley had ever seen.

He double-checked the name on the charts, just to make sure the weasel wasn't trying to pull a fast one. When he was sure it was Granger, John reached out to check the man's vitals himself. He never made contact. His hand stopped roughly five inches from his target and the air crackled where his fingertips hovered over flesh. Something was surrounding the man, protecting him from Crowley's touch.

Crowley backed up a bit and looked at the man on the bed more closely. "Well, that little bastard."

"Excuse me?"

John looked at Mr. Weasel and smiled. "Come here." Despite a slightly worried look the man came closer. "Touch him."

"What?"

"Touch the man on the bed."

"Why?"

"Humor me."

The man reached out and placed his hand on Alex Granger's arm.

Crowley nodded his head and looked around the room, carefully scanning the faces that were doing their best not to look like they were watching him. Then he reached out his hand again and tried to touch Granger. The same thing again, there was a pressure and then the air crackled. He pushed harder and the pain started, like fire ants biting down on his flesh. His skin began to cook and he pulled back, looking at the blackened flesh of his fingertips even as it healed.

The hungry ghost was learning new tricks. In this case it had made a duplicate of his very own wards and managed to attune them so that they affected him.

"One little problem with that, sunshine. I would never build something I couldn't tear down."

John placed his hand above Granger's head and spoke softly for a moment. He felt it when the ward collapsed and nodded his satisfaction.

A moment later the people in the medical ward started screaming.

It only took a second to understand why.

---

Most of the Dead God's attention was focused on building a new body. Even a few hours ago it would have been blind to what the old man had done, but not any more.

The ward it had created was gone, and much as it might have liked to do the same to the defenses it had imitated, it wasn't quite capable of that. Not yet at least.

Earlier it had learned that merely by observing, it could cause damage to the skin between the living and the dead. Now it actively concentrated on rupturing that barrier. The shift was easy and if it was lucky, the old man might be too distracted to stop it from finishing what it had started.

---

The change was abrupt and disorienting. One moment they were all locked in the darkness and the next there was light so powerful that it made their eyes ache.

The dead were not always aware of the living. Most of the ghosts of Cherry Hill remained in the same cells where they had lived their last, unaware in many cases that they had even died. Despite Jonathan Crowley's claims that the spirits in the asylum were mostly mere echoes, faint recollections and energies left by years of pain, many of the dead had more coherent thoughts than he imagined.

They were simply not sane thoughts. Simple math, really: crazy in life, crazy in death. They might not have all started out insane, but the dead of Cherry Hill were almost guaranteed to be psychotic. Death had not ended their mental imbalances; if anything, the time locked away within their own minds had distilled whatever dysfunctions they suffered.

For the first few moments, the dead were too stunned by the light to react. It was, in their long incarcerations, something that they had all but forgotten. They had little use for the light in the prisons of their own minds. As time passed, many of them had simply fallen into a stupor, a deep sleep that left them dormant. The Dead God had changed that a bit when it fed on them, but there were many who simply had no reason to respond, even when they became food for the unborn deity.

This, however, was something completely different: this was stimulus.

It was enough to wake them from their slumbers.

For some it was nearly a miracle. The sudden awakening let them remember things from their pasts, let them see that they were free from their wretched pasts, allowed at last to escape from the prisons that had killed them in life. For others, it was an annoyance, an awakening from the only peace they had ever known.

The dead woke from their long naps, and looked into the light with absolute fascination. They did not act in unison, but they did act. And this time around, the living noticed them.

---

The buildings that made up Cherry Hill had been built and rebuilt several times over the years. Originally there had only been the large wood and stone building where the central hub of the structure stood now. Over the course of time it was taken down and replaced with brick and stone. Later still, there were additions put in place and the hub was dismantled and rebuilt with three additional stories. As time went on, there were security additions put in place. More than one person working within the facility had joked about falling through the basement and into the older asylums buried below. Happily that wasn't the case. There were no substructures that were unknown and the newer buildings were all on the same ground level and in some cases even used the original foundations. A little digging here and refinishing there had taken care of that sort of problem.

That led to the odd changes in perception that the people in the asylum quickly became aware of: Little changes, like patches of building that no longer existed showing themselves through the newer structures and what happened to Clifford Donald Hummel. Cliff was a strong man-at least in his own slightly delusional mind—and a pious one as well. He believed that he led a righteous life and that the Lord watched out for him as a result of his piety.

In a perfect world, Cliff would have been playing for the Phillies and blasting a few hundred home runs out of Veteran Stadium every season. In the real world, he had just been promoted to head custodian of Cherry Hill. The only time he ever got to use his baseball bat these days was when he was smashing the heads and bodies of the occasional field mouse or rat he found wandering around the basement area. If he could kill them with one blow it was a home run. So far he'd managed about fifteen for the season. A lot of foul balls, too—where the little bastards crawled away after he wounded them—but you took the bad with the good and thanked the Lord for both if you were smart. Say Amen.

He took what he could and called himself lucky. At least the administrators were letting him keep his baseball bat around for just such unpleasant situations.

It was starting to seem like the season was going to be over earlier than he'd expected. He hadn't found a single living critter to smash in the last few days and he'd made it a point to go looking for them. Luck would be with him eventually and he'd find a few of the bastards where they belonged, but in the meantime, he decided it was time to check out the attic storehouses and clean them out properly. It took a few days but he'd gotten permission to clear the rooms of their potential fire hazards, which meant he had a damned fine excuse for killing a few critters. That they were paying him for it was a sweet bonus. Say Amen.

The day wasn't too hot when he got there and Cliff gave himself the hardest work assignment, which put the rest of the custodial staff grateful to their new boss. They got to handle the light work and cleaning and he got the hard tasks. He'd never minded heavy lifting; it kept him in shape for the ladies, right? Say Amen.

He'd been going strong for almost two hours. He hadn't actually thrown any of the boxes out, but he'd moved most of them and found a nice nest or two, of mice and rats alike. Only two home runs, but not a single foul yet. Not even the pinkies were fast enough to escape him and those things could move fast if they were scared. He could have done without the spiders, but the little fuckers were everywhere and impossible to escape. Say Amen.

Cliff sniffed the air and stalked his prizes like a bloodhound. The nests always smelled the same way and judging by the odor, he figured he must have hit the mother load when it came to colonies of vermin. In the far west corner there was a stack of boxes that he guessed hadn't been moved in over fifteen years, and the odor of rodent droppings was so pungent it almost made his eyes water. Say Amen.

His stomach fluttered with anticipation and nervous excitement. On the one hand, he hated mice and rats. On the other hand, he loved bashing their little bodies into bloody pulps. Besides, he was looking forward to at least doubling his home runs for the season.

The boxes were heavily mildewed and smelled of rotting paper. Even the outside of the corrugated paper containers had that nasty green powdery stuff on them. He pulled the first box off the stack carefully and grimaced at the stench of the nest down in the boxes below. It had been strong before, but now? It was like walking into a cave full of bats or something. He could hear the rustling of the nasty little buggers and felt the thrill of anticipation grow brighter inside of him.

The second box didn't come off the stack the way he wanted it to, and the cardboard container slid across the bottom and spilled its innards all over the front of his clothes and the floor directly in front of him.

"Motherfucker!" The papers that spilled out were not intact. Most of them had been chewed into new shapes by the mice that were now crawling all over his body. They squealed in protest as their home for at least a few generations crumbled all over him. The mice were on him, too, and his skin shivered with revulsion as the creatures used tiny claws to hold onto his clothing and to climb up his shivering form like his body was a big old tree and the ground below was a raging flooded river.

Cliff let out a decidedly girlish shriek of his own and stepped back, reaching for his Louisville slugger. "You little shits!" The creatures were everywhere, and while he knew there weren't really thousands of them moving all over him, it sure as shit felt that way. He swatted madly with his left hand even as his right claimed its prize. Furry little bodies, hot and squiggly, slid off his shirt and one tiny set of teeth sank into the web of flesh between his index and middle fingers, drawing a hot line of blood from inside him. Great! Now he had to worry about rabies, too!

Cliff looked down at the mice as they fell, some of them landing with the grace of cats and others bouncing like half-deflated rubber balls as they hit the cold stone floor.

He lifted his left leg and stomped hard, even as his right leg rose. His feet hit like hammers, smashing as many of the nasty little buggers as he could, his heart beating faster than he would have expected.

Finally, with the baseball bat held up and just over his right shoulder, he added his trusty weapon to the foray.

It should have been the most glorious day of his entire baseball season. Say Amen! Instead, the floor disappeared from under him and

Cliff let out another much louder scream as the mice, the files and Cliff himself all took a forty-five-foot plummet to the roof below.

In the world of the living, Cherry Hill was seven stories high in the hub and four stories elsewhere. In the realm of the dead the rules were a little different. The original structure that had been built on the land was still there, a ghost of the past as it were, and it was far more dilapidated. The Dead God was changing the rules of reality, and in the process, Cliff Hummel was the first living person deliberately thrown over from one reality to the other.

He crashed through the roof of the ancient structure and plummeted down another ten feet before the floor stopped him and the rain of vermin and papers that cascaded down with him. The impact shattered bones throughout his body and crushed half of his internal organs. The trauma done to his body should have killed him on the spot. At the very least, he should have been knocked unconscious as a result of shock.

Unfortunately for Cliff, the laws of reality were in flux. His body lay shattered and dying, his spirit lay with it, unable to break free of the mortal coil and proceed into death properly.

Cliff learned soon after his impact that the dead could scream. They were screaming even as they entered the ruined cell he'd broken through on his descent. They screamed as they crawled over him and touched him, unfamiliar after so many years of being locked in their own personal hells, with the notion of flesh and what it was for.

---

The walls shimmered. All around the medical ward, the air grew cold and the whitewashed surfaces changed, merging with the landmarks from the past as seen through the eyes of the insane. Barriers that were never meant to be breached weren't merely opened, but completely destroyed as the entity that Jonathan Crowley had tried to stop did exactly what he'd been afraid it would do and opened wide the proverbial gates of Hell.

The dead didn't come from a great distance, they simply appeared. Death was not kind to the dead. Many of them looked nearly normal, but the majority were broken things, wretched shadows of what they had been in life.

Somebody behind him let out a scream that was almost instantly echoed from a dozen living throats. The dead cringed at the sounds but did not flee. Misshapen forms looked toward the source of the sounds and studied them carefully. A few of the braver spirits moved closer, fascinated by whatever it was they saw when they looked at the living.

And then one of the things reached forward and struck Weasel in the side of his head. Had the dead thing known the man? Crowley had no idea. What he did know was that the thing was pushing an arm into the man's face and that while it seemed to cause Weasel a lot of pain—judging solely on the way the man fell to the ground and flopped like a fish on dry land—the dead thing seemed to enjoy the sensation.

He wanted to help Weasel. He wanted to move over and rescue his new pal from the bad dead thing, but he didn't have time. What was happening now was just the first stages and if he didn't do something soon the asylum would be the last of his problems.

If the medical ward was any example, the dead in Cherry Hill far outnumbered the living. If he didn't put a stop to the madness soon, he knew the dead from other places would be drawn here. They'd come to feed the thing that had summoned them. Worse, they might come to feed themselves on the living people they met along the way.

Jonathan Crowley could have told his doctors something if they were present in the room with him. He could have explained that the hungry dead never stop being hungry and that from time to time they lead by example. He was already dealing with one powerful entity. If he didn't stop the rift from growing, it was very possible that he might have to deal with more of the dead things that wanted to eat the spirits of the living and the dead alike.

# Chapter Twenty-Three

There are things that can go unnoticed and things that cannot. The sudden appearance of the dead qualified as the latter. Inside their cells, the inmates at Cherry Hill were open game for their predecessors. Most of the patients were heavily medicated to keep them from hurting themselves and others. Unfortunately, that left them unable to defend themselves.

Not all of the ghosts attacked. Some merely watched and others ran their hands over whatever they could find, fascinated by textures and sensations they had long forgotten about. Others touched the living people they found, just as amazed by the sensations.

The dead had texture now themselves. Without the barrier that kept them from this world, they could touch and be touched. The sensation wasn't pleasant for the recipient. Being dead meant having no mass. The flesh was replaced by a thick substance that the local coroner would have been very familiar with: ectoplasm. Jonathan Crowley could have explained to the people around him that ectoplasm is a simple generated protein capable of mimicking human flesh: with it the dead can create bodies, touch the material world and interact with the living. The catch is, it takes a great deal of energy to generate and to maintain. Without enough energy, the substance collapses and quickly breaks down. In most cases, ghosts can only manifest for a short time before they are exhausted. Few are powerful enough to incorporate in the world for very long. Ectoplasm is not flesh. It can look like flesh, but it will never be flesh. In any case, the fights didn't go as planned.

The ghosts did indeed build their bodies from the ectoplasm, drawing on whatever memories they could to rebuild themselves. The results were seldom-accurate examples of what they had been in life.

The patients were usually kept in a mildly drugged state, but not nearly all of them were blind or unconscious. The immediate reaction was what would be expected: panic.

In several cases the patients simply curled in on themselves and tried not to see what was right in front of them, but in most instances, they reacted violently to being touched by things that simply should not have been possible.

One Bruce O'Reilly, incarcerated and then remanded to Cherry Hill after torturing several men to death in his basement, thought he could fight back against the four ghosts that had been haunting him since he killed them. They had always lacked the power to make themselves known to him, except in dreams.

That situation was rectified. They took turns beating on him and cutting him until he was at the edge of death himself. They did not kill him. His death might have given him power and none of them wanted that. So they left him where he was, pinned to his bed by his own entrails, and merely watched him as his body functions ceased.

It might have actually become a problem for them. Bruce might well have come back as a ghost himself and rained down his fury on the four smaller men, but the Dead God was still hungry and devoured all five of them as it continued to build its body.

Throughout the asylum the inmates hid, fought, or tried to flee. Those that fought usually didn't fare well. Those that hid soon discovered that a ten-by-ten cell is not a good place to curl up and hide away. Those that tried to flee encountered the barriers that kept them imprisoned but did nothing to stop the dead from coming for them.

In the corridors and offices of Cherry Hill, most of the employees discovered the same difficulties. The dead were simply mad. Some paid no attention at all to the living, as if they had not just been allowed access to a forbidden place. Others took their revenge on anything that happened to be nearby.

And while the hospital patients and staff dealt with the dead, Jonathan Crowley dealt with the living as directly as he could.

He looked at the body of Alexander Granger and shook his head. He'd hoped to fix everything before the sanitarium could become a war zone. He failed. Left with no other options, he reached out his hands and grabbed Granger's head in his fingers.

Alex Granger opened his eyes and stared blankly at John, his face registering only the slightest shock at the contact.

He looked into those unsettlingly empty eyes and concentrated on what was going on inside the brain held between his fingers. There was activity, and a lot of it.

All around him the screams continued as Mr. Weasel and the other workers at Cherry Hill were confronted by the dead. Some of them held it together and tried to handle their patients first while others chose to run for dear life. Crowley did his best to ignore the noise and come up with a proper solution.

In theory, he could heal Granger and reverse what had happened, but it would take time and energy that he didn't know if he could spare. The man was a lunatic to begin with. He'd read the file and knew that Granger was exactly where he needed to be. He also would have guessed that, thanks to the gentle surgical hands of Phillip Harrington, the only way that Granger would ever come back was if he took the time to repair the damage done to the man's brain. He wasn't actually sure that helping the man would remove the monster that had come from the wreckage of Granger's mind.

In the end there was only one logical choice. He firmed his grip on Alexander Granger's chin and slid his other hand to the forehead before wrenching the man's skull violently to the left. The snap of vertebrae separating was loud enough to hear, even if he hadn't felt the jolt through his hands.

Granger's eyes lost what little focus they had and the man died while John looked at him.

Unfortunately, the screams continued around him. His simple solution had just failed miserably.

---

The Dead God felt it when Alex's life ended. It focused on the death of its host and trembled until it realized that it was still there.

Had it the need to breathe, the Dead God would have held its breath, dreading whatever would happen next. And when it realized that it still existed without Alexander Granger to anchor it to the world, it let out a roar of jubilation.

All that fear for nothing. All that wasted time being cautious, when it was now strong enough to survive away from Granger.

"Poor Alex." It could have captured his spirit as it left his body, but chose not to. Long exposure to Alex had left it feeling tainted by his mind. It wanted nothing more to do with the man who had given it form and purpose within his twisted mind.

Still, it hungered. The body it built made great demands of both the physical and the spiritual realms. The ghosts were easily consumed and the flesh was taken from anyone who caught its attention.

Soon, it knew, it could be born into the world. It would be powerful, nearly unstoppable. All it had to do was finish the task it had given itself and it would have life of its own.

At first it had planned to build the body from nothingness, but now it reasoned out a better way of handling the situation. Now it understood that there was no reason for it to strain so mightily when the answer to its woes was already in the asylum and waiting.

The living people in the asylum were already screaming, fear and pain leaving them no choice in the matter.

What was one more scream among so many?

With the power it had gathered, the preparations it had made, the Dead God reached out and touched the target of its hopes and dreams.

Only forty feet away from where Jonathan Crowley had just murdered Alex Granger, Leslie Anne Hampton opened her eyes as she felt the baby kick within her womb.

---

Leslie felt the strange sensation and was puzzled. Ever since she'd been moved to the new room, she'd been treated carefully. Her medications were administered and she was fed and left to herself a lot of the time. These days, she even had a television, but she thought that was mostly because she kept asking questions when she wasn't distracted.

Her belly felt funny, hot and tight. She moved her hands and felt something moving inside of her. Whatever it was, it seemed agitated. She'd had bad gas a few times, who hasn't, but it had never felt like this.

Puzzled by the sensation, she moved her hospital gown out of the way and looked at her stomach. It used to be flat, but now it was moving as something swelled and burbled inside of her. She poked it, and felt a sudden sharp pain where her finger touched the skin.

She closed her eyes for a moment and then decided she should call for the nurse. One of the nice things about her new room was that she could push a little button with a nurse's cartoon face on it and the nurse would come to check on her. She pushed several times but got no response.

The pain was getting worse, so Leslie lay back on the bed and closed her eyes, hoping it would go away.

It didn't. If anything, it was worse than before. Her belly was growing so fast that she couldn't even lie on her stomach and hope to make it go away. She looked like her older sister Nancy had looked before her nephew Tommy—*we don't talk about Tommy, Leslie! NOT EVER!*—was born.

Leslie tried to sit up, but couldn't. Her belly weighed too much. She lifted her gown again and saw that her breasts were swollen, but they looked like anthills next to the mountain of her stomach. The skin was stretched and red, and the weight of the mass was heavy enough that she had trouble breathing.

When she tried to reach out with her hand she found she lacked the strength.

Leslie closed her eyes and soon found herself drifting mercifully into sleep.

She was not conscious as the form swelling inside of her continued to change and grow. Despite the energies fed into her from beyond, the growing child demanded sustenance. When none was provided, it began to cannibalize its mother. Proteins and body mass were stolen away, drained to keep the growing god alive.

Leslie Ann Hampton died five minutes after the Dead God touched her.

One minute after that, her corpse gave birth.

# Chapter Twenty-Four

Carl Branaugh hadn't planned to go to work. He'd intended to play hooky. Funny how things never seemed to work out quite the way he wanted them to. Instead of calling in sick and grabbing his fishing pole, he got dressed and went into the office. There was just too much damned guilt involved in sneaking away when his caseload was bigger than it had been at any time in his past.

He was at the office and almost ready to just take the paperwork with him and finish it at home when the phone calls came in from Cherry Hill. This time he decided to demand back up. He was readying himself for a nice shouting match with the captain when the man came to him and told him to take two cars along for the ride. Four extra cops did a lot to make him feel better about going back to the asylum.

Murphy, Liebowitz, Chapman and Wendt came along for the ride. He warned them about the weird goings on and they listened. It was hard not to take the warnings seriously when over thirty people had been killed according to the phone calls.

The ride was strictly business. All three cars left the station with sirens going and lights flashing.

Carl knew things were going badly when he saw the covered bridges on the way to Cherry Hill. Rather than try to explain it to the others, he simply got on the radio. "I don't know what's going on here, guys, but the bridges are…wrong."

"When the hell did they put those things up?" Liebowitz was sounding as puzzled as Branaugh felt.

"No idea, Johnny. Just keep going. Captain said he'd have back up for us as soon as he can."

The air grew darker as they moved and Carl felt the start of butterflies winging around in his stomach. Nerves. He wanted to turn around and toss his badge over the captain's desk, but couldn't quite bring himself to do it. He'd sworn an oath to protect and serve. Besides, there weren't a lot of high paying jobs in the area, unless he wanted to work at Cherry Hill.

"Is the sun going down?" That was Liebowitz again. Branaugh thought he'd been imagining things: the sky was clear except for a few puffy clouds and those were nowhere near the sun, but everything seemed darker anyway.

"Look, there's been some weird shit going on at Cherry Hill. That's why we're going out there now. Just be prepared for anything that might come along."

Moments after he finished speaking, Branaugh saw the people moving along the side of the road, just past the last bridge. He kept driving and kept his eyes on them, puzzled as to how they'd gotten there. The asylum was ten miles into the middle of nowhere and he hadn't seen any cars broken down along the side of the road. Of course there were bogs all around them. It was always possible someone had gone over the side.

He passed them by at high speed and then pulled over, ready to render aid if needed.

The people looked out of focus and he rubbed his eyes, wondering if it was time to break down and see an eye doctor. The other two squad cars pulled over in front of his and the four uniforms climbed out.

It was Liebowitz that noticed what Carl missed at first. "Why do they look fuzzy when everything around them is fine?"

He looked again. It wasn't his eyes; it was, in fact, the people. He tried to stare at them hard enough to make out details, but they were too blurry.

"I don't like this." Chapman spoke softly, even as he reached for the butt of his .38.

"Neither do I." Liebowitz was frowning as he spoke, but kept his hand away from his holster.

Branaugh cleared his throat: "Do you folks need assistance?"

For the first time, the oddly blurred people looked up at him. He felt his balls try to pull inside as he realized what they were. Ghosts.

Every last one of them was a dead thing and if he was counting right, there looked to be seven of them looking his way.

---

Jonathan Crowley looked around the ward, trying to figure out where the impossible monster might be hiding. He still couldn't quite wrap his mind around the idea of a living hungry ghost and that delay was costing him valuable time.

He was certain, absolutely sure, that the man he'd just killed was responsible. Now he was having second thoughts.

"No. I'm right about this. There aren't any other options."

Frustrated and fed up, he turned toward the exit to the medical ward, planning to stop only long enough to dispatch a few of the ghostly things that were moving around the room.

He'd seen ghosts manifest before; he knew what he was looking at. They were shapeless until they concentrated, and then they took form. Most of them seemed to have a few strange notions of what they were supposed to look like, but considering they were in a nut house, he wasn't too surprised.

The thing on top of Mr. Weasel was letting out a continuous screech, a wailing note that grated at Crowley's nerves. Mr. Weasel on the other hand, was motionless. He was alive, Crowley could see that much, but decidedly unconscious or even comatose.

There was no way he could exorcise every spirit in the building, but he could make things difficult for a few of them. He spoke under his breath, pleasantly surprised at how quickly he could access the ancient spells. His mind was clearer than it had been in a long time and he wondered if that was because he was finally recovering, or simply because he had to focus to handle the current situation.

It didn't much matter. Either way, he spoke the necessary phrases and the thing sitting on Mr. Weasel bucked, leaping back from its chosen target as if scalded.

"That's right. Get away from him. You want someone, come for me." The unevenly shaped thing stared for several seconds, wide eyes bulging in its lopsided face, and then charged. It had about the same level of finesse as it did good looks. John caught it as it stumbled past him and pinned it against the edge of a gurney. The thick skin of the thing was an illusion, touching it was like holding onto a balloon made of wet leather and filled with water.

The strength it possessed was far more real than its appearance and it caught him a solid blow across his jaw. John staggered back, taken off guard by the ferocity of the attack and then he retaliated, driving his fingers into the gelid flesh and puncturing the body it had created for itself. While his hand was buried deep into its spectral insides he cast a second spell and trapped the spirit, drawing it in against his palm. Without the weight of the body it generated from the air, it was easily held and captured. What was left collapsed on the ground and began to decay at high speed. Crowley stepped over it and moved on, prepared to weave as many spells as he had to in order to keep the people around him safe.

"No, damn it all!" His fists clenched, and the one spirit he'd taken out of commission burned against the palm of his hand. "I don't have time for this!"

The people around barely noticed his comments or his actions. They were too busy trying to stay alive.

And that was exactly the problem. To save them he had to find the thing behind the newest dilemma. If he left them, they would likely all be killed in the meantime.

He looked around with eyes that could see so much more than most humans, and tried to find the source of what was happening. The spirits that moved around him came into sharper focus, including the ones that had not yet dressed themselves in ectoplasmic flesh. The very walls of the building pulsed with spectral energies for a moment and then the glimmer that emanated from the asylum disappeared as if it had never been there.

And finally he understood: The enemy he sought was everywhere at once, spread thin and not locked into a single location.

"You sly bastard." He couldn't quite keep the admiration out of his voice. Jonathan Crowley wasn't easily fooled and somehow the thing had kept him in the dark for a long time.

"Where did you go?" He looked around again, checking the ceiling, the walls, the floor, but whatever had been filling the whole of Cherry Hill was trying something new.

Was it hiding? He doubted it. The feeling in the air was different now, darker. The living hungry ghost was doing what he'd feared it would do all along. It was trying to be born. This time, it seemed like it might actually succeed.

---

The Dead God rolled away from the ruins of Leslie Anne Hampton and tried to stand. And failed.

It fell to the ground on muscles that had never attempted motion before and shivered, unprepared for the effects of gravity on its body. Still, it grinned. Life! It was alive; it could feel for the first time instead of merely studying the memories of sensation. There were senses it could barely comprehend, waves of input that were fascinating and almost painful in their intensity. It had acknowledged that walls existed before, had seen them in stolen memories, but the four barriers that surrounded it on all sides were so much different then what it expected. Like a blind man seeing the colors of the spectrum for the first time, it was briefly overwhelmed. Sounds were much louder than it had imagined; smells were more intense. The organs inside its body were functioning perfectly, but they were so very bothersome and distracting. Its heartbeat was a dull thunder that seemed ready to break its body apart with every pulse. Light was unsettling and the feeling of falling, of lying on the ground was both a wonderful new sensation and agony.

It had access to so many memories and it employed them now, teaching itself motor function at a speed that was unheard of in human history. Though the process still took almost five minutes, it was soon moving its arms and legs, reveling in the sensations.

Outside the room it still heard screams, but inside its mother's small prison all was calm. It looked back at Leslie's remains and frowned. What little remained of her was wet and bloodied. It hadn't planned to kill her, merely to use her body as a vessel. Still, both she and the unborn child she'd carried were now a part of it. They would be together.

It breathed in the scent of her death and exhaled a charnel stench from deep within itself. The world waited beyond the whitewashed concrete walls and the steel door that separated it from its new domain.

The door resisted its first attempt to open the handle, but yielded as soon as it pushed.

Outside the dead and the living were locked in a mad dance, some fighting against each other from time to time, though few of the living remained capable of defending themselves.

Most of the humans in the room barely noticed it at first, but when they did, they made their appreciation vocal. The dead and the living alike saw the Dead God for the first time, and knew that the being standing before them was superior, powerful, and deserving of worship. It knew because they fled just after seeing it.

The Dead God lowered its head to move from the room that had been its birthplace. The body worked perfectly, but the size of it made access to the larger room a challenge and it felt the top of the doorway break to its will.

"I AM DEAD GOD. WORSHIP ME." The words were thunder as they spilled from its lips. The people trembled and clutched at their ears, wincing in pain.

All save one.

Sight was still a new thing, barely understood and confusing, still it could look upon this one and know him anywhere. The once old man stood still, slowly turning his head to look upon the splendor of Dead God's perfection and bared his teeth in a wide and unpleasant smile.

"Hi, Dead God. Great name by the way. I bet you're gonna' be a lot of fun at church picnics."

Dead God didn't understand the meaning of the words, or the sarcasm with which they were spoken. It only understood that the man before it was not trembling and did not feel the need to worship it.

*Perhaps, it thought, the once old man does not understand. He will, given time, but for now he must be made to know me. "I AM DEAD GOD. WORSHIP ME."*

"You're not supposed to exist. Fuck off." The once old man came closer and stared Dead God in the eyes. It looked down at him physically, towering a head and shoulders above the once old man. It thought carefully about what the strange man had said and realized that it had been insulted.

Once more it tried to reason. "I AM DEAD GOD. WORSHIP ME."

"Oh please, you're already getting boring."

Enough! The man was offensive. The Dead God swung one arm forward and caught him in the chest. The once old man let out an involuntary noise and flew across the room, his body striking the ceiling and then falling, bouncing off of a metallic table and finally to the ground. Dead God heard the bones break, saw the blood that escaped from the wounds where the once old man hit the table, and saw him fall to the ground in a way that it knew meant he had been damaged beyond the human body's ability to mend itself.

If the confusing old man was not dead, he would be soon and then the Dead God would eat him.

It looked at the people where they trembled and tried to hide. It watched as the dead instinctively fled from its presence, and it smiled. "I AM DEAD GOD. WORSHIP ME."

The once old man stood up and wiped blood from his mouth with one hand. Even as he moved his face healed and his teeth showed in a savage grin.

"You have no idea how much I wanted you to do that."

---

Amelia crouched in the corner of her room and shivered. She could feel the panic that came from the living and the dead alike in waves of emotion that pushed into her, even through the wards that Jonathan had created to protect her. Much as she wanted to help him in some way, the fear was crippling. She could barely make herself open her eyes and the idea of standing, of seeking out Jonathan was too much for her to handle.

Just when she thought she would be able to overcome her paralysis, she felt the Dead God being born. The fear was bad, but the sensations that ran through the poor soul that was forced to give birth were too much for her, Amelia held herself tightly and shivered as she was hit by wave after wave of agony. She experienced echoes of what Leslie

Anne Hampton endured, but they were worse for Amelia: she was conscious throughout the process.

The fear intensified even more as the newborn made his presence known. She sensed the thing's mind, its emotions, but could not fully understand them: whatever it was, a ghost or a demon, its mind was powerful and its emotions struck her like physical blows. She felt her skin burn as it walked somewhere above her.

Amelia knew secrets about Jonathan Crowley that few people knew. For instance, she understood that he would recover from almost any injury that was not natural. He had lost a leg years ago in a purely mundane, if violent, method and he had not healed from that, but she'd seen him cut and bruised and broken in other ways and watched his flesh mend from all of it.

She was not that lucky. The pain she felt was real and would stay with her until her body could recover from it. Unless it killed her first.

Amelia collapsed on the ground, barely even realizing that she'd moved in an effort to escape the pain.

Her eyes fluttered briefly and then she was unconscious, incapable of thinking or feeling anything. Her mind sought out protection, reaching for anything that could save her body, even as she was struck by more pain and physical damage.

Her attempt at salvation was purely instinctual and she sought the only person she knew could help her. The only man who had helped her in the past. Her lips formed his name and spoke so softly that even if she'd been conscious she wouldn't have heard herself.

"Jonathan, help me."

---

Easily eight feet tall and almost as wide, the creature pushed into the room and looked around with eyes that had barely formed lids. It looked like a psychotic's dream made into an uneven reality. When Crowley considered its probable origin, he supposed that made sense. All of it looked like it should have been cooked for a little longer. The skin was thin and pasty, and every vein and artery was clearly defined under that hide. The face was uneven: the mouth hung slackly on the left side, and the nose was too small. One eye was larger than the other and neither of them were where they should have been. Thin, baby fine hair covered its scalp in odd patches.

It wore no clothes, so figuring out the gender should have been easy. While it had no breasts, it seemed that whatever the thing was, it got a little confused when it designed itself. Fully formed male and female genitalia were readily available for all to see.

For all of that, it looked intimidating as hell standing there and demanding to be worshipped. He studied it carefully, assessing as much as he could while it looked around. Even though it seemed incomplete, he knew that wouldn't last. Even as he watched the skin was thickening, becoming more of a proper epidermis. The thin hair was becoming fuller and spreading like a lawn across the overly large head. The rest of the body was catching up: it was just born and maturing rapidly. It demanded worship again and he made a snide comment to get its attention. If it was looking at him it wasn't mauling anyone else and John had no doubt it could ruin a person with one swipe of the massive hands it flexed as it stared in his direction.

Once more it demanded worship and once more he taunted it, hoping he could dodge any actions it might take.

Jonathan, help me.

Three little words that came at the worst possible time. He recognized the source immediately, and let himself get distracted. That was when the oversized thing that had just knocked its way through part of a wall tried to send him into orbit. Crowley slammed into the ceiling, ricocheted off a metal table and slid across the ground.

He laid perfectly still and felt the fiery itching start as his body mended itself. He couldn't afford another distraction from Amelia, so he kept low and wasted precious seconds casting reinforcements for the ward he'd already set in place. He didn't exactly have time to run down and check on her, so John had to hope it was enough.

Dead God shouted out about wanting to be worshipped, and Crowley decided he'd had enough. He stood back up and wiped the blood from his face, careful to get it out of his eyes.

The idea was to sneak as close to the thing as he could and attack it. The problem with that concept was the small group of people that the thing was looking at.

Just to make sure he got his way regarding the end result of the thing looking at them, he made noise as he stood up.

"You have no idea how much I wanted you to do that." Blatant lie. He wanted it to politely lie down and die.

The thing stared at him for a few seconds and Crowley sidled forward and to the right, making sure it was looking at him. The medical ward was at the end of the wing. If he could maneuver things the right way, he could take what was about to happen away from everyone's sight.

The Dead God had different ideas. It was big and it looked stupid, so Crowley made the mistake of thinking of physical confrontations. Instead it looked his way and lashed out with its mind.

All of the memories he'd managed to suppress became fodder for the thing towering over him. It reached into his skull and pulled everything it could from inside, only to thrust the recollections back into John's head. Elizabeth died again a hundred times. Each of his children screamed and suffered as he was forced to watch. His grief was renewed and cut into him, weakening his resolve, crushing his will. Why had he wandered down the middle of a street half-naked and picked a fight with the local cops? Because he'd wanted to die and that feeling came back, overpowering his senses and dropping Jonathan Crowley to his knees.

The oversized beast came closer, and he didn't have it in him to care. Let it crush him! Let it end this misery once and for all. He wanted his family back and knew he could never have them. If that was the case, why not join them in the darkness?

As quickly as the feelings assaulted him, they were gone, replaced by a screech of pain.

John blinked his eyes and shook his head and then looked at the thing that had just played inside his mind.

The Dead God was not looking at him. It was staring instead at Mr. Weasel, who was not only conscious—surprise, surprise—but holding an IV stand like it was a baseball bat and getting ready to swing a second time. As powerful as the thing was, it was new to the world and ill-prepared for the pain that the man had inflicted. It held onto one arm and glared at Weasel with a pout on its face. The IV stand had a dent near the base that cocked it at a strange angle.

Crowley shook his head, amazed that anyone in the room would consider fighting for him, and then he attacked.

Jonathan Crowley used his magic when he had to, but in a pinch, he still preferred a physical confrontation. He moved up fast and drove his knee into the crotch of the giant, satisfied with the way things crunched under the impact.

The monster looked down and roared. Its face had taken on a lot better symmetry as it kept maturing, which in this case merely made it look even more intimidating as it glared at him.

It brought both arms up over its head, ready to smash him into the ground, and Crowley smiled. As soon as it was ready to pulp him, he stepped in close and kneed it again.

"Not a very fast learner are you, bright boy?"

It was faster than he thought. It brought up a knee of its own and shattered Crowley's ribcage. Having the ability to heal is a wonderful thing. It doesn't do nearly as much good when you aren't given a chance to recover. John bounced a good fifteen feet, and the thing followed quickly, knocking aside two patients still strapped to their beds and several pieces of functional but unattractive medical equipment in the process. It kicked him again and sent him into the wall. He gasped as the force of the blow pulped his internal organs. Blood flowed inside his battered form and he knew there were parts of him that had been torn apart.

It kicked him again and this time he caught the worst of the impact with his forearms but still took enough damage to make the world go all gray and fuzzy.

The Dead God looked down at him and mimicked his grin with surprising skill. Then it drew back to kick him again as his body tried to recover and Jonathan resorted to playing dirty once more. The foot that tried to crush his body still managed to hit him—hard enough to crack the wall behind him in fact—but instead of touching his flesh, the foot stopped half an inch away, blocked by an invisible barrier.

Crowley stood up, wincing as his broken bones shifted back to where they belonged.

The thing swung again, and Crowley moved to the side. The oversized hand smashed through the wall instead of his head. There are disadvantages to being the size of the creature that had just come into the world. Among those flaws, happily for Crowley, is not knowing your own strength. The thing looked at its hand where it had ruptured not only the drywall but also the thick bricks behind them, and let out a scream as it pulled back its shattered flesh and bone. Before it could recover from the new damage it had done to itself, Crowley shoved it against the weakened wall, letting its weight take care of the rest.

The wall collapsed, falling away from the side of Cherry Hill and taking the living hungry ghost with it. Several hundred pounds of meat fell to the ground and hit hard amidst a shower of ruined bricks and mortar.

Jonathan didn't bother to think about it as he stepped out of the building himself and dropped down toward the Dead God. One way or another, he wanted to finish his task.

# Chapter Twenty-Five

Kimberly Walker stayed at home when the insanity truly came to Cherry Hill. She was still overwhelmed by what she had seen and having troubles accepting it. Worse, she couldn't quite get over everything that the monstrous voice had said to her.

Long after it had finished ripping Walter Sawyer into pieces, it had stayed with her, speaking into her mind without words, but with images both vile and endearing, as if she would understand the mental assault and be grateful for it in some way.

Even thinking about it made her hands tremble.

She finally got out of bed a little after noon and stumbled into the kitchen of her small efficiency apartment to make herself a pot of coffee. She needed the caffeine. Without it she knew she'd spend the whole day in bed, if not the entire week.

Her mother had called her the night before and they'd talked on the phone for almost three hours, despite the cost. Her mom wanted her to come back to Florida and quit school. Kimberly wanted nothing to do with that. Still, it had been nice telling someone all of her problems.

She set the Mr. Coffee to brew and sat down at the kitchen table while she waited, contemplating whether or not her stomach was up to actual food. She'd tried pizza last night, but not long after she'd eaten she thought about poor Walter again and lost her dinner.

She stood up when the coffee was finished and reached for a mug with hands that were still shaking far too much.

That was when the voice started in her head: *Kimberly, come to me. Be with me and I will grant your every wish.* Of course she recognized the voice. How could she not? If she never heard it again it would stay with her, haunting her every waking moment for as long as she lived. The mug she'd plucked from the cabinet dropped from numb fingers and shattered across the tiled kitchen floor.

Kimberly walked over the broken pieces without even feeling them and, still dressed in only a t-shirt and a pair of underwear, she reached into her purse and pulled out her car keys.

She didn't want to go to Cherry Hill. That was just possibly the last thing on earth that she wanted to do, but her body moved anyway, following orders she could not resist.

Kimberly Walker ignored Mr. Darby's fish-faced expression as she pulled out of the apartment complex. He was a nice old man and very conservative; seeing her half naked had probably damn near given him a stroke.

She drove carefully, following every rule of the road. She cried her eyes red and puffy and had to wipe them almost constantly. She did not want to go to Cherry Hill. She just had no choice. Her body was hers to command only as long as she followed the will of a nightmare.

She had her orders and try as she might, she could not deny them.

Kimberly wondered exactly when her world had gone to hell.

---

The seven dead people came closer and Carl shook his head. "Screw this. Let's go to the asylum."

"I think we're already there."

"Not funny, Liebowitz. I mean it, let's go!"

None of the officers argued with him. They moved back to their squad cars as quickly as they could, doing their best not to take their eyes off of the out of focus shapes that were coming closer. Carl didn't wait around to see who would follow. He hopped into the idling car and put it into gear. He only burned a little rubber. Both of the other cars made a lot more noise as they took off.

There was only a short distance to go before they reached the parking lot. It should have been enough to leave the ghosts in the far distance, but it didn't work out that way. By the time Carl was parking, he could see them coming up the road, moving faster than humanly possible.

Chapman had his revolver drawn by the time Liebowitz parked the car. He was out and facing the approaching things before anyone else was ready.

So Chapman got to die first. He didn't wait for orders, but screamed at the things to stop where they were. They ignored him and kept coming. He fired one warning shot over their heads and when they didn't respond, he cut loose with the rest of the shells in his Smith & Wesson.

Carl watched as the bullets passed harmlessly through the figures. There was no sign of impact, no hint that they felt anything at all. Then, as he watched, the images changed. They became more defined…solid. In the near darkness of the day he'd barely realized they had no color, but now, as he watched them become substantial he noticed the rich hues that ran over them.

The one closest to Chapman opened its mouth and let out a howl as it came for him. Chapman froze, uncertain how to deal with the sudden transformation, and it cost him everything. The creature grabbed the younger officer's face with both hands and drew in a massive breath. In the process, it took something vital from its target. Chapman let out a small moan of surprise and fell to the asphalt parking lot surface, his eyes staring blankly.

Four officers pulled their weapons and opened fire without a word spoken between them. Whatever the things were—Branaugh was still banking on them being ghosts, but they were solid now and obviously dangerous—they had just killed a cop.

When the bullets hit this time they did damage. Holes blasted into the damned things and staggered them back from the officers.

None of them, not a single one, looked completely right. They had humanoid shapes, but there was something off-kilter about their looks. He didn't have time to deal with details. There was too much going on around him.

Somewhere behind them he heard a loud cracking noise. He turned to look as he started reloading his revolver and saw what looked like a fist sticking through a brick wall forty or more feet up.

"Oh, bullshit! This is just fucking bullshit!" He turned back to the immediate problem at hand. The ghosts looked down at where they'd been shot and he was happy to have them distracted. One by one they lost the focus that had made them clear and he saw thick fluids spilling to the ground. He couldn't tell from a distance, but damned if the liquid didn't look like the weird crap that had shown up a few times inside of Cherry Hill. *Great. Whatever it is, it's outside the walls now.*

A moment later the damaged wall exploded outward, dropping something the size of a small car with it. A shower of stone and debris smashed into the grass at the edge of the parking lot and the big pale thing went with it.

Liebowitz looked over his way with half-wild eyes. "What the fuck did you get us into, Carl?"

Carl looked his way and saw the ghosts, once again blurry and distorted, behind him. They stood perfectly still for a moment, all of them focusing on whatever had fallen through the hole in the outside wall of the asylum.

He looked at the pile of rubble and saw the whole mass of debris tremble.

Something big started to move under that mass, and Carl decided he could do without knowing what it was.

Then the ghosts let out a few sounds of their own, wails of terror or pain.

Carl looked their way again. They were still in the same spot, but their bodies were distorting even more. The seven figures seemed to pull back, trying to resist a force that had them caught and didn't seem to want to let them go. Then one by one they lost whatever battle they were having. The spirits were torn apart and drawn into a stream like a whirlpool cutting through still waters. The end of that vortex was in the same spot where he saw the oversized thing fighting free of the rubble.

"What the hell?" Liebowitz was watching too. Carl studied the process and tried to remember everything that Crowley had said about ghosts. None of this made the least bit of sense to him.

Something big burst away from the broken masonry and stood up. It was a nightmare, easily two feet taller than Carl and covered with dust, the creature looked like something out of a bad dream.

A quick motion caught his attention from higher up, where the wall had fallen apart. He watched as Jonathan Crowley looked down at the thing below him and then just stepped out from the opening and let himself drop.

"Crowley! No!" The words were out before he could think. He didn't like the man, but he didn't want to see him dead, either.

Crowley did not fall to his death. Instead, he landed with both feet on the head of the thing standing below him and struck like a pile driver. The beast let out a roar and fell into the ground for the second time, landing roughly in the ruins it had just climbed free from.

Jonathan Crowley scrambled away from the behemoth and pointed his finger at it. "Do me a favor, Branaugh, and shoot the son of a bitch!"

He didn't even hesitate. He should have been considering everything that was going on, everything that had already happened inside of Cherry Hill. Instead, the detective aimed and fired, blowing chunks out of the thing that was trying to stand up.

Liebowitz looked at him for a moment and then joined in.

The pasty white thing bled and screamed, staggered by each bullet that blew through its body, but not killed, not yet. Carl called to Murphy and Wendt and they looked at him for a moment before finally taking aim. Whatever they were shooting, they could plainly see it was big and deadly. That was enough for now.

Branaugh used every bullet he had and so did the rest of the officers. Twenty-four bullets smashed into the grotesque flesh and most of them came out the other side trailing blood and meat.

The thing looked up when they were done. It did not fall dead or even stagger. It simply stared at them. In fifteen years of service Carl Branaugh had never fired more than two bullets at a living target. He'd just used every single bullet he carried to try to stop a monstrosity and the fucking thing just looked at him.

"Hey! Fuckface!" Crowley's voice was loud in the growing silence. The thing turned to look at him again. Then it moved, pushing away from the ruined wall, bleeding profusely as it charged, the brutal slab of meat caught Crowley in its oversized hands and rammed him into the wall.

Crowley wasn't moving.

The big thing was.

---

None of the memories it had taken from anything, living or dead, had ever prepared it for the pain it felt. The Dead God was dying; its body failing after so much time and energy devoted to building it.

And the Dead God was not amused.

Its hand caught the once old man and squeezed, feeling bones creak and break under its grip. But that was not enough. It needed to kill the old man once and for all, to get rid of him so that it could try again. It had made a body before, there was no reason it couldn't make another now that it needed to.

Still the man struggled, thrashed as it slammed him into the wall. He fought with every breath, his fingers trying to peel back the Dead God's flesh and break its grip.

It would not let him escape.

Once more it reached into the once old man's mind and sought a way to stop him. It found just the right memory, the perfect way to make him stop struggling, and forced the man to relive it again.

---

John felt the bones grating inside his body. He heard the break and couldn't even manage a groan. He'd underestimated the thing a second time and it looked like it might be the last time. He was almost grateful. Maybe this time death would come for him properly.

He'd accepted it. He welcomed it.

Then it got stupid and made him angry.

Whatever it meant to do, instead of simply crushing him it shoved his mind back into the memory of his family dying. Elizabeth's screams echoed through him and tore at his heart. Jeremy's pain-reddened eyes looked at him and ripped through his mind. His little boy was helpless and there was nothing he could do to stop the pain. Theresa's last rattled breath cut into him and the sound of Wendy's legs breaking, mixed with her wail of pain to freeze his blood anew.

John Crowley felt it all again with all of his senses, felt the anger, the sorrow, and the shame. His body was too broken to move, but his mind screamed for him, raging at the futility, the feeling of helplessness.

Jonathan Crowley let out a growl and looked at the face of the thing that mocked his memories and forced him to relive them. It was bloodied, yes, dying even. But it looked at him with hatred and reveled in his pain.

"You asked for it; you bitch."

The Dead God looked at him with a shocked expression. It must have thought he was dead.

No such luck.

As has been stated before, Crowley preferred physical confrontation to mystical. Now and then something happened that changed his mind on the subject.

He touched the hands that were still wrapped around his chest and spoke softly, uttering words he had not spoken but twice before in his life.

The Dead God didn't even have a chance to scream. Flesh boiled away from the oversized hands as streamers of smoke rose into the air. The monster dropped Crowley to the ground as its skin seared away.

It looked at the damaged meat and shivered. The blackened skin spread across the forearms and then upward as the monster looked on.

From his new perspective on the ground, John smiled as best he could through the pain of regeneration. He felt bones shifting back to their proper positions and the wreckage of his muscles and organs knitting themselves back together. Was it painful? Oh, yes. He didn't care. He just pushed the pain aside and watched as the Dead God burned.

Panic rose in the demon's eyes and Crowley stood up, his smile spreading wider and wider. The thing looked away from its ruined, smoking arms and then toward him with an expression of pure confusion. It didn't understand how this could happen, didn't realize that any physical body can be destroyed.

"You like that? Does it feel good?" John's voice was shrill and he didn't care. All thoughts of public appearance were gone from him. All concerns about the people in the asylum had been dismissed, replaced by the sheer pleasure of watching the sick fuck that had brought his worst pains back as it was incinerated.

The scorching heat spread, charring muscle and bone and blackening the pale flesh in a growing stain. Soon the whole form was blazing. Crowley stood near it, watching as the flesh bubbled and then finally burst into flames.

On the other side of the fire he could see Branaugh and a few other police officers staring in wide-eyed horror.

Finally he shook himself out of his rage and looked at the mess he'd made.

"Shit."

The body was gone. The spirit was still out there and that meant it could still cause trouble. It would make another form if given the chance and it would make one even more powerful than the last.

The rift between life and death was still there, still growing, and as a result Crowley and all of the men present saw the hungry ghost as it rose from the remains.

Crowley called out past the shape that lifted and ordered Branaugh to get his ass inside and handle the situation there. Partially it was because he knew the chaos in Cherry Hill was probably reaching the point of no return. Dead and living alike were having it out. Mostly, he wanted the detective and everyone else away from him when he finished his duty.

The form that rose up was not quite shapeless. It towered up into the air, much larger than the body it had occupied, and stretched roughly shaped arms into the air above it as it howled its rage out into the ether.

In most cases Crowley had an advantage. He knew that he could survive almost anything. This was different. He'd never actually entered the place where the dead dwelled. That particular location was off limits to him as it was for every living thing. The Dead God had changed those rules and Crowley didn't know exactly what would happen now, or how he would handle dealing with a giant that could potentially rip his essence out of his body.

He was about to find out.

---

Though it had sampled life and was intimate with death, it had never been killed before. The pain of being destroyed still echoed through its mind and while it was as strong as ever, the Dead God was having trouble recovering from the destruction of its body.

Senses that had become adjusted to the physical realm were suddenly altered and it saw not colors and shapes but energies. The once old man still glowed with a ferocious vitality, while it had been diminished. The man still had form and could move his body, while it stared down at the remains of the majestic form it had created.

It accessed its memories of the living and dead alike and chose a trick of the dead this time. Rather than creating a permanent body, it chose to use the ectoplasm all around it to achieve a temporary form.

Dead, yes, but not defeated. It pulled in the spirits around it as easily as it had inhaled oxygen while alive and it drew in the ectoplasm it wanted to gather mass.

The man looked up at it with that same strange smile in place and it felt weight again, however temporarily. This body would be less vulnerable. This form would be designed solely for destruction. The once old man would know pain and then death and it would swallow his soul, devour his wretched little life.

---

Branaugh and his men ran through the front doors of Cherry Hill's main entrance and stared at the carnage. There was little left around the area that wasn't battered in some way or another. No people, just furniture. That was as close to good news as he'd had in the last day.

"We're not spreading out. We're doing this together, guys. One room at a time."

"You hear me complaining?" Liebowitz was looking almost as pasty as the thing they'd shot.

"Let's just do this, okay?"

They hadn't even reached the end of the hallway when the lights started flickering. Carl decided to worry about the people inside instead of the power outage. They kept moving, and he wished he'd thought to bring a few hundred extra rounds.

They had no keys, which meant they either shot the locks off the doors to gain access to most of the building, or they found actual people who had keys. The first option wasn't going to work very well because, if they were lucky, they might have ten bullets. And thinking about that fact, he checked with the rest of the officers. Sure enough, they had seven bullets. He took two of them.

That only left finding someone with keys. When in doubt, find food and you'll find people. That was his philosophy in college and it had never failed him. He went for the break room.

He found people. Sort of. They were in the same shape as the first victims he'd seen, but the attacks on them hadn't been quite as extreme.

Liebowitz looked at the survivors and groaned, his face going chalk white. "What the fuck happened to them?" He touched one of the fleshy masses with his foot and then backpedaled and screamed when it let out a moan of pain.

"Calm down!" Carl realized he was screaming and forced himself to take a few deep breaths. "This is what I've been dealing with in this place for the last week. We don't know what causes it. The only good news is it's not contagious."

That said, he walked over to the first of the victims and tried to figure out where, exactly, the pockets on the slacks might be. There was an ID tag on the shirt that identified the whimpering lump as Phillip Harrington. Carl didn't even try to suppress the shiver that ran through him as he reached into the pants pocket and fished around for the keys he needed. Harrington tried to say something, but all that came out was a faint whistling noise. His mouth was open and gaping, but Carl couldn't see any hint of either teeth or a tongue.

"Shit, Harrington, I'm so sorry…"

He found the keys and stood back up on knees that threatened a rebellion. "Liebowitz, you need to call the station, now. Call them and tell them we need back up and ambulances." He should have done that before, but he wasn't thinking as clearly as he would have liked. Something about monsters and ghosts took away his normal calm.

Liebowitz didn't respond. The lack of words coming from the younger cop was enough to make his neck hairs raise into hackles.

"Liebowitz?"

None of the others were responding. He didn't want to turn around, didn't want to see whatever was keeping them quiet. Carl had the purely childish desire to ignore whatever was over there and hope it would go away.

There were sounds, but they were faint, almost inaudible. They were wet noises, bloody snippets caught by his ears. When he couldn't stand the near silence for even a moment longer, he turned and looked.

The three men with him were all crumpled to the ground, surrounded by the blurred, nightmarish shapes of the dead. A veritable army of ghosts held onto them and pulled at them. Parts of the living men twitched and shuddered as the ghosts sank hands into their flesh as if it were merely water and pulled away, taking something more with them. Each time a hand withdrew away from one of the uniformed officers, the cop flinched and trembled as if in pain.

"What the fuck?" Branaugh didn't waste time thinking. He reached out to grab at one of the imperfect figures and felt his fingers pass through it.

The shape—he thought it was male but couldn't be sure—ignored his presence completely. Its hand just kept reaching into Wendt and pulling, ripping something loose from inside of him. That something—*his soul? His life force? His spirit?*_—left no marks on Wendt's flesh or clothing as it was torn free.

Carl tried again to touch the ghosts and failed. He grew frantic. He screamed, he tried to lash out, but nothing worked. Liebowitz had stopped moving and all Wendt did was shiver uncontrollably.

Desperate, Branaugh grabbed Wendt by the ankle and pulled him away from the ghosts that attacked the downed officer.

That got him all the attention he could have ever wanted. The things hovering over Wendt turned to look at him, their misshapen faces contorted with rage.

"Oh, shit." One of them lunged toward him and Branaugh raised his hands to block the attack. The thing moved through his arms and reached into his chest. Spectral fingers caught at him from the inside: hot knives of agony ripped into him and sent him to his knees. He felt it when a vital part of his spirit was torn loose from the rest and watched in horror as the hand pulled back and the ghost shoved some fragment of his soul into its greedy mouth.

That was the moment when Carl Branaugh knew he was a dead man.

One moment later, before his prediction could come true, the ghosts throughout the room were torn away, caught like wisps of smoke in a tornado and pulled through the wall.

If he'd had the strength, Carl would have gone after them. He would have seen that his suspicions were accurate: the ghosts were drawn to the Dead God as it tried to summon the strength to fight against its enemy. Throughout Cherry Hill the dead fought to keep their places and failed.

The Dead God was hungry and demanded sacrifices. The dead were chosen to fulfill its needs.

Carl Branaugh crawled on his hands and knees, aching and weak. He made it most of the way to the door before he collapsed into unconsciousness.

---

Crowley stood still and watched as the thing that called itself Dead God began rebuilding itself. Even without the unusual abilities he possessed he would have seen the ghosts being drawn to the monster. They came from inside the asylum and from farther away, like iron filings drawn to a powerful magnet, their energies drawn into the coalescing blackness. With each spirit the Dead God absorbed John could sense the power increase inside of that endlessly hungry pit.

He also saw it start to solidify as it generated the ectoplasm it needed to make a body.

As Crowley watched and recovered from the damage the thing had inflicted his smile grew bigger and brighter.

"That's right, bright boy. You just keep making this easier for me."

At first he thought he might have to deal with a giant again, but this time it seemed the Dead God preferred to play on a more level field. Instead of forming a body meant for intimidating mountains, it concentrated on adding mass to itself. It was still a little taller than him, but not gargantuan in its proportions. Thick ropes of ectoplasm wove themselves together around the spirit, forming a body that was close to human, but not quite there.

Crowley felt the itching heat fade from his muscles and knew that he was healed. His muscles hummed with energy and he paced around the thing as it finished recreating itself.

Dark, sleek skin covered a muscular frame. The face, malformed before, was nearly perfect now. A strong jaw and broad features surrounded eyes that were the same color as the flesh, and he saw the slack expression on the Dead God grow animated as it looked in his direction.

It spoke without opening its mouth: You must be destroyed.

"Yeah? Well, if you feel that way, I guess we should get this done, Peaches."

The new and improved body was much faster and far more graceful. The Dead God stepped toward Crowley and drove its fist toward him. Crowley sidestepped, blocked the blow with his left arm and then caught the wrist as it passed by his face. His right arm lifted and dropped as he twisted the captured limb. A moment later, the Dead God screamed in pain as newly formed bones were shattered under the impact. Before it could properly recover, Crowley wrenched the broken limb in a half circle and yanked the hungry ghost in closer. His next blow broke the creature's neck. He brought his knee up quickly and drove it into the shocked face of the thing and felt more bones fracture. Three well-placed kicks shattered the spinal column, the left fibula and the right side of the creature's pelvis.

The Dead God fell to the ground again, face down, and Crowley spat at it. "First rule you should have learned, moron, is how to actually fight." Most of the blows he'd delivered would have either crippled or killed a living being. The Dead God was not alive, not any more, and it started to rebuild the new flesh again.

Crowley didn't give it the opportunity. He reached out with both of his hands and drove his fingers into the mockery of flesh, reaching past the ectoplasmic shell and into the very essence of the hungry ghost, before it could finish the task of healing itself.

"The second rule should have been how to stay hidden from me."

He caught the spirit in his hands and pulled it from the body it had created. It burned, Lord, how it burned, but Crowley kept his smile going as he captured the thing.

He wove his spell quickly and efficiently, capturing the Dead God in his grip and stripping it of its power. He had fought demons on countless occasions and while the Dead God was powerful, it was nothing compared to a true Infernal.

"You cheated, sport. You didn't play by the rules. Now I get to spank you and send you home."

Oh, how it struggled. It tried to break away from his hands and when that failed it tried to force its way into Crowley's body, but he was no longer a weak old man and he was ready for it.

What are you doing?

"I'm killing you once and for all, you little shit."

NO! Please, I want to live!

"Not an option. You killed a lot of people and you broke the rules."

I didn't know! I didn't understand!

"Yeah. You still don't. You never will."

It stopped trying to speak and sent waves of emotion into him, desperate wordless pleas for mercy. Crowley endured them and scowled through the process.

"Oh, stop it. You're being a baby." In truth—and John had to acknowledge that it was the truth—the entity was a baby. If he'd figured out the details as well as he thought he had, it was less than six months old and had spent that entire time getting a very skewed view of the world.

Magic. It always came down to sorcery in the long run. He could have destroyed the thing and called it done, but as he'd already accused himself of several times, he was getting soft. He tightened the wards around the spirit and severed its ties to the worlds around it. It took time; the connections it had made to both the living and dead realms were powerful. When he was finished, Crowley waited until he was sure that the spells were working properly.

The rift between the worlds closed itself. The dead that had survived being drawn to the Dead God were pushed away, forced back to where they belonged. There were no people around. Crowley could only hope that none of them were stuck on the wrong side when the dimensional barriers were sealed.

"Okay, 'Dead God,' I have a deal for you and it's a one-time offer. You say you've barely lived. You say you want to keep on living. I can see that. If I decide to let you live, there will be a few changes. Do you think you can accept that?"

He felt its desperate desire to live. The saddest thing about the situation, as far as Crowley was concerned, was that it really hadn't understood what it was doing. That didn't make it innocent, per se, but it was not truly malignant, either.

"I'm going to regret this later, I just know it." He looked at the thing in his palm and shrugged, not caring that it couldn't see him. It sensed the intent behind the gesture, that was enough. "Okay. I'll deal with the details later. Meanwhile, this is going to hurt. Let's call this payback for all the damage you did."

One more simple spell: the power taken from the dead and the living alike was released from the hungry ghost sent back to where it came from. Very little of the essence stayed around or moved back toward Cherry Hill. Crowley knew it was likely that when he went inside he'd find more corpses than living beings. He had to content himself with the knowledge that it could have been much worse.

What was left of the hungry ghost was weak enough that his hands finally stopped burning from trying to contain the energies: he watched his flesh reform until the itching stopped completely.

"That's it for now. You stay right here and we'll work out the rest of the details when I'm done here." Dead God was weaker indeed. It whimpered its pain and stayed where he had placed it. There was little it could have done in any case.

"Now, let's go clean up the rest of your mess."

# Chapter Twenty-Six

Amelia finally left her shelter shortly after the worst of the emotional barrages came to an abrupt halt. There were still people around her that were alive and feeling pain, but the endless assault she'd felt while the Dead God walked was done with. The difference was so powerful that for a while she almost felt numb.

It was a wonderful change of pace.

Physically she was not at her best. She felt like she'd been sunburned over most of her body and walked carefully to avoid the friction of her clothes rubbing against her skin.

The hallway was empty, so she walked toward the front of the facility. More than ever, she wanted to leave Cherry Hill behind. The building was a house of madness and she no longer wished to feel the side effects in her mind or on her flesh.

She didn't know what Jonathan had done earlier, but she had no doubt that he'd saved her life with his intervention. Another reason for her to be in his debt, to be sure, but she also knew that he'd never make any demands of payment.

One of the front doors to the facility opened and she saw Jonathan as he came in. He moved with a cocky saunter that she was not used to, his head held high as he scanned the main area and started in her direction. His eyes when they met hers were calm, but she could tell it was a mask. He was trying to hide away from the turmoil that still raged inside of him, a tempest of grief and anger that Amelia doubted would ever go away.

"All finished," he said as he reached her. "The big bad bogeyman isn't such hot stuff when he gets his butt properly whupped."

"Are you all right, Jonathan?"

"Couldn't be better." His tone dared her to contradict him. She wasn't feeling all that adventurous at the moment and declined the dare.

"Did you kill it?"

"Not really." He held out his hand and showed her the pulsing light that was all that remained of the Dead God. As much as she understood about Crowley and his abilities, she couldn't understand how he simply dismissed the carnage around them. She'd seen him berate her father until he was in tears because of bringing her into the world, and now he held the cause of immense suffering in his hand and showed it to her like it was a prize.

"What will you do with it?"

He stared hard into her eyes, and whatever he was feeling was shut off to her. "I'm not sure yet. Something. It'll never be a problem again."

She didn't say a word, but her expression must have spoken volumes. For the first time that she could remember, he was the one who broke eye contact.

"In any case, let's take a look around. Maybe there are a few survivors."

"There are. I can feel them."

"Yeah? Good. That'll make this go a lot faster." He walked past her and headed down the corridor. Much as she wanted to leave the asylum, she followed. She knew it was what he expected of her.

He stopped after half a dozen paces and turned back to face her. He reached out and touched her arm gently and spoke under his breath. A moment later she felt the burns healing on her body. She hadn't wanted to ask him for anything—he'd already done so much—but she accepted the gift with a sigh of thanks.

From then on, she led and he followed. They moved through the whole of Cherry Hill finding the living in a house of the dead.

---

He couldn't scream any more. He didn't have the strength.

Phillip Harrington suffered in silence and wondered how long he would live in his current state. Through eyes that had been twisted into new shapes, he tried to pay attention to everything going on around him. Though he saw blurs of light and darkness and heard the muffled sounds of voices, the sensory input made no sense to him.

Hands touched him, moved his wrecked form around and onto the curved ruin of his back. He found the strength to scream again when it happened and wished desperately for an end to his suffering.

A moment later he got his wish. All that had been done to him was undone. His bones became whole and his body was restored.

Phil let out a shuddering breath and closed his eyes, uncertain if he was dead or alive for a moment. The end of his agonies was a staggering moment in his life.

"How ya feeling, Doc?" Jonathan Crowley's voice cut through his momentary peace and he felt his blood pressure soar to new heights. All the pleasure he'd just experienced faded away in an instant, replaced by his rage at the cocky tone of his patient's words.

He opened his eyes and looked at the bastard kneeling over him and the Dunlow woman who may as well have been his mascot.

"How is it that you're still walking around, John? Shouldn't somebody have caught you by now?"

Crowley's expression said he'd just smelled something foul. "Is that your way of saying thanks, Doc? I could have left you the way you were, you know."

Harrington felt his pulse pounding in his ears. He wanted nothing to do with Crowley. "Am I supposed to thank you for making my life so much better? Is that what you're expecting from me, John?" He stood up and brushed at his dirty clothing—none of which was sitting exactly in the right place; his pants were twisted at an angle on his hips and his shirt was riding up—then readjusted the way his belt was situated. His anger was so powerful that his eyes were stinging with unwanted tears. "You're the one that brought this...this curse to Cherry Hill! Everything was fine before you showed up!"

"What did you say to me?" Crowley's voice had dropped a full octave and that nasty smile of his had vanished. If he didn't know better, Harrington would have thought the man sounded shocked, as if the truth of Phil's words could ever get past the lies that spouted from Crowley's lips.

"Other people might think you're some divine miracle worker, Crowley, but I know better! You did this! You and your sick little mind games!" He yelled so loudly, with such fury, that spittle flew from his lips and sprayed across the front of Crowley's bloodstained guard's uniform.

Jonathan Crowley trembled with rage, his face reddened and his eyes bulged. Maybe once Phil would have been intimidated, but after everything he'd been through he was beyond being afraid of a mental case.

"You little shit." Crowley stepped toward him exactly two paces, until they were inches apart. "You sick little bastard. You did this. You cut into the minds of people with your little knives and you tried to stop their violent tendencies. But you weren't happy with that. You had to go a little deeper, see if you could add just a little more pain to their lives and you set something loose that shouldn't have ever been set free."

"What are you talking about?"

"I'm talking about Alexander Granger. His mind wasn't normal, Doc. I don't mean he was crazy, I mean his mind was something special. If you'd performed a lobotomy without adding a few extra slices, that thing you let free might have never gotten loose." Crowley's eyes blazed with anger. "Don't you dare lay this at my feet. I had to clean up your mess, Harrington. I had to fix your mistake."

"Utter nonsense. Delusions from a warped mind." He smiled as he said it. Knowing it would piss Crowley off even more.

Instead of getting angrier, the comment seemed to calm Crowley down. That little change made Harrington nervous.

"You're right. I'm the bad guy here. I should have never given you anything. So I'll take it back."

Harrington froze: Crowley had healed him. "You can't possibly be that vicious!"

"Oh, you can keep the flesh, Doc." John's eyes narrowed. "I'm taking back the other gift I gave you."

Crowley turned his back and headed for the door.

"What about everything that happened here?"

"Not my problem." Crowley crossed his arms. "I don't even work here. Have a nice life, Doc. For your sake, I hope we don't meet again."

As Crowley walked away, Phil noticed the other people in the room for the first time. Detective Branaugh was staring hard at him, his face locked into a stony expression.

"Well don't just stand there, Detective! Arrest him!"

Branaugh shook his head and moved away. "Arrest him yourself, asshole. He just saved your life."

---

The car stalled just after Kimberly crossed the fourth covered bridge. She hadn't bothered to fill the gas tank, even when the warning light showed on the dashboard the night before. Despite her desire to stay where she was, she climbed out of the car and started walking.

Ten minutes later she felt the world change around her. The already darkened sky grew darker, and the air took on a wintry chill.

She should have been afraid, but she was elated. The voice in her head vanished along with the light. Kimberly kept walking, but chose to head for home instead of to the asylum. She was free and walking a dozen miles didn't seem like that bad a thing if she could stay away from Cherry Hill.

It was only after she crossed over the first covered bridge that she realized she hadn't seen her car._*No matter,*_she thought._*I can always come back for it later.*

It was hours later when she was cold, exhausted and nearly delirious that she realized something else had gone wrong. She'd made it most of the way back to her apartment and seen no one. Not even a car in the distance.

The first of the dead people wandered in her direction only three blocks from her front door. She'd known Alan Stephenson in life, had gone to school with him and sent a condolence card to his family along with flowers when she attended his funeral.

Alan looked at her for a long time before he spoke.

Kimberly didn't hear a word he said. She was too busy screaming. The monster was gone from her head. The dead were not so easily dismissed.

The police cars, fire engines and ambulances all saw Kimberly's car as they drove to Cherry Hill. No sign of the nurse was ever found.

---

Crowley looked around the parking lot for several minutes and then settled on a car that struck his fancy. He nodded with satisfaction and threw the spirit attached to his hand directly at the vehicle while speaking under his breath again. Amelia could feel the power that flowed from him as he cast his incantation.

"What did you do?"

"Just now? I decided I need a car and Dead God here needs a body." He stared at her and then shrugged. "What? It's temporary. I'm still trying to figure out what to do with the damned thing."

Amelia stared at him for a few seconds and then looked on with a dumbstruck face as the station wagon he'd chosen as a target began to change shape. In a few seconds the old woody had become a Dodge Charger.

"You possessed a car?"

"No, I let the car be possessed." His voice took on the more familiar tones she'd known when she was young. He spoke with the patience of a teacher. "There's a difference." He walked around to the passenger side door and opened it for her. "Need a lift to the airport?"

"Yes, please." What else could she say? "But that wasn't what I was asking about. I meant what did you do to Dr. Harrington?"

"Oh, that." Before taking care of the doctor, Crowley had done what he could to heal every living person in Cherry Hill…there weren't many left. Mostly they ran across corpses. Jonathan had tried, she knew that, but the deaths barely even seemed to affect him. She felt like crying for every last one of them, but if he felt anything at all, he hid it well. Amelia had watched him walk past Harrington several times before he finally restored the man to a body that was intact. She had no doubt in her mind he'd known exactly who he was saving for last. Jonathan could be very unforgiving when it suited him.

Despite everything he'd seen and endured, Jonathan was smiling. "I just gave him back his little talent. The one I took away from him."

It took her a minute before she realized what he meant. "You let him see the dead people again?"

"Yes."

"Why?" She couldn't keep the horror out of her voice.

"Because it's the least he deserves. He's lucky I didn't ruin his body a second time. He did this, Amelia. He may not have meant to, but he brought it around."

Crowley climbed into the driver's side seat and Amelia slipped into the car as well. The engine purred when he started the Charger and roared as he pulled out of the parking lot.

"You can be a vicious man, Jonathan."

"If you're expecting me to argue with you, you're wasting your time."

"How could you do that to him?"

Jonathan was quiet as they drove down the long road away from Cherry Hill. He didn't speak until after he'd pulled aside to let a battalion of emergency vehicles roar past.

"I'm fond of the truth, Amelia. He doesn't much like the truth. Now he gets to deal with it. Leave it at that."

She nodded her head and stayed silent for a while. Jonathan said nothing at all, he simply drove.

They were just moving onto the interstate and heading for Philadelphia before she spoke again. "What will you do now, Jonathan?"

"What else? Sit at home and wait for phone calls or letters, just like I did before—" His voice caught for one moment and his throat worked as if to swallow a very bitter taste. "Before I tried to settle down."

She looked away from him before she spoke again. "Will you try to have a family again?"

He snorted and shook his head. "No. That's all in the past. No friends, no family. No chance to get caught in that insanity ever again."

"Not ever?"

"There's no point to it, Amelia. I'm not a social creature to begin with. I'll go back to my research and let people go on with their lives."

She didn't have to ask if he would be lonely. She already knew the answer. He would be miserable, and if she knew anything at all about Jonathan Crowley it was that he'd probably be happier that way.

"No friends, Jonathan?"

"I have a few. I'd like to keep them. And yes, Amelia, that includes you."

"Are you driving back to California?"

"Well, I've got this new car. Seems a shame to dump it on the side of the road, don't you think?"

"So let me drive with you."

He was silent for a while, but he turned off of the northbound interstate when he found a proper road heading west. California was days away and she was glad to spend the time with him.

# About the Author

JAMES A. MOORE authored more than forty novels. The first decades of his career focused on his love for horror, as seen in many novels including the critically acclaimed *Fireworks, Under the Overtree, Blood Red,* and the Serenity Falls trilogy. Later, Jim earned a reputation as the "prince of grimdark fantasy" with his hugely popular Seven Forges series as well as the Tides of War trilogy. The author loved collaborating with other writers, most frequently with Christopher Golden on the Bloodstained Worlds trilogy and with Charles R. Rutledge on the Griffin & Price series, among others. Nominated for the Bram Stoker Award twice, Moore won the Shirley Jackson Award for co-editing *The Twisted Book of Shadows*. He first came to prominence as one of the principal world-builders involved in the World of Darkness from White Wolf Games, most famously Vampire: The Masquerade and Werewolf: The Apocalypse. At the time of his passing, Moore left behind one completed solo fantasy novel, as well as completed collaborations with Charles R. Rutledge and Mary SanGiovanni. Plans are afoot to bring those to readers soon.

## Bibliography

### NOVELS

**The Black Stone Bay Series**
Blood Red (with "Blood Tide"
Blood Harvest
Bloodlines

**The Bloodstained Series (w/Christopher Golden)**
Bloodstained Oz
Bloodstained Wonderland
Bloodstained Neverland

**The Chris Corin Series**

Possessions

Newbies

Rabid Growth

**The Chronicles of Jonathan Crowley**

Under the Overtree

Writ in Blood: Serenity Falls, Book One

The Pack: Serenity Falls, Book Two

Dark Carnival: Serenity Falls, Book Three

Cherry Hill

Smile No More

Boomtown

One Bad Week

Where the Sun Goes to Die

**The Griffin & Price Series (w/Charles Rutledge)**

Blind Shadows

Congregations of the Dead

A Hell Within

**The Seven Forges Series**

Seven Forges

The Blasted Lands

City of Wonders

The Silent Army

The Godless

The War Born

**The Subject Seven Series**

Subject Seven

Run

**The Tides of War Series**

The Last Sacrifice

Fallen Gods

Gates of the Dead

**Standalone Novels**

Deeper
Fireworks
Harvest Moon
The Haunted Forest Tour (w/ Jeff Strand)

**NOVELLAS**

Dear Diary: Run Like Hell
Homestead
The Wild Hunt

**SHORT STORY COLLECTIONS**

Slices
This is Halloween

CROSSROAD
PRESS

www.ingramcontent.com/pod-product-compliance
Lightning Source LLC
LaVergne TN
LVHW091022080826
845145LV00002B/329

* 9 7 8 1 6 3 7 8 9 2 8 6 2 *